A Hero In His Time

The University of Chicago Press • Chicago & London

A Hero In His Time

A NOVEL BY
ARTHUR A. COHEN

The University of Chicago Press, Chicago 60637
The University of Chicago Press, Ltd., London

University of Chicago Press edition 1988
Printed in the United States of America

97 96 95 94 93 92 91 90 89 88   5 4 3 2 1

Library of Congress Cataloging in Publication Data

Cohen, Arthur Allen, 1928–
A hero in his time : a novel / by Arthur A. Cohen.

p. cm. — (Phoenix fiction)
I. Title. II. Series.
[PS3553.0418H4 1988] 87-26201
813'.54—dc19 CIP

ISBN 0-226-11252-7 (pbk.)

To Isak Babel, Peretz Markish, Osip Mandelstam

for James Scully

PART ONE

1. Above Pushkin Square

Yuri Maximovich Isakovsky returned home from the office that Sunday in January and fished in his pocket for the key to his apartment, fatigued, his mind muddled with unanswered letters and solitary lines of poetry. He was about to turn the key in the lock when he became aware that something was wrong. The door was not properly closed, and from the merest pressure of his hand upon the knob it opened. His ancient dog, invariably seated behind the door awaiting his arrival, was nowhere in sight, but the instant he entered the room he heard squeals of fright and knew that Nastya was hiding under the bed, something she had done only when Irina Alexandrovna had been in residence and they were making love.

Squinting about the room suspiciously, Yuri Maximovich was relieved that his first fear was not confirmed. Not a burglary, but something else, more subtle to his accounting, had taken place. He noted that the bookshelves were disordered. Whole sections of books had been removed from their shelves and replaced in a manner indifferent to the intimate harmonies their owner had devised for them. Indeed, the complete writings of this hero of the revolution or that master of the literature had been lifted out and returned, leaving the books uneven, eight volumes of twelve jutting out, the remaining four and two from another series lagging behind, as though his library were a phalanx of marching soldiers, the second row wheeling several paces behind the front line. And the desk to which Yuri Maximovich came immediately—there the usual mess, but with a difference, for some papers which he knew he had crumpled and thrown into the basket were once again lying on top of the desk, and the manuscript pages of his poems, which over the years since his first book had been published had accumulated very slowly, were wrinkled, their corners bent, an alien thumbprint upon the first poem.

His apartment had apparently been interviewed that Sunday by State Security, he concluded. Only a matter of time, he thought, before the interview would be conducted in person. Everything fell into place. Seven times the previous week he had received phone calls and when he lifted the receiver the caller had clicked off. It was not uncommon to bracket the pattern of movement of someone under open surveillance by telephoning him in the mornings and evenings to determine when he arises and when he leaves for the office, when he returns home, whether he goes out in the evenings, and in Yuri Maximovich's case, whether he is in the habit of working Sundays at the office. A series of telephone calls answered, another series unanswered, and the regularity of habits can be confirmed. Easy enough. If Yuri Maximovich were suspected of some criminal activity, the agents would simply arrive at any time of day or night (preferably night) and ransack his apartment, shoveling his books and manuscripts into a potato sack and taking both them and him away to the Lubyanka for interrogation.

Yuri Maximovich was relieved, therefore, to know that he was simply being watched and investigated without circumspection, the little signs of the agents' visit being sufficient warning to establish an understanding between State Security and Comrade Isakovsky. Obviously the unidentified authorities were watching him for other reasons than the suspicion of crime. He would find out in time, he had no doubt. For the present, he could only be cautious, all the while observing his anxiety mount, his pulse throb, heart thump, blood vessels constrict in fright.

That evening Yuri Maximovich ate his dinner seated at his desk, scrutinizing his room slowly, noting one or another mound of dust that had been disturbed; a patch of oven soot which had settled on his bookcase bore a palm print unmistakably larger than his own, and a mop which had stood in one corner of the room had been moved to another. Fortunately, Yuri Maximovich sighed, they had not found his journal. He had taken it that day to the office, as he had intended to be ready in the event his Zeus poem began to move. It could be called incriminating if that is the correct description of its contents. The journal contained, as will be seen, notations which reflected the individuality of a man, conceivably dangerous in a society where it is preferable that men be differentiated by little more than the color of their hair, the song of their mother tongue, the slope of their backs.

Having paced the small apartment a dozen times, Yuri Maximovich left off speculating about the implication of the interview conducted in his absence and went back to his poem. He worked ferociously until the early hours of the morning—a standard practice—spitting out words to the framed pictures of personal saints and beloved sites which hugged a corner of the desk, racing to the bookshelf to consult a line or two of a favorite poem, peregrinating his dictionary in search of a word, drinking tea, writing a line and hating it, bunching the paper, and weary at last, dropping into his bed to sleep.

It was morning by the clock when he awoke.

Yuri Maximovich, the son of Maxim Osipovich Isakovsky (these Russian names, these Russian Jewish names which sound of history, families, places, migrations), fifty-four years old last July, on the cusp between the crab and the lion, arose and moved barefoot about his apartment on that particular morning in January of 1972. He walked as he always walked, indecisively, skittering forward for an instant as though intent to smack an especial fly or wipe a smudge from the door; and then darting to one side, forgetting fly and dirt, he seized his razor, left open upon his writing desk, where one can only imagine that he had contemplated suicide the previous night for the four hundredth or three thousandth time, when the four hundredth or three thousandth poem he had been trying to write refused to come forth from his forehead. If not suicide (for Yuri Maximovich rarely shaved), why then did he leave the razor open beneath the mass of balled papers?

After one of Yuri Maximovich's combats of composition, his desk resembled the armory of children readied for a snow fight—a dozen or fifteen balls of paper, perfectly rounded as though he had crunched them with one hand and shaped them with the other into perfect balls, modeling those discarded papers after having failed to mold his words into poems. The razor? Perhaps, indeed, he had intended to shave? Who knows? In all events, on this occasion, a morning in January 1972, he took up the razor from his desk, carried it to the window, and there, without benefit of mirror or reflection in the frosted glass, cut an errant hair which had grown long and disgusting from his earlobe.

Yuri Maximovich stood at the window and frowned at frozen Moscow below, a Moscow laden with snow, borne down under the snow like the skin man whom he saw sometimes in the market, wearing a score of animal pelts, his face hardly visible, peering like an American Indian from beneath the bear's head that shuttered his eyes. From where Yuri Maximovich stood he could see down into Pushkin Square, and he spat on the wooden floor. Pushkin's head, majestically bowed from genius, was covered with a square Polish cap of snow (Mickiewicz and Pushkin often exchanged banalities), and a pigeon sat upon his head, feeding from his bronze skull. Yuri Maximovich thought for a moment and scratched his balding head, spat again and flattened a dust ball that rolled across the floor, gusted by a secret wind that blew from nowhere discernible.

It was six in the morning. He had begun his aimless ambulations about the apartment a half-hour earlier, roused from a fretful sleep which had almost overtaken him at his desk. He had neither slept properly nor profoundly. Not the surveillance nor the search had agitated him as much as the difficulty of writing his new poem. He knew where to find the KGB; the KGB knew where to find Yuri Maximovich; but where would he find his poem? Where was it? Nowhere at all. (Yuri Maximovich hunted images like birds pecking for seed in snow, false forage which fattened neither birds nor poets.) It was six o'clock precisely, the usual hour of his *levée*: hand-washing in the kitchen sink, a warm rag to his sinuses, a rapid pass with the toothbrush, close examination of his chin to determine if its two-day-old bristle demanded razoring, and lastly, a brisk massaging of his gums with both index fingers, agitating the blood which tingled through his mouth, prickling his exhausted, somnolent brain. Yuri Maximovich considered himself awake and risen.

The apartment of this poet was a treasure of minuteness, by Soviet standards luxurious, since he managed to live in it alone, without friends or relatives, and until the evening before, without unbidden visitors. It was large enough to allow his pacing, its corners generous enough to encourage periodic scrutiny and appraisal; it had light in the morning and an old-fashioned Russian stove which enabled him to cook his food and gave him heat at night. At an earlier time, during his brief marriage to Irina Alexandrovna, the stove had stood in a small room which had once been a cleaning closet of the fourth floor of a private house, converted during the twenties into an apartment house, but since Irina's departure, Yuri had moved the stove into the so-named living room/study and inserted his bed into the vacated kitchen. His bed literally filled the former kitchen. It really was a *bed*room—or rather the mattress and wooden frame which he had had specially constructed completely filled the space—and when Yuri Maximovich decided to sleep he could if energy sufficed dive to sleep or if dead-tired simply crawl from the living room under his blankets.

The kitchen (for how did Yuri Maximovich eat?) was merely a name given to a space, an example of creative flat, a permanent name affixed to a constantly changing space—sometimes a spot cleared upon his desk, sometimes a niche on the bookshelf, most often the top of the stove, where he kept his few pots and a frying pan.

His food was simple. Tea and rusks, an occasional soup with a stripped marrow bone, an egg, or a compote of fresh fruit—the only thing, in fact, which Yuri Maximovich cooked properly. (He adored fresh fruit, lovingly savoring their plum skins, their wrinkled prune faces, licking sap from his hands when he squeezed them in the vegetable and fruit stores; and he guarded sugar and cinnamon and cloves for the mating of fresh fruits into the mess that would become his compote.) Not having many, Yuri was not generous with his pleasures and few of his friends (excepting Irina Alexandrovna, who had introduced him to this natural delight, and Ilia Alexandrovich Kolokolov, the celebrated poet who had once been his closest friend but whom Yuri no longer saw since Ilia had become famous) had ever enjoyed Yuri's subtle knowledge of the nuptials of pears and cherries, apples, cloves, and lemon.

Ilia Kolokolov had eaten compotes with Yuri Maximovich and Irina Alexandrovna after their wedding, and later, when Irina had left him for the Major, Ilia would sometimes drop by to bring his friend green apples and peaches from the south or a plum or two, and would say, "Old friend, stew us up a compote and let's visit awhile." At the beginning, Yuri would be truly pleased with Ilia's thoughtfulness. In those early days Ilia had published little more than Yuri Maximovich. Both of their books had come out in 1957, and although Ilia's had sold out in six weeks and Yuri's had taken more than two years to disappear, Ilia Alexandrovich remained reasonably modest.

In those days enthusiastic Ilia, younger by seven years than his friend, continued to bring poems in his head to Yuri, and seated, would recite them, using only his hands for additional information, occasionally slapping out the meter on his knee or tapping a simple anapest on the wooden floor. And what is more important, he still listened to Yuri's reactions, lifting his right eyebrow and tilting his broad-boned face toward Yuri

Maximovich, who always criticized in motion, pacing, standing up, sitting down, touching and fingering, flicking imaginary crumbs off his leather chair or mopping up authentic dust with his bare hand, and talking nervously about this and that word, the true and false, the felt and fabricated qualities of the poems Ilia spoke. But as time passed and the next decade opened, the sky lowered upon Yuri and the horizon widened for Ilia, and where the one disappeared into the cumulus, thrusting his poems deeper into his pockets, the other, favored and employed, stood forth as a Soviet singer, a grand poet, a celebrated poet, who spoke standing now using his body like a pylon, slamming his weight against his poems, using his arms like scythes to cut open the shuddering air about his words.

The last time Ilia Alexandrovich had visited Yuri Maximovich, Yuri had refused to make the compote and stood in the corner listening with petulance and undisguised contempt (it was, he well understood, jealousy full-blown) to Ilia's catalog of triumphs: his enormous editions, his foreign translations, his tours and receptions, his visits with jazz musicians and rock stars, his encounters with the greats of the world. Ilia, self-deprecating, adored his triumph and spoke of it with delight and ebullience, always adding as coda to each sonatina of celebration, "It's foolishness, isn't it?" Yuri Maximovich could not reply at such moments. His agreement would have been too vehement. Ilia remonstrated with his own modesty, fuming and sputtering that it was trying to be so beloved. Yuri said nothing. Ilia left and did not return.

Now it was six o'clock in the morning more than ten years after his last meeting with Ilia Alexandrovich. Yuri Maximovich resumed his perambulation of the modest living room, coming to rest upon the Chair. *A word about the Chair.* The nine pieces of furniture (the desk, a clumsy console table without drawers; a desk lamp with a glass shade; bookcases, two of them; an old-fashioned armoire, where he stored his clothes and a broken radio; the aforementioned bed; two stools, and the Chair), each tagged with a personal history and provenance, the oldest being the Chair, which was found in a street near the river where it was about to be burned for fuel during the cruel winter months of 1943 when Yuri Maximovich was on leave from the front for the burial of his mother. His mother, Mira Babininskaya, had died in Moscow at the apartment of her brother's daughter, and although these kin had at first refused to allow the guild of old Jews who called themselves a Holy Brotherhood to wash her and watch her through the night, Yuri's angry telephone call had stunned them into grumbling acquiescence. His mother was buried with the ancient words, and Yuri, remembering childhood chants, had said the right prayer for her every day, though never in the same place: once on the subway, once on the street when he saw a young Jew with sidecurls hidden under his worker's cap, and once, would you believe, while he was brushing his teeth. In any event, it was that month in early 1943—on leave from the front, where he loaded shells into enormous cannon—that he acquired the Chair. That Chair, that *magnífico* of a chair, with tasseled corners and gilt feet, with threadbare mauve seat and leather back, with carved rosettes into which varnish and finger dirt had been rubbed with a loving thumb, that marvel of a chair was, as he called it, the Poet's Chair, and when he approached it every morning, saluting and imploring it, it stretched out to receive him, its arms firm, fists of lion's paws clenched to receive his prideful palms. Yuri Maximovich approached his chair as though it were the throne of Erasmus saluting Wisdom or the necromancer's source of power, shooting the energy of poetry up through thighs and buttocks. If Boris Pasternak required a desk to write poems, Yuri Maximovich required a chair. Of course the difference was that in order to compose, Pasternak needed to clear off the admirers and friends who crowded his desk like spirits on the head of a pin, whereas all Yuri Maximovich had to do was remove his ancient rheumy mongrel, who loved the leathern smoothness of the Chair and the familiar smells of Yuri's body.

Yuri Maximovich left off his morning salutation to Pushkin and began to circle the Chair. He knew what it meant. It always meant the same. Before he could have his morning tea he forced himself to remember what, if anything, had transpired in his dreams, to bring to consciousness the bits of paper and wisps of smoke that clung to memory after his nocturnal struggle with the shades of forgetfulness.

Yuri Maximovich daily seduced himself into poetry. He used everything in his apartment—the furniture, the configuration of dust, the shape of the twisted bedsheets, the arrangement of the previous night's balls of scribbled paper—as a haruspex would examine a rabbit's entrails, to divine something that had been missed. Each morning now for the past ten days he had come to the Chair, brushed off the sleeping Nastya (who briefly fought against his hand and then hopped off, yawning and yapping with annoyance, to settle near his shoe), and the same line in variance and rearrangement returned to him:

> *His courage was an unembarrassed dawn*
> *Light rising without reflection,*
> *A sun, unabashed.*

But today for some reason he rummaged in his memories more ancient than he had ever plumbed, and he suspected the prying of the agents and the imaginings of sleep and the sheets which had nearly tripped him, wound as they were about his ankles, when he fell from his bed. He could add another line:

> *Zeus does not fear the center of the universe.*

"Yes, friend Nastya. Zeus. That's a splendid god. Zeus, Zeus," he whistled the name as the kettle he had set to boil began to hum. Yuri poured himself the tea and dropped a chip of green apple, slightly browned from exposure, into its murkiness. He sipped and felt warm. What a delicious god, he thought. Now Zeus, an ample figure of the Hellenes: so much a god, but so comprehensible in his magnificent vulnerability; so like a man, so much a god.

> *He accepted heaven as his place.*
> *Why do I have difficulty with my feet?*

Yuri Maximovich put his back to the Chair, straight like a cavalier upon his steed. A pad of paper lay upon his lap, and with his right hand he measured the air with his pen, marking out the words of the half-composed poem. Suddenly he remembered that while he had been struggling at his desk the night before, several lines had moved easily to the paper, but he had not recognized them as his own.

Yuri praised time and the brevity of sleep. The lines were fresh. The teacup almost fell from the armrest where it was balanced as he jumped up and drove into the air the balls of paper hunting for one sheet, the last sheet of the night, on which the lines stood, serried like an army of St. Cyril:

Atlas bore the universe,
But could not move,
The immense weight of fragile worlds
Lodged like apples between his shoulders.

There is no point to feet
If I cannot move.

The eye joined the fragments and the union was agreeable. The imagination construed unawares, bits of this and shards of that unite, and from the secret conjurations, the lines like hard lead type stand forth ready for the paper of eyes. Almost a poem, almost a poem, the first—that is, almost the first—in so much time, in so many months of time. Yuri Maximovich fell back into the Chair, away from the desk and its muzzled lamp light, widening with the birth of day, encompassing more, peering less.

Dawn crept over Moscow like a cautious marauder, stealing up upon Pushkin and putting out the artificial lights that made him glitter, replacing his refulgence with a dull-gray cloak of darkening snow.

Dirty dawn. Moscow dawns deepen suspicion. One confirms the hermeneutics of suspicion in Moscow dawn. The suspicion is not circuitous, as Westerners might think, shrinking lines of argument, widening bulges of paranoia fed by hunger and dizzying dreams of luxuries preserved in literature. It is quite simply the refusal of the dawn, the turning back of sunlight by overpolished marble, by massiveness of architecture, as though Nebuchadnezzar's ziggurats had joined with God's Babel and the city had been rebuilt as a giant commercial office building waiting to be filled up with the products of progress. (If God made light, so can we, the city seemed to say; however, qualifying that arrogance was the caveat that God did not exist, and we in fact might well be scarecrows and inventions.)

The light of Moscow dawns is dirty in the winter. It sneaks in and suffuses and there's a moment—ten minutes or so—when all the lights are extinguished in order to conserve fuel, and dawn waits in the suburbs. That is the hour when early men like Yuri Maximovich are filled with suspicion, tense with uncertainty, not knowing which is gone forever, the lights of men or the muted sounds of divine speaking (light, being for Russian poets, another form of speech).

The moments when the lights of Moscow disappeared and the filaments of dawn inched, like centipedes, across the Moscow sky were always the most terrifying and exhilarating for Yuri Maximovich. He sometimes dreamed that this was what death would be like: the transition between the artifice of anatomical apparatus and the free kingdom of sourceless breath—breath, like light, having no familiar origin and no perceptible end.

That particular morning, January 17, 1972, was different than it had been for a year of mornings before. A conjuction of terror and hope. His apartment had been searched and a poem seemed to be shaping in his blood; the bubbles of verse tingled in his brain, the vein above his right eye bobbed like the gullet of a fish, and words, beloved words, fell from his lips like manna in the desert. Why today? he wondered. But he reined his incredulity and accepted it, and that too was unusual for Yuri Maximovich. In the past, all those unproductive years between 1957 and 1972 (he salvaged at most two dozen poems from that period, all unpublished, most not even read at public recitals), he would take a broken line, a handful of words, a solitary image as omen that the dry season was over, that the great waters of verse were rising within him and the flood would soon begin. He would, not unlike this moment, sit still upon the Chair and speculate upon the causes, but within a week the waters had settled again and playful little streams licking visible stones, covering the ground moss of his soul (thin, insubstantial, lightweight, definitely lightweight), would be all that remained. After each of these false alarms or stillbirths Yuri Maximovich would generally subside into despair, and with despair would come a foray into self-deception, a bit of toadying, a conspicuous maneuver of ass-licking—currying favor with some fourth-rate hack in the Union of Soviet Writers, badgering for a mention of his first and only book of poems in a minor roundup of a quarter-century of Soviet verse. But after fifteen years of this he had learned his lesson. He had been slapped about like a fly—no, not even a fly, a gnat who buzzed and hummed and flitted from ass to ass, picking up occasionally the morsel of his name. He had the nine clippings in which his name had been mentioned, all but one in provincial journals—the one exception being a mention of him in Kolokolov's enormously celebrated memoir of poetry in the fifties, which Ilia Alexandrovich had called with orotund clarity and a bell-like tinkle of modesty, *Footnote to My Poetry.*

From the journal of Yuri Maximovich Isakovsky
March 11, 1962

Ilia Alexandrovich has published his memoir. *Hoc fecit.* The bell is ringing throughout the land. Four hundred thousand copies in a month. Bedkin, that vermin, put a note under my door. The note was filthy. Filthy with Bedkin and Bedkin's leaking pen and smudgy fingers. Filthy with the truth.

"Did you know, Yuri Maximovich, that Kolokolov has four hundred thousand readers?" Yes. And the next morning he had one more. I put down my two rubles for that book. I found myself on page 102. It reads:

> There were eleven people at the dinner. Sasha Lebyedev, the *metteur en scène* of the Bolshoi, the great Nina Isakova, our soprano, Boris Lipmansky, Secretary of the Union of Soviet Writers, Nikolai Koramazin, director of one of our distinguished publishing houses (and my own publisher), Yuri Maximovich Isakovsky, a poet and musicologist, old Konstantin Paustovsky, my wife Lena, and myself. It was in a private room at one of our new Moscow hotels.

> The conversation turned to poetry. I had just published my fourth book of poems, *Tough Talk*, and many people thought I had taken my life in my hands. But they did not understand the resilience and power of our people. Most of the guests were a little fretful. We had all drunk a great deal. It was then my old friend, Yuri Maximovich, said, "Ilia, tell the story of your life. Tell it straight out and everyone will understand that *Tough Talk* is not a knife at the jugular vein, but a loving pinch on the cheek, a lover's chafing with his mistress." I thought a moment and knew he was right. That's the true origin of *Footnote*. It was an old friend's suggestion.

And so it runs on. I became the origin of that document in self-congratulation. Can you comprehend how he writes? He writes prose exactly as he writes poetry. He thinks he's profound because he can't see the bottom. Of course he can't see the bottom! It's covered with mud. Slime, tadpoles, algae, pure murk and mud. And he thinks it's profound. Can you believe a paragraph like this—the opening paragraph, mind you—"A poet's only life is his poems. Everything else he writes, everything he says about his life—his origins and history, his parents, friends, lovers—are so many footnotes to his poems. They explain a line or establish a marginal fact, but the only truth, the real truth of the poet's life is in his poems. A poem should be so whole, so total that everything the poet is, everything he feels, all that he stands for should be in that poem. Read the poem and you know the poet. It is for that reason that everything which follows here is a footnote."

If only I had known my Marx and Lenin well enough, I would have put my clapper to Kolokolov's romanticism. But of course I wouldn't do that. That's precisely the point with me. I don't use such language well at all.

Here on view, neatly arranged, I have a well-thumbed complete writings of everyone. "Well-thumbed." What a joke. If Irina Alexandrovna had ever told. She wouldn't. She left me for the Major but she also helped me assemble my show library when we married in 1954. Her father, an instructor in Marxism-Leninism for the union of electrical workers in a small radio factory in Volgograd, sent me a whole library. They arrived in two packing cases, the week of our wedding. The complete writings of Stalin were still in tissue paper, so fresh and pristine that for weeks I kept them on the shelf in their swaddling clothes. But when we were finally organized—that is to say, when Irina had reorganized this apartment to accommodate me and my possessions to her arrival—it became necessary to assimilate our new literary hoardings.

Friday morning when Irina returned from shopping (we were having friends in to visit Sunday evening for the first time since our marriage) she motioned to the books and said, "Yuri, don't you think they should look like they've been handled a bit?" I realized then and there it would be dangerous to have all those unread books sitting on the shelves, clean, unscuffed, virginal, when just beneath them on the bottom two shelves were anthologies of American and English poetry, and much Russian belles-lettres and verse by considerably more mortal figures of our times. I decided I had to take care of this, so I sat down with the various student's guides to the readings of the masters of the revolution and began to annotate the standard editions my father-in-law had provided. It was quite easy but took more than twenty hours to complete—and it had to be done skillfully.

The first thing I did was to determine that certain of the texts could be underlined casually, and so for Marx's controversies with Feuerbach, I used a rather thick, soft pencil, whose graphite spread and smudged. The lines were undulant and casual. Marx's destruction of Feuerbach could be regarded as a super-addendum—not crucial to one's education but indicative of one's serious regard for the literature. No less for Engels's history of the textile workers of England. *The Communist Manifesto*, on the other hand, required many careful readings: for the first a sharply pointed drafting pencil and a little ruler were crucial. The text was thoughtfully underlined, whole blocks of the text enclosed within double-ruled rectangles, and an occasional underscoring in red suggesting that a second reading had been undertaken; in the margins, when the plight of the proletariat was exposed, the vices of the bourgeoisie exhibited, or the criminality of the ruling oligarchies inveighed against, I would pencil such profound exuberances as "splendid," "well-said," "to the point," or simply "*nota bene.*" In due course I worked through all of Marx and Engels, Kautsky's Erfurt program, Rosa Luxemburg, the trial speeches of Vishinsky, later the manifestoes, pronunciamentoes and exortia of Lenin, and the lectures, position papers, and addresses to Party and the nation of Stalin himself. I had acquired to fill out this sound and reasonable library the novels of Alexei Tolstoy, Sholokhov, Paustovsky, Ehrenburg, and many others including safe lives of the leaders, and early adventurous works by Bukharin and Lunacharsky, even though they had later passed under the knife. And when all the underscorings and jottings were done, all the "fines" and "splendids" written in the margins, all the page references to often-cited passages copied in the front of the flyleaves of the seminal volumes, I took each book and cracked its binding repeatedly, coffee-stained an occasional page, rubbed dust upon their backs, and returned the volumes, now violated, to their original places.

It was only the morning of the party, Sunday morning, that Irina said mockingly, "Did you notice, Yuri, that Papa sent us only the most recent editions?" Then it was that I realized for the first time that the Stalin Codex, for instance, had been published only two months before, the Lenin was six months old, and the Marx-Engels, the only one of vintage, had been published towards the end of the war. Indeed, if anyone had bothered to notice, my education was rather complete and phoenixlike, rising full-blown from the ashes of my indifference. Fortunately none of our guests ever proved curious about my knowledge of the sources of the Revolution and the history of the Party. Bedkin, the spy, might have noticed the books, but he was too illiterate to have discovered my ruse, and anyway I didn't know him personally nor would I have invited him to such a family festivity.

Clearly, I was in no position to chastise Ilia Alexandrovich for his bourgeois romanticism—if indeed it was simply bourgeois romanticism. At the most, poor Ilia Alexandrovich is guilty of metaphysical stupidity, a misunderstanding of what the Greeks call the *ontos on*, the very being of being. He thinks of his poetry as the precipitate of life, the by-product of retorts and burners, the congealment of all of life. Poetry for Ilia is mined gold; he thinks the rest of life, its shale and clay, is to be chipped away and discarded in the deep mining of making verse. His mistake is to think of the poem as more perfect than the life. Ilia's romantic delusion is a conceit, as if to say, "My poetry is pure, though my life be an impurity." That's nonsense. Poetry is nothing if it is not the transcription as truth

—adamantine, clear, impassioned, and above all, intelligent—of everything that life demands in immediacy, confusion, promptness. Poetry is silent breathing, unhurried, a contemplation of sources.

I would be called a metaphysical poet were I not so nervous. My friends think my dogginess, fingernail biting, shaking hand, tipping teacup behavior incommensurable with metaphysics. What they miss, of course, is that being makes me nervous. Anyone who takes sleeping for death and waking for paradise is not simply making metaphors—which nonpoets read as making mistakes—but making metaphysics. I think life is chancy. Perhaps that is the reason why I have done everything to avoid being murdered, murder being the normal means of dying in this country, natural death being unnatural and rare among the intelligentsia and bureaucrats (and I am both, as poet and editor, and sometime English translator).

No, I take it back. I am in no position to put clappers to Kolokolov. My wood clapper would be shattered on his iron bell. I am too vulnerable to chastise. I stay alive. I endure. I bury poems in my head like diligent ants dragging provender for the winter to the deep caverns in their hills.

2. At the Office of The People's Voice

Yuri Maximovich always walked slowly from his little apartment above Pushkin Square to the offices of *The People's Voice*, the quarterly journal of folk music that he had edited for eighteen years.

Yuri became editor of *The People's Voice* in 1954 shortly after the death of Stalin, when the lower echelons had begun to feel the tremors of relaxation before Georgi Malenkov opened the trap door beneath himself, in the midst of the famous thaw during which the ice softened but, alas, froze again before new tendrils could begin to grow. Yuri's predecessor in this sinecure, a specialist in Armenian folk music, had unfortunately disappeared after the degeneration and death of Stalin because the late President of the Independent Socialist Republic of Azerbaijan had been denounced as an insurrectionist Armenian nationalist and executed; unfortunately old Comrade Adam Sagatelian—who had come up from Sevan in his middle years, called to his position at *The People's Voice* at the recommendation of the now-deceased President—met too frequently with that late aforementioned to discuss the Islamic sources of Armenian music of which the former sang a considerable repertoire (accompanying himself on a strange stringed instrument) and which the latter parsed and examined laboriously, all the while mopping his perspiration with a large silk handkerchief.

Yuri Maximovich had met Comrade Sagatelian only once, at a reception held by the same late President of Azerbaijan in 1952. Yuri was delighted to meet someone who came from the island of Sevan, since he knew the accounts of its geography and history written by Osip Emilievich Mandelstam twenty years before when Mandelstam's sometime protector Nikolai Bukharin had sent him to Armenia to get him out of Moscow at a time when the campaign to discredit that poet had become vocational training for Soviet journalists. Yuri Maximovich had been introduced to Comrade Sagatelian, and the moment old Adam had mentioned his island of origin, Yuri had asked, cupping his hand against a pretended cough, "Did you by chance meet the poet—what was his name? Mandelstam, I believe—when he visited Armenia?"

Comrade Adam smiled as Armenians do, his eyes creasing while chin and lips slept impassively, and nodded affirmatively. "Yes. Oh, yes," he said, the words coming some seconds after the acknowledging nod. "Tell me about him. Do those monastic mud huts he described still exist in Sevan?" Comrade Adam nodded once more. Their conversation was not productive. The Armenian committed himself to nothing more than several nods. The inquisitive Kievan Jewish poet betrayed nothing more than a fleeting, surreptitious curiosity.

Several years later, when Yuri Maximovich applied for a change of position (at the time of his marriage to Irina Alexandrovna Narcissova), the Ministry of Culture's office of placements and positions, having duly examined his credentials and starred on his bibliography that he had once written an essay (admittedly fanciful) on the possible connection between the music of the Kazan Jews and the Islamic trope in Armenian music (the connection being that all these had converged at a remote time in the eleventh century when the Caucasian king and his court and people had been converted to Judaism, as set forth in history books and mythologized by the Jewish philosopher of Spain, Judah the Levite), sent him over to take a look at *The People's Voice.*

The offices of *The People's Voice* were located about forty-five medium and long blocks from Yuri's apartment. The first morning that Yuri set out from his apartment to visit *The People's Voice*, he decided to walk. It was material to his well-being that he have a long walk to work. The comfortable hour that it took him—through broad boulevards, a small garden, and an old district of Moscow which boasted a street on which Lermontov, Herzen, and Pushkin had all at one time lived—delighted him. He suspected that he would find the position acceptable.

The offices of *The People's Voice* were located in an old wooden building, not even then scheduled for demolition, and at the time of this writing, still standing. The brass plate in the hallway near the apartment of the concierge directed him to the third floor; there he found the lyric quarters in which he was to spend nearly two decades. The door rattled open and he entered.

The rattling apparently disturbed the bird. The moment he entered, a finch began to chant indecisively, starting and breaking off, running a whole scale perfectly and then meandering to an abrupt halt, mouthing its message along with birdseed that it flung around the cage as though demented. A sensible precaution—a security system appropriate for a music magazine, Yuri thought, amused.

Directly behind the door he observed the cage on top of a large, glass-fronted bookcase which sheltered bound volumes of *The People's Voice*. It was only after he had come around the partition separating a species of semiprivate office from the small sitting room that he noticed a young woman, of dark cast and splendid face boned like an Arabian steed (all flaring and flushing), with deep-set vast eyes, black like ebony beads. She faced him but did not disturb herself to look up, though Yuri Maximovich was directly above her, waiting for the bird to stop singing and for the young beauty to acknowledge him. Several moments passed. At last she lifted her face from the large sheets covered with clef and stave marks, and having blottered her fingers one at a time, leaving behind five neatly rounded fingerprints on the absorbent paper, she removed the green visor sheathing her hair and smiled. The hair spread and curled about her face like a liberated wraith, accentuating the lean boniness of her steed-mien. She had been copying some music for the printers.

"You must be Isakovsky, Yuri Maximovich," she announced cheerfully.

Momentarily shocked by her inversion of his name, Yuri replied with unconventional eagerness, "Yes. And you?"

"Alegrini, Lydia Yegorovna." She answered in the same way, but her attention was distracted by something slightly to the north of Yuri's forehead. Yuri looked over his shoulder, thinking perhaps he had brought a bug with him to the offices.

"Forgive me, forgive me. It's your hair. Do you know, Isakovsky, that you have a shock of hair standing up like a scarecrow."

"Yes, I know. The wind does it. The wind has always done it. I don't mind," Yuri replied and, embarrassed, patted the top of his head, flattening the scarecrow.

"It's amusing. Yes, very amusing. You will be amusing, won't you?"

"Really? And how will I amuse you," Yuri replied, nonplused but enchanted. It seemed an odd way for a secretary (even if she was totally alone and therefore superior to everyone and no one) to conduct herself, to behave in such an informal manner before a total stranger—indeed, before someone who might well become her superior.

"You're replacing Comrade Sagatelian?"

"I don't know yet. I've been sent here to find out if I want the job."

"Oh, you know better than that. How long have you been a Soviet citizen? I should suspect all your life. Well, certainly you know this is no inspection. They may call it an inspection, but in fact it's an appointment"—she pointed to a letter in the wooden file box on the desk—"and, I should add, quite clearly an order. You have been ordered to run *The People's Voice.* That makes you my superior. It is a pleasure to meet you, Comrade Editor."

"I see," Yuri Maximovich answered, glazed by the rapidity of events. "I see. Well, now. Appointed. Ordered. Yes. Hmm. Is that quite so?" he mused aloud.

"Oh yes, Comrade Editor, quite so. No doubt about it. It's right here." She practically speared the paper on an eccentrically sharp index finger, using her thumb like the supportive mandible of a crab, and began to read rapidly. " 'Yuri Maximovich Isakovsky, Soviet journalist, musicologist, translator, and poet, has been appointed the new editor of *The People's Voice*, effective November 19, 1954.' Well, that's today, isn't it? So you see, the inspection is no inspection." She paused and then asked, her eyes focused now upon his scuffed black shoes, "You're not a party member, are you?"

"No. No." Yuri replied distracted.

"Well, I shouldn't think that would matter too much. I am. It helps to have a party member about when it comes to printed matter, don't you think? It's all a bit easier now that we've put the gods and demons to bed, but we can still make mistakes if we're not vigilant. And we don't have hoards of editors like our other journals, do we? So, instead of collective responsibility, we have ceaseless vigilance. I'm our ceaseless vigilant and a pretty one, don't you think?" Lydia Yegorovna paused but did not wait long enough for Yuri to confirm the obvious. "You're not married, are you? Yes, well, I know that too. I have your whole record right here. Born in Kiev. Jewish. Soviet Army. Artillery. Front lines. Decorated twice. Wounded at Kharkov. Demobilized in 1946. And then articles, articles, articles. Parents dead. No brothers. One sister. And you have a two-room apartment. That is important, isn't it, Comrade." The acquisition of that treasure of an apartment, like the Chair, came back to him. Accidental good fortune. Six years earlier an old woman had died at the precise moment Yuri was making inquiries of the House Chairman. Yuri waited until the funeral was over, helped her dolorous grandson pack up her belongings, made a contribution to the House Chairman, and moved in. Did she know all that, too? But Yuri's curiosity outweighed his inclination to acerbity.

"What's important, Comrade Alegrini?"

"The apartment. A two-room apartment?"

"If you wish. Yes. A two-room apartment, although one room is a converted broom closet."

"As I said, a two-room apartment."

"Yes. And all two rooms, all four hundred and fifty-three paced-off and measured feet of it are mine. Not large rooms, as you can surmise. Modest, very modest and stuffed with books. Books everywhere."

"You probably read endlessly. Every night, I should think, read and read."

"And write," Yuri interjected, a bit sadly.

"Your poems?"

"Yes, my poems."

"And whose poems do you like? Whose?" Yuri felt the down on the back of his neck flutter. His electrostatic shield had been violated. The radar went on, scanning the ether about him. "Oh," he gestured vaguely, with a lazy arm, "the young singers, the tough young singers, the Leningraders, I suppose, although they seem on occasion mannered and a trifle aesthetic, as though the old style had inched back undetected. Yes. I like loud, husky voices."

"I agree," Lydia Yegorovna pronounced, satisfied.

She stamped her feet on the floor, pushed back her chair, and stood up. The power of the gesture, its astonishing decisiveness, further jarred Yuri Maximovich. The masculinity of the movement was at such variance with the slender and lovely figure which stood up from behind the desk.

Lydia Yegorovna Alegrini was not an athletic Marxist, so familiar about Moscow, the young women whose bodies were left to the vagaries of fate and the demands of labor. This young woman, this woman in her twenties (he later found out from the files that she was twenty-seven), cared for her body. It was hosed and shod, girdled and brassiered like he imagined every stunning French girl, Italian girl, American girl he had coveted in magazines was assembled.

"May I ask you something?"

"Of course, Comrade Editor."

"Forgive me," he began deferentially, "but Alegrini? An Alegrini in Russia? If you don't mind. A beautiful name, and evidently the right one for you." He smiled, his even teeth showing through cautiously parted lips.

"But of course. You know the ancient company of Rossi, Rinaldi, and Rastrelli, our great imported architects. That fraternity hired by Peter the Great and Catherine II who built in Old Leningrad, in Kiev, and raised up churches and palaces and noble homes. All Italians. They brought with them draftsmen, marble workers, carpenters, craftsmen of all sorts. I think over the years they lived in Great Russia they must have invited more than a hundred craftsmen to the court. Well, then, my great-great-grandfather, or was it my great-great-great-grandfather—who can be certain?—in any event, a distant paternal relative, a mason from Genoa who was responsible for a lovely patch of floor in the Stroganov Palace, was my patronymic ancestor. Over the years, although my father's family did think about changing names in the middle of the last century when the unpleasant Nicholas was at the height of his xenophobia, their neighbors protested and persuaded them to stand fast. Everyone loved having the Alegrinis about. Such a lovely Mediterranean name for a family on the Neva. Is that enough, Yuri Maximovich?"

"Oh, yes. Yes, indeed. A lovely story. Perhaps I will even give you a poem in return for that story." Yuri smiled again and the smile was received with a smile, and all smiles exhausted, the tour of the offices began.

The People's Voice was a modest but influential journal, distributed throughout the world to every institute of folklore and ethnic culture, to every library of musicology, and throughout the Soviet Union to every school, to every Center of Rest, Recreation, and Culture, and naturally to every foreign press bureau and embassy. It had a remarkably large distribution in Kenya, although it was never discovered to what possible use eight hundred copies could conceivably be put in Kenya, except, as one wit in the post office had commented, to hide the nudity of the prime minister's tribe. All this enormous culture—this culture of thirty thousand copies quarterly—was produced out of an exceptionally small office run by a Comrade Editor working as reader, stylist, exegete, prosodist, and researcher in two large gabled rooms of an old Moscow apartment house, which tilted southwards against the sunlight (damn the land slope, for it denied the room at least two inches of sunlight on good days); the rooms were furnished with three vast tables standing on bulging legs, file cabinets, uncomfortable chairs, a birdcage, a desk with six large drawers in which previous editors had hidden boiled eggs, sweets and nuts, gloves, caps with earflaps, pipe tobacco, and packets of *makhorka* stinking like rotted rope, all of which contents Yuri Maximovich emptied out the first day (one of the disagreeable aspects of losing one's job by arrest was that the prisoner—in this case, Comrade Sagatelian—did not have the opportunity to empty his desk of debris and the police, observing that the drawers had no papers nor hidden compartments, were uninterested in gathering up the decomposing rot and stuffing it into their evidence bags), a cleaning boy and runner—always of eighteen years of age or thereabouts, invariably a relative of some high official, with a name like Vanya or Vassily, and lately (so Lydia observed), with a running nose which was wiped on manuscript envelopes—and the same Alegrini, Lydia Yegorovna, who had come to the journal at the age of twenty-two, direct from university. Having studied the kithara (the ancient form of zither on which Comrade Sagatelian had excelled) and having learned how to copy music, write neatly, and use the typewriter, she was immediately hired when her employer learned that she had been recommended by Boris Pepinka Kaltangorov, who administered all subsidies for the various Soviet troupes of performing singers, dancers, acrobatic bears, and circuses. Young Lydia, it seems, had also had an affair wtih Comrade Kaltangorov, which helped matters and insured that old Sagatelian would have pass tickets every Friday night to the Moscow Circus, which he adored (the poor old Comrade was in fact picked up by the police as he left a performance of the circus).

There you are, then, two large rooms: one partitioned into secretarial space where Lydia Yegorovna typed, transcribed, answered her telephone, monitored Yuri Maximovich's telephone, dispatched the nose-wiping V on his errands about Moscow to collect and deliver manuscripts and post, fed the watch-bird finch, and administered the Comrade Editor, who occupied the other large room, connected to her own by a door upon which one had to knock and a slot in the wall through which calls and shouts could be delivered and messages dropped and occasionally an admonishing or beckoning finger could be pushed.

An aside about the slot in the wall. It was an opening after all, an incision cut by design into wood and plaster flesh that had remained unprotected, naked and uncovered, from 1823 (when the particular house in which *The People's Voice* was domiciled had been constructed) to the present. Probably for hot dishes fed from kitchen to dining room, Yuri Maximovich surmised. The cicatrix was like the mouth of an automatic food dispenser, so popular in the fantasy of Russia ever since the Tramp had added *Modern Times* to the legacy of the October Revolution. The wound had gaped until Yuri Maximovich discovered that Lydia's ear was invariably inserted in its void whenever he answered or made a telephone call. He then, contending to Lydia that cold drafts and refugee flies made their way into his office from the space beyond through the medium of the naked aperture, demanded that there be affixed to either side a metal strip, flexing on spring hinges. On Lydia's side the metal flap bore the little legend "Lift to Open." On Yuri's it read: "Keep Closed."

The conviction that every office in the Soviet Union had its own security police did not diminish with the knowledge that one's office had only three inhabitants. It simply meant that one's suspicions need not extend beyond the obvious. Lydia Yegorovna Alegrini, party member, mistress of notables, had denounced her predecessor and Yuri Maximovich was presumably next in line. It fitted naturally and Yuri was not unduly alarmed. He was only disappointed that she was so beautiful an agent. It was prudent then for Yuri to speculate and to wish to verify Lydia's extracurricular vocation. He couldn't seal off the opening precipitously. It required several weeks of sneezing and beating at flies with rolled papers before he could announce straight out that he had to close off the opening. Before that, however, fair man that he remained, it was necessary to confirm his suspicions of Lydia Yegorovna.

The morning of his first official day as editor of *The People's Voice*, Yuri had spent perusing back issues of the magazine. It was still inconceivable to him that the eighty-page journal —filled as it was with essays and notations, discographies and bibliographic entries, critical annotations of musical transcriptions, musical examples and complete notations, diagnostics of diseases of the language which rendered modern versions of old folk-lyric traditions either formalistic and unspontaneous or stylized and indulgent (that essay had been the last written by the *disparu* Comrade Sagatelian), editorial invitations to free submissions, contests for unregistered folk songs with special prizes to ethnic communities having less than a population of one million, and photographs of singers, performers, bards, hymnists, and musicologists—could possibly be put together and published by a staff of two and a minor. But that was the case. It was only him, Lydia Yegorovna, and boy.

There were of course numerous contributors: contributors who wrote letters, contributors who sent recordings which had to be played at Lydia Yegorovna's flat, since *The People's Voice* lacked a phonograph (or, it should be noted, Lydia Yegorovna's cumbersome machine was really borrowed State property or property on extended leave of absence at her apartment from the office), or as sometimes happened, as for instance on the second morning of Yuri Maximovich's long tenure, a personal visit from a contributor—in this case, the virid and purplish Yasha Isaievich Tyutychev.

Comrade Tyutychev descended on the office in a whoosh of cold air and steam shortly after Yuri Maximovich arrived for his second proper day of work—that is, November 21, 1954.

Yuri had just collected his mail from the wire basket that hung beneath the open and as yet unshielded mouth of the aperture and begun to sift through it, muttering with confusion, not knowing which letter to open first, for all were addressed to Adam Sagatelian, the decedent, or to Comrade Editor, or to the editor's letter column, and Yuri had no idea how to cope with such a volume of mail—twenty-three letters in all. He had gone through nineteen of those letters when to his amazement he found one addressed to him by name, Comrade Editor Yuri Maximovich Isakovsky. He called to Lydia Yegorovna and saw her eyes, like those of a lynx, suddenly peering at him through the slot.

"How is it possible that one Yasha Isaievich Tyutychev could have known that I was to be the new editor of the journal? Have you any idea?" No sooner had he finished his question than the door flew open and into its expanse stepped a transfixedly ugly man of middle years, his body draped in dog fur which rose up to a mottled collar, upon which his jowls (jowls so slack that one imagined each contained the lees of trampled grapes) rested comfortably. The eyes peered around his nasal promontory like telescopes; his hair was cut in bangs which descended to his eyebrows. That was Comrade Tyutychev.

"Quite simply, Comrade Editor—she told me, the beautiful Lydia told me. Don't you know me? I am the gypsy editor, the contributing editor for itinerant music, vagabonds and ne'er-do-wells, nonpolitical convicts, recusants of all types, as long as they sing. I'm written on the masthead. That's my name on the inside left page, between Miukov and Vinogradin, and it would seem correctly middle, since Miukov handles the urban idiom, songs of draymen and costermongers and tailors, and Vinogradin the laments of the gypsies. I am the link between them—the country mouse come to the city, the city mouse fleeing to the country. I've been waiting for you to arrive. I've come every day since your predecessor passed on, hoping that somebody new, young, lively would be appointed." Tyutychev talked on and on, moving around the desk to shake Yuri Maximovich's hand, opening his dog's fur to reveal his vest, gold watch, and worker's trousers, his black high-button shoes and white silk socks, the sore on his nose, the hair in his ear, and the sheaf of papers which he pulled from his pocket and lay open page by page from one end of Yuri's desk to the other.

At the conclusion of his address Tyutychev motioned to Yuri Maximovich not to speak and began to sing his little essay—a combination of expository text on thieves' songs of the Ukrainian markets and their tunes, all sung together, basso like the rumble of an Orthodox deacon reciting the Credo and fluent tenor as the melody parted from the words. Yuri could not help but listen, amazed and not a little intimidated. How could such an oddity exist in the Soviet Union—no, not an oddity, such an out-of-step, such a parody of decadence, such a madman.

"Excuse me, Tyutychev."

"Comrade Tyutychev," Tyutychev reproved, smiling, "and if not Comrade, then colleague. The masthead remember, Comrade Editor. And my forty rubles. Do you remember those?" At this recollection of his unpaid fee he shouted, "Lydia Yegorovna, remember my forty rubles. You owe me bread and rent. Forty rubles, that's what it takes to keep Tyutychev hunting in the sewers for culture."

"Good Comrade Tyutychev," Yuri Maximovich began, interrupting Tyutychev's singsong. His own voice was low, even condescending, for he was hoping to cut beneath the unsettling enthusiasm and bluster of Tyutychev. "I am sure Lydia Yegorovna has not forgotten. But that's not the reason you've come to see me unannounced, without an appointment. You must understand that editors are busy men."

"But of course, of course, Comrade Editor. It is precisely because your colleague understands all these things that he has come the second day after your investiture. The article, that's what I've come about. My article." For a moment Yuri had no idea to what article he referred, but Tyutychev helped him, turning to the desk again and gathering up, like wash left to dry, the sheets from which he had hymnically descanted the woebegone laments of his Ukrainian thieves. "Ah, yes, that was very much an article," Yuri acknowledged distractedly.

"Your first editorial decision. I have come for a decision. Our dear departed Comrade Sagatelian—may he rest in seraphic arms—was considering the article. I had sung it to him three months ago, but he was unable to complete his decision. Oh, did Adam deliberate and deliberate." Tyutychev pulled at his jowls with a blubbery hand. "He never could decide in the twinkling of an eye. It was difficult, so very Marxist of him. He had to figure out the bearings of this upon that, the implication of each phrase for the groan of history. Every time I would try to hurry him along, he would say—you must know the terminology—'Wait, wait, Tyutychev, we must reflect as parts of the superstructure whether it enlarges the basis.' What incredibly amusing language that is." Then he whispered to Yuri in a voice surely bassoed through the aperture to Lydia's enlarged ear, "Forgive me, Comrade. I shouldn't say such things. Lydia hears all, remembers everything, even writes down counterrevolutionary observations like housewives making a shopping list." Tyutychev was clutching his papers to his breast, occasionally raising them like a fan to his face to cover some questionable remark or shield one or another of his outrageous adjectives from rising with the whole sentence to Lydia's attentive ear.

Tyutychev's monologue continued while he roamed about the office, opening his dog fur when he became agitated and slamming it shut when he rose to his full height to drive home some weary point about the inefficiency, pusillanimity, or sheer indifference of Soviet editors. At last, after circling Yuri's desk in ever-diminishing swathes of space, he came to rest before him, and putting his puffy face right up to Yuri's nose, he muttered, "So? So what is it, Comrade? What's the answer? I eat today. But do I eat next week and the week after? It was a fifty-ruble essay for Sagatelian, but for you, since you're new, a special fee. Forty-two rubles. How do I arrive at forty-two? Well, this way. My lodgings, so they are called (I share a bed with a worker in the turbo-electric plant who does the night shift), come to two rubles a week. Food. Not much. I beg food, steal it occasionally, or turn up uninvited at gatherings where there's a bit of scrapple for grabs. Let's make food eight rubles. Tips for itinerants who sing songs to me. One ruble distributed in numerous kopeck benefactions. The rest goes for *kvas*, cigarettes of the cheapest kind, and vodka twice a week. I get by on twenty-one rubles and make the difference from doing errands for newspapers, poets looking for an image (I hunt up images, you know, Comrade?), entertainers wanting a new folk song (that's where I make the most, sometimes one hundred rubles for a good song). But you, you're my two-week man. Forty-two rubles. Heh. What do you think? It's a nice piece. I sang it without the footnotes. Nine footnotes with fabricated references to lost versions. Readers love my stuff."

Tyutychev spoke all this about an inch from Yuri Maximovich's forehead, the words curling about him like the buzz of bees, the flutter of hummingbirds, the whisper of little lizards. Tyutychev's dog fur smelled, but Tyutychev was irresistible.

"Yes, yes, of course we'll publish you. Have no fear. I'll take the essay. That makes eighty-two rubles we owe you."

Tyutychev, delighted, embraced Yuri Maximovich and in triumph raised his voice. "I told you, Lydia Yegorovna, he bought it. A draft for eighty-two rubles." Yuri Maximovich realized that he had been foxed, but it did not embarrass him. It was only after Tyutychev departed, promising to return again the following day for his money, that Lydia Yegorovna descended upon him.

"You were an idiot, Comrade Editor. Oh, yes, I know. I shouldn't call you an idiot. It's rude and insulting. But do you know what you've done? You've put a bad mark on your record. Tyutychev is not really too long for our world. The police have been looking at him for some time now. He consorts with the low and corrupt. He's a fence, a thief (he confessed it, didn't he, stealing food), a good-for-nothing. We don't need Tyutychevs."

"That's a question, isn't it? dear Lydia Yegorovna," Yuri Maximovich remonstrated, smiling at her anger.

"Not to me. It's no question to me."

"I'm sorry about that. I thought there was something marvelous and exotic about him."

"Like cannibal plants and noxious gases. Exotic. Phew. He stinks, that Tyutychev does."

"I have to agree with you there."

They didn't pursue their disagreement. When she had left, grumbling that she hated to pay out good money for such drivel as Tyutychev's, Yuri Maximovich found himself vaguely anxious. He was unsettled and distressed. He belched, covering his mouth with a handkerchief lest the sour smell of his discontent waft through the aperture into Lydia Yegorovna's cubbyhole. Tyutychev not long for "our world"? Not only was Lydia a viper, it appeared, but she was determined to bite such harmless and innocent men as Tyutychev. Granted he was improbable, disconcerting, not of the Soviet world, but that had as much to say about the Soviet world as it had to say about Tyutychev. Yuri Maximovich tried to find Tyutychev that night to warn him, but he was not at the address he had written out for the office records. Somehow Yuri Maximovich suspected he might not see Tyutychev again. He didn't return the following day as he had promised.

After several weeks had passed, Yuri gathered up the manuscript which Tyutychev had left behind and put it in one of the drawers of his desk. Many times over the coming years he reread the essay, and as time passed, he converted the essay from a lean and parsimonious exercise in fake scholarship into a kind of private liturgy, concluding each month of his stay at *The People's Voice* by opening the drawer in which it lay and looking at its florid hand, its curlicues and elaborate delicacies, checking a trope or tune, looking up one or another bit of Ukrainian slang in which the thieves' songs abounded, reconstituting on each occasion of inspection the energetic and impassioned presence that had been Yasha Isaievich Tyutychev.

It was like that for fifteen years. Yuri Maximovich was continuously muddled; even after his marriage he remained muddled. Lydia Yegorovna liked nothing about Yuri Maximovich except Yuri himself. She disliked his poems. She disliked his vagueness. Perhaps it was because Lydia Yegorovna could control him that she suffered him. Indeed she could. Yuri Maximovich had no certain proof that she was an informer, but she conducted herself like a spy. One of the curiosities of Soviet life he had long observed was that anyone and everyone could be an informer. For most informers it was not a professional activity; they received no plain envelopes with neatly folded bills for their services. But the fact that it was never known for certain if so-and-so *was* KGB meant it could never be ascertained. Only the closest of close friends could discuss the matter, and even among them it was possible that a slip could be made. Everyone in this society is part-time. Life on suffrance makes for part-time corruption. Almost no one was exempt, for the system worked better that way. Only the top was exempt. The masters were never spies. But Lydia, most definitely Lydia of the circumspect, was an informer. Perhaps, Yuri once thought, she was merely curious, constitutionally curious, committed to the hearing of every conversation and the reading of every scrap of paper that passed across his desk, but he disabused himself of that fantasy. He found her one day winnowing his wastebasket; she claimed that she had misplaced the address of a correspondent and was hunting for the envelope that had accompanied his letter. But he couldn't believe her. That particular day he had occupied himself working on the draft of a poem, and the basket was literally filled with discarded texts, bunched and now flattened out. She had the temerity—admirable, he thought—to convert her nosiness into a virtue, quoting to him a line from the draft she had found and urging him to persevere.

Yuri Maximovich was surprised on the anniversary of every year of his summary appointment to *The People's Voice*. He was surprised that his masters renewed his appointment, which is only to say that they had never harassed him, never contested his editorial decisions and innovations. He was permitted to conduct his life in the unsupervised and leisurely atmosphere of his apartment and his office, occasionally traveling to the small dacha which he had been allowed to buy in Peredelkino, and once, when he had managed to save some money, spending two weeks at a recuperative sanitorium on the Black Sea, where in the company of two dozen other exhausted intellectuals, he took walks in the fields and hunted birds' nests. Yuri Maximovich persevered as Yuri Maximovich despite endless invitations to cease to be himself, to become something slightly different and unfamiliar. He had passed through changes in heads of state, shifts in foreign policy, showdowns and confrontations with foreign enemies, and at home, the harassment of dissidents and malcontents—many of whom, he thought with relief, were now out of the way in exile —and the protests of Jews sitting down in Red Square or demonstrating before the synagogue in Bolshoy Spasoglinishchevsky Lane before Passover and during Purim and Chanukah. He had read accounts of these demonstrations and shook his head both sadly and in disbelief. Something in his nature understood perfectly well what it was all about, but he felt, quite reasonably, that there was little point in trying to join them, to shout out a slogan or two before the KGB hustled them into fast little cars and sped them away to oblivion. And so he kept these feelings to himself, stoppered with silence and grinding teeth. Even when Lydia Yegorovna would try to find out his opinion of this or that, his view of Aleksandr Solzhenitsyn or Andrei Sakharov or the poor Jewish dancer with the Kirov Ballet, he would say something prudent and intelligent, but finally evasive. His favorite phrase, which he issued with a dismissive authority, was "courageous, but misguided." Anyone who tried to do something to moderate the magisterium of the official view was courageous but misguided, and therefore a fool. And fools, of course, one suffered. They were part of daily existence, and like Tyutychev, one bore them like one endured the taste of nettle tea when real tea leaves were unavailable.

On that particular morning in January 1972, Yuri Maximovich arrived at his office covered with snow. As he crossed the street near a disused monastery, a snowdrift which one moment had seemed calm and at ease suddenly, as if agitated by his presence, rose up in a swirl and fell upon him. Yuri cursed the winter and bit his lip to distract him from the freezing cold. Fighting his way against a screaming wind which beat at him again and again, he reached his destination and trudged wearily up the stairs to *The People's Voice*; the finch sang out his arrival, and he dropped, stunned, into a chair in the visitors' foyer. He looked a sight, like the negative of a photograph, Lydia said several times: everything that should have been dark—hair, eyebrows, chin bristle—was clotted with snow, and Yuri's pasty complexion, matted patches he attributed to a poor liver, was reddish and raw. Lydia Yegorovna, no longer as agile nor as slender as she once had been, helped him take off his coat, heated a washrag over the samovar, and applied it carefully to his inflamed face.

"Poor Yuri, poor Yuri," she whispered.

Lydia Yegorovna had never married. Between Yuri and the succession of finches which occupied the entrance cage and the train of V's who had given way, their company exhausted, to a half-dozen I's, two of whom had been erroneously named Innokenty, Lydia had no apparent private life. At the beginning, when she was still quite young, there were lovers or at least affairs, not the least of whom had been the aforementioned Kaltangarov of the Circus, but after Yuri Maximovich had been seduced in the inner office of *The People's Voice*, literally thrown from his editorial seat late in the evening of the first month of his editorship after he and Lydia had completed dummying *The People's Voice* for the winter number of 1955, he had lost track of Lydia's amours. Lydia had come up behind him while he was rereading Tyutychev's essay, and screening his eyes with her damp palms, had whispered huskily to him, "Guess?" It was so ridiculous he couldn't help smirking, but for Lydia love was no jesting matter; avid, systematic, well disciplined in all things, Lydia had devised to wrestle herself—working from headlock to crooking to caress—into Yuri's embrace. It did not require rape. Rapine, ravishment were quite sufficient terms, and with the infinite syntactic subtlety of Russian verbs it was possible for them subsequently—even beyond the two years of Yuri's marriage to Irina Alexandrovna—to refer with amusement to the night that Yuri had been rapined. Yuri Maximovich hardly encouraged Lydia Yegorovna. It was not in his character to think about feelings—indeed, to experience them outside of his poetry. He tended to think about feeling the way children are sometimes trained to think about self-abuse (as the nineteenth century called that preliminary pleasure)—as though there were some kind of metaphysical plumbing which connected the phallic juices to the electrical charges of the brain: waste one and you consume the other. Masturbators cannot be poets, Yuri's mother had once said *à propos* of nothing that he could then discern, although he recollected later that his door was open while with pen in right hand and left otherwise occupied he had been trying to force a rhymed epic from Gogol's *Taras Bulba.* He dismissed his mother's declaration as one of several idiocies, among which he numbered her announcement that "Writers are not necessarily Authors," or later, "Jews without Yiddish are like chickens with cut throats," or, "It may be that revolutions can't be made without breaking eggs, but culture can't be made without scrambling them." Mira Babininskaya would always issue her proclamations after long periods of silence during which she listened carefully to everything being said, having contributed nothing but an occasional grunt or the refilling of cups, and then referring to nothing—really nothing —she would announce something about the writing or Jews, or culture, the principal subjects to which she had given her attention. She knew everything of the Yiddish writers and had mastered Russian to the point of following the debates between the various sections of the Bund at the turn of the century; later, she even believed for a time that the Jewish Section of the Communist Party [the famed *Evsektsia*] would really help the lot of Russian Jews. Mira Babininskaya was, in sum, the only thinking member of Yuri's family, his father being a miserably harassed auditor in a leather-working factory in Kiev. It should be noted, however, to the credit of Maxim Osipovich, that it was through him that Yuri had found his way to poetry and not, as you might think, through his mother. The fact is that Yuri's father, auditor in the Pinskoff Shoe and Bag Factory, had had correspondence with one Emil Veniaminovich Mandelstam of St. Petersburg, who was a wholesaler of leather skins—a real specialist in suedes—and Emil Veniaminovich had written a proud postscript to a letter to Yuri's father announcing that his son's first book of poems had appeared and that he was sending him one as a gift. That first edition of *Stone*—with the benign lion on its faded green cover, over which, hanging in a leaden field, was the word AKME—had stayed in the Isakovsky library unread for twenty years until Yuri found it when he was sixteen and gulped it like a claustrophobe let loose in pure oxygen.

Yuri Maximovich was warm at last. The snow puddled about his chair and his galoshes were put to dry upended upon two broom handles that occupied the corner near the birdcage.

"Any mail?"

None.

"Any telephone messages?"

None.

"Any calls without callers?"

No reply.

It was a typical day. Utterly boring. Deadly. He would perhaps go on with his Zeus poem. He went into his office and shut the door. It opened immediately. Lydia had brought another glass of steaming tea to his desk, had opened one of the drawers, found a bag of crystal sugar and broke off a piece, which she laid next to the tea on a paper napkin. God, she was boring. God, she was motherly, familiar, saturnine. She anticipated everything he wanted except his need for a poem, one good, round, fat, delicious poem.

"Yes, thank you, Lydia Yegorovna. A thousand thanks."

She said nothing, smiled, and left. Yuri realized as he watched her sway out through the door that she had put on some weight, that her backside was a little thicker than he had remembered it when he had studied it last—some time ago, he recalled. He really hadn't looked at a woman in so many months, hadn't thought of a woman as more than a different kind of obstacle that one had to deal with on lines for the tram or a taxi or in a restaurant or at a shop.

Yuri Maximovich tried, but he didn't manage another line of his Zeus poem that morning. He wrote instead a journal account of the wordless interview conducted the evening before in his apartment. His journal, an oddly shaped notebook more like an accounts ledger than a writer's notebook, was nearly full. Another would soon be required, he thought when he put down his pen. It was nearly noon and time to start thinking about a hard-boiled egg or a plate of soup down the street, but he hated facing the cold again and thought perhaps it would be easier to ask Lydia Yegorovna to bring him back a portion of mushroom soup in the metal container they kept for such errands, or perhaps, if she was reluctant, to wait until one o'clock, when Innokenty Tikhonov came in for his three hours of scurrying and laziness.

The phone rang in the outside office, but Yuri Maximovich didn't care about the damn phone. He drummed his fingers on the desk. The phone rang again, and although he could have depressed his phone button and picked it up himself, he waited for Lydia Yegorovna to summon him.

"Comrade Editor," he heard her say, arousing his attention with an uncommonly official formality. "It is for you, Comrade Editor. Urgent."

Yuri Maximovich smiled, expecting at most a long-distance call. He was awaiting one from a correspondent in Tashkent who was late with some notes on Tartar musical instruments. He picked up the phone and said, a hint of unction in his tone, "Yes. Isakovsky speaking."

"Comrade Editor?"

"Yes, this is Isakovsky of *The People's Voice*."

"One moment, please."

The speaker's voice hummed with efficiency, but the voice which succeeded hers—a woman's voice—was shrill with authority.

"Isakovsky? Is this you? Isakovsky—what is written here?" (He could hear her querying with irritation the presumably illegible script before her.) "Ah, yes. Yuri Maximovich—is that correct? Yes?" (Yuri grunted assent.) "So then. Is this Isakovsky, Yuri Maximovich?" (She did not wait for an answer.) "Yes? Good. My name is . . ." (She paused—was she looking up that as well?) "First Secretary Bassinova in Comrade Furtseva's office. I have the pleasure . . ." (She paused again, and he heard her clear her throat.) "*No.*" (She remonstrated with herself.) "Pleasure, yes. Duty, more so. Exactly. I have the pleasure and duty to inform you that you are going abroad." (Yuri was instantly terrified; he became dizzy and reached for the carafe of water on his desk, which quite naturally he spilled, the water dripping over the edge of the desk into his lap.) "There is commencing five days from this day, in New York City in the United States of America, the International Congress of Music and Ethnology. You will be the Soviet representative. The chairman of the gathering has been notified. English you know? Yes, it says here. You translate from English. It must be rusty. Practice, please. But if English troubles you, there is translation into French and German." (She exchanged these opinions with herself.) "You can go? True, Isakovsky?" (The voice inflected with polite circumspection, but the question—like all of Comrade Bassinova's questions—was circumstantial and rhetorical.) "Of course, you can. No wife. No children. No family. Nothing to hold you here at all, except of course your well-known patriotic fervor and the fact that you are an able editor, a good Communist, and—what does it say here?—a poet. But poetry is the least of your ties? No?" (Yuri Maximovich wanted to say no, but it would have been an irrelevant and misunderstood response.) "Good, then?" (This was the first and only point at which it was obligatory that Yuri Maximovich say something besides grunt or wheeze into the phone. He said yes.) "Excellent. You will not be traveling alone. Several others are in your party, all doing various things in New York, some more exalted, others less." (Did she mean "exalted"? Yuri thought, but came to no conclusion.) "Kolokolov, for one, the Soviet poet, is reading to a vast audience and is being given a dinner by his fellow poets and littérateurs. You know him?" (Yuri could not begin to to answer. A terror and a horror in one.) "Well, then, Isakovsky, today is Monday. You leave Moscow at eight A.M. on Thursday. Your passport, tickets, travel documents, and the necessary funds and instructions will be delivered to your office Wednesday afternoon. I wish you a pleasant journey and we" —the change to the collective, the eternal collective of impartial power was underscored— "look forward to meeting you on your return, which will be, let us see, eleven days from today. Bon voyage, Comrade Editor."

Yuri Maximovich Isakovsky fell back in his chair, forgetting to replace the telephone. The water from the spilled carafe had wet his lap and dripped down his leg. But he was stunned. It was clear now why his apartment had been searched. He was being sent abroad. Lydia Yegorovna had quietly opened the door and was about to congratulate him, but seeing his face suddenly drained of color, she put a hand to her mouth, sighed, and disappeared.

The list of improbabilities jostled in Yuri's head, desperate for an order and arrangement: New York, fabled New York; a week of meetings with world intellectuals; his first airplane trip out of the Soviet Union, beyond the seas; Ilia Alexandrovich Kolokolov, seeing again his old friend, the celebrated poet, Ilia Alexandrovich Kolokolov, in an atmosphere unstrained by the palpable anguish of Yuri's unproductivity; and lastly the reason for it all, the reason for it all, the reason for his deputation. Why he among Soviet musicologists—a mere editor, let us say it, an editor of no particular passion or interest in the music traditions of his country, in music even, who had by happenstance (which occurs more frequently than one imagines in the lower strata of Soviet life) come to occupy dominion in a neglected corner of the national pasture? There he was, a minor, neglected poet, a Jew of unstable chemistry, without family and children, being allowed to wander abroad, where every Soviet citizen and most assuredly every Soviet Jew without solid profession and title was invited—not at all politely, the newspapers hinted—to defect the homeland. Yuri Maximovich found himself squinting, sighting the reality beyond his desk with suspicion and disbelief, hunting for the giveaway of motive and intention as though every taxi driver, every newspaper vendor, every hotel clerk, every passer-by he might encounter over there was observing his various parts—his bulky overcoat, his ill-fitting blue suit, faded and shining, his unprepossessing black tie, his white shirt with removable collar, his gray hat with the vast brim—and peering out the secret of his presence, that he was a Jewish national of the Union of Soviet Socialist Republics loose at last in the great world of bourgeois temptation. He shuddered, not alone at the unconfirmed innocence of his fantasy, but more at its tired, weary imagery. Yuri Maximovich was afraid.

Several relevant entries in the journal of Yuri Maximovich
January 17, 1972

Late afternoon. After waking from a dream.

I am a real atheist. I don't believe in God. God is an idler, a lay-about, a real loafer, and our new society is founded on work. But I was born to Jew believers. My mother and father were both Jews. Down inside me they locked up a secret name. Yes, God may be a loafer and a good-for-nothing, but not my *Adonay*, not my real-named God, who has a distinct personality and character. When people ask me, thinking of some poem in which I make a universal person out of a simple quality, "You sound in this line, Yuri Maximovich, like you're a God believer?" I can answer, "Not at all, not at all. It's just a manner of speaking. It's a bit high-flown, don't you think?" Yes, a bit high-flown and I take a pencil and bite its point and strike out the line. I am very compliant to criticism. It doesn't pay to say anything which anyone can misunderstand. That's one reason why I despise our big Soviet poets. No one can possibly misunderstand them. The only difference between us is that they're on to a good thing—ancient Russian blood, whereas I'm a national mongrel, a cur of a Jew, neither fish nor fowl and certainly not a red herring. The point is that God is just a universal word, a word in every language, a general word like "man" or "table," and what does it really matter if God is *just* a word like "man" or "table." There are no men and no tables and no God, but there is a very particular man—in my case, Yuri Maximovich—and Yuri Maximovich has very specific qualities which include a wart on my cheek, a thinning hairline, a bald spot, and the sixty poems that make up the work of my life, each with a different tone, each with different charms and certainly different titles, and then over there, far away, some extraordinary person who is not God, but my Lord, my *Adonay*, my *Elohim*, my *El Shaddai*. And he has many other names as well, most of them I cannot remember, but they mean love and father and spirit and creator and good person. So you see, one more trick of Yuri Maximovich. I don't believe in God, but I believe in my God and he has a name and that very special name I say to myself every day—sometimes, twice or three times a day. When I nick myself with my razor, I say his name with a certain amount of annoyance. Or when Olga Petrovna, the cleaning woman, spills the garbage, I think that my God is not very bright. But for all and sundry, for everyone else I'm plain atheist. And the other side of the truth is equally devastating. To prove to myself that I was really an atheist, I let myself be baptized one afternoon in my youth in a monastery in the Ukraine. When it was done and the priest kissed me solemnly I nearly burst out laughing.

The baptism hadn't mattered at all. I had, oh yes, taken the trouble to do my homework, to memorize the catechism and whatever else was required of a young Jewish convert, but it was all a malign inversion, a further way of showing contempt.

It has been my theory all along that Russian history is the warfare between the Byzantine sword-wielders, who wanted to keep everyone inside the borders of the land in order to prevent us from escaping paradise, and the Westernizers, who knew that Russian angels and saints all had holes in their socks and lived with pigs in their bedrooms.

The same warfare goes on today, only the names are different. Can anyone imagine that the KGB's manual of subversion is much different than the calendar of heresies in the Middle Ages? Not much. Atheism and the Russian Church go hand in hand. Build the churches with slave labor, tear them down with Bolshevik enthusiasm, only to rebuild twenty years later on the same land a rest home, a hospital, an asylum—again with slave labor. The surest way of remaining a Jew, even an ignorant Jew as I am, is to pretend to be on the one hand an atheist and on the other a True Believer.

I loathe unbelievers and True Believers with an endless fury. What I like about the Jews is that they know that history is a concubine and the surest way to keep her tricked is to pretend to play her games. So much for my baptism by old Father Ignatiev, who was so blind he first put the communion wafer in my ear before realizing that it didn't fit. I am sorry I didn't believe in transubstantiation. I was so hungry in those days.

That night. Before leaving for a party.

The books of Great Russia, those miraculous tales of civil servants from the ninth to the fourteenth grade, those tales which shatter our composure and beet our faces with laughter—all those stories are about the hysterics of nonentities. It doesn't matter whether they hide in the sewers of Moscow or skulk in the courtyards of old Leningrad or spill out their dyspeptic guts in the provinces or in insane asylums, they all amount to the same thing: how horrible it is to be a nonentity when one's rage, jealousy, envy, viciousness, talent, ingenuity—the orders and rosettes of genius—pinned upon one's scruffy lapels qualify one for the Court or at least bedchambers of the most extraordinary of whores.

The point is that all of my predecessors in this terrible art of writing were absolutely clear how glorious and miserable was their gift. Gogol couldn't stand it, so he burned it, and others dueled it or Siberianized it, consumped it or burned themselves out one way or another in order to get free of their miserable golden skin. They couldn't bear to be nonentities, so they created them instead as if to say, "Me, a nonentity?" Not at all! Akaky Akeivich maybe, that idiot Kovalyov maybe, but not me. I am their maker, don't forget; my nose smelled them out with the pig's infallible snout for the truffle.

What could possibly excuse a Yuri Maximovich? What could possibly excuse my decision to become a nonentity, not of the ninth grade, not even of the fourteenth grade. What excuse can I give to myself, and why don't I simply cut my wrists and stop throwing up against the wall my puffballs of paper with half a line, half a stanza, half a poem, but without a single poem finished, recited, published, in more than ten years?

And now they reward you. Yuri Maximovich, now they reward you for being a nonentity. You haven't protested anything. You got through the hairs of his mustache without so much as a scratch. You haven't even developed a rash from having climbed about in his mouth for thirty years. Great ones are slaughtered for a rotten stanza in manuscript, and that just because vicious admirers laughed and the Great Bristle got word he was made fun of. But Yuri Maximovich, child of survival, how did you get to your fifty-fourth year? Now, maybe it's because you're really a terrible poet. While others were touching the acme, you became a nadaist, a nyetomane, a nadirist—in a word, a nonentity. They made the line and the square supreme and you made the empty page pure form.

3. Collecting One's Terror and Other Belongings

Yuri Maximovich left the offices of *The People's Voice* without his soup after recovering from the shock of his conversation with Comrade Bassinova of the Ministry of Culture.

The invitation to visit New York City seemed so incredible that he speculated it might be a hoax. Only one person, he imagined, could be devilish enough to conceive and execute such a prank, but Linka Popiukov (a professional clown, as it turns out) was playing the provinces and would never go to the expense of arranging, long distance, for someone to impersonate an official of the Ministry. Linka always enjoyed being on the scene when one of his pranks was being enacted, not just being on the scene as an observer, but starring in it. No. It wasn't Linka, but it could still be a trap.

Yuri Maximovich had heard reports of the KGB arranging such things. It happened daily when he was a young journalist toward the end of the Stalin years. In that time everyone told lies and friends informed on friends, even though most of what they said was no more incriminating than the jealous report that so-and-so always managed an egg for breakfast (Where did he get such a steady egg if he doesn't keep a laying hen in the closet? Where, I ask you?) and buttered his bread on both sides (and butter, fresh butter? Where from, I ask you?) or that Engineer K read old books which contain the two outlawed letters of the czarist alphabet or Citizen D sometimes livened his conversation with Russian proverbs that mention the fantastical name of God. That's the way it went, for the most part, although to be sure it occasionally happened that the brush picked up more than lint. That's where the danger comes! Every apartment house had its house spy and still does, as you will discover when you encounter Vovka Bedkin, Yuri Maximovich's own—indeed, personal—spy.

In that time, however, when Soviet citizens were still telling lies like breathing, most neighborhoods in the residential districts of Moscow had a pair of KGB operatives skulking about with their ears hanging out like the hands of Charon. Invariably the KGB was satisfied. There were rumors, tips, denunciations enough to provide full employment for the secret police, and Soviet society guaranteed full employment. "No smoke without fire," everyone said, from the Chief Procurator on down to the victim's family, but no one seemed to question who lit the fire in the first place and who smelled and reported the first puff of smoke.

It took nearly a half-dozen years following Stalin's death for word to be released that indeed many who were condemned and packed off had in fact been innocent—or put otherwise, that there had been smoke without fire. But the important consequence of all this for our story, for the situation of Yuri Maximovich Isakovsky, is that in January 1972 he found it hard to believe a perfectly good telephone connection between himself and a rattled lady in Comrade Furtseva's office giving him a bona-fide all-expense-paid trip to the land of giant buildings and vivid lights.

The first instinct of any well-trained Soviet is to be suspicious—in fact, to suspect a plot to entrap him, to catch him out singing the American national anthem, rushing to change rubles into dollars on the black market, or accosting American tourists walking through Red Square with questions about the customs of New York cafés and cloakroom attendants. Any sign of excess enthusiasm, any mark of unjustified optimism, excitement, anticipation would be misconstrued as at the least vulgar, or possibly, at the worst, anti-Soviet behavior. Who knows?

Of course, none of this happened with Yuri Maximovich. He behaved exactly as he should have behaved. He showed no exuberance. He was quite simply terrified, which is the right way for a Soviet citizen to receive word that he is going abroad for the first time in his life. He was terrified to be leaving Moscow (and fantasized that his apartment would be expropriated by the time of his return); terrified that misbehaving or deciding to defect (or both) he might be drugged and forced into the luggage compartment of Aeroflot 101, compelled under guard to return. In a word, terrified, terrified, terrified (thrice-spoken) of nothing and everything, the unknown, the mysterious threat posed by travel beyond Yuri Maximovich's bit of Muscovite universe. Like every sound and solid citizen, Yuri was an orthodox puritan—not a divine Puritan blessed by God with unshakeable principles and austere limitations, but a simple Russian puritan who could not abide spitting in the street, paper on the sidewalk, lascivious dancing, electrified guitars, unhoused female breasts, outlandish clothing, indiscreet language, delicate sauces, Turkish sesame candy, aromatic wines, pictures with flesh tones, photographs of cripples, cripples themselves, expensive cigarettes with gold tips, license, permissiveness, anything which would be considered "*ne kulturny.*" What to do with such high-mindedness? More extreme still if one recalls that it was distilled from familiar socialist rigidity conjoined with a Jew's atavistic memory of ancient restrictions. You can therefore imagine the terror with which Yuri Maximovich received the news of his travel orders. New York City was more frightening than a moon walk.

The terror, of course, was unconfirmed by the facts. The surveillance was over. There were no KGB agents in the vicinity of *The People's Voice* pretending to be street idlers or hall porters before, during, or after the telephone call. Only Lydia Yegorovna observed and heard, and nothing she could report would be damaging. Perspiration, a bouncing pulse, a slight reddening about the ears—all attributable to the aftermath of the blast of snow which had begun his day—was the extent of Yuri Maximovich's response to Comrade Bassinova. And to be sure, a hurried departure without his soup shortly after midday. Not unusual. But the feeling that the invitation was a hoax did not disappear with such rational temporizing.

The theory of Soviet truth which Yuri Maximovich had several months earlier sketched in his journal under the heading *General Considerations on Daily Survival* came back to him in waves of nausea. He thought for a moment, as he rushed down the stairs holding on to the rickety banister like a child clutches the mane of a rocking horse, that perhaps he had a serious flu, that he wouldn't be able to make the airplane on Thursday morning. But even if he had the flu, it had come too early to be of much use. It would have to develop into something serious for him to be allowed to beg off. He knew perfectly well that his symptoms were not flu—only queasiness, nerves, an attack of anxiety—and he stood panting at street level, waiting for his stomach to settle down.

It was at this moment, while he was leaning against the heavy vestibule door and waiting for his composure to return before taking on the winds of Moscow, that he recollected his encounter with an old short-story writer about whom he had written in his theory of Soviet truth. Iskurtsky's predicament was exemplary of most of its basic tenets. Praise, Yuri had noted in the *General Considerations*, is excellent when it comes from familiar quarters, from people who have no apparent reason to lie—that is, close friends or family, and they only when speaking under circumstances that cannot be misconstrued, or if misconstrued at all, will harm the praised less than the praiser.

It was in the above light that Yuri Maximovich interpreted the praise which Lydia Yegorovna offered him while she puffed on a cigarette following love-making in his apartment the third or fourth time she had spent a night there. Referring to his old poem "Pushkin and the Stone Guest"—in which Yuri Maximovich had laid over the image of Pushkin's statue in the square beneath his window (an obsession of his) the figure of Mozart's stone Commendatore before his mausoleum, and animated both according to rules devised by Pushkin for the interpretation of Mozart and the jealous Salieri—she had said that the poem was "provocative and deep," adding that "I have learned more from that poem than I ever learned in my Russian literature course." Now that praise—delivered by a responsible Soviet secretary, probably the office spy and consequently in the employ of State Security, from a position beneath the poet—was certainly injurious to the praiser. If Lydia Yegorovna were ever to denounce him he knew that he would detail to his interrogators, ungentlemanly though it might be, the curious angle from which Lydia Yegorovna seemed most comfortable spying. The revelation of her promiscuity would compromise her as much as her disclosures might damage him. A stand-off. Hence he realized the principle that one should always estimate the relative authority which both praiser and praised possess in order to assay the truth of the praise.

Praise, however, from *uncertain* quarters delivered in a public place could be a means of entrapment and must consequently be regarded circumspectly, as the old short-story writer from Gorlovka made clear when Yuri Maximovich accosted him in the street, calling to him over an open space of ten feet and asking whether he had *really* written the little tale which had appeared in Alexei Tolstoy's paper *Nakanune* during the twenties.

The writer in question, now dead of natural causes—what was his full name? . . . anthologized three times . . . yes . . . Stepan Nikoleyevich Iskurtsky from the city of Gorlovka in the Ukraine—had indeed written the sweet little fable of the candy-maker of Lepinsky Street during the concluding year of NEP. Yuri Maximovich had come upon the back issues of *Nakanune*, discovered the story, read it, liked it—yes, liked it—and when he ran into Iskurtsky, hurrying for a streetcar in Yuri's district, had called out to him: "Hey, Stepan Nikoleyevich, I read your old story in *Nakanune*. Lovely." The old man stopped dead in his tracks, turned around slowly, his head buried in his overcoat, and peered at him over a vast lapel. Yuri was about ten feet away, as I've said, and it was not until he came within six inches of Stepan's stumpy nose that his acquaintance acknowledged who had called out to him.

"Yes, Oh, yes, hello to you. But I was running, you know? And now I've missed the tram. What was that you were saying?" Yuri Maximovich repeated his compliment. "Did I write that story?"

"Well, if you don't know, who would?" Yuri Maximovich was laughing, but for Stepan Nikoleyevich it was not a laughing matter. He appeared to take the compliment as an accusation, but then Yuri—younger man that he was—did not realize the implications of Iskurtsky's delicious evocation of a Russian *baba* making licorice braid and selling it on Lepinsky Street, in exultant celebration of small capitalist enterprise.

"Maybe I did write that story. But then maybe I didn't write that story. Didn't it cross your mind, Isakovsky, that another Iskurtsky from Gorlovka could have written a story about the Lepinsky *baba*?"

"You either did or you didn't write it, Stepan Nikoleyevich. If you want my compliment, it's yours. You have it. If you don't want it, forget I praised the story. In fact, go the whole way, forget I ever met you. No! I can't do that to an old friend and distinguished Soviet writer. The plain truth is I liked that story, whether you wrote it or not."

"Perhaps you should, perhaps you shouldn't."

"What? Like the story, whether you wrote it or not?"

"Precisely. If I wrote that story, perhaps you shouldn't like it and I apologize for having written it. That is, if I wrote it in the first place. And if I didn't write that story," (". . . and I'm not saying that I didn't," he whispered) "you shouldn't be congratulating me in a public place with dozens of people whom we don't even know scurrying past, listening."

That, of course, was the key to the matter. Listening! Objectively speaking—down the lens of a camera, so to speak—

nothing could be safer than talking to a friend on a public street with no possibility of anyone picking up the sound of your voices and recording it. But it had come to the point—that was in 1968—when listening, mere listening, had again become dangerous. The best place for a conversation was in the dead center of a forest, and then only if you were talking to yourself. But who knows? If you were crazy and there were two of you—one who listened quietly while the other spoke outrageously—it was possible for the benign and passive self to leave the forest, write it all down, denounce the loud-mouth, and bring it to trial. A Solomonic decision for non-Solomonic judges. Which do you send to Siberia? It wouldn't matter. Both would be sentenced. The malign and morose self would go along with the garrulous and imprudent to a tenner of hard labor and rehabilitation.

All madness. This kind of speculation ends in craziness, medieval hairsplitting, Buridan's ass, the razor of Occam, nonsense, absolute nonsense. But make no mistake, my friend, it happens every day. Exactly like this. So commonplace in this country that one is led to believe that the only people who really manage to tell the truth are those who have lost their sanity. It's exactly as Yuri Maximovich says in his *General Considerations on Daily Survival.*

This madness is also the reason that in our country, right alongside the thriving business of concentration camps, detention centers, rehabilitation programs, there is a whole network of insane asylums. If someone misbehaves he is often given the choice between having his body broken or his mind stretched to the breaking point. It amounts to the same thing.

In the Urals, it is known, for instance, that in the vicinity of the city of Z (an alphabet letter is used to protect this neat little postwar city that houses and provides work for eleven thousand worthwhile citizens) there is a large work camp (six thousand inhabitants), and a stone's throw away—protected by the same electrified barbed wire, the same large lights, the same wolfhounds and soldiers—an insane asylum for those Soviet citizens considered to be more or less insane. They have, informants report, a shifting population: some detainees in the work camp whose bodies are less susceptible to corrective punishment are sent off to be "insanitized," while others, dumbheads to begin with, are given a dose of hard work clearing forest and working on pipelines for natural gas.

In the old days, days beyond the recall of Yuri Maximovich, days described and intimately detailed by the great wanderers of the last century, lingering ambiguously in the travels of the early part of the new Socialist world—the journeys of Esenin and later Mayakovsky—pilgrimages to the West were orgies of celebration and victory, emptied bottles of champagne, dishes of black olives and pressed caviar, women languishing upon chaises with floating eyes and delicious perfumes, draping the great poets with adoration as though they were all Phoebus Apollo, merry sprites of song and sound. All that was past, irretrievably. How does a middle-aged Russian Jewish poet, editor, sometime English translator, with a racing heart, balding head, watery eyes, and uncertain digestion go abroad? Not as a hero, not a celebrity. At most, as a functionary of a society that is its own legend of self-congratulation.

In those olden days, when the glorious traveled (and one forgets that many went abroad never to return, ignominiously, desperately, hiding a diamond or two—all that remained of wealth and station—in their bosoms, ending their lives as busboys and starvelings in cafés with balalaika music), they spent days preparing for the departure, gathering their documents, organizing their finances, visiting friends who owed them money, pressing their clothes, selecting their traveling literature, attending last-minute celebrations in the private rooms of restaurants or small dinner parties in the houses of those who adored them, bidding goodbyes and throwing kisses from train windows. Yuri Maximovich knew all this from literature. It had nothing to do with his life. Nothing. No need to arrange a passport or call at the visa bureau. It would be done for him. No need to secure funds, letters of introduction. They would be delivered to him. Nor an itinerary, hotel reservations, flight schedules, travel information. Everything was prepared in advance.

Detail and festivity beside the point, there was nothing to do but ritual imagining, and when Yuri reached his apartment in midafternoon, he informed his mongrel of his traveling orders and set about composing a letter to the Chairman of the House Committee with instructions for the care of Nastya (that was the bitch's name), the watering of his two dieffenbachias, the collecting and disposition of his mail, and an indication of the day and probable hour of his return. The letter took a quarter-hour and by three-thirty in the afternoon Yuri Maximovich had finished preparing for his trip to the United States.

Yuri Maximovich had made himself some tea and was munching a rusk when he heard coughing at his door. The coughs were deliberate, evenly spaced, staged. There had been no knock; Yuri ignored the cough, although it came at regular intervals. He counted ten little coughs accompanied by shoe-shuffling. At last (three or four minutes had passed) the shuffler cursed softly and there was an indecisive knock at his door. Whoever it was clearly knew that Yuri Maximovich was at home, had somehow followed his movements, and decided (unusually, Yuri thought) to introduce himself in the middle of the afternoon of an ordinary day.

There was a second knock. A weary "yes?" escaped Yuri's lips. "May I have a word with you, Comrade Isakovsky?"

"One moment, one moment." Yuri arrived at the door as the handle began to turn from the outside. His importuner was also impatient. Yuri threw the lock and opened the door. "So it's you."

"Yes, Comrade Isakovsky. I am Vladimir—called Vovka, I'm afraid—Bedkin. I will be accompanying you to the United States."

Until that moment, Yuri Maximovich had never met Vovka Bedkin face-to-face. He had encountered Bedkin many times (unavoidable in a building with only eight stories and thirty apartments chopped up like kindling wood), but the encounters had been more sleeve-to-sleeve, in the darkened stairwell late at night, where Bedkin sometimes lurked pointlessly. The first time that he rushed by the huddled figure, his face hidden by a scarf, Yuri had thought to accost him, demanding the reason for his presence in a private building at three in the morning, but he was so tired he hadn't bothered. The next morning he inquired of a neighbor who it might have been. "Vovka Bedkin" was the unhesitant answer. All of them knew of Vovka's suspicious habits and correctly concluded that not he, but they, were suspicious and inquired no further. Once, indeed, Bedkin and Yuri Maximovich had met rather more directly, but still not face-to-face ("Buttock-to-buttock," Yuri had described it). Yuri had just returned from a midnight walk and had passed his former wife, Irina Alexandrovna, strolling on the arm of the Major. He had returned to his apartment in a vicious mood. Passing Bedkin rummaging in a trash can (For what? Incriminating evidence or cigarette butts?) that stood in front of Galyakin's door on the landing three floors beneath his own, Yuri had sent Vovka sprawling with a push from behind. By the time Bedkin had picked himself up, cursing, Yuri, ascending the stairs by twos, had reached his own apartment. But that was all—a few meetings *en passant*, so to speak. And of course they knew each other by notes, by little scrawled messages, badly punctuated and ungrammatical, which Bedkin slipped under Yuri's door, notes not at all dissimilar from the gloating message which Yuri had found a month after the publication of Kolokolov's memoirs.

You may wonder, correctly, why Yuri Maximovich had never confronted Vovka Bedkin face-to-face, why he had never done more than send him sprawling in rear-guard action when clearly, for at least a decade—that is, from 1962 until January 17, 1972—Yuri Maximovich had known of his miserable existence and his even more disgusting, but commonplace, vocation. It is hard to understand, given the various provocations he had endured, why in all that time Yuri had never punched his stuffed-up little face or twisted the ugly nose that now sniffed at his doorstep in the middle of the afternoon.

The forbearance of Yuri Maximovich had little to do with his eccentric privacy, his willingness to tolerate any humiliation rather than enter into relations with a stranger, or with his odd hours—his habit of going to sleep at four in the morning and rising before dawn, which in January is about nine in the morning—or with his unconventional but faithful attendance to duty at *The People's Voice*, or with his disinclination to move about in public, to eat in restaurants, to go to the cinema, to visit plays or museums, to hear the readings of fellow poets or listen to musicians play their instruments, or even, most plausible, with a fear of assaulting an agent of the secret police. No. The simple fact of the matter is that they had never met because they were on different schedules. While Yuri worked at his office, Vovka Bedkin spied at home, and when Yuri returned to his apartment—usually at about eight in the evening—Vovka had already left to take up his duties as a file clerk in the accounting office of GOOM, a suitably trivial job, but one which allowed him to be slack when he was pursuing an enemy of the State or diligent and industrious when spying was slack. They were really ships passing in the night: Yuri a nocturnal tug, Vovka a fishing smack.

It sounds, does it not, that Vovka Bedkin was really inconsequential and harmless. Yes? An idiot, a fool, not even worthy of being sent flat on his behind? Let me tell you, friends, fools with a vocation are a greater menace than venal savants. Since they have the sensibility of a horse (which thinks from the front that every irritant in the rear is a fly), they make no distinctions. To Vovka Bedkin everyone except himself, a few superiors, and Comrade Brezhnev were flies. His only concern was to discover if the vast number of others are big or little flies (for which distinction he was no doubt rewarded from time to time with envelopes containing coveted little packets of surplus rubles). Because Yuri Maximovich was a poet he was a potential fly *ab initio*, as a once-published but now silent poet, a small fly; as editor of a Soviet journal, a biggish fly; and now, imminent fly abroad, a large and potentially dangerous fly. The time had obviously arrived for a face-to-face visit, most especially because Vovka Bedkin had himself been informed that day that he would be on the plane as companion, bodyguard, manservant, counselor, instructor in recusant ideologies, flagellant of the faithful—that is, as aide-de-camp or truly as personal spy to Yuri Maximovich Isakovsky.

Vovka Bedkin was, as we've implied already, a free-lance house spy in the eight-story building where Yuri Maximovich lived and has lived for twenty-four years, ever since he was granted his residence permit to settle in Moscow.

Vovka Bedkin has a limp. He claims it was a war wound, the result of a piece of shrapnel which severed a valuable muscle in the thigh of his right leg. Others in the building—notably Katerina Golopkin, who lives in the back apartment near the skylight in one room with a blind alley cat whom she walks on a leash—think otherwise. Katerina claims with a laugh that he got his leg caught in a door while he was pretending to deliver a package to a suspect. Vovka was one of that disreputable legion with which the country was overrun, useless factotums whose low intelligence, deficient imagination, and careless manners made them ideal for special assignments of the secret police. It would appear, judging from the existence of innumerable Vovka Bedkins, that his was a country in which the worthless were allowed to keep track of the mediocre, the mediocre of the competent, the competent of the gifted, and the gifted of each other, lest one become outstanding.

Vovka Bedkin's triumph and eclipse had occurred during the Doctors' Plot, so-called, of January 1953. He had been living at that time in the country, about thirty miles from Moscow. He worked as a janitor-gardener, more the one than the other because you could loaf and spy more efficiently if you swept up and carted trash. Gardeners, Bedkin decided, have to be outside with their heads bent low over flower beds, which makes spying—an upright or at least a crouching profession—difficult.

In all events, Vovka had been posted by a vigilant captain in the local constabulary to keep his eye on a pharmacist who had moved into the community—not an ordinary pharmacist, but a researcher, a somebody who had sufficient authority to keep a little mixing workshop in the shed behind his house. There, when the pharmacist, a Dr. Yakov Moysevich, was home from his laboratory in the city, the lights would burn night and day. The captain from the constabulary thought something funny might be going on, so he put Vovka to looking in on Dr. Moysevich from time to time and even, when the doctor was out, to noting down what was written on the bottles and vials and tubes the doctor was in the habit of using. Twice, Vovka Bedkin had limped into the doctor's workshop, noted down what he found on the blue-bordered labels, and transcribed them to a report which he brought to the captain. The captain (a virtual illiterate, but a special kind of illiterate: highly trained in the martial arts, excellent war record, decorated and now promoted to the constabulary of the new suburbia in which the ennobled proletariat lived, but for all other purposes totally useless) received the list from Vovka and examined it, pulling at his cheek with authority. Vovka waited, anxious to have the matter deciphered. Naturally the captain could make no sense out of the formulas and Latin names, but promised to send them on to Moscow for translation. In the meantime, his suspicions aroused, he congratulated Bedkin on his find and urged him to redouble his efforts, to draw Moysevich into conversation, to insinuate himself into the doctor's life and perhaps find out something useful and important.

Vovka now had a purpose. He did as he was asked. He returned to the district that very night and hid in the orchard until he saw the doctor had settled himself in his shed and begun to work. He saw the lights go on and off in the doctor's laboratory, and all he could think about was that fame was slipping through his fingers while he waited, surrounded by denuded apple trees and rotting cores. In Moscow, on the other hand, Bedkin knew that swift little cars and large, cumbersome limousines were picking up treacherous plotters and speeding them to the Lubyanka. Doctors. Doctors. Everyone was a doctor. And Jewish doctors, too. His eyes inflamed,

Vovka Bedkin thought, "What if this Dr. Moysevich was one of them? What if he was working every night, like the Protocols said they did, concocting potions and poisons to do in the whole Secretariat of the Party and even Comrade Stalin? What if Dr. Moysevich was really pharmacist to the greats of the land and was plotting their deaths?" All Vovka could think of was the dreadfully mysterious Latin names on the amber vials and the perking retorts bubbling with purple and green mixtures. Oh how Vovka must have skulked, skulked an hour or more until he could stand it not a minute longer! He arose from the concealed position from which he was able to see only a small bit of the doctor's laboratory, and limped closer. He was tired, and what with his pigeon-toed left foot nearly overlapping his dragging right he must have made something of a racket, but Dr. Moysevich heard nothing. The wind blew; the trees shook. That was all the noise that could be heard. Vovka was able, therefore, to lift himself into a position where only his nose lay visible upon the window sill where he had drawn himself up to rest and snoop.

Dr. Moysevich was seated in front of his burners, and a whole network of tubes and glass containers hummed and belched, but he seemed to be doing nothing but making notations in a very small leather-bound notebook. Once Dr. Moysevich held the book up in the air, his thumb holding it open, and Bedkin could see that the pages were filled with formulas and symbols. This only enraged Bedkin more, and like every ignorant man, the exasperation of ignorance only served to confirm suspicion. He kept muttering to himself, "The notebook, the notebook. It's all in the notebook." Had he not restrained himself he would have rushed in and snatched the notebook from the amazed doctor and fled with it to the constabulary. But that was out of the question. After all, Vovka Bedkin was a professional, even if free-lance. He knew perfectly well that patriotism sometimes had to be constrained by patience, so he continued to wait, his nose freezing; droplets of water drained from his head, forming whiskers of icicles above his lips. At about midnight his chance came. Dr. Moysevich had, quite simply, to relieve himself, and since his little shed had neither running water nor toilet, he had to walk the hundred paces or so to his cottage. The innocent doctor put down his leather notebook, put on his overcoat, fitted a cap securely upon his head, wrapped his face in a scarf, and left the shed for his cottage. Vovka figured he had at least five minutes, but one was all that was necessary. As soon as the doctor disappeared, Vovka entered the shed, picked up the notebook, peered about but saw nothing else of interest, and ran from the laboratory, his body bouncing upon his uneven legs as though his trunk were a piston rising and falling upon two moving shafts.

He only learned his glory the following evening. The captain of the constabulary, a tall officer with a complexion like a swamp and a mustache unevenly razored so that his smile seemed like a sneer, took the notebook with condescension and promised Bedkin that it would be forwarded in the morning to Moscow for decoding. Bedkin returned a half-dozen times the following day to check in at the constabulary, but there was no news. He was more than ever convinced that he must have landed a big fish, for any innocent man would have promptly reported the theft of an innocent scientific notebook. To his delight, at precisely ten o'clock the following evening he learned that Dr. Moysevich had been taken into custody and delivered to Moscow for interrogation.

Two days later the newspapers, already filled with accusations against the nine doctors, carried additional allegations against one, Dr. Yakov Moysevich, a pharmacist accused of having prepared false medication which had been used by the other conspirators, Professor Yegorov and the Lenin Prize winner, Professor Vinogradov, in murdering Andrei Zhdanov, Aleksandr Shcherbakov, and many others. There beneath a photograph of Dr. Moysevich was the glorious caption: "Apprehended through the vigilance of Citizen Vladimir Bedkin."

It appears that on the last page of the notebook Dr. Moysevich had written the names of the conspirators who had been apprehended in the Doctors' Plot, and beside their names, their addresses, positions, and rank. Moreover, the formulas that Moysevich had inscribed so laboriously in his notebook apparently reflected arcane enthusiasms, the permutation of substances and metals. In a word, the distinguished pharmacist, who it was proved had known several of the conspirators, was an alchemist, and he was trying—as Jews are always known to try—to convert base metal into gold. What could be better? A pharmacist. A friend to conspirators. A Jew. Another doctor. And an anti-Soviet profiteer trying to make riches out of metal shavings. Well, you can just imagine how it went. Vovka Bedkin, now outfitted in a brown wool suit, greeted the press in the company of Captain Grigory Gribatnikov, and both shared honors for the new revelation.

It all lasted a little over two months. On March 5 the Great Leader died of a stroke. On March 6 Georgi Malenkov became Premier, and on April 4, only a month after he had gotten used to his desk and chair, it was announced from the great Kremlin that the Jewish doctors had been falsely arrested and accused; the lady doctor who had concocted the plot lost her Order of Lenin and was promptly demoted. Yes, Dr. Moysevich was sentenced to one year—commuted to three months—in jail for unlawful experimentation, a vague charge akin to profiteering, which was all that his alchemy would warrant, and Vovka Bedkin, like all the spies and confidants and agents who had been instrumental in fabricating the charges against the doctors, was tried and given a prison term for producing evidence by impermissible means (theft, in Vovka's case). Captain Gribatnikov was reprimanded for having encouraged Vovka, but he was not punished, since fortunately for him the KGB had whisked the doctor from under his jurisdiction and all the impermissible means of extracting confessions were laid at their authority. And so it ended. Instant glory. No less instant demise. Vovka served his term making slippers out of rush reed in some distant climate and returned to Moscow thin as a rail, limping worse than ever, pigeon-toed so badly he looked like a warped stick. After some rushing about and string-pulling (frayed strings at that), he was finally given permission to stay on in Moscow, allowed to serve again as house security—

originally for four buildings, now reduced to two—and given his minor job checking inventory slips in the dress department of GOOM.

Vovka Bedkin stood before Yuri Maximovich, his nose sniffing about the room, for it was the only appendage of Bedkin's body of sufficient vitality to enter a room without the whole of Bedkin following.

"So it's you," Yuri Maximovich acknowledged—a bit too confidently, he thought afterwards.

"Yes, Comrade Isakovsky. I am Vladimir—called Vovka, I'm afraid—Bedkin. I will be accompanying you to the United States."

Yuri Maximovich could think of nothing to say but "Why?"

" 'Why?' you ask. A good question," Vovka Bedkin replied, not a little pompously. "Should I come in?"

Yuri was struck by his use of the conditional tense, and it pleased Yuri—no, relieved him. Vovka Bedkin was not all that confident. The events of 1953 still abraded him, and the recent transfer of two of his buildings to another operative made him chary of being forward. He wasn't less dangerous for those reasons. It was just that one could count on a little extra time while Vovka decided whether or not his position was secure. "Should I come in?" hung like an afterthought, for Vovka Bedkin had already raised his pigeoned foot and was preparing to shift himself into Yuri's apartment.

"By all means. Do come in. You already know it, don't you? No need to ask for an invitation now." Yuri had decided that undoubtedly it had been clumsy Bedkin who had made the phone calls of the previous week and disarranged his apartment the day before. He was so unimpressed by Bedkin he determined to allow his intrusion to pass unremarked.

Vovka Bedkin was invited to enter Yuri Maximovich's apartment for the first (and it would be the last) time. "Lovely room, yes, very lovely, very poetic," Vovka Bedkin exhaled, sniggering with little bits of contempt. "Very poetic."

"You find it poetic. Whatever does that mean?"

"Books, everywhere books, and a large desk and an enormous chair and plants and Pushkin out the window. And is this your book?" Vovka Bedkin had spied a copy of Yuri Maximovich's book of poems, which bore the title *The School of Song* (Yuri had not dared to use the Latin—although he had wanted to and indeed had written *Schola Cantorum* on his own manuscript—since he well knew the danger of archaisms).

"It has my name on it. It is my book."

"To be sure. Yes. Of course." The little flutter of unsureness again. Three strophes of embarrassment when none was really called for. "So then, that's what I meant. Very poetic. Yes. May we sit down and chat for a little?"

"Of course, but only for a little. I have a number of errands to do before Thursday. Yes. I'm sure you have other things to do yourself." Yuri could not bring himself to acknowledge directly that this creature descending into the poet's Chair was really going to be on the plane with him to New York. Already New York seemed more forbidding; as though it were not enough to sleep in foreign beds, one had to bring bedbugs from home to make them familiar.

Vovka Bedkin, seated upon the Chair, had difficulty arranging his body. Until he watched Bedkin, Yuri had never been quite that aware how alien a body can be, how mysterious it is that some men can contain the variety of limbs, appendages, extensions, imposing upon them something more than rudimentary intelligence, whereas others—the vast number of others, most particularly Bedkin—have no capacity to perfect an even elemental unity. Bedkin's handicap, his pistonlike motion, his dragging right foot, his interfering left, were really commentary added to an already well-expressed confusion. Bedkin didn't work, and clearly Bedkin's deficient intelligence was the cause. He could impose order on nothing, wagging his head, wriggling his nose, flicking his tongue about his lips as though to catch flies, his spare and rampant hair, blotchy skin, and his limbs functioning like advanced music—the notes shrill and discordant, the unity all in the intervals between sounds, as if in Bedkin's case the only lucidity were in the undifferentiated spaces of skin and bone from which poked his disarticulated arms, legs, head. Yuri Maximovich had observed Bedkin shifting about uncomfortably for several minutes, examining this and that, his eyes bulging forth as they discovered an object of curiosity or narrowing as they discerned the concealed—the books on the bottom shelf, the bunched balls of paper left in disarray upon the desk. Clearly Bedkin was so excited with his new assignment that he could not settle down. He was enjoying his new responsibilities, and the more enthusiastic he appeared the more ludicrous and insignificant he became. Yuri could hardly take him seriously, but he had no doubt that the little cacophony in front of him had a most assiduous and efficient conductor who would make of him some species of music, even the most unbearable. So then, watch out!

Vovka Bedkin settled down at last, steadying the game leg against the desk, and averting his body from Yuri Maximovich, stared down the line of his shoulder toward him, complementing the chaos of his body with a rigidity of look which one finds only in the most arch of Caligari's expressions, as though reality were truly the play of extreme light and dark, rather than, as poets believe, the play of shadows. "And so, Yuri Maximovich, let us begin our chat."

A moment passed. Was Yuri expected to begin? "You first," Yuri said.

"Me?"

"But of course. You came to my door. That is my Chair. This is my apartment. You came to call. In that case, Bedkin, call. What is it you want?"

"To know you, of course."

"Now let me explain. To accomplish that you have to show interest, tell something about yourself, provoke curiosity in me. Don't you see? That's the way you do it."

"I understand. Well then, how should I begin?"

"It's up to you."

"Quite right." Bedkin paused. "What's New York like?"

"How should I know? I've never been there. It will be quite a surprise."

"Yes. Quite." Yuri couldn't figure out what the "quite" meant.

Silence began. The undifferentiated interval in the score. What a bore, Yuri thought.

"You seem a most cooperative man. Not at all what I had expected."

"What did you expect and from whom did you learn of me?"

"Come now, Comrade. You don't have to ask that. You know about me. We needn't conceal that. It's obvious. I do jobs for our security forces, keeping watch mostly. Did you know, Yuri Maximovich, that I turned in four provocateurs, three exploiters of the working classes, and a major profiteer during the last two years. Quite a record. I am very diligent."

"I'm sure you are. But then why me? Why are you interested in me?"

"It's clear, isn't it? I mean it should be clear. You're an educated man, a writer, a translator, an editor, a poet. You have credentials which people from your nation worked hard to get for themselves in the old days and gave on to their children. More than I had from my parents."

"I see." That is all Yuri did.

"In any case," Bedkin continued, "you are a privileged man, and privileged men are very often—it is our experience—tempted to take advantage of their privilege. You know what I mean. Get a little extra out of it. Now, I'm not saying that applies to you, but you must be aware, Comrade Isakovsky, that many people of your race are trying hard to make life difficult for us Russians, demanding something extra."

"I see." But Yuri had ceased to do even that.

"Staging demonstrations, doing hunger strikes, contacting foreign press, circulating damaging petitions, and most of all trying to leave the country for that terrorist state of theirs. I say 'theirs,' since I know that little bug of a country isn't yours. But still, no matter, you were born into that race."

"It's a nation, perhaps not even a nation," Yuri speculated aloud.

"As I said, you were born into that race and you may have a drop of its taint on you."

Yuri Maximovich remembered for an instant old Father Arkadi Ignatiev dropping water on his forehead when he was nineteen. As Yuri wrote in his diary about that episode, "The waters of baptism washed away nothing; neither did they stain." Yuri Maximovich lifted his arm and was about to silence Vovka Bedkin, but Bedkin rushed on undetained.

"That's the reason why I'm supposed to go along with you: to make certain you don't embarrass the Soviet people in any way. You see, we don't really have a hold on you. You don't have much family left, certainly no direct blood relatives; you're divorced and you have no children. We have no guarantees, but we are certainly trusting and we have no reason to doubt your loyalty."

"Then why are you going?"

"Insurance. Pure and simple. I'm an insurance policy. Or rather I'm the inspector for the insurance company that makes certain the policy terms are fulfilled."

"I see *now*. It goes like this. Jew by birth; Jew forever. Jew forever; bad Russian. Jew and Russian: oil and water. Never mix. Never mix at all."

"Quite right. You have it in a nutshell. One can see you are a poet. You get to the heart of things so quickly."

"Well then, we've had our chat, haven't we?"

"Do you think we're finished? I thought we might talk a little about poetry. I'd like to learn about poetry. It wouldn't help me in my profession, but it might make me a bit more light-hearted if I could understand poems."

"You think so, Comrade Bedkin? I'm not sure it would help you at all. You are so vigilant, after all. You have little time for poetry."

"I suppose you're right."

"I know I am."

Vovka Bedkin retrieved his body from the Chair, strained himself up, and nodding goodbye, dragged himself from Yuri Maximovich's apartment.

From the journal of Yuri Maximovich Isakovsky

"General Considerations on Daily Survival"

It is a human mistake to imagine that the impulse to tell the truth is inborn, or even that it is subject to the instruction and nurture of decent homes and sympathetic mothers, fathers, and teachers.

The telling of truth—in a socialist society—is no less subject to the laws of economic and social well-being than the quality of one's black bread and kasha. If one is a ruler in such a society, one is given the option of taking chances, and the range of chances is considerable—not yet, however, requiring the telling of truth, nor for that matter requiring the tale of lies. The options involve one's *classless class* (a classless class in a socialist society means that anyone can get into your class—hence its classlessness), but very few who are in can get out with a whole skin (hence its reality as class). Movement is upward from the nonclass of the lower classes—from peasants, kulaks, the petit-bourgeoisie, the privates and drovers of the army, the sweepers in universities, the retort cleaners in laboratories—to the top classes of the nonclassed—the university professors, the technicians, inventors, scientists, computer programmers, engineers, newspaper directors, publishing house executives.

Since I am a poet and have always been a poet, I understand perfectly well the history of lies which clings to my vocation. I know, for instance, Plato's condemnation of poets. Poets were illusionists and therefore liars. Later, of course, when the Greek historians went to work and Aristotle tried to figure out what to do with these two species of literary imagination—the writing of poems and the writing of history—he reversed Plato, according a higher station to poetry than to history, since poets tried to elevate character while historians tended only to explain and justify the miscreancy of rulers.

Of course Plato and Aristotle were both wrong. They didn't know class theory. They weren't Marxists. They didn't understand that between poets and historians, it's like choosing between rotten fish and meat with maggots. The only people who understand what poets and historians should be doing are the people who employ their talents, who determine the "true" truths and the "true" lies and arbitrate who is given the privilege of telling which and to whom and for how much. Now, this is the way Soviet literature has worked for a half-century. The only times a poet (or anybody else, for that matter) tells an honest truth or an honest lie is when he's between classes, when he's graduating from university and looking for a job on a newspaper, when he's left journalism and become a translator, or when he's taking on a bit of interviewing and radio lecturing along with translating or writing free and spontaneous letters of condemnation to *Literaturnaya Gazeta* about someone everybody is out to destroy. At such moments he is telling authentic lies, true lies.

The reason why these are true lies is that at least what he says is helping him, his family, his career—providing for his children, guaranteeing better vacations or cheap tickets to the Bolshoi, one or another of the useful privileges which are guaranteed to those moving between classes. The higher one gets, the more one commands of the goods which the rulers are free to dispose. (I have sometimes imagined Comrade Brezhnev with a box under his bed filled with tickets to the best seats at the opera, the ballet, the circus, spending the last minute before going to bed shuffling the tickets and putting them in envelopes along with a little printed card which reads, "With the Compliments of Your Ruler.") In other words, when you are between classes, truth and lie are objectively interchangeable and whichever is told is deeply felt, self-interested, and therefore as relatively true as it is false.

My theory of operational truth (social truth) and operational lies (social lies) is based upon a clearly Marxist conception of the floating class. Our whole purpose is to guarantee that there should be no proletariat; that there should be no abject poor, no one unfed, unhoused, unclothed. What we want is to empty the proletariat and transfer everyone by decree and work into another class—the lower-middle class (the upper proletariat). The upper proletariat does not want to return to the lowest class (which anyway has been abolished); the members of the proletariat (which is now only an honorific title) strive to stay where they are and to push higher. The drive of the Basis is to become the Structure; the passion of the worm is to consume and thereby to become the flesh on which it feeds.

Whatever the accuracy of this description, it does not explain why it is so difficult for my friend, Stepan Nikoleyevich Iskurtsky, to accept my praise of his story.

The only way this can be made intelligible is if we analyze the situation:

	Yuri Maximovich Isakovsky	*Stepan Nikoleyevich Iskurtsky*
Age	54	77
Nationality	Jew.	Ukrainian.

Residence	Moscow.	Visitor.
Profession	Editor.	Short-story Writer.
Salary	Ample.	Pension + modest royalties.
Dependents	Self.	Four (wife, unmarried daughter with bad eyesight, centenarian mother in nursing home, himself).
History	Virtually none except that which goes along with being a Russian Jew (which is quite enough).	Once a mild Menshevik sympathizer; had friends who got killed; traveled abroad and spoke French, which he claims to have totally forgotten; received letters from foreign publishing houses in the twenties.
Career	Published one book of lyric poems, *The School of Song*, translations of four stories by Jack London, and an anthology of literary criticism from the American periodical *New Masses* that was pulped before publication.	Three collections of short stories, all of which were praised and chastised.
Status	On the borderline between a safe and stable reputation (recognized in better literary cafés, unchallenged membership in the Union of Soviet Writers) and utter undistinction.	Unsafe distinction.
Theory of Truth	Nobody has asked for any major declarations; none have been offered. Why not admit it? It hasn't hurt so far.	Never thought of the question—a provincial condition, but he has had difficult times, particularly when the longitude-latitude of his Ukrainian home city of Gorlovka isn't on Moscow time.

In other words, we get beyond operational truth (a function of class mobility) to the truth of one's situation (the fact that Stepan Nikoleyevich and Yuri Maximovich are in a comparably *mezzo-mezzo* circumstance). I offset the advantage of my being in Moscow with the vulnerability to which one is exposed. I offset being a Jew to Stepan Nikoleyevich's age, insecure income, and dependents. His modest fame offsets my undistinction, but his fame may come from being a writer from Gorlovka, which gives him the advantage of being published in two languages—Ukrainian and Russian, the former of which is his native tongue. The language of situation is the language of offset—striking out and balancing.

I can go on with this, but you get the idea. If you were to magnify this a hundredfold, you would get the sense of how I live.

I have a notebook filled like a bookkeeper's with double entries on virtually everyone I know—the details of their situation offset by the variables in mine. For some of them the fact that I am a Poet is irrelevant. What matters to people like Lydia Yegorovna is that I have a two-room apartment (even though one of them is a closet bedroom); for others—women, by and large—the fact that my member is circumcised (a modality of being Jew) is both relevant and exciting. The "by and large" stems from the fact that when I was younger I knew a soccer player who made the Olympic team in the Mexico City games; he insisted that circumcision would help athletes store energy and once asked me for permission to do close inspection of my denuded member while we were showering after a match (yes, I was once an amateur soccer player for a year until my shins got bashed in). Grigory Beletsky was dropped from the team after the Olympics apparently because he had begun to pursue his examination of penises with less scientific seriousness.

So much for some of the variables. Multiply them and you can imagine how I had to spend time documenting my situation before I could make a move. It also had a harmful effect on writing poetry. Doing one's ledgers takes time, and my pockets were always full of little pieces of paper on which I had set down a new fact to be entered when I got home—the bank clerk who cashed my checks keeps racing pigeons; Natasha Plinyak, whom I dated occasionally, has a brother in prison for extortion; Anastasia Nazarinskaya will go to any length, including theft, to find flower bulbs; and so on and on. But whenever a year was done—usually in the early hours of the New Year after I had gotten back to my apartment from a party—I would open my ledger of the year and go through it carefully. At the bottom of each entry page I would write "Account Closed" if I had stopped seeing someone during the course of the year, or more ominous, "To Be Closed." The only accounts which I kept open for a number of years are those whose names figure continuously in my journals. There were several names on whom I could not make a determination—either "Closed" or "To Be Closed" because they had disappeared. One of those is Yasha Isaievich Tyutychev, whom I hardly knew, who mystified me, whom I have grown to miss.

4. Packing for Travel

"Nastya," Yuri called out several minutes after the door had closed on Vovka Bedkin. "Nastya, dumb friend of mine, where are you?"

The mongrel bitch, her tail wagging, crawled out from under Yuri's desk where she usually slept during the day and came to his feet. Nastya licked a toe without much satisfaction and looked up at Yuri. Yuri bent down and gathered her into his arms and began to kiss her ear. "You are a real friend, Nastya. A real friend. The only friend I have in this whole country." Yuri sat down in the Chair with Nastya and looked about gloomily. It was past six o'clock, and although the city had not begun to darken, it had slowed down a bit. Sullen apartments showed their lights, and the few pedestrians that one sees in Moscow were beginning to leave the city's center and return to outlying districts. Yuri Maximovich was very tired.

Shortly after six o'clock in the evening Mira Babininskaya called for the midwife, a bubbling woman with flaming-red hair and strikingly beautiful hands, veined like old porcelain. Mira Babininskaya was content to deliver her baby without her husband pacing nervously at her bedside. Maxim Osipovich did not strike her as being indispensable to childbirth, and although she had sent word to him at the factory, she was certain the child would be born long before he would have his desk cleaned up and the accounts ledgers put away. The midwife arrived, called for the hot water and towels, and immediately went to the room on the top floor of the apartment house on a street a stone's throw from the Podol, where the poor folk of Kiev lived. She entered Mira Babininskaya's bedroom just as her moans elongated into screams, spread her beautiful hands on Mira's stomach, and began to press gently. Gradually, with urging and coaxing, the baby's head emerged, and within an hour the child was fully withdrawn into the thickening dusk. He was clean and unblemished, and Mira Babininskaya approved of his existence. The older child, a daughter, played in her room by herself during the birth of her brother. She was indifferent to his existence and would remain so.

Yuri Maximovich, son of Maxim Osipovich Isakovsky, was born on July 21, 1918.

To come into the world between the February and the October revolutions and to pass one's childhood in Kiev during the ferocious wars of the Reds and the Whites—the city periodically under siege by one or the other, captured by one or the other, abandoned to famine and disease by one or the other—would seem to make a child's world eventful. Perhaps, but not necessarily. Most people are spectators. History eddies about them, scarcely penetrating the tightly knit fabric of their days. They rise, go to work, make their living, return home, speak, eat, read their books or play cards, go to sleep. It would not really matter to them if the world turned inside out (or even, worse yet, intrude into their living rooms). They would persist in regarding such a world as impolite, perhaps cruel, but finally irrelevant to them. The Isakovskys endured the Revolution like a badly planned theatrical, checking the program for changes of cast and replacements, annotating the performance, affixing critical plaudits and condemnations; only after it was done and the stage dismantled did they determine whether the drama had been, after all, well-played.

Mira Babininskaya had too much to do taking care of her family to become involved in the Revolution, and moreover, despite her curiosity about the outcome and her explicit sympathies with the Bolsheviks, she really considered the Revolution as an occupation for gentiles, not Jews. She reduced all of the activities of General Denikin and the variety of Red commanders who opposed him to a simple question, "What does it mean for *Yidn*?" and she received a speedy reply. Absolutely the same thing. Despite promises and proclamations, the new Soviet resembled the old Russia. The Jewish proletariat—and virtually all Jews were somehow poor and without class consciousness and hence by definition proletariat—stood by and watched the Ukrainian Whites mount small pogroms in the Jewish quarters of Kiev, followed by Ukrainian Reds mounting small pogroms in the Jewish quarters of Kiev. The Jews were never just right, never to anyone's taste.

Yuri Maximovich was not harmed throughout his childhood, but he learned how it was done—that is, how people were harmed. And make no mistake about it, it is much more shocking to witness others brutalized than to pass through it oneself. To stand by, as he did when he was four years old, and watch out of the window a Cossack brigade execute two old women who lived on the next block and then put around their necks placards reading "Jew Hoarder" was more devastating than to confront the Cossacks himself. And only three months later he watched a brawny young Red guardsman dragging a rabbi along by his beard to a court convened by the provisional Bolshevik government. The old man had been caught trying to bribe an official to get his son out of the city and through the lines to Odessa, where he hoped he would be able to leave Russia for good. Yuri Maximovich observed these episodes with mouth agape and eyes wide with amazement. He never asked about them, but their significance wasn't lost upon him. He knew, his mother knew, his father knew (his sister managed not to know, and whatever she perceived she ultimately managed to forget) that in place of the old women or the bearded rabbi any one of them would have done as nicely. Fortunately for the Isakovskys their apartment wasn't very large, their furniture not very new, their belongings not very bright and enviable, their food as scarce as their neighbors', and the number of their enemies so few that they were never directly assaulted or denounced, their apartment never invaded or occupied.

The Isakovskys got through the Revolution and its aftermath by going about their business inconspicuously, and by the time it was all over and the Reds had won, they had calmly become supporters of the Revolution. Mira Babininskaya never gave up reading Yiddish stories, although she made certain her children knew Russian well and she did urge her son to join the Komsomol when that Bolshevik youth organization began to organize Kiev. The factory in which Maxim Osipovich worked was taken over by the State and began making shoes instead of bags and gloves. No matter, he continued to do his work diligently and took to wearing a little red flag in his lapel. He didn't want anyone to mistake his loyalties.

During the month of August—it was 1934—Yuri Maximovich went off with a group of his friends, all young Communists, on a labor walk through the Ukraine. It was late summer, bitterly hot, and the paucity of rain had brought on a severe drought in parts of that vast wheat field. The land was dying and all Komsomols were urged to help on the land, carrying water from deep and protected wells to the fields, assisting the various collectives in whatever way they thought useful.

One afternoon about two hundred kilometers south of Kiev, he and two other friends stopped along the road at a wooden house that appeared empty and abandoned. They came into what had been a large kitchen and lay down on the earth floor to rest in the cool. They had just lit up cigarettes and were leaning on their elbows talking drowsily when they heard a low moan from the banked oven which stood in the corner. Suddenly they saw the head of an old man poke through the oven opening, his face filthy, dirt caked like grease paint exaggerating the furrows of his cheeks, his unkempt hair long and gray.

The old man saw them and tried to retreat into the oven. Yuri begged him not to be afraid, and coming toward him, offered a sip of water from the canteen the boys shared.

The old man, it turned out as he told his story, was not yet fifty. The wooden house had been his home, and the parched fields beyond had been tilled by him and his family and friends for more than two generations. At one time his family had been serfs, but for nearly fifty years he and his father and two other families of freed men had worked the land, bringing up good crops of barley and rye. He hadn't understood the whole idea of collective farming. The year before he had been told by a young commissar traveling through the district that his farm no longer belonged to him, that it was now part of a large collective established four miles away and that he should report there for orders. He didn't understand. He did nothing. A month ago, while he was in the forest hunting wild turkey, his family—wife, mother, three children, younger brother and his wife—had all been rounded up, packed into a truck, and delivered to a railway siding outside of Kiev for shipment to somewhere in the East. He understood that he would not see them alive again. That was that. The only question he had to answer was whether he would continue living or kill himself.

The young Communists didn't know what to say. They left him a cup of water and departed as quickly as possible. One of the boys—he was later killed at Stalingrad—said, reassuring himself, "Dirty kulaks. They get what they deserve." Yuri Maximovich, a spectator, thought to himself, Is this what it means to be deserving?

The spectator of the sorrows of the race has rather fewer alternatives than the participant. Knowledge liberates, but no less constrains. Given an awareness of the endless culpability of the race, each breath becomes theft, each cigarette a luxury, each kiss treachery. But that's how it was with Yuri Maximovich. He could not, as others did, clarify the visible injustice of the new order by elevating the specters of the old. He had only the Jews of the Podol to consult, and they, unlike his own family, were made up of passionate Communists, young like himself, born into the heat and welter of the Revolution, imagining that it was a great furlough from history. They painted signs, organized rallies, marched to the barricades, and shouted their slogans when they had no bullets for their guns. Some were killed and they were all heroes. The older people were poor and getting poorer. Whatever imagination they possessed had fed upon the thin gruel of the Bund, the Zionists, the Labor Orthodox parties, the Yiddishists—all of which were crushed by the end of the twenties; Yuri Maximovich was too young to know that these movements had been the lifeblood of his people. He was simply a Russian Jew, a Komsomol destined, he was told, to party membership. Notwithstanding, he was still a boy without a point of view. He wasn't religious; he didn't know any Hebrew; the few books that he had read on the history of the Jews frightened him; he knew some Yiddish, but aside from stories by Peretz, Babel, Shoilem Aleychem, he had little contact with the Jews. His family made an abbreviated Passover, but that was their only festival and it was little more than a "racial throwback," as Yuri called the little service that preceded the eating of a very large meal and the drinking of too much wine.

By the fall of 1936 life in the Soviet Union had become clear to Yuri Maximovich. The middle-aged kulak in the oven was now joined to the great of the nation passing in review before the iron fist, confessing their crimes unsmiling as the fist fell. Whatever illusion he might have had that Communism was to become his religion dissolved into a dull, persistent headache whenever he read the morning newspaper. It was at this time that he gave up reading newspapers.

It was no surprise to Yuri Maximovich, however much it may surprise those who consider the events of his life, that he determined upon a curious course in that year. He became a poet and he passed through the rites of conversion to the Holy Russian Orthodox Church. Both decisions shared an ultimate privacy, for he discussed his resolution with no one; moreover, both were motivated by the same disgust for the institutions which enfolded both poets and believers—namely, State and Church.

Yuri Maximovich knew perfectly well that in olden days

the Church had been the master of its own slaves, but now the Church was persecuted, and he knew no less clearly that Russia elevated and destroyed her poets and had been doing so since the days of Pushkin. He therefore decided to join himself to two societies which he knew would give expression to his own persuasion that it was all—all the life he saw about him—unjust.

The conversion would have been an offense to his parents, but it was not to offend them that he appeared at the Monastery of the Mourning Mother, a small conventicle which struggled on with four aging brothers and an abbot hidden in a rural wood near the Ukrainian village of Gradizhsk. The abbot, a vague old man named Arkadi Ignatiev, catechized him for a whole week from morning until night and then late in the evening of the seventh day baptized him. When Yuri asked him for some food, the Reverend Father ordered him to leave, telling him to go and beg like all pilgrims before him. Yuri Maximovich had seen the four freshly baked loaves and the wooden bowl filled with red onions, garlic cloves, and radishes in the refectory and had imagined that there would be enough for five old monks and himself, but that was not the case. In a way, Yuri was relieved by Father Ignatiev's pious advice. It confirmed him in the inversion he had determined for himself. He knew that the Church was really as contemptible as the State, that there were no settled orders of power upon whom one could rely, that he had to go it alone. He left the monastery laughing.

The dawn was a glow of red and a brilliant sun rose over the Ukraine, drying up everything except Yuri Maximovich Isakovsky, who, given the baptismal name of Mikhail after the Archangel, slept through it all. When he awoke Yuri could not remember the name that had been sealed with chrism into his brain, his eyes, his mouth, his ears.

The decision to become a poet, not unrelated to the whimsy of his baptism, grew from the conviction that the only way to endure as a man in this country of his was to become wholly useless. He could not conceive for a moment how the powers arrayed about him could get to the soul of a poet. A poet, Yuri reflected during the months following his baptism, was someone who was so wholly unresponsive to the possibilities of power that creating poetry could not help but be the only vocation for men who wanted to be just. It had to be that way. Whenever Yuri would speak to himself the various invocations he had created to pacify the gods of the city or the deities of the countryside or the great God of the universal pantheon, it was always a prayer that the poet remain indifferent to the uses of the world. But of course the education of a poet long precedes the decision that one has the gift to make poems. The writing of the first good poem on the flyleaf of a book, on the back of a notebook in a trolley, on an envelope—that mysterious crystallization that results from years of fiddling and diddling with the languages of sensibility—has no discernible origin. Is it a wound that never heals? Most certainly not. And if not a wound, then a scar? More likely, but still dramaturgy and dramatics has no place in this. Reading, most certainly, dozens of poems over and over again until the fabrications of others became the husk of his own words and the utter delight of a language—dark and mysterious languages, with subtle connections and rhythms, so hopelessly stressed and beaten with the short grunts and elongated sighs of the race of men that became Russians—passed through him like the milk and bread his mother set out each morning for her family.

The Isakovskys did not have many books, and those they had reflected less choice and selection than the bequests of history—the Hebrew Bible of a grandfather from Vilno; the large Russian Bible bound in tooled leather that his father had earned as a prize for being an excellent mathematician in high school; an odd volume of Pushkin which Mira Babininskaya thought sufficiently worthy to set beside her beloved Peretz; an illustrated periodical and compendium of the wonders of the world, *Universal Panoramas*, an antediluvian publication found in odd copies in those cranky bookshops that survived into the twenties—all these along with bric-a-brac and earthen jugs with dried flowers, filled the single bookshelf that stood in the corner of the family common room. And, of course, unopened, the volume which Emil Veniaminovich Mandelstam had sent to his father from old Leningrad in 1913. That book —it was called *Stone*—Yuri Maximovich discovered the same summer that he encountered the kulak.

Unfortunately, by the end of his youth it had already become the assumption of the times that poets did not need the education of the history of man in order to make poems. Enough, the new prosodists argued, to breathe along with ordinary men in order to make poems. What was not understood then, or perhaps even now, is that breathing garlic may be excellent for a head cold, but not for poems. There were in fact so many splendid poets—of course many others were shot or in prison by the end of his youth—who had taken the sensible suggestions of the state about advisable themes for poetry, healthy beats, and right meters and measures for the instruction of the masses that a young poet like Yuri Maximovich was not lacking for instructive models. He rushed to buy the reviews which carried verse and for many months would follow a single career with enthusiasm, only to find that the poet had passed on, had turned to translation, had decided to write children's books, to teach linguistics or Russian grammar, which signaled something more ominous than the laryngitis of the muse. He concluded (indeed, he stated it once—quite forcefully, some of his friends thought—and he omitted it from his first and only book of poems) that fame—which he symbolized by a blinding stage light, immobile, always directed to the same enlarged circle upon a slatted floor—never budged. In the conceit of Yuri's little rage poem, fame was an empty circle of light into which one or another poet stepped, speaking his poems like a hierophant or a bird or an actor, and whether good or bad, noble or base, the poet had no life unless he stood within the circle of the light. The light of fame was not indifferent, nor was fame whorish. It was only a spotlight for the sake of whose illumination men would tear each other to pieces.

Nastya coughed and wriggled in Yuri's arms. She was hungry. It was past her feeding time, but Nastya had lain still while Yuri Maximovich snored.

It had clearly been a mistake to sleep. For several minutes

Yuri stared dumbly at the wall above his desk, a particular spot stained with a drop of matted blood and dried wing where he had smashed a fly with a truncheon of manuscript several days earlier. The sleep which had overtaken him was a rare sleep in late afternoon. On normal days he would have been drinking tea with Lydia Yegorovna and summarizing the events of the completed day, tidying the piles of boredom which lay upon his enormous desk. Something, Yuri recollected, had brought him home early, something had dismayed his schedule, and a disagreeable visitor had passed in and out of his apartment. Limp, crumpled by the fatigue of a restless sleep, his body edged forward to examine the little mounds of paper which huddled behind the foggy dusk of day's end. A light from far below in the street cast a shadow on the wall, but Yuri, not yet completely awake, continued to stare. There was something that eluded him, a piece of his sleep that fled before his wakening, burying itself once more in the shifting sands of forgetfulness, like the ridiculous saint who unconcernedly walked into the marsh of the southern Nile and shouting words of contrition sunk into the quicksand until he perished. There was that bit of quicksand within him, shifting restlessly until it seized and strangled magnificent images, brutal memories.

Yuri shuddered and hugged Nastya to himself. He remembered. It was the old dream. It had come back again, revisiting him like the rancid beggar who made the rounds of his building once a month, but receiving no alms from Yuri stayed instead to play dominoes and drink tea. The dream smelled like the beggar, but it was familiar and somehow not unwanted. Yuri had had this dream (or rather its mode and variation) sufficient times over the past twenty years or so since the funeral of his father.

Maxim Osipovich Isakovsky, the inconsequential and muddled father of Yuri Maximovich, had survived Mira Babininskaya by six years, the last—after an accident in which he broke his hipbone—spent in a home for the aged and infirm located in a dreary park in Kiev, where the local children planted radishes and lettuce usefully.

Old Maxim had decided, Yuri learned after his death, to

become religious. Maxim Osipovich had quite simply reverted. He hadn't known a great deal about Jewish practice to begin with, and what he remembered at the age of seventy-one, when all this took place, was thin indeed, but whatever it was that he recalled he magnified and exalted, turning such a trivial recollection as having two rolls to bless on the eve of the Sabbath into a fetish requirement (going to the length, you see, of buying for an outrageous price the dinner roll of a gentile roommate—an ancient man with no teeth at all who couldn't possibly have chewed up the stale rolls the hospital received from the local baking cooperative, but who loved to suck on sweets, for which Maxim's thirty kopecks was more than adequate). But that's the way it went with father Isakovsky. Fortunately for Maxim Osipovich, a rabbi occasionally dropped in at the home on the pretext of seeing the ailing brother of his wife, and while there he would go through the wards checking for Jewish names and a chance to help. He was, you might have guessed, a follower of the great Hasidic master of the Ukraine, known generally as "the Lubavicher" after the village of Lubavich where the dynasty had been founded and where the first rebbe was interred.

The rabbi—his name was Mendel Iskovitz—was grave, but did not look religious. He was shrewd enough to wear a cap instead of a broad-brimmed black hat, and he kept his little twisted tassels of hair shirt virtually invisible to all but the meticulous and foreknowing; his frock coat was more frayed gentility than a badge of belonging. The retired rabbi—who kept himself together by receiving and losing and receiving again the only license granted in Kiev to bake unleavened cakes for the Passover—caught Maxim Osipovich's interest by whispering, "*Shoilem*," to him late one day. From that brief salutation—a flicker of recognition which linked Maxim to something that he longed to recollect, for it had been Mira's greeting to him when he returned from the factory—a friendship began which left him a few months later happily religious, thinking about God and the Garden of Eden in a way he was unable to think about the shrieking Komsomols planting in the radish garden outside his window. His religiosity had not, of course, gone unobserved. Maxim Osipovich, even though indifferent to the niceties of Jewish law, tried to obey them in the large by refusing to eat meat. Unfortunately, the soup which he received once a day had bits of fat and bone floating upon its surface which he could not ignore. Rarely was the soup rich with vegetables, rarely could he persuade himself that no forbidden animal had boiled in the gruel. He resigned himself, not unhappily, to ignoring the soup, and the rabbi—good man that he was—brought him several times a week a hard-boiled egg which supplemented his meager diet. The point of the matter—and there is no reason to exaggerate the tale of Maxim Osipovich's conversion—is that the old man, as pious as ignorance will allow, grew increasingly bored with living as the colors of paradise became more vivid. One evening, not long before the New Year, 1949–1950, the festival which the Jews call Rosh Hashanah, Maxim Osipovich Isakovsky died.

The funeral and interment in the cemetery of Kiev would not normally have been well publicized. After all, death is commonplace. The rabbi, however, was proud of his convert, and word of Maxim Osipovich's pious last year had gone out among the Jews of Kiev. Instead of the conventional twelve or fourteen mourners, more than sixty people crowded about the burial site, Yuri Maximovich among them.

The rabbi spoke quietly and simply of Yuri's father. He spoke in Yiddish quietly and simply, saying:

"*Yidn*, you should know something about Maxim Osipovich Isakovsky. He wasn't much to look at and he hadn't made much of his life. He began as a clerk and he died as one. Not much really. A worker, pretty much like all the workers in this country. Not much sorrow, thanks to God, but not much joy either. He loved his wife, who died six years ago, and he loved his son, the writer Yuri Maximovich, whom he didn't see very often, and a daughter he loved also, but she has disappeared.

"What makes Maxim Osipovich important is that he changed his mind. He thought for most of the years of his life that *Kodesh Boruchu* didn't matter, that if he existed he was so elevated and high up in the councils of heaven that he couldn't possibly take a look at how Maxim Osipovich was doing down here. In other words, Maxim Osipovich didn't bother much with God and God didn't bother much—so he thought—with him.

"I guess what changed Maxim Osipovich was that he fell down and broke his hip, and with that he began to feel pain and his body fell apart and he could see the end of his life approaching more clearly than he ever thought he would. He told me once that he had imagined death like a surprise. He hoped he would simply be overtaken by death like a distance runner who is suddenly passed by a sprinter whom he hadn't even noticed. But breaking your hip and getting put to bed for a year, hobbling about on crutches, wearing hospital clothes—all this tends to put an old man in mind of death.

"That's what happened until I came along.

"I guess I helped change his mind, although as a rule I don't go about changing people's minds. I don't make propaganda for God. God doesn't need me to do that. I have enough to do without that, but from the very first day I spoke to Maxim Osipovich and wished him a "*Shoilem*," I knew that here was a man who wanted to change his mind. He had lived all his life —seventy-one years of life—without ever really thinking. He grew up when the cursed czar was tormenting us and he continued doing the same thing when our country became Communist. It didn't really change anything that he could see. The Messiah hadn't come. There was no difference, and unless a man sees the real difference, it's hard for him to be a political man. And Maxim Osipovich wasn't very political, although he didn't cause trouble for anyone, and he never missed workers' meetings or deadlines for his figures. No. No. Maxim Osipovich never gave a thought to why and how and what for. And I confess I didn't really give him any big idea. I simply began to tell him a little bit about what it has been for a Jew like him to endure into the twentieth century and to complete a decent life. I showed him that the odds were all against him —against him, and against all of us, and against me, but that it happened anyway. One morning, Maxim Osipovich said to me, "Reb Mendel, what you're saying is that I'm a survivor." I answered him, "Yes, a survivor."

"Of course, from that moment on, although his hip still wouldn't mend and he grew weaker, he began to think maybe his life had been remarkable, maybe it had been courageous and worthwhile. And maybe (and he thought this out all by himself) some *Kodesh Boruchu* had helped him simply by being the head of the council of all the great, dead Jews who attended to the living.

It was at this precise moment in Reb Mendel's grave-side speech—who knows for what reason—that a middle-aged man wearing a trench coat and a curiously old-fashioned black derby began to whistle. Another, standing to his left, took up the whistle, his fat index fingers jammed into his mouth. The rabbi stopped for a moment, but reconsidering his initial silence, dropped his eyes to the coffin which lay before him and said loudly: "You will not interrupt me. I have used up little of my time and I will continue to the end."

The man in the trench coat shouted back, "Four minutes!"

"I will speak to the end of my time. I am allotted thirty minutes and I have spoken less than five. A man has died and deserves thirty minutes of our time. If you, you whistlers, have no respect for the dead, these before me have come to pay him and each other their respects, and you will be patient, whoever you are and from whomever you come."

The derbied man stepped back away from the crowd before the grave site, and four others—three dressed as he, in tightly belted trench coats with caps or hats firmly upon their heads, each with brim or visor pulled down over his eyes—joined with him to confer. After a moment they took up positions about the mourners and readied open notebooks and pens for the conclusion of the service. Beyond the circle of mourners, beyond the thin company of these deputies of the police, in the road beyond the gates of the cemetery stood a bus, before which lounged a dozen or so militiamen with carbines and side arms.

"I have told you some things about the last days of Maxim Osipovich. He began his life as a Jew and in the concluding days of his life he thought his way back to the *Kodesh Boruchu.* He tried to bless God in his eating. He tried to think nothing that was forbidden to the mind of a Jew. He tried to bless God with his thoughts. In this he remained cheerful and joyous to the end. He made his last confession to me. He unified the Name of God, and by joining himself in the end to the whole body of the Jewish people, Maxim Osipovich Isakovsky completed his return."

The rabbi then began to sing the last prayer, calling out to the God Who is Full of Mercy, but as he made his way through this prayer the whistles began again, and looking up, the mourners could see that about them stood now not just the five deputies of the police but the militia as well. They whistled, their faces puffed red, distorted, grimacing. One who, unable to whistle, was spitting against his dirty index fingers finally stopped in rage and began to shout, "Kike, Kike, Kike!" until his dirty little word sounded like a rhythmic cheer.

The funeral of Maxim Osipovich Isakovsky ended. The mourners passed through the ranks of the police, leaving their names and addresses as well as their identity cards, which each was required to collect from the police station later that afternoon.

When Yuri Maximovich—cold, weary, and dispirited—stepped into the office of the district officer to retrieve his identity card that afternoon, he had resolved to make clear his disgust with the party officials who had cheapened the funeral of his father. Unfortunately there was no one there to meet him. A young girl, the officer's secretary, sat smoking a cigarette at her desk. He annouced his name and she handed him back his identity papers. Yuri Maximovich was about to say something to her, something about outrage, scandal, disgust, but she smiled at him and mumbled her thanks to him for coming on time so she could go home early to make supper for her children. There was nothing left to do, and shrugging his shoulders, Yuri Maximovich left the police and returned to Moscow on the plane, hugging the leather briefcase in which he had put his father's scruffy wool prayer shawl which the rabbi had handed him before the funeral.

One last recollection. The rabbi—Reb Mendel Iskovitz—was tried the following month and sentenced to a long term for religious agitation and anti-Soviet propaganda.

Yes, that was the whole story that Yuri Maximovich had tried to remember. The same thing had happened to many people, to many people more famous than his old father—to dead poets, novelists, newspaper editors, old revolutionaries, loyal Bolsheviks; to many, many others who were buried amid acrimony and bitterness, the words of their friends and mourners drowned out by hoots and shouts, microphones cut off in steaming halls, funeral buses diverted so that old people had to walk miles to the grave site, priests embarrassed, rabbis humiliated. Oh, yes, it had become quite common. The occasion of death found people very vulnerable, or so the police thought, but they were often mistaken. Somehow death gives mourners courage, and very rarely, very rarely indeed was a funeral of the famous or loved ever really disrupted. People became solid and strong, monolithic in the respect and reverence they were determined to show the dead, and one supposes that united in their loss, at such moments, they too would willingly have joined the dead. That's at least one view of grave-side heroism. But for Yuri Maximovich the memory of his dead father's burial amid such clamor and disrespect—that old, thin father with the face of a confusion—tormented him. He dreamed of the middle-aged man in the trench coat and black derby, of the frustrated whistler shouting expletives, of the laughing militiamen whistling, and of the austere Reb Mendel Iskovitz somewhere in Russia paying for the burial service of Yuri's father.

Yuri Maximovich was stroking Nastya, stroking her, stroking her, hugging her fur and not listening. The phone, which he kept in a drawer of his desk, had begun to ring, but Yuri Maximovich didn't hear it at first. The sound finally got through to him. Yuri opened the desk drawer and lifted the receiver. He didn't speak. He didn't say a word.

"Yuri Maximovich?" the strong voice inquired.

"Speaking. And you?" Yuri asked. He hated the telephone.

"Major Kolyakov."

"Major Kolyakov?"

"Yes. Irina's husband."

"Yes. Irina's husband. So?"

"Irina and I are giving a party this evening. We know that you are leaving for the United States of America in three days, and we should like to say goodbye to you."

"I don't think so, Major. I don't have any celebrating to do with the Kolyakovs."

"Colonel Bobov of State Security will be at the party, and he thinks it would be a pleasure to meet you. The party begins at nine o'clock. Irina and I will expect you no later than ten. Until then."

The phone was replaced and the desk drawer slammed shut. Yuri said aloud to the major, "I see."

The journal of Yuri Maximovich
January 1972

I suspect—my memory about dates is vague—that it was late in the fall of 1956 that I read my poems in the aula of the University of Moscow. There were four of us reading that evening. I only remember Kolokolov and myself. A young Dagestane poet threshed out poems against lies while telling them. I thought at the time that one poem against lies might be the truth, but four in a row, like fake pearls, glittered without persuading me. The fourth I cannot recall at all. He was born (that I remember, oddly) in a mountain village in Upper Cheghem, and his jacket smelled of goats.

The hall was very dark when I came out to read. I read five poems that night. I don't remember which and it doesn't matter. I don't even remember which poems Ilia read. But the point was that when I finished my turn at the podium, the polite applause was pierced by a whistler—not a derisive whistler, not a whistler of hoot and disdain, but someone whistling to rise above the applause to my attention.

At the end of the evening while we were drinking tea with the students in the lounge, a young woman with the face of a moon shadowed by a falling wave of black hair (which made her, I suppose, a three-quarter moon) approached me. I had been talking with a fledgling engineer who wrote verse, and he was extolling the qualities of some poet whose work I detested. I was listening, I confess, distractedly, hoping for someone to break in and cut me off from his enthusiastic spittle. There she was. My protector, I thought. To which she replied—perhaps reading my mind—"No. You don't know me. It was I who whistled."

"Didn't you like the poems?" I asked, smiling, not at all upset if she had replied negatively.

"No, No. I liked them. That's why I whistled. I do things in a contrary way." She laughed and with a gesture that I came to recognize as typical—a way of attracting and holding complete attention—she used her brightly painted fingers to push back her rampant wave. The engineer smiled dumbly, showing his neat teeth. He was about to depart. I did not turn back to him. I liked this woman. The truth is, I had nothing to like at that moment, and she was exceptionally beautiful and—it seemed to me—open.

"May I introduce myself? My name is—"

"Yuri Maximovich Isakovsky," she inserted immediately.

I laughed. "Of course. My shyness. I'm damned awkward. Forgive me. And you? . . . for I can hardly know *your* name."

"Irina Alexandrovna Narcissova," she answered, suddenly serious. "May I speak with you for a while? Not here, if possible. At your apartment. Is that possible? Will I keep your family up if I come home with you?"

"Not at all. I have no family."

"Perfect," she answered.

"That I have no family?"

"Ah. You are not only a poet, but a quick poet, and not quite as shy as you make it. Is that not so, Yuri Maximovich?"

I can only presume that in those days she was right. I had recently left journalism. I was the editor of a Soviet quarterly. I had a two-room apartment, so to speak. And my book of poems was being considered for publication, although three years were to pass before it appeared. She was right for that time. I wasn't generally shy. What I meant and knew was that I was shy with women, the more beautiful the more shy, and with Irina Alexandrovna, shy to the point of stupidity. To stupidity, I must admit that! (*Damn, but I have no wish to set foot in her house this evening. Damn them all!*)

Irina Alexandrovna came home with me that evening.

She came into the apartment and dropped her wool cape to the floor, never retrieving it from the cascaded pile into which it descended until, as it turned out on the following morning, she hung it up in my closet. Oh, yes. She decided to stay. That is to say, I admitted by morning that it would be lovely if she stayed. That is to say, I asked if she would honor me by staying. That is to say, the real truth was that by morning I could not bear to have her leave.

The night had been luxurious, a *luxe*, an unendurable *luxe* which she knew quite well how to provide, all the time effacing herself—her eyes (large like cavities on the surface of the moon) wide and disbelieving, her breasts (a range of young mountains with twin peaks) pinkish and succulent—denying precisely the exquisite control which she practiced like the diesel locomotive that runs between Moscow and Leningrad, anticipating every switch, every shift in the track, acceding to them all, having anticipated them. Oh, she was surprised, endlessly surprised.

"What a joyful surprise," she said after we had made love the first time that night, and as she said this she cupped a hand over my mouth and I kissed or nibbled or bit at it. How the hell should I remember my goatlike behavior? No poet from Upper Cheghem, but I nibbled like a goat. I made tea, walking about the apartment with my underpants on, although she told me to go naked. I couldn't. I wanted to, but the idea of making tea naked shocked me. I picked up the fag end of a cigarette she had snuffed in the corner of the bed closet. She had libertine habits, I suspected, but I would have cleaned up after her like a trainer behind an elephant if she had demanded it. What stupidity! How stupid!

She had said she wanted to talk. For hours I waited for her to say something. She had nothing to say. And yet I could not believe (then nor even now, for that matter—fourteen years after she left me for the major) that she had deceived me. Deceive me? The Idea—and it is a capital, major idea—so appalls me that I reject it. A month after she had picked up her cape from the pool of sunlight that collected by the foot of the Chair and had hung it in my closet, borrowing my leather jacket to fetch her belongings from a friend's apartment, I rejected with disgust Lydia Yegorovna's aspersion to the effect that it was "salvation that she's found an apartment at last." All I could reply—angrily, I admit—was that Lydia

Yegorovna had shown considerable and irrelevant interest in my two rooms when she interviewed me for my job. But there it was. Irina Alexandrovna moved in upon me, later with me, and finally at the end of the road, through me—to the major.

The story—stitched together like a Ukrainian patchwork, fragments and bits at a time—emerged as such a waste of human beauty, such a traducing of human imagination and ingenuity, that I put it down ultimately not to Irina Alexandrovna's personal corruption, quintessential and defining like a birthmark, but to the rusting of conscience to which Irina and millions upon millions of other citizens of this nation have succumbed. A cruel judgment, but then not cruel, since I do not judge people, only juggernauts of iron.

Whenever the law was passed—early in the thirties, I should think—the housing shortage had reached the point where it could no longer be regarded as a shortage, but as an indispensable stage of socialist development; the breakdown of housing in this city ceased to be a consequence of revolution, a source of humor and inventiveness, an object of inevitable vexation and crossness, and became an institution. Everything in our country which breaks down and cannot be fixed or reconstructed becomes necessary, and through necessity becomes doctrine. To scrounge for apartments in the twenties was commonplace and nasty, but a highly individual talent, calling upon all resources of cunning and skill. But by the thirties and surely by the end of the war, when Moscow was jammed to the bell towers, flooded by refugees, fortune seekers, and job-hungry demobs, the collapse of old housing and the insufficiency of new could no longer be turned over to the imaginative entrepreneurship of the early days. Not to have an apartment meant something—a failure of identity, a mark of impermanence and instability, a genetic defect. Joined to this moral deformation was a law which restricted the maximum population of all our major cities and obliged any itinerant to produce proof of work in the chosen city in order to be assigned an apartment, and yet the possession of an apartment and the various permissions and licenses to reside in the city was crucial to securing a job. The Gordian knot. For Irina Alexandrovna Narcissova, I was Alexander the Great.

The first night I thought I was Alexander. I behaved like the conqueror. I was treated like a conqueror. And like a conqueror I was betrayed.

Irina, with the face of a moon and eyes like the green of lizards, had come to Moscow from the south at the suggestion of a film editor who had befriended her (no doubt as I had befriended her) and promised her an audition for a movie director. She arrived, and several months after her audition, hearing nothing, she had made a *skandal* at the film cooperative, denouncing the morals of the film editor (who, it turns out, operated a splicing machine, doing nothing more exalted than snipping and gluing film). The poor man (who had a wife and three children) disappeared for a time, but Irina went right to the top of the system howling corruption and bawling innocence.

The turn in the story comes at this juncture: Irina Alexandrovna came to the attention of an official in the State Security in charge of embassy surveillance. Since Irina had somehow learned a smattering of Turkish and Greek—how, I did not dare to ask—she was employed by the KGB in Moscow to do odd little tasks, minor seductions, and trivial entrapments, and in return for each and every one she was promised a residence permit. Unfortunately it's one thing to denounce the bad form of a film splicer and quite another to suggest that all the initials of the awesome mnemonic, the K, the G, and the B, were each and severally liars and cheats. The fact is, beautiful Irina didn't do her last job well at all. She quite forgot that she wasn't supposed to enjoy herself while she was in bed with a naval attaché of the Turkish embassy. She forgot to give the signal, her enraged "husband" never appeared, the trap was never closed, and she lost not only her dark Turk but the favor of her protectors. When she met me she was in the last three months of her temporary permit. All would have been lost had I not succumbed.

I did.

Why she chose me—beyond the obvious, and the obvious I disbelieve—remains a mystery. I could have pressed to lift the edges of the shroud which disguised the truth, but I did not dare to. I did not question her. I could not bear to lose her. She was my first and last carnality. I discovered that bodies locked in love produced sensations so exquisite that crushed roses, mountains of perfumes, a sea of sweet-smelling tears, the mauve and scarlet silks of Arabian sheiks—in fact nothing of the sensuality of the worlds dreamt and felt in dreams could equal it. The redness of red and the blueness of blue that gave all the paintings of Matisse in the Hermitage their clarity and light were nothing beside the blue shimmer of her skin bristling in the morning cold or the red-purple of her lips bitten by her desperation to yield pleasure.

Irina Alexandrovna was an angel of sexuality, amorphous and ambivalent as angels, shallow and unprofound as angels, duplicitous, I am afraid, as the angels, who one minute link themselves to Satan—an angel, after all—and the next turn upon his sinfulness like wicked termagants. Oh, Irina Alexandrovna, how I loved your using me, how I admired your skill and deftness, how stupid I was.

You said nothing that first night except how marvelous you found my penis—slender as the arm of an athlete, you said; how strong you found my hips, strong as a young sapling. I believed you. That was virtually all you said that first night, extolling some portion, part, piece of my natural machinery as though I, since my youthful soccer days, had paid any attention to the disarticulated equipment that is my body. My penis—yes, that lackluster artifact of mine was no more "slender as the arm of an athlete" than my wart was a black pearl, as you called it. You seasoned my vanity like an expert chef and you gave me joy.

Which lasted exactly two years, from the night you returned home with me. You proposed to me the tenth night and by the thirtieth we were married. You acquired a residence permit to remain in Moscow, and I—I acquired a complete library in Marxism-Leninism.

A little more than two years later, 1958, winter, you left me for the major, the very major who as a lowly captain had first recruited you into the State Security.

He, son of a bitch, he is the major who just called, to whose apartment (stuffed with the thievings of high administration, spilling over with second-rate appliances and machinery imported for our elite from the warehouses of Western factories) I am ordered to go. They have decided that I be celebrated, fêted, and no doubt employed by Colonel Bobov, who among other things controls exit visas.

A children's country. A nation of children playing the grand game of life and death.

I'm in the right mood to leave Russia. I've had an eventful day. This day in my life is worth a year of other days. If it had happened slowly, unrolling over a span of days, I would have had time to flatten each event, desiccate it with explanation and interpretation, return it to the file of forgetting, but all in one day—a poem, Comrade Bassinova, writing in my journal, meeting Bedkin, dreaming of my father's funeral, speaking with Kolyakov, recollecting Irina, and now going to meet Colonel Bobov. That's a day, isn't it? Indeed, it is. I feel reckless, like an endangered species that has to improvise its survival.

5. A Party in Honor of Yuri Maximovich

Everything about Irina Alexandrovna (née Narcissova, briefly Isakovska, currently Kolyakova) was convenient.

Most obvious, immediate to sight, was the convenience of her beauty. And convenient it was: efficient, easy to conserve, and completely superficial. That moon face, the lizard eyes, the strong and long neck, the ankles of a dancer, the size 6 feet were all of a piece, nothing awry, no defect to convert her beauty from simplicity into depth, rewarding the beholder with the suspicion that perhaps these placid waters ran deep. No—nothing about Irina Alexandrovna was incommodious, angular, suggestive. She was a bore, or rather her beauty was boring; beyond succulence and delectability, the pleasure past, the slack remains of her spreadeagled body were boring. Too even! Too regular! Too perfect to be delicious again without a respite!

"I could never make love to her twice in the same night—after the first night, that is. The passion was all in *me.* Her body was a receptacle—a gravy boat, a demitasse cup, a bud vase, all smoothness and marvelous design; but after the Act, to look upon her, exhausted and motionless, I was always bored. No. No, it took a day or two before my brain and my penis agreed to want her again. She, however, being nothing more than a complete set of imperial service, was ready at a moment's notice."

Yuri Maximovich's opinion. After the fact, after the divorce.

But this impression of Irina's character, limited to two years and a bit of marital convenience, was nothing beside the conviction which took hold of Yuri Maximovich as he ascended in the elevator to the fourteenth floor of the skyscraper on Vosstanie Square that Monday evening at a little past the hour of ten. Yuri Maximovich had been able to moderate and contain the diluted solution of Irina's existence for two years of marriage, and for fourteen years of aftermath, but confronted with the real presence of Irina Alexandrovna Kolyakova, living in that skyscraper—not at all like the photographs of Chicago skyscrapers that he had pondered in the U.S.I.A. magazine to which *The People's Voice* subscribed—Yuri was obliged to renew his respect for Irina's shrewdness. Clearly it had been Irina's decision to live in the center of Insurrection Square (that is what "Vosstanie" means), celebrated from the year 1950 by a twenty-four story building culminating in an uninhabitable gilt spire which rose an additional one hundred and sixty meters above the central shaft. The conception of two enterprising architects, respected Pisokhin and assiduous Mindoyanets, the building was the nearest Moscow would come to a complete American center of culture, rest, and recreation, housing a movie theater spacious enough to accommodate most of the residents of the apartment house (if all decided to be recreated at the same showing), a large *Gastronom* that supplied the tables of its privileged inhabitants, and a profusion of turrets and pinnacles in the style of the thirties, from which, wearied and depressed, at least one citizen threw himself each year into the square below.

The domicile of the Kolyakovs was clearly an Irina decision. Irina had no doubt treated the major, as she had treated Yuri, to eyes like saucers when they had driven through the square during their apartment hunt, and the major, his hands deep in his trousers or clutching the fabric under his armpits with a crooked thumb—serenely dumb—had probably asked, not yet acclimated to her beseeching eyes, "You want an apartment there?" "Oh, yes, Oh, yes," she had no doubt replied. "Oh, can we? Oh, please, please, my Major." Hear it? Can you hear it precisely? The major removed thumb from his armpit or hand from his pocket and stroked hers. "Of course, immediately." The apartment was arranged. Such things were easily arranged if one was well situated in the hierarchy, and a month later the Kolyakovs had moved in and begun acquiring the furniture and appliances that Yuri Maximovich would soon encounter, and most particularly, the clever iron bootjack in the form of a paunchy officer of the extinct armies of Russia, which, nailed to the door, served it as insignia and knocker.

At ten minutes past the hour of ten that Monday evening, three days before he was to depart for the United States, Yuri Maximovich—called to the home of his ex-wife, whom he had seen *en passant* only a half-dozen times in the fourteen years since their divorce—lifted the booted legs of an iron general and rapped on the thick wooden door. He sighed and opened the jacket of his blue winter suit. He already felt steamy and uncomfortable, although he had left his overcoat, shapka, galoshes, and gloves in the vestibule below. The door was opened a minute later by an old woman who could not possibly have been a house-worker—more likely a spinster aunt or perhaps the the major's mother. She examined Yuri Maximovich with appraising insolence, and without introducing herself, attached her hand to Yuri's; digging a sharp nail into his palm, she dragged him down the entrance hall toward the smoke and noise that rose from the bog of human beings that had gathered ostensibly to celebrate Yuri Maximovich's departure from the Soviet Union.

It was impossible for Yuri Maximovich to see into the room. Not only was it was dark and ill-lit, but people were clutching each other as though seeming to dance. Insanely, the only music to be heard was a ballet suite of Tchaikovsky, light and elegant as a spacious ballroom decked in firs and pine boughs, whereas there, atop Vosstanie Square, the fetid room was like the meanest *boîte*, as crowded as a *sakusochnaia* serving sprat sandwiches, or as it was, the living room of a highly placed Soviet officer who had the culture of a footman. What Yuri Maximovich could see of the room, swarming with people, was sufficient indication: promos of the Revolution in ornate frames, a branch of lilac rising from a water jug upon the mantel, and a row of folk dolls—promising, but inspection dissipated one's hopes, for they were meticulously fabricated miniatures of soldiers, sailors, cavalrymen, sappers, what have you, all tricked out in little caps and boots, and finally martial and drab.

"Hello." A hand shoved out of the gloom, seized his own, and pumped it energetically. Yuri could not see his greeter but replied appropriately. And another, clapping his back, was invisible behind a tall woman with a wool muff knotted about her neck. Yuri tried to see around her but managed little more than a detailed inspection of the river of red that surrounded her tongue, which she was waggling for some unaccountable reason at a little fat man who held her hands and swayed to Tchaikovsky's flutes. Yuri Maximovich, his hand still mandibled by the bony old lady, was being led through the room of visitors and dancers. At last passed through, they turned down another short hall and into a study lined with bookcases holding the Soviet Encyclopedia and loose-leaf binders marked only by serial numbers. The room was plain and almost empty of furniture. A leather couch placed against the right wall was occupied, but Yuri could not see its occupant in the gloom. Behind the desk which Yuri presumed belonged to Major Kolyakov—for two telephones with numerous buttons rested upon its glass-topped surface—there sat not Major Kolyakov (or at least in Yuri's recollection the figure did not resemble the major escorting Irina Alexandrovina whom he had twice passed in the street) but an ascetic-looking tall figure in uniform. The old lady released his hand and disappeared. He had not learned her name. The occupant of the divan rose up on an elbow and called to him, "Did Mother introduce herself?" The voice was unmistakable, and when he turned, a hand stretched toward him; he took it, first thinking perhaps he would kiss it, but decided instead to shake and release it. The hand returned to its owner. "Mother?" Yuri mumbled apologetically. "I'm sorry. I didn't know it was a mother." Irina—for it was Irina Alexandrovna—laughed. He still could not see her properly. She lay like an odalisque, her left leg raised, her right outstretched, her body turned three-quarters like her face, contorted to the room, each angle dictating a different perspective. Foot up to head she was crunched in the chiaroscuro of the study, lit as it was by an antique lamp upon the desk; viewed frontally, she was a marvelous head, two breasts stacked like soft rolls, one atop the other, and her smile, a breathing sneer. The old lady returned and handed Yuri a goblet of sweet champagne. "Thank you, Mother." The face, stretched like crackled parchment, creased about the eyes, as much expression as it could muster. "Thank you, Mother," Irina echoed. "To you, Yuri Maximovich," the occupant of the desk called out, producing a bottle from the floor and filling his tumbler with vodka. "To you, to America, to Moscow, to the Soviet People." There were four toasts without intermission to which Yuri meekly assented by sipping the sweet champagne. His glass was emptied; the old woman returned with a full bottle and set it on the table with a dish of *zakuski*, red and black caviar sandwiches covered with chopped eggs and bits of onion. She disappeared again and the room subsided into silence. Behind Yuri Maximovich stood the major, before him the unknown toaster, and upon the divan Irina Alexandrovna.

"Do I stand?" Yuri asked after a moment flushed with unease.

"You never were certain what to do with your body," Irina announced, not concealing her sarcasm.

"Forgive me, gentlemen, Major, but your wife is a bitch." Yuri was relieved by his outburst—a reprisal, he reasoned, for one event of the day.

"You are speaking to my wife, Isakovsky," the major spluttered as though the information was both unusual and sufficient reproof.

The officer behind the desk (whose identity one has guessed) smiled with amusement, more at the silliness of the major than at Yuri Maximovich's comment. He was not offended by Yuri's insult; Yuri had been insulted first, after all.

"Of course I know it's your wife, Major. I also know that you are a major. I know this other gentleman is a colonel, undoubtedly the Colonel Bobov who wished to meet me. That covers everyone except me. I am Yuri Maximovich Isakovsky, editor, poet, translator, and now, it appears, international traveler. That's everyone. All of us. Now to our interview, if you please, so I can leave this party and go home to Nastya. Nastya is the other bitch in my life. A dog, a loving bitch dog, with virtually no teeth and little bite."

"Madame Kolyakova, if you please," the colonel said, finally weary of the little tableau. Irina Alexandrovna rose from the divan, lifted a chiffon scarf which had fallen from her shoulders, wound it twice around her neck, opened her mouth to say something, shook away the words, and left the room. "Good. It is best that we talk alone, and then you can enjoy the party. It has been arranged for you, my friend. It would be very rude to your hosts and to me—since I suggested the gathering and (permit me to admit it) the appetizers and drink do not come from the *Gastronom* downstairs but from our own commissary—if you were to leave without enjoying yourself. So we will talk and then you will enjoy yourself. Soviet citizens not only have the right, but on occasion even the duty to enjoy themselves. Understood? Yes? Excellent!

"Now to matters at hand. You are going, my friend, to New York this coming Thursday, and you will be there about a week. You will be staying at a decent hotel where many of our visiting poets and literary figures lodge. You will be attending your conference. You will go to a dinner for Kolokolov, where you will applaud his genius. And you will also give a poetry reading, a reading of your *own* poems, old ones and perhaps new ones. One of the new poems that you will read is being prepared. It's a short poem called 'Ripe Times,' an optimistic, hopeful poem composed in our cipher room. When the reading is over, you will be approached by someone who will say, among other things, 'Yes, indeed, Mr. Isakovsky, the times are quite ripe.' You will acknowledge the warmth of this sentiment, and when asked to see the text of the poem you will offer it as a gift. That's it. Very simple, I think. Very simple. That's all we would like you to do."

"That's all. That's all. Very simple." Yuri Maximovich looked about him for an open window, not that he had any intention of jumping. At that moment he wanted to be able to see out of the room, to look beyond the lean, drawn face of the colonel and his leaden subordinate to the sky above Moscow, to open space, to dark clouds. Unfortunately the panes of glass were all painted black. "I *must* do this thing for you, Colonel?"

"Do you have any question on that score?"

"I dislike spying."

"Spying? Who said anything about spies and spying. My friend, your are being too poetic, too dramatic. Spying?" The colonel laughed, his voice rumbling with contempt. "No, no. A simple matter of transmitting a lovely poem. Very short. I guess it must be a half-dozen lines. Quite innocent."

"Colonel Bobov, sir, I should not like to do this thing," Yuri Maximovich said slowly, comprehending his words, comprehending their meaning; each word—formed like a rock over the millennia of geological time, shaped by the weight and pressure of fires, gases, universal fissures—fell from his mouth, each by itself, and each word—a jasper, a crystal, a sapphire, a carnelian, an amethyst, a diamond, a coral, precious in the value of men, but aged and formed in the center of creation—was caught in the palm of the colonel, where it shuddered, terrified of the power of this new man of the century.

The colonel turned his back on Yuri Maximovich and stared at the bookcases, suddenly reaching out and withdrawing the volume bearing the serial numbers Z10073–Z11068. Flipping the pages, the colonel settled down into the chair behind the desk and began to read quietly. "You know, this is interesting reading. It is work for the major, but as the head of the section it is reading for me. Do you know, Major Kolyakov, for whom I worked?" The major acknowledged that he did. "The austere General Ivan Ivanovich Agayants, an astonishing man. It was he who first spotted your predecessor, Isakovsky. Sagatelian, I believe, was his name. Both Armenians. They had the smell of that region, except that the general smelled better. Well, I mention him only because he taught me a very great deal about how to get our way, quite legally, quite honorably, except that the recipient of our displeasure is uncomfortable for a time. For instance, let us take the situation at hand. Let us say that you remain firm, that you decide not to read our little poem, not to transmit it—let us say, in a word, that you remain uncooperative."

Yuri Maximovich could not contain himself. He knew the litany. He had imagined it like every Soviet citizen; every Soviet citizen with the intelligence of an adolescent could imagine it, but nonetheless he interrupted with a frightful pleading. "But, Colonel, I have done nothing. It's that simple. I haven't done anything. I don't want to do anything."

"Precisely, Yuri Maximovich, you haven't done anything, and it is for that reason that you will do this. And if by some mistake of judgment you should decide that you will not do us this little favor, you will still not have done anything, but you will receive your deserts for disobedience. Now, how would we arrange that? Let me think aloud. No, I needn't do that. I have it all before me. Case No. 10091 did nothing, but we didn't like him. That was in 1962. So let me tell you what happened to case No. 10091. We arranged a traffic accident. Then we asked his employer—in your case, your secretary—to warrant brutal habits at work. A minor matter. Three years quite far away. Yes? Then . . . here, let us take case No. 11034. A perfect case. Let me read to you. 'Citizen So-and-So was arrested in January 1966 for circulating *samizdat* copies of disreputable and anti-Soviet literature,' such as you have, Yuri Maximovich, buried in the old icehouse of your dacha." (Yuri was aghast. His face fell apart in confusion and he was about to interrupt the colonel.) "The contents of your apartment are quite harmless, but the dacha? That's another matter. Don't worry about it. The books don't amount to much. We have their titles and your marginalia are absolutely harmless. *We* should care if you have all of these useless poets, these Tsvetaevas, these

Gumilevs, these Akhmatovas, these Mandelstams? What do we care if you choose to read shit? But the point is that it's an offense in any case. So then, what happens? From little acorns we plant trees, whole forests of trees. In the matter of Case 11034, the subject was sent away for a tenner. This week—punishment enough—he was recalled and his case canceled. Rehabilitated. We apologized to that wreck of a man. We gave him a pension. It won't surprise us if we bury him within the year. He did nothing but annoy us. Had he done worse we could have saved a fortune in time and money, but we do have standards, criteria of justice. Not your ancient justice, to be sure, but our justice. Our justice is to make this country work, to make it tick like a precision watch, and for that we are quite content to shave the edge of sentiment which clouds the crystal, slows the mechanism, befouls the steel and plate of the instrument. You understand?"

"Do I have to go abroad? Let us say that I decide not to go, become ill, develop a catarrh, a rash from head to toe that makes me unsightly, or perhaps, sir, a disgusting open wound that festers and belches green slime."

"Are you making fun of Colonel Robov, Yuri Maximovich? I am unamused. I have no time for jolly amusement. If you become ill, my friend, it will be a sickness to death, you may be sure of it."

"I don't have any choice, do I?"

"Soviet citizens do not have choices except to be obedient and live. They can always choose to die and we are quite prepared to accommodate them. That's the only choice they have."

"I have no interest in dying just yet," Yuri allowed, warming to his compliance. There was no use to further protest.

The colonel poured himself a tumbler of vodka, drank it off, and slammed the glass down on the table. The tumbler shattered; the thick green-white glass of the desktop screamed but did not yield. "So then. The poem will be sent along with your traveling papers. I trust it will go well with you. One last thing. Bedkin is quite familiar with your assignment and is authorized to do what is necessary to ensure your compliance, or at the very least the impossibility of your noncompliance.

He will be about you like a blanket. Ugly mutt that he is, you won't shake him. Kolokolov, on the other hand, is a useful utensil. He's better at poems than at this kind of prose, so I would not trouble his brain with your difficulties. All clear? I look forward to seeing you upon your return. You will return, won't you? I think so. Somehow I think so. Good evening for now, Yuri Maximovich, and *bon voyage*."

Colonel Bobov rose and came out from behind the desk to Yuri Maximovich, to whom he extended his hand. Slowly Yuri received it, grasping it lightly. What a mistake. The colonel nearly crushed the hand. Yuri winced with pain. "The power is in the will, my friend, never in the hand. Goodbye and good luck. Outside is a party in your honor. Join it." With that the colonel exited down the hall into the miasma of celebrants.

The major had stayed behind. Yuri Maximovich collapsed upon the divan and drew his legs up, crushing his head to his knees. Words began to fly through his brain, enormous words of anger, and he stuttered to speak them, but only sounds—at most, unintelligible syllables—emerged from his confusion; nothing precise and sensible could be heard. He had lost the strength of the ages. Only stupidities of rage remained.

"And what's more," the major began, "I didn't like at all the way you spoke to my wife."

"Goddamn your wife, Kolyakov. Goddamn you, Kolyakov," Yuri replied instantly, focusing his anger upon the major's inanity. The major reached down and picked Yuri up by his tie and slapped him. "It doesn't matter at all, Major. Slap me around. You're used to that kind of thing. It doesn't matter at all." The major released his tie, and bursting into laughter, left the room.

"He's in there," he heard the major say to someone at the end of the hall. Yuri had no wish for another interview, but before he knew it he was face-to-face with Kolokolov and two others, a youngish man with ambulatory features whose eyes roamed, whose nose had a remarkable tic, whose virtually hairless face was still blubbery with baby fat, but otherwise, if one could endure his androgynous ugliness, seemed intelligent, and a woman in her early seventies whose gray hair had been rinsed with an orange dye, giving her dead-white skin a lunar glow. They entered the room, provided Yuri with a full glass of warm champagne, and sat down on the floor before the divan. Only Kolokolov stood, and it was he who began: "Why are you going to the United States?" His voice was unpleasant and irritable.

"It's nothing I asked for, I assure you."

"That's beside the point," the orange woman observed acidly, lighting a cigarette.

"What are these people, Ilia Alexandrovich?"

"Friends, I think you'd call them. Just friends. This is Anatol Paukinsky. He's a journalist. He reviews my books in the provinces. And this marvelous lady has been friend to most of the great poets of our time. She is none other than Liudmila Brilova, sometime lover of our poets, including the great Mayakovsky."

Yuri had heard of her. Everyone had heard of Liudmila Brilova. She had notoriety. What she lacked in distinction or talent she had at one time disguised with beauty, but now, her beauty fading, she conserved its remnants in a formaldehyde of rinses and unguents. Her apartment was known to be decorated with drawings of herself executed by Sudeikin, Yakovlev, Goncharova, Larionov, and even Mayakovsky (who drew quite competently), when she was a revolutionary starlet, and featured an enormous chaise longue on which she received, recumbent. Her husband had been a famous critic in the twenties, but he was dead. During the sixties she had undertaken, rumor had it, a different profession than courtesan. She was known as a security mouse—that is to say, apparently harmless and insignificant, she encouraged her admirers to speak their minds freely, confidently, in her drawing room, and then repeated her findings to a small dictating machine and passed the tapes along to the right office. Everyone knew of her duplicity and she was loathed and feared, but this neither embarrassed her conscience nor prevented her informants from continuing compulsively, like scorpions stinging themselves to death, to unburden their cramped souls in her boudoir.

Liudmila Brilova smiled sententiously at Ilia's introduction, extending her arm and tapping the ash of her cigarette on the floor. Paukinsky immediately produced a small ashtray from his pocket. Yuri could not determine whether it was one he had filched from the apartment, for it was common practice to pilfer anything small that was left in view—from pencils and lipsticks presumably to ashtrays—or whether it was not in fact a service which Paukinsky performed for Madame Brilova, offering her the ashtray in taxis, elevators, corridors, or in this case, the study of Major Kolyakov. "Yes, how I remember Vladimir Vladimirovitch. He was an extraordinary poet, a fact that compensated for other deficiencies to which I am afraid I can attest. What a miserable end. How sad. How very sad. I miss him from time to time. You shouldn't speak of him, Ilia Alexandrovich, in such a manner. You make him sound foolish and as for myself, you make me sound wanton and a bit necrophiliac."

"But it is a fact, is it not? It is one fact among many in your exhilarating life which fascinates strangers, so why not mention it?"

"I have no wish to impress people by intimate details," she replied, drawing once again upon her cigarette and tapping the ash into the metal receptacle which Paukinsky dutifully extended.

"You're so modest, Liudmila." Ilia congratulated her once more, chuckling with delight. It seemed to Yuri as though he mocked her, while flattering her no less.

"I'm not a foolish woman, Ilia Alexandrovich. I am vain and self-preoccupied. I was beautiful. No doubt I still retain the outline of beauty, compromised by age, but recognizable; however I know perfectly well when I am being used by you. Don't forget, famous Soviet poet, that I'm not one of your adolescent claque." She said this with determination. Clearly she was not a woman to be trifled with. She turned to Yuri Maximovich, having disposed of Kolokolov, who leaned back against the bookcase. "And you, Yuri Maximovich, why has there been nothing since *School of Song*?"

"I have had nothing to say. I'm afraid that's the truth." Yuri was telling an obvious truth, but one not usually admitted and therefore unlikely to be believed.

"Remarkable, remarkable," the journalist hummed.

"Why so? Why remarkable? Nothing remarkable about it. Poets dry up like unwatered fields," Ilia observed sourly.

"It is not from lack of water that I am dry, old friend. Not at all. I've had water enough. Or to change the image, if you please, I have not been without inspiration."

"What then has been the matter?" Liudmila demanded.

"Lack of courage, I suppose. Lack of courage. That's the real truth."

"How odd," the journalist commented, scrutinizing his unpolished black shoes.

"In the old days there was too much courage. These days there's too little," Liudmila observed, not a little provocatively.

"You're right, I suppose," Yuri said cautiously, suspecting the trap of her accommodating complaisance, "but then even in those days the excess of courage led to empyrean loftiness, the style of mandarins and hierophants—vague Khlebnikov, succulent Kuzmin, lofty Blok—while nowadays we have barrel chests of courage with not much to say. That's why I keep quiet."

"Damning with faint praise, I call it." Paukinsky's clichés were at least accurate.

"You think so?" Yuri Maximovich said.

"Of course he's right. We're not all empty-headed showmen. All of us? Vosnesensky, Yevtushenko, myself, barrel-chested with nothing to say. There's a touch of jealousy there."

"Undoubtedly. I've never denied jealousy. A clean emotion. But no envy. I don't envy you."

"You don't envy! How very noble," Liudmila interjected.

"Madame Brilova, you don't know me and you're in no position to judge."

"But of course I am. My position is the position of any shrewd Soviet observer. And I might say, my position is more favored than most. I knew all the poets. All of them that counted for anything. You, my friend, are the most recent poet I have met. Behind you is a line of two generations at least.

Literally scores of poets have made a path to my door. I made poets famous, and others whom I neglected stayed neglected. So that's that. *I know.* I judge correctly."

"One thing is certain, Madame, you have no self-doubt."

"Exactly, Isakovsky! There is no room in my life for self-doubt—no room in this city or this country for self-doubt, as you call it. An indulgence which rebuilding the world cannot tolerate."

"What she means, Yuri Maximovich, is that we all have a socialist task, even poets."

"Oh, my God," Yuri had begun to remonstrate, but Paukinsky, alert as a foraging insect, cried out, "There's no room either for that tired word in this conversation," but Yuri ignored him and rushed on, sipping his refilled glass nervously, speaking between sips, "Poets . . . and socialist tasks—the very language is mad . . . Poets have no responsibility to do anything but tell the truth and take the consequences."

"So that explains why you haven't written!" Liudmila had pounced upon his phrase.

"How so?"

"Afraid of the consequences."

"Did I say that?" Yuri Maximovich heard the phrase, naked as a light bulb.

"You did say that."

"You certainly did."

"My ears heard it. My pencil takes it down." That was Paukinsky, who indeed had taken from his jacket pocket a little notebook and pen and had begun jotting furiously.

Yuri stood up from the divan and stretched his legs. He almost fell. One leg had gone limp and he shook it violently, even resorting to giving it a pound.

"So, Yuri Maximovich," Ilia spoke like a judge at a summation, "you admit to being afraid of the consequences."

"My leg, damn it," Yuri replied, annoyed by its refusal to awaken.

"Forget your leg," Paukinsky said, anxious to proceed with his note-taking. His pen dripped ink.

"It's *my* leg, after all, and I can't walk."

"In that case sit down."

"It's functioning now." Yuri stamped on it; it didn't give way. "What's that? What have you been saying?"

"The consequences?"

"Yes. The consequences. I was saying that I was afraid of the consequences? Is that what I said?" Yuri Maximovich wrinkled his nose thoughtfully. "Well, it's the truth. I am afraid. It goes against my nature to think of poems as shaking the foundations. I should like to make poems that shore up the foundations, root trees more firmly, strengthen nature, resuscitate gardens and forests."

"Very poetic," Liudmila said slyly.

"You think so, Madame Brilova?"

"An evasion. Everything you say evades the point. We singers have a job to do," Kolokolov observed smugly.

"Well, yes, you singers do, but poets like myself have no job. We write poems by necessity, not duty. Nobody tells me to write a poem, but I cannot think of not writing them. My problem is that I have an image a day which flies through my brain, refusing to settle down into a poem. I run after it with my net, dashing about the streets with an open net, hoping to trap it, but off it goes on its blue wings. When I think I've got it, translucent, it becomes invisible against the sky. Here. There. Gone."

"You have no social duty?"

"I told you that I'm afraid of the consequences."

"Your lack of courage again?"

"Yes. My lack of courage. I should hate to be thought a parasite on the healthy body of Soviet letters."

"You work."

"Very hard, I think. The hardness magnifies with the boredom."

"*The People's Voice* bores you?"

"The voice doesn't bore me, but *The People's Voice* does. It's the difference between the song and the singer. The truth is, Ilia, that you bore me, but you've written an occasional good poem."

"You attack me now."

Yuri did not reply.

"His envy again."

"My jealousy. Not envy, Madame Brilova. Never envy. I don't want a hundred thousand of my books sold. I don't want to scream through microphones at slack mouths. No. No. Never. And no need to worry. I'll never have it. Never. So there's no envy of what I could have, but don't. I don't *have*! Pure and simple. I don't have Ilia's talent for the big throat."

"You're off the track again," Paukinsky put in, his pen poised for new quotations.

"Yes, friend, back to the main line. No social duty to poetry? Eh! I see. Do you remember our poet Mayakovsky. Remember what he said in his poem 'Homewards':

> *I want*
> *the State Planning Authority*
> *to sweat,*
> *Debating my quota for the year.*

That's what a poet wants. A quota. A bushel, a tumbler, a cartload full, no matter. Whatever he's told is needed. That's the poetry he gives the people." As she completed her peroration Liudmila raised a clenched fist and brought it down on her bony knee.

"So you *believe* Vladimir Vladimirovitch? You take him at his word." Yuri Maximovich began to giggle. He drank off his glass and refilled it. His giggles became heavy laughs and his face was red with drink and ridicule.

"You idiot woman. You believed him. You know poetry like a cow knows udders—a thing to suckle and drain off. God knows you're an idiot. If I believed Mayakovsky meant that I'd join him with the bullet. Poor man. He meant just the opposite. He knew better. I know he knew better."

The three were horrified. The first to reply to Yuri's attack was Liudmila Brilova, who rose with difficulty to her feet. Coming up to Yuri Maximovich, she stood before him and examined his face carefully. "I will remember your face. I will remember it in detail, and you will remember mine. You will have years to contemplate it. You may be sure you will regret this insult. Are you coming with me?"

Anatol Paukinsky retrieved the ashtray, emptied its contents behind the chaise, returned it to his pocket, closed his pen and folded his notebook and put them away, and—equipment gathered—stood up from the floor, glowered at Yuri, and followed after the old woman, who walked magnificently on her *démodé* patent heels down the hall, the click like a single melodic grasshopper, into the gray mist of people who shouted and sang in the beyond.

"What's become of you? What *has* become of you, Yuri Maximovich? You've written your death warrant. You better apologize to her. You had better, I warn you. That bitch has power and she'll use it. Mind, she will."

"Never. I will never retract a word I said tonight."

Yuri Maximovich had not forgotten the interview with Colonel Bobov throughout the conversation with these friends, and it was now once more before him, fully recollected. He knew that he had drawn a line through the moiling sea and that he had no choice but to walk through. His only concern, like those who preceded him in this perilous enterprise, was whether the waves would cave in upon him or the enemy reach him before he came out on dry land.

"So this is the way you are leaving for the United States. What a frame of mind! You're as nervous as a sparrow. Do you think you should go?"

"Of course, all the more reason now. I am going and I will be a good man there and I assure you, I assure you, I'm coming back. Whatever the music I'll be back to hear it. I don't guarantee to face it, but hear it, yes, I'll hear it all right."

"It's your neck, old friend. Better yours than mine."

"A Kolokolovian line, if I ever heard one. You know, someone called you not long ago, a 'useful utensil.'" Ilia flushed with anger. "Don't be angry. I don't agree at all. I wouldn't say you're useful. You're a leaky utensil. A utensil, yes, but riddled with holes."

"You want my enmity, too? You've been looking for it for a decade now, sniping and sniveling by turns. Well, you've got it. We're enemies at last." Ilia Alexandrovich arrived at momentous recognitions more slowly than most, but when they dawned upon him—his sudden illumination before Yuri Maximovich's disdain—he announced them like sunset, all lights and tremors and flutters of the horizon.

"As the French say, *soit*! So be it. One more enemy. I've made several in one day. It frees me from the necessity of having to worry about friends. I embrace you. I love you as an enemy much more than I ever loved you as a friend." Yuri Maximovich began to laugh again. "Eech, I sound like one of our novels, but they're all true. It's part of the great tradition, the underbelly of the Russian spirit, loving enemies." He embraced Ilia, grasping him around the waist and clasping his hands behind him, hugging him, his head resting on Ilia's shoulder.

Kolokolov broke away, backing off down the hall. "He's mad," he shouted. "Yuri Maximovich has gone mad."

The room beyond buzzed, the noise rising and falling like a swarm of bees whizzing away and then turning, wheeling, bearing down dizzily upon Yuri Maximovich. Yuri saw them all. There must have been a dozen people left in the drawing room, all shouting at once, each in his own way the recipient of a separate insult of Yuri Maximovich: the old mother, Irina Alexandrovna, the major, Paukinsky, Liudmila Brilova, Kolokolov, and the strangers to whom, with venom and invective, they had transmitted Yuri's insults and defamations.

Yuri stumbled down the hall toward the swarm and as he entered, standing posed in the doorway between the corridor and the drawing room, the swarm hummed distantly, voices trailed off, and a miserable silence fell upon the insulted. "A marvelous evening. A miracle. A revelation. I must thank all of you. I have never felt so celebrated, and for you, on your behalf, to spare you having to express your heartfelt feelings for me, I wish myself a *bon voyage* and a safe return. And may God bless Yuri Maximovich Isakovsky." He steadied himself, straightened up, and gleaming with a smile walked soundlessly across the thick carpet runner and out of the apartment of the Kolyakovs.

6. A Traveler Returns

It was about four o'clock in the morning, Tuesday morning, fifty hours more or less before his departure for America, that Yuri Maximovich stepped out into the January cold of Vosstanie Square. It was dark and empty. A car moved out of the shadows of a side street and swept the square with a searchlight. A police patrol car. It did not stop. For some reason Yuri Maximovich must have appeared above suspicion. It surprised him, since he had never felt quite as suspicious as he did that morning. He had gathered for himself, in the course of one night, a coven of powerful and influential enemies. He could not help but remember, weaving drunkenly down the street leading out of the Vosstaniya in the direction of the river, the extraordinary campaign which had successfully driven his beloved Mandelstam from Moscow. The campaign had been waged by men of letters, critics, translators, publishers, all bonded to the task of humiliating and destroying a poet. Obviously it was a worthwhile political enterprise—destroying poets—for it was devised and executed with reptilean cunning.

No need to rehearse it for you. You couldn't check it anyway. It is not to be found in any Soviet books of literary history. (Indeed, you can't even find Mandelstam in their books, leastwise not as a poet. A minor translator, a maker of children's books perhaps, but not as the greatest poet of modern Russia.) That was part of the problem. There was no way of establishing the record of history. Even the *School of Song*—Yuri's first and only book, now out of print (four copies in his own library)—could be obliterated so easily that all trace of Yuri Maximovich Isakovsky could be struck from the record of Soviet times. Libraries burn, archives shred, private copies can be confiscated, and within a decade all trace of a Yuri Maximovich Isakovsky could be removed. It had been done before, and unfortunately for him he had no widow, no son, no beloved to preserve the record. He dared not think "canon." One book of thirty poems is hardly a canon. It wasn't the loss of greatness that he feared or the destruction of his life's work, for he hadn't really done a life's work or for that matter completed a full measure of days. He was fortunate. He had been given time to waste, and fool that he had been, he had wasted it, but now it seemed to him he had stumbled upon a different course.

The street led Yuri Maximovich through Smolenskaya Square, and as he wandered through the garden that had been grown on the remains of the old haymarket, he found himself mumbling that it was as unreal, as ugly and artificial as had been the miserable hovels against which Tolstoy had inveighed a century before. Anything unsightly to the consciousness of the rulers was leveled and replanted with neatly arranged trees and flower beds. Moscow had nothing old any more. If it couldn't be buried it was planted. He wove down the Smolensky Boulevard, which merged into the Zubovsky before it reaches the Krimsky Bridge over the gray-green waters of the Moskva. It was very cold, but the early morning air felt brisk and elevating.

Whenever Yuri Maximovich wanted to leave Moscow he went to the Krimsky Bridge. The bridge, a bridge, any bridge, suspended over a city joins but also severs. During the springtime the kiosk near the bridge offered almond-flavored ices, and Yuri would stand—one foot upon the bridge, the other upon the bank—licking at this delight and dreaming that the bridge was severing him from Moscow and bearing him like a magic carpet down the Moskva and then upwards across Europe to Paris. That was when he thought of the bridge as a gangplank or causeway connecting formidably large and lumbering land masses that stayed put, while he and bridges in general were roaming things, set down from time to time and forced to do the menial work of serving as path upon which others jostled and rode their way over and upwards. In other words, the Krimsky Bridge. The Krimsky Bridge, recent though it was, with its stern pylons and gracefully fanned embroidery of steel rising in elegant arabesques, was a place of refuge and consolation for Yuri Maximovich. No wonder, then, that at five in the morning, his head dense but clearing, weary and confused, he should make his way to the bridge's center and there, standing over the river, begin to cry. Not sadly and not with self-pity, I should think. More in relief and consummation, for he had come to the turn in the road and he had taken it, resolutely, perhaps desperately, but not innocently and unaware of its consequence.

The wind of the night had settled. It was exceedingly cold, but the dying of the wind and the warmth of the champagne made it bearable. Yuri's coat was warm, but not that warm; he had pulled his fur hat down about his ears, covering his forehead against the occasional blasts that still found their way out from their entrapment beneath the bridge. But he was indifferent to the cold and finally gave up slapping himself to fend it off. His mind had whirled as wildly as the winds, but as they settled down before dawn, his exhausted mind expanded into somnolence, and dead-eyed he stared off down the river in the vague direction of what in earlier times had been called Sparrow Hill, to the south where dimly the sky parted from the earth to admit the thinnest line of dawn. It must have been past seven in the morning, gusting toward eight, when the sky began to stretch and free itself from the night.

Yuri Maximovich had not seen the figure coming to his side.

The figure, cloaked by an immense coat of bear fur depilated by a mange, came to rest beside him but made no move towards Yuri, neither to close the half-dozen-foot gap which separated them nor to speak out over the space. The bear seemed content to shake and stamp slowly, one foot rising and the other descending in a useless little dance too deliberate to combat cold and too clumsy to be a jig. It seemed but a ritual movement before the cold. The coat was at ease with the cold. Indeed, at its top was the head of a man, but the coat was more like a tent, inhabited rather than worn. Yuri Maximovich could not see the sleepless little eyes streaked with red veins staring out at the river, tipping upwards toward the boomerang moon, which appeared against the shifting clouds as though aimed at a target in the west, or glinting from their sockets in Yuri's direction, examining his strained face and his slack and wearied body leaning against the railing.

The bear began to move by inches down the railing towards Yuri Maximovich. "Do you mind if I stand by you for a time?" it asked.

Yuri Maximovich was startled by the voice and turned to see who spoke. He saw nothing but the peak of the fur and the estranged eyes peering out from a crack between the top and the second button. "Do you have to?" Yuri replied, not unkindly, but with evident exasperation.

"I thought you wouldn't mind."

"I do. That's a fact. I do mind."

"Well, in that case, I'll put a few more inches between us." The bear moved a foot away.

"That's still not enough. You're close enough to be beside me. The bridge is nearly a quarter-mile across and you think three feet isn't crowding me."

"It's a free bridge, old friend."

"As free as anything can be . . ." Yuri was going to add, "in this country," but thought better of it. It wasn't necessary to be denounced by a bear at seven o'clock in the morning. "But," he continued, "it would be a lot freer if you left me alone. You see, if you left me alone, you'd also be alone and then we'd both be free."

"You have a point, but with all that's happened to me since you saw me last, I could use a bit of closeness."

Yuri Maximovich was startled again. The voice had not importuned. It had slipped the intimacy in between a breath, the voice neither having descended emphatically nor risen to the decibels of an important announcement. If the stranger had indeed been acquainted with Yuri Maximovich it was not a knowledge upon which he relied. In fact, the stranger began to move down the railing away from him, sliding his glove-covered hands in front of him like a child running its hands down a banister.

"Hey, wait up. Hold on a minute." Yuri had turned toward the stranger and shouted after him, but a rush of wind drowned his words and the stranger must have heard little more than a jumble of sounds within his bear's cage. Yuri walked quickly toward the coat, and catching up with it, put out his hand to halt the retreating figure.

"I'm sorry. I've been here several hours now and I suppose I'm freezing to death."

"In that case, come with me and I'll brew some tea for us and then I can emerge from my ridiculous coat and visit with you."

Yuri Maximovich was attracted by the stranger's reasonable invitation. He wanted a cup of steaming tea and since the stranger claimed to know him, he thought to himself, Why not? and followed along at his side. The cadence of the voice seemed somehow familiar, but it was muffled by its furry cavern. They walked side by side a few miles down along the river until they came to an embankment near the Bolshoi Bridge, at which point they climbed up to a broad boulevard on the other side of the Kremlin walls and entered a garden surrounded by a ring of iron gates that were locked at nightfall and reopened each day late in the morning. The stranger produced a metal device (not a key, but a bent spoon twisted like a corkscrew), and inserting it into the lock, twisted it about for a moment until the mechanism sprang.

"Come," he motioned to Yuri, who had been watching him attentively. The light now covered the ground, although the sky was still dark. They entered the garden. His companion closed the gate behind them. The coat led Yuri toward a group of trees and bushes which formed a small enclosure, and entering it, they found themselves suddenly cut off from the wind. After a moment the stranger sat down, opened the bottom button of his coat, and from a series of loops that were attached near the hem of his fur removed a half-dozen or so sticks of dry wood, a small teapot, and two small metal cups, and from his outside pocket a small packet containing tea. The stranger disappeared and returned with the teapot filled with water (presumably from a tap which the gardeners used), dropped the tea into the water, and lit the sticks; within a few minutes the tea was brewed and they began to drink it quietly. The head had emerged from the bear's coat, and for the first time Yuri saw the ugly face, the sparse white hair, and the viridescent jowls, thin and lined but still preponderant, dominating the ridiculous face.

"Do you enjoy your tea, Comrade Editor?" the figure spoke, cupping the metal container with both hands and lifting the brew to his nostrils, where he sucked in the warming steam.

"It can't be." The face smiled and nodded happily. "But it is. Really! My God! It's you! It really is you! I don't believe it!" Yuri Maximovich was exuberant. He almost shouted with joy, but the face warned him with a pleasant frown.

"Shshsh. They might hear you. It's dawn now. The patrols begin very soon now. Can we go back to your apartment? I should like a bath and a nap if that's possible."

"Is it you? Is it Yasha Isaievich?"

"I do think it is. It is he. It is I. I am Yasha Isaievich Tyutychev. Just returned to the Little Mother of Russia. I have slept in here three nights now. My bear's coat and my tea and my thieves' tools keep me protected, but I have to do better than this, Yuri Maximovich."

"Was it by chance that you found me?"

"Not completely. I called by your apartment, but you were out. I figured you hadn't moved. I phoned the splendid Lydia Yegorovna—what a viper!—and pretended to be some official or other looking for you. Apparently you've been having some doings with officials of late, because my invention was enough to set her teeth chattering. I said I was an inspector general. She didn't know her Gogol, poor little dumb thing. I don't even think we have inspector generals now, just generals. In all events she took it gravely and apologized that you weren't at home and told me with whom you were spending the evening. I waited in Vosstanie Square for hours until you came out and then followed you to the bridge. It looked as though you needed to sober up before we met. Well, you did and you're sober now and I am so happy to see you."

"And you, Yasha Isaievich, *you*, I am happy to see." Yuri stretched out his arms and clasped old Tyutychev's wrinkled face, kissing it with unmistakable affection. And then he let go and sat back to stare at Tyutychev's splendid ugliness. The bulbous nose full of pocks and spots, the cheek jowls flaccid like a starved monkey, the hair sprouting from his ears were more than offset by the bright, darting eyes, the intelligent forehead creased from a life of perplexity, and the sprigs of white hair rising from the center of his head like date palms clumped in a desert oasis. "Oh, Tyutychev, what became of you? Whatever became of you? I never ran that eassy of yours, although I've read it a hundred times. You promised me the footnotes and they didn't come, so I assumed you had changed your mind."

"I didn't change my mind. I could run off the footnotes now. No. No, I didn't forget. My mind—how shall I put it?—was detached from my body. My mind didn't change, but my body did."

"What are you saying?" Yuri laughed, suddenly tickled by the image of that splendid ridiculousness separated from its remarkable intelligence.

"Well, what shall I tell you? I'm back from a very long stay in the country."

"You're from another century, Tyutychev."

"Indeed. From another century and from another Russia."

"Turgenev."

"Turgenev is at best a euphemism. Oh, yes, a long stay in the country. For my lungs, for my collapsed feet, for my bilious liver and blotchy skin. I can't eat sauces any more. I've grown uncomfortable with sauces. No more Béarnaise; never again *crème fraîche*. My stomach is a shadow of itself, but I imagine that I can survive to a very old age now. I've mastered the fragility of the flesh. Nothing can damage my body any more. Do you realize, Yuri Maximovich, that I'm seventy-three years old? Seventy-three and still picking locks, acting the tramp, rummaging in trash cans for a bit of supplemental diet. I'm one of God's marvels. I exist and I prove the existence of God. Forgive me, but perhaps you don't believe in God?"

"I'm not offended. And I do believe in something which is not man. If the bit extra that, thank God, is not man is really God, then I believe in him."

"That's good to hear. I would hate to bathe in an atheist's tub. The water would be too heavy. God's fresh waters. That's all I want."

Yuri Maximovich got up and shook himself. The damned left leg had gone off again, lamed by the cold and inaction. But the circulation started quickly, and after a minute of running in place he was ready to join Tyutychev, who by this time had tamped out the little fire, replaced the equipment in the lining of his coat, and buttoned himself up. As they came out of the garden they saw a policeman walking away toward the Kremlin. They increased their pace until they had turned into Frunze Street and finally made their way to the apartment house of Yuri Maximovich.

The sun had risen by the time they unlocked the door to Yuri's apartment. Nastya hopped down from the Chair and barked at Yuri, dashing about happily until she was picked up and hugged. Yuri set the kettle to boil and fixed warm milk with a bit of a hard cracker for the dog; then the two weary men sat down in silence and drank their tea. Yuri gave Tyutychev the key to the bathroom and a half-hour later, his head turbaned with a white towel, he returned clean, fresh, warm, and tired. Yuri was happy to give the old man his bed, and within a few minutes he was snoring soundly. Yuri lifted up Nastya to his lap, and seated before his desk, began to compose.

Thank the stars for light.
They have no other work
But they do it well.
Diligently winking in consonance,
They pretend an ignorance of our plight.
Below, we watch them from the Krimsky,
Taking comfort from their glitter,
Forgetting we burn out
And their life has no time.

He did not bunch the little lyric and throw it against the rampart formed by earlier nights of failure, but slowly his head dropped over the desk, the pen slipped from his hand, and he fell asleep.

"Wake up, Yuri Maximovich."

The voice was very close to Yuri's ear and for a second, although hearing it, eyes still firmly closed, head resting on folded hands, he was not certain who had spoken. He pressed his eyes more firmly shut. He was not confident that he should awaken.

"Wake up, my young friend."

Then he remembered where he was, unaccustomed as he was to falling asleep in broad daylight at his desk, unaccustomed to having a stranger with a gentle voice speaking in his ear. It required an effort, but he succeeded: slowly he lifted himself up from the desk, stretched his body, threw out his arms and breathed deeply, yawned, rubbed his eyes and sat back awake.

"Did you sleep well?"

"Without dreams. Yes. What time is it, Yasha Isaievich?"

"I no longer have a timepiece."

"By the bed on the floor, there should be an alarm clock."

Yasha Isaievich walked to the entranceway between the room and the broom closet and called back, "Nearly three o'clock."

"Lord, Lord. I should call in at the office. Lydia hasn't rung me. Shall we call Lydia?" Yuri said suddenly, addressing

Nastya, who lay curled upon the desk. Yuri opened the desk drawer and dialed the office number. "Lydia Yegorovna. It's I. I slept very late today . . . Yes. A very long night . . . Satisfactory? I should think it might have been." Yuri Maximovich was dodging about the clever probings for which Lydia Yegorovna was notorious. "Evasive, am I? Someone else called me that not too long ago. But no, I don't think so. It's simply that there's nothing to report." Yasha Isaievich had made some tea and brought a cup to the desk, setting it down beside Nastya, who sniffed at its steamy aroma. "I won't be coming in. No. Not today. Late tomorrow most certainly, but not today. I'm going to the dacha, I think."

"But I've just come from the country," Tyutychev said, smiling, after Yuri had replaced the phone and shut the drawer.

"Peredelkino. That's where we're going. I've had a dacha there for six years and I need it now. A day in the country, that's what we need. A quiet day, a walk, and although the secret is gone, a visit to the icehouse and a look at the books. Come with me. I need to talk to you."

Tyutychev nodded thoughtfully. "All right, but I'm not supposed to leave Moscow without permission, and to tell the truth, it's uncertain whether I'm allowed to remain here at all. I jumped the train that brought me back at Zagorsk and walked most of the rest of the way. But why not? I'd like to be with you before you leave."

"Leave? Did I tell you I was leaving?"

"No, but I've had a chance to see the preparations. The note of instructions to the building committee, the pile of shirts and underwear near the window, the suitcase. Whatever for, if not a trip?"

"You notice everything."

"Of course. That's my business. That's what makes me marvelous. Noticing everything."

"Let's go. Put the tin of tea in the basket there. There are some others in the chest above the stove. Throw them in, all of them. Vegetables, eggs we can get out there, and fresh fruit sometimes. I'll make us a compote." Yuri Maximovich fished a leash from under the desk and trussed Nastya. They were ready. It was late in the afternoon. They would be there by six if they hurried. It wasn't difficult getting a taxi to take them on the Minsk road to Peredelkino, a short distance, not even twenty miles.

Peredelkino is settled in the countryside, amid copses of trees and numerous ponds. At this season, frozen and laden with snow, the roads were slow and hazardous, but the driver managed it easily, dropping them a mile from the settlement a little before six. Yuri Maximovich knew a farmer in the district who occasionally sold eggs and pullets, and bought from him a fat little hen, which the farmer butchered and dressed, along with four speckled eggs. The two men and the scampering dog, whom Yuri had unleashed, slid and skittered down the road, which branched and branched, rivulets of roads wandering off into the trees, until they came to a wooden house with a low porch set back from the road. That was the dacha of Yuri Maximovich. He had been given permission to buy it seven years earlier after his tenth year in the Union of Soviet Writers had been acknowledged by a little celebration, four speeches, a minor award, the publication of his picture in the newspaper, and the reprinting of one of his more innocuous poems. He had wanted a place in the country, somewhere to escape, but the terms of escape were never clear and at best always exorbitant. He had applied to buy a dacha a few years after his father's death with the little insurance money that he inherited, but he was turned down for unspecified reasons. During the early sixties, when Pasternak had become troublesome, dachas were no longer regarded as a safe reward for Soviet writers. Several, indeed, with questionable consciences—that is to say, with some solid achievement to their credit—withdrew their applications, fearing they would be turned down, and Yuri Maximovich, honored with undistinction, was allowed to purchase one. Yuri's dacha wasn't located in the choicer sections of the settlement—that is, in the vicinity of the celebrities of the Writer's Union—but for that reason was more secluded. One large room, an old stove, solid planking, a fireplace, and out in back, falling into decreptitude, the icehouse. How the dacha got there in the first place was no surprise. That is easily explained. At one time the servants of larger estates had these wooden cottages for their use when the great families were in residence nearby. The houseman of this or that prince kept his wife and infants at the dacha and walked home once or twice a week to visit with them. But the icehouse—since there was only one of them in that community—was something of a mystery. Yuri Maximovich had inquired of its origins, but it was of such modest proportions and in such bad repair nobody had bothered to trace its history. Without envy, there is little historical curiosity, and the twenty square feet covered with sawdust, the rotten planks smudged with tar, and the slanting roof stuffed with a mixture of dried dung and fabric tatters were unenviable. Nobody had evinced the slightest interest in Yuri's icehouse. He was free, he thought, to make use of it as he wished. It was not visited in his absence, callers showed no interest in seeing the icehouse on his property, and in consequence he had felt safe to convert it into a treasure house, where secretly and silently he contemplated his own gold and silver, his own rare jewels and statues coveted by generations but winnowed and selected by his own fancy and imagination.

No sooner had the three settled into the dacha and started the fire, Yuri lighting the samovar—an old pewter affair—then Yasha Tyutychev asked to see the icehouse. Yuri Maximovich waved off his suggestion. He was not yet ready to explore its contents, and moreover, for the first time since he had purchased the dacha, he was afraid of what he would find. He remembered Colonel Bobov's sly reference to his old trunk and the treasures it contained. *They* had been there. Those agents had been out back rummaging for evidence of some kind and undoubtedly had found it, although the colonel had dismissed his jewels as paste, characterizing its contents with a commonplace obscenity. It was a fact, however, that his secret was now known. The icehouse had at least aroused historical curiosity. He preferred to wait before he visited the icehouse.

"Let's fix supper. Afterwards we'll do some drinking together in the icehouse."

Yasha Tyutychev, it turned out, was a superb cook. He knew exactly what to do, and within a few hours there was a feast before them, a chicken swimming in a thick stew of vegetables; with one egg lightly beaten with white vinegar, herbs which they had carried from Moscow, a few potatoes and onions, the chicken appeared golden and delectable, so they fell to devouring it, giving the bones and leavings to Nastya. The bottle of Yalta wine which they found in the cupboard near the stove was sweetish but potent with the food and compote which Yuri had assembled, and by late evening the two men, sated and pleased, had forgotten the secret anxieties which had carried them to the country for their holiday.

It was Yuri Maximovich who revived them. He had guessed something of the truth of Yasha Isaievich's long disappearance, but had not wanted to probe it. It was not unusual behavior. Everyone knew someone who had gone away. Some never returned, many never returned, but occasionally friends and neighbors were startled by the reappearance of one of these travelers. One of his friends, the editor of a literary journal, referred to the vanished as "vagabonds." He intended to convey his sense of their estrangement, their difference from ordinary settled folk, their condition as eccentrics with odd careers, unsteady habits, questionable characters, but he did not wish to acknowledge straight out that he had any conception of precisely what they had done to earn their vagabondage. He preferred to describe them simply as vagabonds and let it go at that. It was a limbo term and those who returned from their wanderings were indubitably in limbo, having achieved neither the paradise of reward and elevation in life nor the definition of hell, from which no one returned.

Yasha Isaievich Tyutychev was, in Yuri's ordinary estimation, no different than a vagabond. He was a vagabond before he disappeared and no less a vagabond now that he had returned. It was uncomplicated therefore to reaccept him, to cherish his return—indeed, to bring him as a guest to his country home, where, it should be clear, only the tame does and the placid sheep were allowed free run in the game preserves of the leaders.

"So now, old friend, tell me about yourself. Where have you been all these years?" Yuri had settled back, drunk off the lees in his glass, and drawn a blanket about his knees, for the fire in the stove had died down and the wood in the fireplace had burned to coals.

"Are you prepared to know?" Yasha replied instantly, keened and excited by the prospect of telling his story.

Yuri Maximovich thought it over for a bit and then replied thoughtfully, "Yes. Yes. I am prepared to know."

"You will learn something. It's not anything that you don't know in outline, so to speak, already, but like my absent footnotes it will tell you much more than you can read in the main body of the text."

Tyutychev dragged his wicker chair over to Yuri Maximovich, and knee to knee, in a low but conversational voice, began to speak.

"You know nothing of my origins, Yuri Maximovich. You met me in my dog-fur days, when I was still in possession of a whole person, with gold watch and high button shoes. I was, as one of my comrades told me the day of my arrival out there, an elegant bum, and he burst out laughing the moment I began to unpack my little parcel of belongings. I had brought with me a stolen silver spoon, my own teacup, a pair of purple silk socks, a collection of shirt stays for my one shirt, which shredded in the cold water of its first washing. Oh. I was an extraordinary sight out there. And that was how you knew me. I must have said, 'Contributing editor in charge of criminals and vagabonds.' But that was true. It was also harmless. Or at least I thought it was harmless. May I have some tea?"

Tyutychev had stopped suddenly and sat back in fright. He had come to a juncture in the narrative that presumably needed a breath of air, since he jumped up and went outdoors without overcoat or winter gear. He returned minutes later, his face red with cold, shut the door, and sat down again. Yuri had poured his tea and set it on the floor beside his chair. Yasha picked it up, clasped its burning sides, rubbed the cup against his cheeks to warm them, and set it down again without taking a sip.

"I'm sorry. But I remembered something from that first day, and it was for a moment unbearable." Yuri Maximovich extended his hand and grasped Yasha's knee, holding it for a second and then releasing it when Yasha Isaievich resumed his story. "My career, which ended in a dozen years of hard labor in the East, began as a harmless obsession. Have you ever heard of the Yiddish writer Rappoport? No? Well, let me tell you that Solomon Rappoport was a great man. He was and remains my hero, the man whom my life honors and perpetuates. You know Rappoport, but you don't know him by that name. You know him as Ansky, the man who wrote *The Dybbuk*. Rappoport (and I will call him Rappoport) was a Ukrainian Jew like myself. When he was a young man at the end of the last century he saw everything that was to come, everything, and not the least thing he saw was that Jews would be destroyed, that the West would destroy them and the East would destroy them. What do you do if you see something like that on the horizon, if you know how to read the times in labor and recognize that everything that will come into existence will be deformed and crippled? If you're a politician, you do one thing, and if you're a saint, you do another, and if you're a man of letters, you do a third. Well, Rappoport was a man of letters, but he was also from his boyhood a scrap collector. He saved everything. He collected autographs; he rummaged for newspapers, for announcements of speeches, for bulletins of distress tacked to the walls of rooming houses, for records of births and circumcisions, and marriage and death notices. Anything and everything that had a Yiddish expression or a Hebrew word in it, Rappoport saved. He went after the letters of the holy alphabet like an archaeologist—spading up a letter and cleaning it until he had reconstituted a document. It didn't matter whether it was valuable or trivial. The fact that it had one smudge of the ancient alphabet on it meant that it was a treasure. By the end of the century he was already a grown man. He was a writer, a dramatist, a journalist, a poet. Everyone knew Rappoport and everyone confided in him. What they didn't know was that he was not only a writer, but also an archivist of Yiddish. Every time someone died or moved away or went to America, Rappoport would come to the auction sale or contact the relatives that survived or stayed behind, or call upon the junk dealer and rummage for bits and pieces for his archive, until by the time of the Revolution he had accumulated the greatest treasury of Yiddish newspapers and ephemera that existed anywhere. No one could contemplate the enormity of his archive. There was not a room in his house that wasn't filled with boxes, crates, or piles neatly tied and marked. I think only his bedroom must have been empty. His wife saw to that, but then under the bed and behind the curtains and in the closet—papers everywhere. Naturally the Revolution had no interest in Jewish sentiment. They could only think of Rappoport as a reactionary. He wanted to preserve the past, they said. What he really wanted was something entirely different. It wasn't the past he venerated—not at all. The past, he always said to me, is only the raw material of the future. He was a socialist. So am I. I have no interest in wealth and treasure—well, anyway, naturally Rappoport was misunderstood. He was imprisoned in the thirties. And his archive? What became of that? Would you believe? Everything he wanted by design was fulfilled by stupidity. For years he had begged that it be preserved. He had gone about like a beggar foraging for kopecks to house his *monumenta Judaica*, but no one had had time for him. The rich Jews didn't and the poor ones certainly not. But when he was arrested and tried for counterrevolutionary activity, whatever that means—for bourgeois reaction, for Western contacts, for sentimentality, for being a Jew with a snout for manuscripts (a hoarder, they also called him)—they packed up his collection, five truckloads full, and brought it to the university library in Kiev. It's there, safe and sound in the basement of the library. So much for the archive. But as for myself? When Rappoport was tried and condemned, I wasn't at the trial. There were so many in those days you couldn't go to all of them. I had seven friends condemned the same week in Moscow, all in different places. I wanted to say goodbye to them all. I couldn't. I sent them little notes of confidence and support and signed them with a symbol they knew was mine. That, I'm afraid, came out at my own trial. I had made a rubber stamp with a little device which an artist friend had cut for me—a lion with a harp in his paws—and I stamped my notes with that. Only Rappoport got a message through to me when I saw him briefly at the railway station before he was boarded with twenty others for the leisurely trip to his death. He whispered to me, eyes straight ahead, not looking at me at all, '*Tzcor.*' That means 'Remember.' That was the last of him.

"Yasha Isaievich took it all very seriously. I was still a young man during the thirties. I had a head full of languages and tunes and a room full of scraps of paper. I went back to the Ukraine, to my hometown, Zhitomir, where dynasties upon dynasties of Hasidim had been raised up and buried, and I began there to do something Rappoport hadn't contemplated. Rappoport put down words; I put down tunes. I began to collect songs, beginning with Yiddish folk tunes and Hasidic melodies. I gathered more than six hundred of these and wrote them down every day when I drank tea in the markets or late at night wherever I put my head down. I didn't work, properly speaking, and that was the beginning of my trouble. I didn't need much to live. Enough for paper and a stub of pencil and a bit of food. In those days you could sleep out by the side of the road and nobody bothered you much. There were millions of Russians wandering in those days, and luckier than most of them, I had papers of sorts. But when the war broke out it became difficult. They didn't take me when I signed up. I had had an embarrassing operation when I was a boy—a double hernia. Would you believe that? So I went to work in a factory in Kiev making land mines, and every evening I went to the markets and hunted tunes.

"And then the Germans got close and we retreated to the Urals and I got work in another factory. But the truth is that by '44, I had finished with the Jews and the Jews were almost finished anyway. No new tunes. No new tunes. I knew it was all over with my Jews when one of my best contacts—a man who used to dredge up tunes for me like a miner panning gold in a riverbed—ran up to me one day in Izhevsk where I was spending the winter and, embracing me, began to sing out the present he had brought me. When he was finished, I had to tell him that he had sung that song to me at least five years earlier. He frowned and then tried another. I knew that one too. More than a dozen. I knew them all. There were no new tunes. Late that night I took a long walk through the snow. I didn't have to be at work until eleven o'clock, when the night shift in the factory started up. I was walking in the outskirts of Izhevsk when I came upon a vodka shop where a group of brightly dressed ruffians were drinking. I went in and had myself a drink. One of the men—a big man with fat arms and a face knotted like a sour stomach—stumbled over to my table and sat down. He looked at me meanly for some minutes. I pushed over the tumbler of vodka to him and he drank it off and then smiled. 'I don't know you, comrade.' I admitted that. 'You're not police?' he asked straight out. I didn't look it, but one never knew how police looked; I said no. And then he said, 'I'm a thief. I work sometimes, but mostly I'm a thief.' I replied, foolishly but fascinated, 'I didn't think we had thieves any more.' He threw his head back and roared. His companions came over and stood behind him, slapping each other with amusement. What could I do? I admitted I was an idiot and they liked that. I didn't know what to say. I had never known anyone to come right out and admit they stole for a living. But then I had a stroke of luck. I asked whether thieves had songs. I had heard one or two from some Jewish thieves I had known long ago in Zhitomir, but I didn't realize that the idiom was so vast. I was such a specialist, I hadn't listened much to gentile songs, but that night I heard songs I couldn't imagine. The big man was the head thief, but he had a marvelous voice, a rich basso of a voice, deep and rumbling like a waterfall in a mountain gorge. He sang and sang, songs in Russian, Ukrainian, even some in Armenian. I couldn't believe it, and what was most astonishing was that the songs he sang to me were like my Jewish songs. The tropes were for the most part the same. I had known that many of my Jewish songs were simply Yiddish transcriptions of folk tunes which every Russian peasant knew perfectly, but I had always thought of peasants like assimilated Jews. They were Jews with a fixed place—a village, a house, a yard. But Russian thieves were like wandering Jews. They had nowhere to go but to prison. That old powerful thief —his name was Pavel Rostopshin—had been born in Vladivostok. He was a brigand in his youth and rode in the Red Cavalry out there in 1919 against the Americans and the English and then turned back to thievery and pillage. But for me he was Rostopshin the Thieves' Voice. I went back to the tavern every night for a month, and before I knew it, I had a couple of hundred songs. Rostopshin ran out of songs in a few weeks, but he brought singers to me. Pickpockets and market thieves, housebreakers and pilferers, gypsies and Caucasian bandits. He got everyone in Izhevsk who was a gangster with a song to come by and sing for me. That's how it began. I became the collector of thieves' songs. And I loved it. I had a new life.

"That carried me a long way, nearly through another generation. I had big notebooks filled with songs, and by then I had gotten back to Moscow and began to publish them in *The People's Voice*. Before I met you, I had gotten into some trouble. You can't help it in a profession like mine. You stay around thieves for fifteen years and even if you don't steal yourself you begin to smell like them. I had become shifty-eyed and odd. My clothes stank. I never bathed. I was too poor to waste money on a bit of soap or a new pair of underwear. I had a few fine things mostly given to me by my thieves, but for the most part, I was a smelly, obsessed man.

"Well, what do you think happened? One fine day they decided I was a reactionary, and what's more, a reactionary who didn't work for a living, didn't keep regular hours, consorted with malingerers and anti-Soviet low types. That happened about a week before I came to the office to see you. Remember old Adam Sagatelian? Oh, I forgot, you didn't know him. A lovely man. A really lovely, gentle old man who adored me and my songs. Lydia Yegorovna couldn't stand him. He was too fatherly for her. She liked either brawnies or pushovers. (I think you're in the latter category, Yuri Maximovich.) In any event, right after old Adam was stripped of his life, she got started on me. She wrote me up in her delicate hand and off it went to the right department. She is very big, you know, on anonymous denunciations. She's done it before, I suspect. I guessed it had to be her because the investigator questioned me about the title of one of my essays which Adam had scrapped before it went to press. The investigator of my case couldn't have known about it but for Lydia Yegorovna. I had called one of my notes for *The People's Voice*: 'The Happy Times of Soviet Thieves.' A wonderfully accurate title for a gathering of a dozen or so festive ballads about courtships and christenings, filled with wonderful lines about robbing the poorbox to pay the priest. Naturally the title was a laugh for Adam and me, but Lydia Yegorovna crossed it out of the manuscript and put in something solid and safe. The investigator asked me about such anti-Soviet tendencies in my work. You see, old friend, Soviet thieves can't possibly be happy. They don't work. Work makes freedom here as it did in Germany. Thieves are just depraved capitalists, perverted entrepreneurs. The government just doesn't see that thievery is part of the human system, keeping the balance. My thieves are just keeping the ledgers of this life clean and neat. Oh, well. How would Lydia Yegorovna understand? How could she? She's a pretty thing. Does she still have a lovely ass, Yuri Maximovich?"

Yasha Isaievich had gone on and on. Yuri had listened absorbed like a child at a magic show, wondering with amazement how it was done. How was the trick of life done? The man was astonishing. A miracle? Not at all. No one had done it for Yasha Tyutychev. It was all of his own doing. Then natural? Not quite. It was simply—and this Yuri Maximovich had no choice but to accept—that here was a fresh spring that couldn't be dammed and couldn't be contaminated. The simple passion of Yasha Tyutychev. A life line thrown to Yuri Maximovich by chance. Tyutychev was so much more than his own fantasy of the mobile Krimsky Bridge. Here was a real way. Not an escape into solitudes and privacies. Tyutychev was there showing Yuri Maximovich how it could be done. There was nothing beaten in that old man, nothing at all, and here he was asking with a smile about the state of preservation of the buttocks of his denouncer.

"Incredible!" Yuri answered, stirred not by the recollection of Lydia Yegorovna but by the question. "Yes. I guess still quite marvelous. Less appreciated than it should be, I suppose. But come now, old man, do asses still delight you?"

"Of course. Even more now. They delight me! Utterly! Although I haven't been with a woman for ages. There was one in the camps in all these years, but that was a lucky break. Nothing to talk about. It took no time at all, and I am, you see—believe it or not—a languishing lover. If it can't take an hour or more I don't enjoy it. But that's out of my life entirely by now. At seventy-three with a dozen years of prison behind me it doesn't make much sense to go hunting women."

The truth is that Yuri Maximovich had no interest in Yasha Tyutychev's carnal invocations. He had permitted the conversation to languish in that direction less to encourage the old man's scatological enthusiasm than because his unease had made him acutely aware that he, Yuri Maximovich Isakovsky, Soviet editor and member of the Union of Soviet Writers, was sitting with a returned exile, a restored prisoner, an ex-enemy of the state. Now that is not really hard to understand—that nervousness, I mean. How many men are there who can calmly befriend a hardened criminal? Temporize: Yasha Tyutychev, a hardened criminal? Nonsense. A wonderful old man wrongly accused and condemned. Nothing to it. Of course you would befriend him. But would you? I think not. A reformed criminal, perhaps; a thief like the thieves of Izhevsk might be amusing and at the most you would keep your hand on your wallet and your silver locked up, but it is very unlikely that you would invite even the most genial of crooks to your country home for an outing. Properly speaking, of course, Yasha Tyutychev was not a reformed thief nor even a political prisoner. He was a constitutional reprobate, an unreconstructed independent, an original, and for that reason presumably a danger to be locked away. He couldn't be contaminated, but he could most certainly contaminate others. Or at least that's the way the logic goes.

In good and sensible societies, where sympathetic winds prevail and conscience is notoriously healthy and well-aired, people are much more terrified of a pickpocket, a thief, or an extortionist than of a fanatic. Here, to the contrary, in this land it is all quite reversed. The thieves of Izhevsk are not simply thieves. If they were simply thieves it wouldn't be difficult. In olden days they were merely thieves and received thieves' penalties—the lash and worse. In Dubai, capital of the Emirate of Oman, the hands of a thief are still cut off and hung about his neck. That at least makes sense, a primitive kind of sense. A handless thief can hardly steal. He has to mend his ways and turn to another occupation, although such a punishment can hardly be construed as vocational retraining, since it's difficult to imagine what anyone can do for a living without hands. But the thieves of Izhevsk are no longer thieves. In this new society, they are social depravities, pathological throwbacks, intractable and ineducable individualists who resist reconstruction. They are in effect political thieves, political housebreakers, political extortionists, and as such as dangerous as counterrevolutionaries or bourgeois Westernizers or capitalist conspirators.

Until that day Yuri Maximovich had never known a criminal. Perhaps he had met criminals, but he had never known it at the time. Undoubtedly he had stood beside them in the subway or on a line for a restaurant but he had never wittingly "consorted" (as the expression goes) with criminals. Nor, for that matter, until that day had he ever really thought about such things. He took for granted the existence of criminals, but knew that there were vigilant citizens who protected the innocent from their insinuations. For the first time, then, in his own dacha in privileged Peredelkino, no less, he was passing the night with someone just returned from the camps of the East. But for some reason, although unnerved by the forthrightness with which Yasha Isaievich described his history and referred ever so casually to his years of confinement, Yuri Maximovich was less agitated than he would have been, say, a week earlier, a week before his conversation with the Ministry of Culture and his invitation to the United States, a week before his meeting with Vovka Bedkin, a week before his enrollment by Colonel Bobov and his embroilment with Liudmila Brilova, his remeeting with Ilia Kolokolov, and more than all of these, his increasingly luminous recognition that all of these encounters were somehow related to the enormous despair he felt before his inability to create poems.

In other words, he was ready for Tyutychev. No wonder, then, as the distraction of their brief foray into the sexual curiosities of old Tyutychev ended and the two men relapsed into silence, the one lifting his now tepid glass of tea to his lips and the other shifting uneasily in his wicker armchair, it should be asked with relief, as if breaking the spell cast by fifty years of circumspection: "Tell me about the camps of the East."

"You want to know?"

After a hesitant moment, Yuri replied with conviction that he did.

"But there is really nothing to tell. That is, there is nothing that can be told. All the telling, for people like myself, is in the method and the procedure, not in the detail of the cruelty. What do I mean? It's important that I make this clear. There is nothing unusual in the way they go about destroying people. It's so conventional as to be unremarkable. It is only remarkable to people who aren't used to these things. *Mutatis mutandis*, I can think of no civilization that hasn't somewhere in its past a machinery of destruction comparable to ours. The French Terror, the Inquisition, the reservations on which the Americans collected their natives and destroyed them, or the enslavement of the black races, or in our time the Fascists. Now, what's so different about us? In the effect, nothing really. One set of people, justified by the deceptions of a giant absolute God, determine that the world shall be converted, and failing to persuade the dispossessed to disappear quietly, elect to enforce truth by the rack. Oh, hopeless confusion. A logical error which ends in brutality. Nothing unusual. The only thing remarkable about our method of doing it is in the preliminaries. They really know how to break the will and the intelligence even before the accused knows his crime.

"Now take you, my friend. We have been together nearly fifteen hours. How many times I have made reference—indirectly, I grant—to the years I spent in the darkness out there, and only now, weary and well-fed, in the country where no one hears us talk, you bring yourself to ask me about my journey to the East. You knew I was there, and it wasn't good manners which prevented you from asking. The truth is, you didn't want to know. All of your conditioning in Soviet bureaucracy is to keep you from even considering, much less asking after the hows and whys of it. And why you want to know *now*, this moment, is something known only to you, and perhaps not even to you. It is a curiosity buried in character.

"The truth is, I have nothing unusual to reveal. The camps out there (and there are more than I can count) have a simple task, an unremarkable regimen. They exist to break human beings of the will to be different, and if they don't succeed by endless work, degrading treatment, scant food and medical attention, dirty quarters, and brutal guards, they are either given another chance later by reimprisonment for a second term or denied a second chance by death. It's terribly simple. They don't expect to gain secrets because there are none. I was questioned for seven weeks about my contacts in the West, the command chain of the underworld, the network of thievery, the code notations of my songs (which they took to be a system of ciphers of which I was the principal decoder, since I knew all the songs), but finally what it came down to was that they wanted to know the names of other people because they had a quota and needed new prisoners and I was literally a mine of information. I gave them a few. I'm not at all sorry about doing it. I gave them the name of one thief who had drowned his child. For him I had no sympathy even though he couldn't afford to feed a child. I'm not for child murder. And another I turned in because he had denounced a nephew of Rappoport. He had accused him of being a profiteering Jew. Pure shit. The boy didn't have a kopeck, but he had some of his uncle's books which he occasionally bartered for food during the great famine. They take strength as recalcitrance and weakness as remorse. A simple morality for a simple terror. Nothing much to it. But if you want to understand something truly amazing, I must make a confession to you. I was happy in the camps."

"Happy?" Yuri Maximovich was astonished.

"Oh, yes, quite happy. Dirty, unfed, freezing cold most of the time, but *mirabile dictu*, happy. Yes. Happy. Now, let me make it clear, Yuri Maximovich, that not many of us were happy out there. Most of the happy ones—and there were a few—were fulfilled martyrs. All the Adventist and Witnesses and Baptists were happy by and large. It seemed to them that the very existence of the camps and their presence in them was confirmation that the apocalypse was at hand, that God was quickening the times, readying them for the great upheaval, and that they, persecuted for their faith, were part of the advance guard of the redemption. They were not much different than the few old Bolsheviks I met there, who felt the same way when they were imprisoned in their youth by the czar. They were in prison for a good reason. They knew the reason and were proud that history had singled them out for special treatment.

"I was completely different from all of these. I had no ideology, no cause, no special set of beliefs, and yet despite that, I was enormously happy. Every morning I was practically the first out of my bunk, the first to be washed and into breakfast, the first ready for line-up.

"The reason is simple. When they picked me up in Moscow two days after I met you, I had gone dry again. I had used up my material. I had turned to invention and fantasy. Many of the songs I gave you in my article I had whipped up myself. You smile, Yuri Maximovich. You knew it. Splendid! Not that I didn't have real ones I could have used. Not at all. But I knew them so well, they had come to bore me. I had more than a thousand thieves' songs, all neatly written out and cross-referenced. I knew where my songs came from; I had traced them all since my days in Izhevsk when I first discovered the genre. By the early fifties I had used them all. I had written several myself. I had ceased to be an archivist and become a composer, and I was disgusted with myself. People like me don't score folk songs for violin and balalaika. We don't write up the laments of criminals for entertainment. And that's what I had come to. When they picked me up I was absolutely ready for a new time. Oh, I was terrified. I thought I wouldn't survive the first month out there. But I kept my mouth shut and moved slowly. I was firm but thoughtful with my fellow prisoners, and lucky for me the first jailer I met was one of my thieves from Izhevsk. You see, they used ordinary criminals as jailers for the political convicts. Ordinary criminals, having no ideology, played no favorites. They had contempt for the politicos. Why go to jail for an idea? they thought. It didn't matter to them that most of the politicos had no idea at all why they were there, that most of them couldn't understand their crime and as a result couldn't repent or be reconstructed; most of these died. They died from the very irrationality of their imprisonment. Those who survived were either regular criminals or people like me who immediately accepted the notion that because they were different from everyone else they were wrong. I spent hours during those first weeks persuading myself that of course—clear light of reason, lightning of intuition—I was out of step with the masses and I had to be brought into line. And the moment I accepted that it was easy for me. I worked hard, but not too hard, and I had a jailer who knew me, who loved my songs, and who often accompanied me on a harmonica while I sang before lights out.

"That was during the first month. There were eighty prisoners in our bunk and more than two thousand in the camp. People died at the rate of two percent a month, slightly less during thaw seasons and summer, and they were always replaced. There seemed to be a line-up of people clamoring for a berth in our camp and new faces turned up all the time.

"One evening (it happened after I had been there about six months) a prisoner came in at nightfall, a Tartar who spoke a little Russian. He was given the bunk above mine. Shortly after lights out I heard the little Tartar begin to cry. I listened to his weeping and said nothing. It was no good to try to comfort a weeper. I let him cry about an hour, and although we only got six hours' sleep and I had wasted one already, I waited it out and finally after the tears had subsided into sniffles and the wiry Tartar had gotten a grip on himself, I whispered up to him in Russian, 'Sing a song. It's good. It's good. Sing a song.'

Why I said that is obvious, I suppose. But the truth is that in six months out there I hadn't once suggested to anyone that they should sing to their sadness. The Tartar became silent for a minute. The tears stopped completely, and then he began to sing a song that he later explained to me was about a wild stallion that breaks away from the herd and climbs a mountain to fall in love with the lonely moon. An absolutely marvelous song with a melody that sounded as gentle as a spring rain yet was beautifully strengthened by the tough syllabic structure of Tartar. A song of natural genius. The next day we became friends. He wanted to learn Russian, since most of us in that bunk were from Western Russia and had at least that language in common, whatever our mother tongues might have been. I resisted until he had taught me the half-dozen Tartar songs he knew. That's how it began. My happiness in prison camp.

"I discovered a whole new literature of song. I discovered that there were Tartars, Uzbeks, Armenians, Turkestani, Mongols in that camp—most of them there for refusing collectivization or for leaving a works project to go back to their village. They had a whole literature I didn't know. Not political, not religious, not criminal. And all their songs came down from ages ago. They were epic songs, full of formulas of heroism and love and kissing gods that were simply astonishing.

"Within a few weeks I had used up every scrap of paper I had saved. And my pencil! The pencil I had hidden in a hole in my mattress was worn down to an inch even though I wet the graphite to get an extra bit of writing power out of it at every use. My days acquired a private logic. I had been assigned to work in the sick bay—cleaning out the beds and the latrines, putting away the dead ones, and washing the laundry. It was a good duty and I had one of my thieves to thank for it, although you thanked no one out there for anything. (If someone did you a good turn you didn't say a word. You just waited for the chance to do him one back and that was that. Scores were settled without toting them up.) The real advantage of working in the sickroom with the prison doctor was that I had a chance to use his pencil. He was issued a pencil only when he produced the stub of the last one, and even though he was reprimanded for using them too rapidly and once the captain in charge asked to see his reports to find out why he had been writing so much, I took care of that. I knew the captain didn't read that much or that easily, so it wasn't hard to trick him about. In any event, paper and pencil became my craft and every night I substituted what remained of my own and took away the good one I had used at work. That was the pencil part of my days. Paper was no less a difficulty, but I managed that too. The sheets we were given were standard-sized, and when a case was done, it was put in a binder with the prisoner's number and filed away. Nobody noticed that with my appearance in the sick bay, the standard sheet suddenly shrank by about two inches. Nobody used the bottoms. Even in our splendidly parsimonious socialist society there is waste, and I imagine I would have defended myself that way if I had been caught. I tore off my measured strips and in a condensed musical code noted the basic melody, followed by the words. That was the premise of my craft—pencil and paper. (Once I had a *Biro*, but it froze and became useless and I buried it ceremoniously in the snow.)

"The material? That was everywhere. If one miserable Tartar could give me six songs, think what thousands of prisoners in fourteen years would give me. Every day I contacted a new prisoner and said hello. Most of them shrank away the first time I approached them. What does this old man want of us? But gradually as my reputation preceded me I became known as Chaliapin. A prisoner who had once met the great basso named me that. Chaliapin loved folk songs. I became Chaliapin and my name went ahead of me. 'Here comes Chaliapin looking for bird shit in the snow,' or, 'Chaliapin, Pyotr over there hums a bit. Maybe he's got something for you.' That was very good. It made me a queer one in the camp, not an enemy, but an eccentric who smiled a lot and paid attention and listened. They liked me and they helped me. We all helped each other as best we could. But when it was all done, I had put together for myself a collection of about three hundred songs. Whenever I got a new one it made me joyful for days. I sang it over and over to myself on the way to work. I made a point of thanking my informant and asking him to think of other songs or point out to me anyone who might have a new one. Every new prisoner became a possible new song, and so I greeted every new face, beaten and miserable as those first-week faces were, with a particular warmth. Get to them early before they hardened up, I would think. Sometimes it worked and I got my song early or heard another version which confirmed an earlier one. It was fantastic. I gathered—would you believe it?—three hundred songs, (three hundred and two, to be exact) in fourteen years. That's more than twenty songs a year, more than one a month. Sixty-seven and sixty-eight were bad years. Only eight songs in two years. I became disconsolate. It's drying up, I thought, and since I didn't know how much longer I really had, I became depressed, and then who should turn up but Hamed Ibraim from Turkestan, a horse thief once upon a time, who arrived with more than a score of songs. I was elevated like the Host blessed by the Holy Spirit, exuberant. Hamed Ibraim carried me into my seventies and here I am. Yes, Yuri Maximovich"—Yasha Isaievich sighed—"those fourteen years were productive. I stayed alive. I did my work and I am rewarded."

"Rewarded?" Yuri smiled with disbelief.

"Rewarded. Of course, rewarded! I saved three hundred and two songs from being forgotten, and every one of those songs will testify for me when I come to the judgment."

"Do you have your notes? Did you come out with them?"

"Of course not. You should know that. I could hide them while I was there, but when I left I was stripped down to the asshole and left with nothing but a suit of rags. Oh, the songs. I memorized them. It took me months of hard work memorizing them. I used the notes to coach my memory. But finally I got every sound and word into my brain and there they stay. I'll never forget them now. Someday I'll write them all down, maybe for you, Yuri Maximovich. When you come back again to Russia after your trip outside I'll present you with an article of songs and you can tell your readers that Yasha Isaievich

Tyutychev is back from the East with a saddlebag full of new songs."

The old man stood up abruptly and slapped his hands together. "I'm so happy being here. You have no idea how happy all this makes me. Being here, being in the country, smelling clean cold. No footprints. No long lines of dirty footprints. Let's go out. I need a walk."

"But it's midnight."

"And so?"

"Quite right. It's only that I hardly ever go out at night." Yuri Maximovich stood up and whistled for Nastya, who had fallen asleep in front of the stove. The two men put on their overcoats, wound their scarves about their necks, disappeared into their shapkas, and stepped out into the cold. The snow glinted in the moonlight and they took off down the road that wound past the dacha. They walked for about a half-hour without saying a word, and when Yasha Isaievich turned about and started back, Yuri and the dog followed him. As they approached the dacha, they heard a noise, and peering into the dark they could make out a little automobile parked under a tree fifty feet from the dacha. Two men were just getting into the car, carrying a heavy sack stuffed—it could have been, if this were an old tale—with the body of a child. The car door slammed and the automobile purred off down the road away from the dacha.

For several minutes Yuri Maximovich and Yasha Isaievich continued to stand motionless in the cold. At the same instant, however, that Yasha Tyutychev reached out to take Yuri's arm, the realization of what must have happened came over him, and with a scream Yuri Maximovich ran toward the icehouse, where the light of a naphtha lamp glowed faintly. The door was open. Rushing inside, he screamed again. The neat little icehouse—empty but for a table and a single chair, beneath which had stood an old-fashioned leather-strapped steamer trunk—was a shambles. The contents of that trunk, all neatly packed and wrapped, had been the secret treasure of Yuri Maximovich. Organized by date of acquisition, the earliest at the bottom rising to the more volatile and available top layer, had been the chest of Yuri's dreams. At the very bottom had been that earliest copy of *Stone*, the book that had brought Osip Emilevich Mandelstam into the world, and alongside it five slender volumes of the murdered Gumilev (*Romantic Flowers, Pearls, Tent, Bonfire, The Quiver,* and a collection of his exotic dramas), and Anna Akhmatova, many volumes of Akhmatova, and the miserable Tsvetaeva, and manuscripts of plays by Sergei Bulgakov, and poetry by Blok, Khlebnikov, Bely, Ivanov, Kuzmin, Sologub, Balmont, Pasternak, and a dozen others, each volume carefully wrapped with oilcloth and written on each a small notation in Yuri's hand describing the occasion of its purchase, the date, his comments and remarks, modified and rearranged upon each successive reading. If the great symbolists had had their Tower, Yuri Maximovich had maintained his icehouse. It had been a sanctuary.

It was a violated sanctuary that he saw before him now. The books were torn apart, their spines, backstrip, covers, end papers, title pages ripped as if by some giant's hand. Yuri Maximovich sat down upon the chair and looked about him at the carnage; the chair swayed back and forth, and like an ancient mourner Yuri began a rhythmic cry, his voice pitched not to an emotion which comes and goes, a grief which can be slaked like a dreadful thirst, but to something immemorial, as though when betrayed by a whole world, the only possible reply is a millennial dirge. Yasha Isaievich, familiar with these things, commenced to gather the pieces together while Yuri kept up his moan and cry, cracking his tongue against the roof of his mouth and pressing out his lament. After Tyutychev had completed the gathering of the broken bones and piled the bits and pieces, the torn scraps, the stripped skeletons, and the now-pointless flesh upon the table, an exhausted Yuri finally stopped his weeping, and clear-eyed, stared ahead of him at the laden table. The naphtha light threw darting glances at the pile, its light shimmering and then, before a rush of air from outside, piercing the dozen cracks in the walls, fled the sight and turned its light to an unviolated portion of the wall.

Tyutychev sat down in the sawdust before Yuri, his feet drawn beneath him, and the dog stood beside him, looking up with confusion at her miserable master.

"Dear friend, Yuri Maximovich," Tyutychev began quietly, his voice almost a whisper, but he spoke so slowly and distinctly that each word was compelled by its deliberation to come to Yuri's ear, and Yuri, gradually at first, turned toward him and listened, dead to everything but that quiet voice. "You think all this so monstrous. Criminal, you think? Brutal? How can this be? you add. Please know, dear friend (and although I sound heavy with irony, there is no irony left in me), that this is nothing. This is common. This is ordinary life here. What is remarkable is not this. What is remarkable, old friend, is that it shocks you, that it brings you to your knees, sends through you shivers of death. Aagh. Nothing. Really nothing. But, truth to tell, perhaps nothing to me. Perhaps I make the mistake of thinking that what I know myself is common knowledge to everyone. I can't number the rapes any more. I can't even remember the number of murders I've seen, seen with my own eyes. I can't recollect how many lamentations I've heard. It's a nation of Jobs, and let me tell you, Jobs without comforters.

"You know how comfort runs in this country: no smoke without fire. That's comfort. Tell anyone about this, Yuri Maximovich, and I'll tell you what they'll say. 'Only books?' One will say, 'Only books?' Another will say, 'What were you hiding?' Yes, precisely that. You are guilty. The State Police is never wrong. You should know that. No smoke without fire. After all, what did they destroy? Oh, yes, I know what you'll answer. But do you need it? Don't you know *A Poem Without a Hero*? Don't you know every line of *Stone* and *Tristia*? Of course you do. A poet's books are his memory. If he hasn't remembered it —perhaps not word for word, but locked in the rhythm of his bones, every word—he didn't want it for his own. What you take all this for is proof of something else, that your illusions are over. That you can hope for nothing more from these people, not even the protection of your illusions. It's a life-and-death country we have. A life-and-death country. It's not quality we have to worry about. That's a problem for the Westerners, who don't remember what it is to deal with life and death. They worry about the air and overcrowding and traffic. What a luxurious life they have. But we Russians still have a nation of life and death. Surrender, we live; complain, we die. It's that simple. Even a whimper of discontent brings death. But it's incredible for that. Incredible, I think. How extraordinary to live in a country where one knows with certainty that he has done his very best if he gets punished. I believe that with all my heart. It's the only thing I still really believe about the ways of this world. I know absolutely that I've done the best I can. You? It's just getting to you and you will do the best you can. I know it. I know you can do the best. I know you won't give up now. You can't. There's no point to it if you do. You might as well kill yourself straight away if you have any doubt about what I'm saying."

Several hours later—it was past dawn when they departed, tramping up the road to the highway, where they waited to flag a bus that came every hour or so—they had exhausted everything to be said. One last time Yuri Maximovich looked back as the road curved beyond the point where he could see the fire that was burning the icehouse behind his dacha. The naphtha lamp, spilled out upon the trunk, had ignited a funeral pyre on which the heroes of his memory burned themselves out, the flames leaping up, bearing scraps of paper on which extraordinary words had been printed, carrying them up in a draft to the skies from which they had first descended.

From the journal of Yuri Maximovich
January 1972

I have said all my goodbyes. The goodbyes are behind me, a thousand miles behind me already. I closed up Yasha Isaievich and Nastya together, and they'll keep each other company. A row ahead of me in the plane is Ilia Kolokolov, spread out on two seats napping, his mouth open. Bedkin has been in the lavatory for an hour now, throwing up. Those are my traveling companions. What an intelligent arrangement.

I went by the office late yesterday after sleeping most of the afternoon. They called me about six to tell me that my icehouse had burned down, but that the dacha was safe. Lydia Yegorovna gave me the news of the fire. I am afraid I dismayed her by chuckling, but that wasn't very smart. She was puzzled but attributed my odd behavior to nervousness about my imminent departure. I did tell her as I buttoned up my coat and finished stuffing the passports, travel documents, tickets, money, and an envelope from Colonel Bobov in my briefcase that Yasha Isaievich was taking care of the apartment in my absence. At that bit of news, her puzzlement gave way to consternation and warning. I replied, "Lydia, for the first time in my life, I know what I'm doing." I thanked her for her concern, reassured her, but told her in the firmest possible way that I would consider any mention of Yasha Tyutychev's presence in my apartment as a personal betrayal. "He's served his time," she replied, presumably regarding the fourteen years given by that astonishing man to his own reeducation as sufficient to rationalize his week of comparative luxury in my apartment. What she doesn't know is that I shall probably invite Tyutychev to stay with me permanently, that I will either arrange to put another cot in my apartment or look promptly upon my return for another and larger suite of rooms. It isn't unusual for old relatives to live out their days with their children. So Tyutychev. We're relatives now. We've adopted each other.

Flying isn't anything like going down the Volga on a steamboat. You can't see anything unless you happen to be someone who becomes delirious about the sight of cumulus clouds or stretches of space infinite. For poets there's no imagery out there. There's no referent in unmarked space except to what's inside us anyways, and that we've been exploring all along. What's the point of looking? My duodenum is as mysteriously vast to me (compelled as I am to imagine it) as is space out there. I thought somehow that you could always see the earth, see treetops and houses, get the measure of things by sighting them from afar. But that was when planes were slower and couldn't get up as high as they do now.

Coming down into Paris, I saw something. I saw a whole city coming down into Paris. I could pick out a few things that everyone can pick out and I was confused and unhappy. I wish I had never seen it at all, knowing as I did that I would never get to enter it. Seeing it all below me and knowing that I would never touch it, that made me very unhappy. I had a vodka in honor of never visiting Paris. After two hours, out on the runway at Orly, we took off again. They never even let us into the transit lounge. I never heard Frenchmen speaking. Apparently everyone on board was going to New York. Engineers meeting with a big construction firm to build a giant skyscraper in Moscow; another group of technicians talking petrochemicals the whole way. Practically all businessmen. One ballet dancer sat by himself. I would like to have talked with him. He seemed incredibly overcast. Kolokolov told me that he was being sent over to complete the tour of a young star who had eloped with an American girl. And besides all those others—not a woman among them—was our little group.

Ilia Alexandrovich sat down next to me an hour out of New York. He had to fill out a customs form and was confused by one of the questions. "What do you fill in here? I never can make up my mind."

"Which question?" I asked.

"This one, about profession."

"That means what you do for a living."

"What are you putting down?" Ilia asked, unabashedly, even rudely and I guessed that his motives were no more pure this time than they ever were.

"Editor, I guess."

"I see, editor."

"And you, Ilia? What are you going as?"

"Me?" His even teeth parted in disbelief and his jaw dropped. Then he began to smile. "You're joking, aren't you? No?"

"Not at all. As what?"

"Poet, of course."

"That's your profession, is it? Does it say poet on your identity card? Whatever it says on your identity card is the way you make a living. I guess Aeneas would register as traveler and hero, or tragedian for Sophocles, and sedentary saint for Simon Stylites. Yes, quite right. You should sign as versemaker. That's a craft and it suits you. What do you think?"

I said all this calmly and intelligently, in the same helpful tone of voice I would use to coax Nastya to eat nourishing soup. Ilia was more amazed than angry. He went back to his seat and thoughtfully tapped at his lower lip with a pencil.

Bedkin had fallen asleep after throwing up all the way to Paris and started again when we took off for New York. He passed me once in the aisle and tried to smile confidently. It was no use. He looked green and pitiable.

The plane is gliding down, circling over a strip of land that ferrets out into the ocean. To the left is a gigantic city of lights, on and off, on and off, and to the right rows upon rows of little houses. In the back of many of these I could see what appeared to be oval but empty ponds. It startled me to think that Americans have ponds in their yards. Or were they frozen over? I could not tell from our height, and by the time we set down they were no longer visible. Perhaps I will investigate that question.

I have missed something. Something I have missed. I know that I should have written longer, more lavishly, more openly about what has happened to me, but the truth is that I am still uncertain of what it all means. I know that most of my old life has come to an end this week, but I have no idea what the end signifies or whether, indeed, the end is to be followed by a beginning.

PART TWO

1. A Series of Accidents

Yuri Maximovich was the last to leave the airplane. As it came to a stop upon the tarmac, before it had turned toward the complex of buildings where passengers would disembark, Yuri became ill—briefly ill, but unmistakeably nauseated (short spasms in his stomach, a sour belch or two, beads of perspiration on his forehead and chin). The moment he was allowed to unfasten his seat belt he went in the opposite direction to the traffic crowding the aisle and disappeared into the lavatory at the rear of the craft. He gagged and heaved but his throat remained dry; he sipped water and dabbed his forehead with a damp cloth. It was a pointless exercise. The nausea was not relieved, but having gone through the motions of contending with it, he felt satisfied and took up his position in the line moving quietly out of the airplane. As he passed his seat, he lifted up his overcoat, his fur hat, and the briefcase containing his documents, his journal, the poem of Colonel Bobov, the slender manuscript of his unpublished poems, and a copy of *The School of Song;* bidding goodbye to the stewardess, with whom he had hardly exchanged a word during the long flight, he descended to the United States of America.

The particular flight which had carried Yuri Maximovich to New York City was filled with Soviet notables and delegations; the waiting lounge where they gathered preparatory to passing through customs was congested by knots of officialdom, representatives of the State Department, the Department of Commerce, the State of New York, and darkly clad, heavily bundled officials from the Soviet Embassy. Since they were not businessmen or government representatives but—if such is ever the case with touring Soviets—private citizens, Yuri Maximovich and his traveling companions were overlooked in the waiting lounge. Only Bedkin seemed occupied, having struck up conversation with a Russian who stroked his chin almost continuously when he was not pulling at the brim of his black hat, forcing it lower and tighter to his forehead.

The customs procedures were meticulous but finally casual. Yuri was struck by the absence of armed militia. The customs man, although wearing some kind of uniform, seemed to be a civilian, more like a bus driver or a trainman than an inspector for security police, which Yuri presumed him to be. He was asked whether he had anything particular to declare. There was nothing, and a chalk mark was made on his strapped valise. A porter appeared; he took the baggage from Yuri, placed it on a cart, and pushed it toward the door. Another official—better-tailored, Yuri thought—at whose side stood an armed policeman smoking a cigarette, nodded to the porter to pass through and eyed Yuri suspiciously, cocking his head to one side, appraising him. As he passed, he heard him say to the policeman, "They look out of date, don't ya think?" The policeman smiled. "Like old Cagney movies." Yuri couldn't make out the comment, although coming into the lounge area beyond the arrival room he was struck by the profusion of colors in the decoration and the people, the bedlam of voices and accents, the unmannered shoving and undisciplined movement of the crowd.

"Would you join us at the press conference for Mr. Kolokolov?" Yuri Maximovich was being addressed by a slight young man with a concerned face.

"Will I be able to sit down?" Yuri replied immediately, for he continued to feel queasy.

"Of course, Mr. Isakovsky. Of course. This way, please, sir." The young man waved his hand in the direction of an entranceway to the right of the lounge, where they passed through a frosted glass door into a room identified as "The Hemisphere Suite."

When Yuri entered he saw that Ilia Alexandrovich was already seated at a long table facing several microphones, the lenses of television cameras, and clicking shutters held by a dozen or so photographers and cameramen. The press reporters, unencumbered with equipment, occupied chairs before the table. Yuri Maximovich was passed through the assembly to the head table and was seated next to a tall and ruggedly handsome man in his early sixties.

"Isakovsky," the man said briskly, turning toward Yuri and extending what he could of his palm, for they were all dreadfully packed at the table and there was really no room for the eight, now nine, persons who sat before it. "I've heard about you. Even read some of your poetry. Very good, very good."

"You know Russian?" Yuri asked in disbelief.

"Of course. I couldn't read your poetry if I didn't. I translate from time to time. Mostly I teach. Bateson's the name. Roger Bateson." He finished the introduction and turned away, apparently uninterested in Yuri's reply. There wasn't one. Yuri was stunned. Little enough had occurred if one considers the face of it, but much more in fact, for Yuri had just met someone outside the Soviet Union, literally minutes after his arrival in the United States, who had read his book of poems, who knew him as a poet.

"Gentlemen. It gives me great pleasure to introduce our guest to you. We have published all of his work and will shortly be publishing—next week, in fact—his new book of poems, with several additional autobiographical fragments, under the title *Plain Songs*. No allusion to the American West,

I should add." At this there were several chuckles in the audience, although no one was quite certain to what the title referred. The speaker continued: "Mr. Kolokolov will answer questions from the press, but first let me give you some idea of the events that are planned to coincide with his visit to New York City. Sunday night there is a dinner planned in his honor at the City University, where a gathering of American poets and intellectuals will read translations of a number of his poems, and Mr. Kolokolov will speak. Next Friday evening at Carnegie Hall, Mr. Kolokolov will read poems from *Plain Songs* to an audience which we have reason to think will be the largest ever assembled in this country to hear a poet read. The hall holds, you know—packed to capacity—almost three thousand people and we are already oversubscribed. This might force us to schedule another reading if Mr. Kolokolov's schedule permit. After this round of activity, Mr. Kolokolov will go to Boston, Chicago, Ann Arbor, and Des Moines for other readings and then do some touring as a private citizen in California. He'll finish up late in January in San Francisco and return to New York City before leaving us for the Soviet Union. It now gives me great pleasure to introduce to you the greatest living Russian poet, much beloved in this country, Ilia Kolokolov."

"Who was that man?" Yuri said, whispering to the professor who had known his poems.

"The publisher himself. They make a fortune off of Ilia," he whispered back.

"The name, please?"

"Harold Paris. He runs the house Anderson, Heartfield and Paris. Old firm, turn of the century, but Paris has it now."

Yuri Maximovich missed much of what Bateson had said. Applause had broken out and the photographers had begun to photograph as Kolokolov rose slowly to his feet. Yuri had caught the name and would remember it, but the rest slid by. He grunted and turned away from Bateson, stretching forward at the table to watch Ilia receive the press. He hadn't seen him since the plane had landed. Somehow he had managed to change clothing. He was dressed in a suit fashioned of some coarse blue fabric, stitched with red thread and tricked out with little metal buttons. His shirt was open and around his neck, in place of the black tie he habitually wore in Moscow, was a blue and red silk scarf, loosely knotted.

"My American friends and friends of poetry everywhere," Ilia Alexandrovich began gently, his arms open as if to receive flowers from appreciative children, "I am so very happy to be once more in your great country. Needless of me it is to say that our two great peoples, joined by so many ties, must learn to speak openly and truthfully of differences which have in recent times put us apart. One way of closing the gap between us is by art. The art most loved by my people is song, whether the song of the people (and we have with us today one of the great enthusiasts and students of the song of Russian people, my old friend and the editor of the great Soviet journal *The People's Voice*, to my right, Yuri Maximovich Isakovsky)..." and with this Ilia turned to Yuri Maximovich and motioned for him to rise, and while the applause began, tentatively at first, Ilia raised his clasped hands over his head and shook a fist of fingers in Yuri's direction. Yuri half rose from his seat and fell back. The nausea had returned suddenly. Ilia Alexandrovich continued, ". . . or the song of the poets who speak out for the people. I have been blessed with the gift of inventing song for the people, and I wish only to use that gift to speak the people's truth, which is for peace, well-being, and harmony among men. Thank you very much for coming today to greet us."

Kolokolov sat down again amid renewed applause. Harold Paris even whistled. Only Roger Bateson, the professor, remained calm, clapping politely and briefly. Yuri had no alternative but to applaud, however, he assumed the Russian style of rhythmic clapping, which among so many spontaneous Americans gave a mocking cast to his enthusiasm. It had been unnoticed, although he caught Ilia looking at him with a quizzical smile.

The questions began.

"Are you looking forward to visiting Boston?"

"You are obviously from Boston newspaper, yes?" Ilia asked.

"It is the birth city of American revolution and naturally of great interest to any Soviet citizen."

"True enough, sir. But you must be aware that you have some critics in the Boston area. One of them has been very rude to your poetry. 'Party doggerel,' he called it."

"The only dog I know is wolfhound. Perhaps I should set it to snapping at the gentleman in question."

There was laughter.

"Sunday night's dinner is certainly one of the greatest testimonials ever offered by American intellectuals to a foreign writer. What is your reaction to this unprecedented event?"

"It would be foolish to deny that I am honored. But, gentlemen, truly it is an honor given not alone to me but to all my countrymen. I am just a man with a gift—no different from a worker anywhere in my country. If you honor one worker, you honor all workers. Not true?"

"True enough, sir. But what I mean is, don't you find any other significance in the fact that so many of our most distinguished poets and novelists are going to offer versions of your poetry?"

"I imagine that it has no other significance than that they like my poems. Don't you think so?" Ilia smiled puckishly and the reporter, obviously embarrassed by the ineptness of his question, sat down.

"Mr. Kolokolov, you are reported as having said that you thought Americans should keep away from the so-called Russian dissidents, that it is, as you put it, 'no business of the Americans how we deal with our internal affairs.' Do you still hold to that view?" The reporter, a short, stocky man with bushy gray hair and demonic eyebrows, looked up above his half-moon glasses at Ilia and fixed him with a stern look.

"I imagine you refer to my statement of November about the hunger strike of the Jewish activists. Yes. I hold to that view. The Soviet government has every right to decide who shall travel and who shall not, who shall reflect credit upon the Soviet people and who might slander it."

"Who shall live and who shall die," the reporter coolly interjected.

"I do not understand. What has living and dying to do with this matter? I speak only about the right of Soviet government to make up its own mind in the best interests of the people."

"So you support the persecution of the Jews and, as Mr. Sakharov contends, other minority ethnic groups."

"Gentlemen of the press, let me be honest, I did not come here to talk politics. Politics separates our peoples. I came to talk poetry, and that is universal language."

"Come now, Mr. Kolokolov. We understand all that well enough," a slow-speaking reporter from one of the wire services chided, "but you are a good enough Marxist, I should think, not to believe in art for art's sake. You talked politics easily enough when Pasternak's *Zhivago* was being attacked. We'd like you to talk a little politics now. Your poetry is full of politics, and probably your politics is pretty artful, so how about it?"

Ilia Alexandrovich began to fuss with his scarf, loosening it with one hand and reaching with the other for a glass of water. "Why is it the case," Ilia began, addressing his words to Mr. Paris, who smiled up attentively to him, "that whenever I greet the American people I end having to do battle with the press. I am, I must say again, a poet and not, as some of you are, political wizards. I am a Soviet citizen and proud of it. You are Americans and proud of it. Why must we be expected to justify our ways to you or—"

"But, Mr. Kolokolov—" the reporter with the half-moon glasses began again.

"May I have the courtesy of finishing up first?" The reporter waved him forward with an exaggerated gesture of deference.

"Why must we be expected, I say again, to justify our ways to you or you yours to us? We both make mistakes, but they are honest and thoughtful mistakes. For instance, your country pursued a disastrous course in Southeast Asia, and you know it now. Would it be right for me to rub salt—how you say—in the wound of that mistake? No. It would not. But I could. Yes. But I would not. I am a guest and the rules of being guest are very strong."

The reporter motioned to indicate that he would pass. He

had lost interest in the press conference and was inquiring into his fingernails. Mr. Paris, taking advantage of the pause, rose quickly to his feet and was about to speak—closing the press conference, no doubt—when a young woman at the back of the room called out, "One minute, please. Would you mind if I asked Mr. Isakovsky a question?" There was a pause, and Yuri Maximovich, hearing his name spoken, returned from the reverie into which he had disappeared and cupped his ear in the direction of the voice, for he could not see clearly which of the three women who were present at the conference had addressed him.

"Mr. Isakovsky? What brings *you* to the United States?" It was a young woman breaching the divide between her twenties and her thirties who was speaking. She seemed very pretty or so Yuri thought, even though the camera lights were blinding. A cigarette hung from her lips and smoke curled about her face like ectoplasm. It was an easy question and Yuri replied matter-of-factly without words of color or particular emphasis.

"But you are also a poet, is that not so?" Yuri nodded. "Will you be at the dinner for Mr. Kolokolov?" she continued.

"I go if I am asked. But you know I am not a distinguished American poet or novelist."

There was considerable mirth at Yuri's answer. Ilia Alexandrovich frowned but then joined in the amusement, calling down to Yuri Maximovich, "Of course you are invited. You will be at my side."

"*Chrosha,*" Yuri replied in Russian, and then as an afterthought continued, "You know, this is first time in my life I have seen how press in your country speaks. It is quite fascinating, I think. You say everything hoping to get people in trap either by their good will or by their stupidity."

"Is that your notion of a free press?" one of the reporters jibed.

"I have no political notions at all. Tell you the truth, I don't read newspapers at all. Not at home. Never. It takes too much time and one finds out too little. So I do never read newspapers." Yuri smiled reflectively.

"Will you be reading your poetry while you're here?" the young woman asked again, renewing her pursuit of information.

"I think so! I hope so! But I don't know where. Somewhere, somehow I will read my poetry, but if there is no English translation going side by side, how will they enjoy it? We will see."

That last reply, speculative and indefinite, concluded the press conference. Mr. Paris rose, thanked Yuri Maximovich, appreciated Ilia Alexandrovich, hoped that the press would cover the dinner and review the reading and the book, and said goodbye.

Two limousines were waiting outside. Into one Yuri Maximovich and Ilia Kolokolov were invited; Vovka Bedkin was in the other with several Soviet officials. All that could be seen of them was animated gesticulation. Their windows were shut against the rain and cold. The Russian with the uncomfortable black hat, who introduced himself as Pyotr Feodorovich Chupkov, information officer for the Cultural Mission, joined the poets.

"I have the invitation for which you hoped," Chupkov said to no one in particular, addressing perhaps even the limousine driver whose partition glass was open. For a moment neither Yuri Maximovich nor Ilia Alexandrovich acknowledged his announcement. The automobile had slid out from the waiting ramp and entered the exit lane which circuited from the arrivals building towards the highway.

"You speak to me?" It was Kolokolov who spoke. His tone was snappish. He had begun to sulk, biting at his lower lip. He was pondering an unreasonable irritation with Yuri Maximovich, whom he had acknowledged more graciously than he believed Yuri had deserved and who had thanked him by usurping the conference and grinding it to a halt. Ilia Alexandrovich lay in a corner of the limousine, shrinking from the more lumbering Isakovsky, whose body occupied space in the automobile like unkneaded dough.

"No, not you, Ilia Alexandrovich. I refer to our friend here, who so desperately wishes the opportunity to read his poems."

"Are you being sarcastic?" Yuri Maximovich questioned, not at all displeased by Comrade Chupkov's churlishness.

"Do I sound it?"

"Unmistakably."

"Take it for that if you choose."

"And if so, why so?" Yuri Maximovich took criticism seriously. He was always willing to improve.

"Your insult to our press. Gratuitous, irresponsible, vulgar."

"All of those. Yes? Well, the truth is that I don't read the newspapers and I won't. Don't you ever miss a day of *Pravda*, Comrade?"

"Of course I do."

"Well? I just go you several better. I miss three hundred and sixty-five days of *Pravda*. A difference in number, not kind."

"Ignore him, Chupkov. He's always like this nowadays. Sour and mean."

"As you wish, Ilia Alexandrovich, but what about my invitation?"

"You will hear about it."

"So tell me now."

"I don't choose to any more."

"You punish me?"

"If you like, yes."

"*Kinderspiel*."

"What is that?"

"He says you play children's games. It's German."

"You know German, Isakovsky?"

"Yes, I suppose, twenty words of German. And probably forty of Hebrew and a thousand in Yiddish and several thousand in Ukrainian and four thousand or so in English and tens of thousands in Russia. So what? I'm a poor linguist."

The limousine had entered the traffic that passed alongside another and smaller airdrome that moved finally to the bridge which coiled about the city. It was dark and the lights of the city, still seen from the distance of Queens, were ominous and unfamiliar. A winter rain, the city's substitute for snow, had begun, and the shapes of the buildings across the river shimmered and shook through the window glass. Yuri Maximovich had been trying to concentrate upon his nausea. It had passed, but in its place another and more desperate sensation had taken up lodging. He felt empty and worn out. The sensation was not simply hunger or fatigue. Of one thing he was certain: he was not doing well. He was not charming; he was not appealing, ingratiating, warm, attractive. He had nothing of Ilia's succulence, and clearly he had inspired the disapproval of yet another Soviet official. His visit was certainly beginning inauspiciously. None of these, however, was the source of his discomfort, and as the limousine moved forward around the bridge, past the tollbooths, down onto the highway that corseted the city, he realized that he was wholly without excitement and expectation. He had somehow been through the experience already. He lay back upon the gray felt cushions of the automobile and closed his eyes. The only image that returned, passing like an old-fashioned moving picture, slowly unfolding, was of the smoke curling up from the icehouse, the very last thing that Tyutychev and he could see above the fir trees as they turned down the road away from Peredelkino. The smoke was filled with bits of paper. The nausea returned in a spasm, and gasping for breath, Yuri cracked the window ever so slightly, lifting his nose to the wind which gusted through.

The last words which Chupkov said to Yuri Maximovich before the limousine eased away from the entrance to the Chelsea Hotel were that he should notify him of everyone who called, left a message, or tried to meet him in person. His tone of voice underscored this "request." It was an order, not a request at all.

Their rooms were ready. On the same floor. Ilia Alexandrovich had a small suite, a sitting room adjoining his bedroom and bath. Bedkin between them in a modest room and Yuri's no less unassuming. A curiously Russian hotel for New York City. The furniture essential and undistinguished but for its age. A cotton bedspread with knotted blue puffs about its edges was the only item of decoration with any individuality, and happily no paintings, no framed promos, no heroic attitudes upon the walls. Yuri remembered the canvas that had been intended to brighten the hotel room he had stopped at in Kiev when he went home for the funeral of his father. A bronzen boy with a scythe, a bronzen girl with a scythe, and golden wheat. Unfortunately that season there was a wheat shortage, and one could only laughingly assume that all was real except the cutting edge of the scythe. It was not correct thinking to suppose that the wheat wasn't there or that the boy and girl weren't bronzen, only that the scythe wouldn't cut. A production failure in the blade factory. Blame someone else for the famine. But here at this hotel, where writers and artists for decades had taken refuge from the moil of the city, no effort was made to supply the rooms with culture. The imagination was allowed to fill the empty spaces; indeed, Yuri found an area over the small desk where he presumed a picture had once hung, for a rectangle of the wallpaper of crimson rosettes was unmistakably bright and clean. He felt comfortable in that room. It was adequate and without character or claim. Yuri removed his shoes, emptied his suitcase, hung out his clothes, washed his face, and lay down on the bed to rest.

It is quite conceivable that Yuri Maximovich had fallen asleep. He had been exhausted and he had felt ill. The plane had set down after a long and boring flight and the press conference had sapped whatever energy he retained. It must have been about midnight when he heard the knocking upon his door. It was a muffled knock, low and slow. Yuri did not reply at once, and after some minutes of stretching and rubbing his eyes, he muttered aloud, to no one in particular, "Just a minute, just a minute." At last awake, he padded to the door and opened it, expecting one of his traveling companions. He was hungry and his watch, his stomach, and real time were completely out of touch with each other. He hoped it was Kolokolov. With him he could at least go to a restaurant. But it was neither Bedkin nor Kolokolov. He had opened the door a crack and saw with one eye a large black felt hat tied with a white sash which dropped down the shoulder of a young woman whose face, for the moment, he could not see. The hall light illuminated nothing but a patch of carpet a dozen feet away. The young woman was in shadows.

"Do you have the right room?"

"Are you Mr. Isakovsky?" The woman had turned toward him and the crack enlarged. It was enough for her to edge through. She had placed her hand upon Yuri's chest and pressed upon it. He had given way and she had entered.

Yuri wondered for a moment whether he was to call Chupkov immediately or afterwards. It was one thing with a telephone call or a message, but a young woman in the middle of the night? Perhaps that became personal, nonpolitical, within the narrow range of permissible privacy. He was logy with sleep and his temporizing with Chupkov ended as quickly as it had begun.

"Yes. I am Isakovsky. But who are you?"

"Don't you remember me?" she asked, removing her hat and laying it on his bed. Her hair, propped within the cavern of the hat, fell about her shoulders. Auburn hair, tangled and snarled, held dissolutely by a red barrette that served no purpose but to withhold a clump from falling over her eyes, swamped her face. He had never understood until that moment the utility of hats with vast crowns: they dissimulate the hair of women. She shook her head madly and the hair fell apart, separated but for a few errant strands, and her face emerged. "Now do you see me? Do you remember me?" Yuri shook his head. He did not. "But the conference. Don't you remember me? I asked you questions."

"Oh. Yes. It was you? But I must explain something, young lady."

"Greta Engel. That's my name. Greta Engel."

"Oh, Madame Engel."

"Not married. Plain Greta Engel," she replied firmly, but with a smile.

"All right, but then what? Agreement. Yes. I shall call you by full name. Greta Engel. Then? Well. We shall see if we are acquainted. Correct?"

"Yes. Perfect." She was incredibly brisk. Yuri had such difficulty getting used to her voice, its curious energy and intensity, that he had still not looked carefully at her face, much less her body.

"But all right, Greta Engel. What is it that you want from me?"

"That's simple, Mr. Isakovsky. I want to know everything about you."

"You must be—what is word?—making joke?"

"Not at all," she laughed. "I'm quite serious."

"But it is a joke to think you can learn everything in six days."

"Why six days?"

"At end of six days, I leave. Poof to Moscow." Yuri was going to say something about disappearing in smoke, but that image suddenly became helpless in his mind and only the "poof" remained, hanging meaninglessly in the sentence. Greta Engel laughed again.

"But that can be arranged, can't it? You don't really need to go, do you?" She was disbelieving, her eyes turning away from the prospect of his departure.

"Of course, dear young woman, of course. I visit only to go to music conference and read poems. That's all."

"Yes?"

"You don't believe me?"

"No."

Yuri was grateful for her disbelief. It gave him the opportunity of frowning, of knitting his forehead, of doing evasive things which helped conceal his curiosity about the young woman who sat before him on the bed, her legs wrapped about each other as a vine about a tree. She was thin; the blue crepe shirt which hugged her ample but unexceptional breasts was tucked into a pair of faded brown corduroy trousers, belted with a strip of green cloth knotted to the side and frayed into long strips which hung down a well-graded hip. Her booted feet were small. Yuri loved small feet. Greta Engel was distinctly odd but undeniably attractive. The frowning which had begun before his ruminations on her breasts was relieved by her feet and disappeared entirely when he raised his head to consider her face. Greta Engel's face was a maze of unreconciled angles, high cheekbones, distinctly European, and a long, almost Roman nose cracked at its bridge, where a bone strong as a condottiere's gave her palpable womanness the confusion of a man's strength. And in the gloomy light her oddly colored eyes, blue-green flecked with dots of red, seemed to give a purplish cast to her face.

"But it is the truth," Yuri replied, his survey completed. "It is the truth. I have come for very short visit. I go to conference. I eat at Kolokolov's dinner. I read my poems. I go home. Immensely short. No?"

"I don't like it one bit. There won't be enough time for me." Yuri Maximovich was mystified. This was not what he had expected of an American woman. He had heard that they were direct and immodest. That was the accepted view. But then Irina Alexandrovna had not been precisely shy and withdrawn. The difference, of course, was that in the absence of intelligence, Irina never entered into conversation. She performed. This girl, this Greta Engel, on the contrary, settled in and talked. Her voice was continuously agitated. Even when she was silent her throat sounded, as though deep in the gorge the waters were gathering and rumbling before they broke. This young lady, he accepted, was incredibly nervous.

"That last, Greta Engel, I find alarming. What is this time you require of me?"

"I've made you a project. An assignment, I guess you'd call it. I work for a newspaper, one of the local city papers. We don't give the news, we organize opinion. Last week, the press release of the Kolokolov arrival came across the city desk. You were mentioned. An 'also-ran,' we call it. Down at the bottom it said: 'Accompanying Mr. Kolokolov will be Yuri Maximovich Isakovsky, the editor of *The People's Voice,* also a poet, who is attending the Congress of Music and Ethnology at the Hilton.' That's what it said. To a word. What caught me was the 'also a poet.' I loved that, and I asked my editor if I couldn't find out what it meant. What's an 'also poet' in the Soviet Union? We have thousands of 'also poets' in the States, but no one would put that down on a job application. A poet here is someone who can't hold a steady job. Fifty years ago, teachers were thought of as poets—people who didn't want to work, couldn't make it. But now it's poets. Even painters are more respected now than poets. At least a painter commands some of the real action—where the money is, you know? But a poet with his images and intuitions. Well, really all the poets I know who hold down jobs—why, those poets have to write in the john during working hours or hide the stuff under the desk blotter. But you people, you Russian poets, even if you've written a poem or two, so long as it's gotten published and been read, you're treated as poets. Being a poet is honorable."

Greta Engel was dazzling. Her words enveloped Yuri Maximovich, but he picked up enough of what she said to become both angry and amused. He considered Chupkov and the possibilities. If he wanted to get rid of her and go back to sleep, he could become enraged and throw her out or call the desk and have the night manager or the floor attendant—he assumed there were floor attendants—throw her out. That was one possibility—distinctly the safest, as he realized later. But as angered as he was by her confusions, he was equally fascinated by her description of the condition of poets in her own land. Perhaps she was equally misguided. Tyutychev's strictures came to mind, Tyutychev speaking about cultures of quality. Poets hiding their poems not because they feared to go to jail but simply because they wanted to appear serious and responsible. What a difference, he thought. And then, of course, she was somehow beautiful, strange and beautiful, and Yuri was exhausted and not really up to resisting adequately.

"I'm hungry." It was not a reply, but apparently the young woman was not at that moment interested in a reply.

"Wonderful. So am I. I'll take you out for a bite." The expression made him wary but interested. It was very late, well past midnight. Yuri had slept very little. He had gone through more than a day now without a proper rest, but he was completely awake. His eyes ached, but his stomach was quiet. He shrugged assent, put on his shoes, and disappeared into the bathroom, where he brushed down his hair. He noticed the prevalence of gray contemptuously. Bundled up, they walked down from the fourth floor, through the somnolent lobby, past the reception desk—which was lit but unoccupied—and out into the street. An occasional truck lumbered by and some private cars, but there seemed a profusion of taxicabs; within a minute Greta Engel had whistled one to a halt and the two of them entered. She mentioned someplace, somewhere, and the cab pulled out and turned south.

The city was quiet, which Yuri found reassuring, and the rain had stopped. The enormous buildings were unlit. There were few pedestrians and not too many automobiles. But then the cab turned to the east and suddenly it was alive. Stores were just closing, scores of people were in the streets, walking, jostling, calling out. A blind black man with an accordion. A strange trio—oboe, flute, recorder—were playing music in front of a bookstore. An old woman wheeling a baby carriage piled high with junk. Yuri leaned forward and watched out of his window. He could see three men—they seemed drunk—fighting with each other, punching and howling. The cab sped by and soon pulled up at a cafeteria, an enormous cavern whose yellow light hooded the street at its entrance. Everything was dark on the block except the cafeteria. Greta Engel paid the driver and took Yuri's arm, guiding him through the revolving door, instructing him to pull his check from the machine, pass through the turnstile, collect his tray and implements, and follow her to the sandwich counter. He was immobilized. Through the glass, he could see steel containers—dozens of them—piled high with foods and mixes, cheeses, fish, and sliced meats, and down the line larger containers with whole meats and fish platters and stews steaming, and beyond those, salads and fruits, and beyond those, puddings and cakes. It was immense. Sixty feet of choices. Yuri was not interested in novelty. He pointed to the sardines. The counterman arranged an assembly of sardines on a seeded roll bedded with lettuce, slid it onto a warm plate, and sped it down the glass countertop toward Greta Engel, who snared it with two fingers and in a single remarkable movement, almost without breaking the speed of the counterman's slide, removed it to the tray. She smiled at Yuri. She took coffee and a pastry. Yuri added a glass of milk and a fruit compote.

They carried their trays to a corner of the cafeteria to be out of the way. The room was remarkably filled for early morning and music was playing in the ceiling.

"An American cafeteria. What do you think?"

"Fantastic. So many choices. More than one needs, no?"

"Not a question of need at all. The choices exist. They're only put on display. If someone had a bad stomach, the choices are automatically narrowed. Or a vegetarian, even narrower. Or on a Chinese diet, narrower still. But the food's all there anyway. The choices make it challenging. Even food is challenging in this absurd country." She bit into her pastry and a jellied strawberry clung to the side of her lip. Her tongue edged out and curled it in. Yuri watched the maneuver with delight, but when she caught his smile, he shook his head in mocking disbelief and turned to his sardines and began to eat. The conversation did not renew until they had both finished and pushed away their trays. Yuri had enjoyed the sandwich, but the compote was imperfect. Greta Engel took out a cigarette and handed a pack of matches to Yuri who accepted them, thought an instant to recollect the implication of the gesture, and at last, removed one, and struck it.

"I like you, 'project,'" Greta Engel began, blowing smoke in a whoosh into the air.

"That's not yet mature." Yuri knew it wasn't the right word, but it was a tantalizing formulation and Greta Engel was aroused by its ambiguity.

"No! What I mean is this. You seem incredibly naïve, or is it innocent? It's that quality which makes poets here anomalous and exotic and perhaps makes them indispensable in your country. The interesting thing about both our countries is that as countries they're very young. Your first poets emerge about the same time as ours. Not even two hundred years ago. Poe and Pushkin were almost contemporaries. Poe died in poverty and Pushkin was edged into a duel and killed. Anyone this country doesn't much like—a fellow out of step, annoying, dismaying, agitating—we do to death by ignoring them. In your country, it's much more direct. The czars and the commissars kill them. Isn't that so?"

"Who is naïve and innocent? Do you really expect me, Greta Engel, to agree to this?"

"Do you disagree with this?"

"Why should I answer you? Do you understand that if I were to agree with you and you were to publish such simplified nonsense, I go to jail."

"But then you agree with me?" She rushed on, ignoring Yuri's scruples. "Here we would do it differently. You would find a publisher and you would be published, but you'd end up with the whole edition in boxes in your basement. Two hundred would be bought by libraries and your family and friends, and the rest you could have in a year at twenty cents on the dollar. That is assuming, of course, that you simply write poems, but don't also sell them. If you know how to sell them—we call it "selling yourself"—it can turn out differently. If you put your poems to music, you become a rock star. If you write perverse poems, you get the coterie of your perversion. If you teach, you can go on the reading circuit and with personality—pizzazz—from sexy blue jeans to elegant tweeds, you can make a connection. It has nothing to do with the poems. They'll make their way without you. Baudelaire saved Poe for the Americans, but it didn't do Poe much good. The point is that here poetry is personality, not power. In your country it's different. Poets make the powerful uneasy. Look at Mandelstam and Pasternak. They made Stalin nervous as hell. Of course, he couldn't stand anyone smarter than he was, and Mandelstam and Pasternak were smart. They were also Jews."

"So am I."

"I thought as much. Isakovsky. Son of Isaac. So is Greta. So am I. Not that it makes it any easier. The Jews aren't a conspiracy, only a smuggling ring. That's what my father says when he's sober. What he means, I guess, is that survival is no conspiracy, only gang warfare."

Yuri Maximovich understood what she was saying and tried to decide if it was true. It was one of those generalizations which commanded an imposing rhetoric, but it hardly seemed accurate in the Soviet Union. The Jews he knew were neither conspirators nor smugglers, and they were not succeeding terribly well in surviving. He remembered the stricture of a journalist his father had known—a Jew from Vilno—who had suggested in an anonymous memorandum to the *Evsekstia* that if the Bolsheviks really wanted the Jews to disappear they should immediately allow them the choice of being Russians. The poor fellow disappeared in the early thirties, but Yuri thought he was probably right. Right for everyone else, of course. It was impossible for Yuri after his father's death, but that episode had demonstrated that it was impossible also for the Russians. The Russians wouldn't let the Jews hide. For them, it only meant the Jews could conspire more efficiently under the cloak of Russian nationality; whereas at present, tired of being persecuted, the Jews were demanding to be let go completely. It was hopeless. The one thing of which Yuri was certain was that if all the educated Jews succeeded in emigrating, within a generation the government would win by default.

"You know, in few years, if all leadership of Jews gets out, two million ordinary, uneducated, working-class Jews will be deserted, left to their fate. No one to worry about them."

"Apropos of what? What are you talking about?" Greta Engel realized that Yuri's silence had skipped the development of an argument and presented her with a conclusion.

Yuri repeated his speculation. "What's to be done? It works for both Russians and Israelis. Israelis want intellectuals and professionals, engineers, scientists, researchers. Russians want to replace Jews with Russians in the same categories. The Russians can absorb two million nice quiet workers and the Israelis can handle several hundred thousand technicians. Perhaps Russians and Israelis have made agreement."

"Fanciful," Greta snorted, taking his irony literally.

"Well, of course, I don't mean it, not definitely, but it has a kind of bitter logic, not so?"

"Yes. It does."

They lapsed into silence. Greta Engel began to smoke again, but she lit her own cigarette.

"Let me ask you a simple question," she began, her forehead strained with concentration, her cigarette marking her works. "If you stripped everything away from being Jewish, every memory of family, every sentiment of history, all familiarity with old custom, tradition, literature, what would you be left with?"

"Justice! Simple justice! Rage for simple justice," Yuri replied immediately.

"And I? You see, I would say mercy." Greta Engel's face clouded suddenly.

"But, Greta Engel, you are not Russian. If Russian, you would know how idle it is to speak of mercy."

"And you didn't survive Hitler." Greta countered. "Not that I did. I anticipated Hitler, or rather my family did. I was born on an ocean liner that came from Danzig in 1937. My father had just built a shoe factory in that city. He had been in the shoe business for years, first as a traveling salesmen for a Polish firm and later as its business manager. I'm afraid my father wasn't a very good businessman. Within six months of opening his own factory—not a very sensible decision at that time for a Danzig Jew—he failed. No one bought his shoes. They accused him of making shoes out of pig leather, and at night the factory was chalked over with caricatures of my father skinning pigs. (An original motif of anti-Semitism?) The factory failed, and broken-hearted, my father gathered up my mother and his parents and moved out. I wouldn't be alive if he hadn't failed. And he's failed ever since. He's a dignified drunk. Beautiful manners, well-read, but he drinks. My life I owe, you see, not to justice, but mercy."

"Mercy is accident?"

"Quite. And that's all we have."

Yuri Maximovich was puzzled. It was an unfamiliar argument. Raised on a different literature, he had always conducted the life of a Jew by dressing Russian conclusions in Jewish clothing. He couldn't bear Dostoyevsky when he was being a Slavophile, a *narodnik*, an Orthodox fanatic, but whenever he began talking about the Russian messiah, Yuri Maximovich substituted Jewish dreams and visions. All the saving women in Dostoyevsky he thought of as Rachels and Rebeccas. Sonia made no sense to him except as the daughter of an ancient rabbi. And Tolstoy and Turgenev—how he admired them, but they were not his writers. They didn't understand the filth of the city; they were too committed to the countryside.

"You are astonishing woman. In Soviet Union we have intellectual women, but Soviet men find such women unbearable. They are all good party workers, with sensible shoes and unattractive haircuts. The other women—those we fall in love with and dishonor—are delighted to be made miserable by gifted man. Any man with talent can have splendid woman in my country. But you are different kind of splendor. Forgive me that. I am not making proposal to you. Only admiring from distance. Yes. Remarkable." Yuri Maximovich was consulting himself. He was excited.

"I'm exhausted. Enough for the first night." Greta Engel put her cigarettes and matches into her enormous carrying bag and stood up. Yuri Maximovich was decisively interrupted. He came to his feet, ran his hands over his hair, buttoned up his overcoat and followed her out into the night. The damp cold, not ferocious like Moscow, was like a lynx, sneaking into every hidden space, whether the hole under the lapel of his coat or beneath the lining of his shapka. He was delighted when another taxicab was flagged and the name of his hotel given to the driver. The driver took a different route uptown. The city was resolutely quiet but for an occasional patrolling police car or lone pedestrian.

As they approached the hotel, Yuri could see another taxicab discharge a passenger before the entranceway. The small man jumped out, looked over his shoulder down the street, and went in. It was Vovka Bedkin. No one else could limp so grotesquely.

Again Greta Engel paid for the taxicab and entered the lobby with Yuri Maximovich. He had expected that she would say good night at that point. It was surprising to him that she had allowed the taxicab to disappear. She would have more difficulty finding another at this hour in that deserted section of the city, but she stayed by his side as they mounted the stairway to the fourth floor. At his door he turned to say good night, but she had disappeared. He stood a moment, listening for her retreating footsteps. There were none. It was then he heard the chain lock rattle on the door across the hall from his own.

2. A Small Talk

Vovka Bedkin was standing over Yuri Maximovich when he awakened the following morning. It was not the way he would have chosen to be awakened. He would have preferred it if Greta Engel had managed to enter his room; but it was unmistakably Vovka Bedkin wearing a proper suit, a white shirt whose collar tips were hopelessly discolored with streaks of dirt, and a brown cotton tie that hung three inches or more below his belt line.

"How did you get in here?" Yuri asked.

"The chambermaid. She let me in. She didn't understand what I was saying. I ended by motioning to her key chain and she obliged."

"Why didn't you use the telephone?"

"I did. You didn't hear it. The operator rang a half-dozen times."

"I hate being awakened by strangers. Positively hate it," Yuri said angrily.

"Forgive me, Comrade. But it was most important. You are

obliged to be at your meetings. They register participants this morning, and this afternoon the congress begins. I am sure you would wish to be on time. And besides, I'm not a stranger, Yuri Maximovich." Bedkin whimpered the last. His feelings were hurt.

"I'm exhausted. I could have slept another two hours." Yuri yawned and his jaw cracked painfully.

"A late night?"

"How so?" Yuri Maximovich had no intention of answering Bedkin. If he had followed him, he knew quite well where and with whom Yuri had been, and if he hadn't, what was he doing out by himself? Either way Yuri determined to let Bedkin's query pass until it was renewed.

Yuri Maximovich sat up in bed and drew the bedclothes up to his neck. He had acquired the habit of sleeping naked when he was married to Irina Alexandrovna and had seen no reason after their divorce to return to sleeping pants and undershirts. He had persuaded himself that the body needs to breath. The truth is that he enjoyed watching the evolution (he actually described the process of aging as "devolution") of his body, its unsubtle, even gross, passage from maturity to middle age, the slackness of his thigh muscles, which had only recently become pronounced, and the gradual thickening of his girth from the tightness of his soccer days to modest corpulence. Now there were times in the morning when, unwilling to forgo his bed, he watched antiquated armies wheeling and maneuvering upon the gentle slope of his stomach. Since he could no longer see the other side unobstructed, it was always a surprise what brilliant siege gun was concealed in his groin waiting to be brought up by the enemy advancing to occupy the woody copse and watering hole which occupied the center of his stomach. But not in the presence of Bedkin. Bedkin would surely note in his report on Yuri Maximovich: ". . . and, Comrades, could anyone be considered reliable who sleeps naked?"

"No chance of your falling back to sleep, is there?" Bedkin inquired with stern politeness.

"Of course there is. But I no longer wish to sleep. It's time to be awake."

"I will wait for you in the lobby."

"Is that necessary?"

"Of course, Comrade. I'm obliged to go about with you."

"You don't know a word of English. Do you expect me to translate the conference for you?"

"When it's important to know, yes. Otherwise, I will be quite content to think Russian thoughts."

It wasn't difficult getting dressed, although if Yuri had had his way he would have sat down before his journal for a bit and made some notes about his conversation with Greta Engel. (It is fortunate now that those notes do not exist.) He had only to dress. It rankled him to recall that he had decided the evening before that he was uninteresting, without eccentric feature or seductive charm. He had displeased a press conference, to be sure; however, he had won the attention of a beautiful though doubtless unsettled young woman in her thirties. To his view she was a dubious conquest, but he had another chance. He was on his way to a Congress of Music and Ethnology—a convention of professionals amassed from Europe, Africa, Asia, South America, and the United States, more than three hundred researchers and investigators into the hums and stammers of myth hidden in the folk music of the tribes of men. They could not be an uninteresting lot. Among them there must be incredible creatures—Tyutychevian, if not Tyutychev. Would not Tyutychev have been a miracle in New York? Within a day he would have found every bum and beggar, every exhausted drunkard and toothless grandmother, and obliged them to sing out their miseries to him. He could not compete with Tyutychev. All he had to offer to the Congress was a rather unremarkable achievement, editorship of *The People's Voice*. By international standards it wasn't a very distinguished journal. It was simply another house organ. The only achievement which it could claim for its existence was the contributions of Yasha Isaievich Tyutychev, the underworld archivist. Besides that, it was little more than another device of the Ministry of Culture to exhibit to the Russian people the legitimacy of self-congratulation. If in the early days of the Revolution, poets, not the least of whom had been Mayakovsky and his admirers, had overturned the standards of Russian prosody in order to attract country boys to the free language of poetry—"every proletarian with the urge to write poetry can write poetry"—*The People's Voice* existed to prove that every Russian can sing if he makes up his mind to open his mouth.

Yuri Maximovich was finally a snob. Slightly pathetic, don't you think? Of course. But then be generous: how do you think—free-thinking, honest, unsycophantic Westerners that you are—that the Isakovskys of Russia stayed alive until this day? Do you think it was done by moral conviction and honor? You would like to think so, but that isn't the case. Those who hung on from the old days, from before the exile of Trotsky and and the ordeal by fire to which the so-called counterrevolutionaries succumbed, all managed to get into trouble because they had read old books, conserved the remnants of old views, survived out of another era when "the revolution" meant something different. People like Isakovsky, born on the cusp of the new era, didn't have the opportunity of a Nikolai Gumilev to stand before the firing squad with Plato in one hand and the Gospels in the other. How splendid! Such heroes make us weep, and Gumilev was such a hero—African adventurer, gunrunner, Acmeist, handsome, and a first-class poet in the bargain. But Yuri Maximovich? A Kievan Jew from around the corner of the Podol with an accountant for a father and a Yiddishist for a mother. What the hell do you expect? A snob. That's all. Trying to find a place to hold fast without the training. No wonder that standing before the mirror of the bathroom that morning, about to present himself to professional confreres and in two days to sally forth beside Ilia Alexandrovich Kolokolov, a poet of whose work and person he was jealous and contemptuous, he was thinking how to dress.

It wasn't difficult to decide. There was pathetically little to choose from. The Isakovsky wardrobe, as such, did not exist. It was a question of deciding whether he wished to be an intellectual worker—the blue trousers that sagged at the pockets and bagged at the knees—or a working intellectual, which dictated the dark corduroys. A blue workshirt which he had bought for himself from a French student who had visited his office to propose himself as corresponding editor for France (such things were occasionally arranged if the higher-ups thought it useful to have a contact among the musical émigés of Paris), and to complete his presentation, a deep-blue knitted sweater, the only thing he retained from his marriage.

About the sweater: Irina Alexandrovna could not knit. The one time she had tried such a domestic recreation she had nearly stabbed a breast with one of the knitting needles, and that had put an emphatic end to such activity. Fortunately, however, she had written to her mother and asked her to execute what she could not. She pretended to be making progress with her knitting while Yuri was at the office, and one evening several months later she presented him with a handsome blue sweater for his birthday. It was only during the course of one of their many pre-divorce battles that she revealed her deception. It was a handsome sweater with a complicated neck, double-knitted and elegantly graceful. With black tie and unmatched suit jacket he was at least unusual for a Russian, not exceptional, but unusual. He was a Russian intellectual, which is all that mattered.

Vovka Bedkin was reading a newspaper in the lobby when Yuri stepped out of the elevator, which functioned, he discovered, during reasonable hours. It was an American newspaper and Yuri was mystified as to Bedkin's curiosity, for he had admitted to a total ignorance of the English language. Indeed, his Russian was not to be congratulated, and any language beyond was obviously a miasma. But there he was with a newspaper, the *Daily News*, in his hands, opened to the centerfold of pictures.

"And Russian you know perfectly?" Yuri asked with amusement, for he was certain the irony would be missed.

"Of course, Comrade. Russian is my tongue. The pictures are

fascinating. Such a corrupt country. Nothing but traffic accidents and murders." He threw the paper aside and stood up with effort.

"We have them too, you know?"

"No doubt, but we don't celebrate them."

They stepped out into the street and began to whistle at the passing taxicabs. A doorman appeared and interceded. A taxicab came to a stop, the door was opened for them, and the doorman stood to one side to let them enter. Yuri Maximovich knew nothing of tips. The door was slammed. They hardly noticed. Bedkin said his one English word, enunciating carefully the name of the hotel—it sounded like the "Heeltown"—but the driver, a Meyer Mushkin, spoke English no differently and understood without difficulty.

The hotel they found astonishing. It was neither those stadiums of marble nor those ancient warrens of highly polished oak and cedar which predominated in Moscow, but something quite original, for it seemed to them, as traffic swirled by foot up and down connected stairwells, that these hotels were constructed not to house travelers, but to ensure that traffic kept moving. In Moscow one could find hotel lobbies late at night where weary travelers waiting for a room to be vacated at the Ukraine waited, say, at the Moskva, while twenty feet away upon another, two friends kept up spirited conversation throughout the night. The Hilton had no apparent interest in encouraging the belief that in the absence of rooms, the lobby could be used as one. Like the great American highways, the complexity of which every Russian grudgingly admired, the Hilton was constructed to compel people to move—no, to force them to keep going, to take the up escalator and avoid the down, to follow the crowds into the bar and through, out onto the sidewalk, to swirl, flow, turn the way the movement dictated. Movement created the illusion of prosperity, and prosperity was the one thing upon which the Hilton clearly depended.

At the moment it was late in the morning of the twenty-first of January, clear but cold, sunny but damp, a brisk wind flowing in from the rivers. The two Russians had little trouble finding the mezzanine floor on which the Congress was being held.

It was hard to imagine that the traffic of musical ethnographers would enhance prosperity, but then the other law of the Hilton, besides traffic flow, was occupancy, and any occupant, however pedestrian his employment or modest his income, was welcome, for there were elaborate and expensive rooms, or intimately small and reasonably cheap ones. It was no wonder, since only three hundred delegates were expected, that the conference space constructed out of sliding walls was unpretentious—a generous auditorium filled with comfortable chairs, fronted by a carpeted forecourt with little booths housed by book publishers, guitar companies, and one audio equipment distributor who featured a surreptitions device for penetrating the secret initiation ceremonies of aborigine tribes "without being caught and eaten" (the advertising placard stated that the equipment, all fashioned of delicate wires and retractable metal, would fit into the crown of a pith helmet). When Isakovsky explained the device to Bedkin, the latter commented that due to the absence of aborigines in the Soviet Union such elaborate technology was unnecessary.

The two Russians had entered the forecourt about eleven o'clock and toured the exhibitions. They were about to take their place in the registration line when Yuri heard his name called from across the room. At first he did not see Greta Engel, but she appeared at his side at the precise moment that a middle-aged lady with a corsage of sunflowers was pasting to his lapel a little identification card bearing his name, his official position, and the initials of his homeland.

"But you left without knocking on my door. I wanted to come with you."

"It was not possible. You see, I have beside me another Russian. You would call him, I think, my watchdog." Yuri Maximovich smiled as he said this, and Greta Engel understood.

Turning to Bedkin she said warmly, "And good morning to you, sir. I hope you rested well." She extended her hand to greet Bedkin, but he did not understand the gesture, thinking perhaps her arm was as stiff as his left leg.

Yuri Maximovich translated the salutation and the question. Bedkin muttered something which was rendered as "Yes, very well, thank you," although in fact Bedkin had made some complaint about the difficulty of sleeping on hard beds.

Yuri Maximovich was pleased to see Greta Engel so soon again. He had already concluded that she did not live at his hotel but had somehow contrived to register there and occupy quarters facing his own in order better to pursue her avowed task of making him a "project." Unfortunately he had little time to contemplate that pleasure, for a distinctly large gentleman with oddly porcine ears approached him, and without bothering to introduce himself, informed Yuri, his irritation ill-concealed though unexplained, that he was scheduled for his remarks at precisely two-twenty in the afternoon.

This was the first that Yuri Maximovich had heard that he was expected to address the Congress. He discovered later that the man of corpulence was the program chairman, who had already spent several wearying hours on the telephone with Chupkov arranging for a translator to be present "to render Mr. Isakovsky's remarks to the delegates," if such proved necessary. Yuri assured him that he needed no translator for prose.

Yuri Maximovich had never been informed that he was to speak. The prospect of a public address was nothing short of terrifying, more terrifying by far than a reading of his poems. He could manage a reading of poems, his head buried in the pages of his manuscript; his hands—ill-used in easy sociality—constrained to the lecturn, only occasionally used to emphasize, where his voice failed, a critical word or the movement of an image. But to rise to his feet amid strangers—without podium and equipment, without darkness—and to speak without text (indeed, virtually without forewarning) in two hours and a bit was positively alarming. Chupkov must have known and, in his irritation with Yuri the day before, have suppressed the information. Damn Chupkov. No matter. Whatever the explanation, Yuri Maximovich was beside himself with anxiety. Perhaps all this will explain his little talk, the substance of which was to prove so accusatory sometime later.

It was approaching noon, and the delegates began to disperse to the restaurants and cafés of the hotel. Isakovsky and Bedkin were at a loss. They had no idea where to eat, and although Bedkin had managed a breakfast, Yuri Maximovich was already weak with hunger now exaggerated by anxiety. Greta Engel suggested a restaurant two blocks away, and within minutes the three were seated in a modest *trattorìa* presided over by a *padrone* with plastered hair and the pencil-line mustache of a different era. Yuri Maximovich had never eaten Italian food. It was Greta Engel who ordered the meal. After it came, the wine had been poured, the pasta distributed, the veal scaloppine sprinkled with cheese, and the three had set to devouring the meal, Greta Engel asked Yuri Maximovich about the time and place of his reading. He replied that he had not been told, but he knew for certain that one had been scheduled.

"But of course, the university seminar in Russian literature at Columbia. Wednesday, I should think. The Congress concludes on Monday evening and you leave Thursday—if I cannot persuade you to remain behind." (Yuri winced, but Greta Engel was confidently aware that Vovka Bedkin knew no English; moreover, it would have been difficult even for the most clever of spies to have managed to eat pasta with such audible enthusiasm and absorb a conversation in a totally foreign language at the same time.) "Oh. You don't need to answer." She looked aside, embarrassed. "I'm being forward, direct. You probably think vulgar. It's not that at all. I'm not asking you to defect, just to change your ticket. Not possible? Well, I tried. All right then. Dinner with you the night before you leave? I'll cook a special dinner for us."

"You are saying too much and you are speaking too fast. I am nervous enough. Now start again. Where do I read? What is this seminar? Tell me about Columbia. Columbia who? Is she hostess? City? What is Columbia?"

"You haven't heard about the reading?"

"Not at all. Chupkov was cross with me last evening and would not tell me. But how did you discover?"

"I called and asked even before you arrived. You see, I have been interested in you for some time now. I got Chupkov on the phone and he was very polite. He told me about the seminar and suggested that if I wanted to report it, he would give me much useful background information. I said I would love that, and this morning the material arrived at my newspaper—a whole packet of documents, a sheath of clippings (in Russian, unfortunately), and a copy of your book, which Chupkov identified as *The School Song*."

"*School Song*?" Yuri snorted. "*School Song*. They are such idiots. *School of Song, School of Song, School of Song*." The mistake made Yuri sick with rage. It was an obvious slight. It would be ridiculous for him to appear in an American newspaper as the author of a book of light verse presumably celebrating some local *gymnasium* or even if the image was supple enough to be elaborated, a party cell, some proletarian league, the Soviet empire.

"I am sorry, Yuri. Forgive me for not understanding." Greta Engel had become suddenly very tender. She understood immediately and touched his jacket sleeve, as if to underscore her apology. Bedkin watched Yuri's outburst with amazement. He turned to Greta Engel and asked in Russian what it was about. She answered him: "I don't understand Russian." Yuri translated her reply to Bedkin, who seemed satisfied and returned to his plate, to which he had added another helping of pasta.

"Do you accept my apology?"

"Not you! My own countrymen. They know English most of them much better than they know Russian. They think English is collection of cheap idioms, and the Russian they speak makes it clear why." Yuri pushed away his plate and drank off a glass of wine in a single swallow. "I feel better. Now, Greta Engel, without mentioning my book if you please, tell me about this Columbia."

"It's not a person. Maybe a thing, but not a person"—she

laughed—"It is a great university. One of the best. The extension college for adults—not young people—has a seminar in Russian literature. The professor, a bright young light who has been to Moscow a half-dozen times, teaches it. He's very original, that guy. I met him once at a party. Simonson. Peter Simonson. Chupkov told me he was delighted to have you. He admires a poem of yours, Chupkov said. One called 'Winter Ride.'" (Yuri saw the poem before his eyes. A short poem of three quatrains, intricately rhymed. He saw the poem, read it, and smiled, for he remembered the night when he wrote it, after returning late to Moscow from the country a week after he had met Irina Alexandrovna. Those were the days when Yuri still thought he could see something in the deep pools of Irina's eyes, something more than the quagmire he later discovered.)

"Good. I want to read before adults. They think better. But who translates?"

"That's arranged, too. You met him at the press conference. Roger Bateson. He'll translate side by side. You read, hand him the poem, and he'll do a prose rendering at sight. He's very good with Russian."

"Roger Bateson? Yes, the man with face of woodsman. Good face. I hope he understands poetry."

"What are you going to say?"

"When?"

"Now. In half an hour. It's ten to two."

"Oh, my God. I forgotten. Good God. I forgotten totally. Out of my mind. Oh, God. I have to speak."

Yuri's panic fell upon him like an avalanche. He stood up from the table and began to pace about near the cloakroom, forgetting the others, the restaurant, most certainly the check, which Greta Engel once more paid. They rushed out into the street, entered the hotel, and joined the swirl mounting the stairwell to the elevators. They reached the auditorium not a minute too soon. The room was filled. Every seat taken. At the center of the dais, which was no more than a series of tables unified by an improbable blue baize, two microphones arched like swans above a stubby lectern and recording equipment purred mindlessly. Yuri Maximovich was instructed by Greta Engel to pass behind the notables to the empty seat two chairs away from the microphones. His head spun slightly and his anxiety, diffused by the wine, gave him a light-headedness and abandon to which he later ascribed the astonishing remarks which he delivered in halting English.

From the journal of Yuri Maximovich Isakovsky
January 21, 1972

Why was it necessary to take me by surprise? It would have been easy for Comrade Bassinova to have told me that the Congress expected a few words from the exceptional Russian delegate. I would have had my moment of fright a week ago. It would have passed, one fright among so many. But such personal considerations cannot be expected, I suppose.

We are all, as Kolokolov stated so succinctly, little more than workers, ordinary workers with a remarkable skill—not different in quality than bears riding bicycles or acrobats tumbling on the high wire. Poets are not special. No one is special. I wish I could learn that. It is a lesson I was never taught. My parents taught me precisely the opposite, but they were old parents from another time. They insisted imprudently that I was unusual. They had no idea in what my unusualness consisted. It was little more than the vague outline of hope, that I would present history with some legacy that would bear the name of Isakovsky.

My parents did not, I'm afraid, understand history. They did not know that history is only a deposit of volcanic ash. Once erupted, once the fires and fumes of the cataclysm have dramatized the dark night with the figurations of hell, they settle by daylight into gray ash covering all, withering and burning away all that lives. I am (and I accept it) "an historical incident." At least (and in this I congratulate my good fortune) I am not an accident. My birth and the birth of any Marxist-Leninist is not simply an accident, interchangeable without distinction with other accidents, but my life, it appears, will never rise to the level of an event. It will remain only an incident, a tenacious blade of grass covered with the desiccating ash of history.

. . .

The program chairman, his jacket unbuttoned because it could not possibly be closed, was completing his introduction of Yuri Maximovich. "It is a pleasure, for the first time in many years, to welcome a Soviet delegate to our deliberations. He has promised, I am told, to say something interesting about the mythopoeic foundations of Soviet folk literature. May I introduce to you the distinguished editor of *The People's Voice* and a notable"—he examined Yuri at this juncture, and observing his tensed face and black hair protected by the overhead lighting from the revelation of its thinning gray—"younger poet, Mr. Yuri Maximovich Isakovsky."

Yuri stood up and opened his mouth. He was about to speak from where he stood. The program chairman smiled condescendingly, and taking Yuri's arm, led him the few steps to the lectern. Yuri adjusted the swans. His hands trembled; he hid one in his jacket pocket and placed the other upon the rim of the lectern. He did not feel protected. He was so visible, most of him apparent above the small lecture desk. The lights glared. His forehead glistened with little bubbles of perspiration, and while someone kneeled down in the center aisle to snap his photograph, he dabbed at his unease with a handkerchief. There had been applause. It began slowly in the front rows and swelled. Yuri did not seem formidable. No one expected much, but were at least hopeful that the talk would avoid Soviet-American tensions, world peace, and Vietnam. The applause was therefore louder and longer than would otherwise have been normal. The applause could not be ascribed to American politeness because Americans did not dominate the Congress. There were many foreigners, many foreigners of white and light and dark skin who were not in awe of the Russian presence. In all events, after a minute or more the applause ended, and Yuri Maximovich, who could quite easily have raised his hand to end the applause earlier, was now obliged to speak. His mind hummed with confusions, for there were now too many things he wished to say.

"Eh, ladies, gentlemen, chairman, I will try to speak short and clear. I am afraid I will quickly use up the several thousand words of English I know. Eh? Well. So let me try to say something very short and, with hope, clear and to point.

"I learn one new word today from chairman. *Mytho*, how you say, *poesis*. This word from two ancient Greek words. Ancient Greeks have no special word for story, execept maybe *historia*. But history story different from story story. Story story in Greek is *mythos*. *Poesis* you think only poetry? But truth is, *poesis* comes from God. The God, he speak poetry, and when, I guess, eh? well, I guess when God speak poetry, he tell story. So *mytho-poesis* means story from God.

"I come to my magazine, *The People's Voice*, because I was sent. I had written a little article about ancient tribe in South Russia, called Khazar. These Khazari made up their mind to become Jewish people because one day their sick king heard God speaking. I figured out some connection link between Jew folk tune in mountains of south Russia and some early-made songs of Muslim believers. In other words, I imagined that my Khazari were the link between Jew believers and Muslim believers. That's how I became musicologist. Truth, I think, well, truth is, I think I was wrong. My little essay nonsense. But I got job at *The People's Voice* because the editor before had gone away.

"Now, eh? well, yes, I am certain most you people maybe, maybe no, believe in God who tells stories. I do, yes. Yes! God not gone away, as my people think and yours think. He only has gone back to childhood of mankind, when Greek people think up *mythos* and *poesis*. God stranger because he sings and our times do not sing, only *study* song. You all—students of singing, but I doubt you sing. You play records of childhood mankind singing and think you know song? Eh? Well. Let me tell you. Not possible at all! Not at all! No song without singing. No song without singers. No God without people know how to hear music, which is different, I think, yes? well, from sitting down with book learning. First come God singing song. Then come man making story out of song. That way we get *mythopoesis*.

"So you see (my last words now), what gives me joy is what my old friend, Yasha Isaievich Tyutychev, greatest Russian walking encyclopedia and treasure box of songs said to me last week—yes, last week, in Peredelkino, where I have little cottage—'Let the big ones listen for thunder in heavens. We know, Yuri Maximovich, that when God speaks stories, he comes up from the earth.' That's where I keep my ear, to the ground, even to the underground, where we can hear God singing stories. Yes? It's true! That's enough. Thank you."

Yuri Maximovich took a step back from the lecturn and blinked. He had gotten through it, and in English even. He had difficulty recollecting what he said, because having spoken in a foreign tongue, the only words he remembered were the last. The tone of his remarks he felt, however, to have been stiff and laden. Applause and whistling. What had produced such an effect? His remarks were too short and schematic to have stunned an audience by their strenuous logic or their impressive scholarship.

From the journal of Yuri Maximovich Isakovsky
January 21, 1972

When a serious man uses the name of the deity—not only mentions that awesome nomenclature, so different in every language, but underscores his mention by a personal confession of belief—it is guaranteed to thrill. Chupkov assumed that I did this purposely, that I willfully manipulated the Godhead in order to produce excitement and pleasure. I must deny that. I wouldn't know how. I explained to him that I am wholly without those gifts of personality. Ilia Alexandrovich could use the name of God or the name of a common weed and produce such electric shock, but not I. He would know how to drop his voice and force us to strain or how to carry a word upwards on the end of a pointing finger or how to lose us in the scratching of his scalp. He knows. He does it magnificently. He has oratory and rhetoric. I? I have no such gifts. I couldn't even hold Irina Alexandrovna's attention. How could I possibly trick an audience of intelligent people, let alone a carefully selected and trained audience of scientists?

The truth is that most of those people, like me, are believers who don't dare speak of it. In our country it's almost a crime for old people and peasants to believe in God, but certainly a crime for an editor of an important Soviet journal. Oh, yes, to that charge, I would plead absolutely guilty. I am guilty of belief. But the amusing thing is that it is also a crime in this country, punishable not by loss of job and income, but by contempt. These people, not unlike ourselves, think such beliefs as all right for children, ladies, and high-strung mental cases, but not for scientists and intellectuals. He—that is, the God—confuses matters. Why, they ask, bring him into it? Believe, if you want, but don't let it get in the way of solid thinking, hard work, clearheadedness, etc., etc. And so—and this is what I imagine happened—when a delegate from the Soviet Union, officially an atheist state, interprets the meaning of a complicated word like mythopoesis as signifying the presence of hoary, archaic belief, it is nothing short of breath-taking, "astounding," as one of the scholars said, or "inspiring," as the art teacher had said. I was inspiring. I breathed spirit into the meetings. I did my own special kind of work, which should have made Chupkov proud of me. But instead, unfortunately, I misjudged my countrymen again. I only tried to make the work of a Soviet editor and Soviet poet creditable to foreigners, who don't appreciate that we are as marvelously various and imaginative and forthright as they are. It didn't work. That's too bad.

Greta Engel reached Yuri Maximovich almost immediately after the meeting ended two hours later. There were several long and splendid papers, one by a Nigerian scholar who had spoken learnedly and intimately of the creation hymns of the Yoruba, his scarification marks glistening and bobbing under the lights. When the meeting was adjourned to make ready for the event of the evening, when a panel of distinguished French scholars was to discuss the implications of structuralism for the interpretation of formulaic tropes in primitive music, spontaneous applause broke out again as Yuri Maximovich stood up to shake hands with the program chairman. It was not victory by popular acclaim. Indeed, not more than a score of people in the front rows rose and applauded as Yuri backed away from the dais, but clearly he had won their approval.

"I'm Miss Janes from the Art Department of the Rhode Island School of Design, Mister Isakovsky, and I wanted just to say, only to you, you were inspiring." Miss Janes said the last, whispering with excitement, directly into Yuri's ear. A tall, thin scholar, his nose gripped by a gold pince-nez, had added "astounding" to the praise, although he called the word over his shoulder as he passed Yuri on the way to an exit door. It was unclear in what his astonishment consisted. A young man with an intense jaw and grinding teeth took Yuri's hand and shook it vigorously. "You really are a poet, sir. That was sure a fine speech, a poet's speech." He disappeared before Yuri could thank him. There were others and there were questions: the historicity of the Khazars interested one, the bibliographic reference to his paper on the musical traditions another, and a query about Yuri's etymological interpretation that perhaps invalidated the supposition of his remarks, but by and large the tone of the greeters—there must have been more than a dozen—was one of praise and excitement. *The New York Times*, the next morning, reported Yuri's talk at length in its dispatch on the congress, and the religion editor of the same paper, a Mr. Spiegel, wanted to interview Yuri about his religious views, an opportunity which Yuri thought prudent to decline. He had decided after Greta Engel's observations and an angered telephone call from Chupkov when he returned to the hotel that he had made enough trouble for one day.

"You were astonishing, Yuri, just astonishing."

"So. You are the second person to say that. I guess it compliment. So thank you. But tell me, why astonishing? Astonishing mean something like frightening, no?"

Greta Engel considered this and then, astonished, admitted the implication. "Yes, you were rather frightening. The passion and all. I didn't think you had all that in you."

"So. What you know about me? Nothing. Absolutely *gar nichts*." Yuri replied, the words more harsh than his feelings.

"That's the point. When do I begin to learn?"

"To learn about me? But why you want all this *informatzia*? Why? For an article, you say, but when you write article and why you write article?" Yuri Maximovich, flushed perhaps from his success, had not noticed that Bedkin was standing behind him, considerably agitated and annoyed.

Greta Engel did not reply to this question. Had she done so, had Yuri Maximovich, flushed and exhilarated by his little triumph, pressed beyond the normal bounds which uncertainty and politeness usually conferred upon his social manners, he might have been more circumspect with that intrusive young woman. Unfortunately he did not compel her reply. He was immediately distracted by the absence of Vovka Bedkin, who had apparently disappeared. Yuri Maximovich began to look about for him. Greta Engel unwillingly joined his search. For some reason Yuri Maximovich felt protective of his incapacitated and somewhat dull-witted little spy.

"What's become of Vovka?" he said to Greta.

"So that's his name. You never introduced him and I didn't want to know. He seemed so menacing."

"Vovka, a menace?" Yuri laughed. "No, no. Poor Vovka just crippled everywhere, from head to foot."

They left the auditorium and wandered through the exhibits, but Vovka Bedkin had disappeared. Later, after Yuri Maximovich had returned to his hotel room, the telephone rang.

"Yes?"

"Chupkov here. You were ridiculous and disgraceful this afternoon. All this talk about gods and myths. What do you think we're running in the Soviet Union, a mumbo-jumbo state like Tanzania?"

"I regret your impression, Comrade. I thought I was quite moving. I almost cried, you see."

That was certainly true. Yuri had been carried away.

"Be sure you don't go on the same way when you read on Wednesday afternoon."

"Is that settled?"

"Yes. Professor Simonson's seminar on Russian literature at Columbia University."

"Then she was right," Yuri exclaimed without thinking.

"Who?" Chupkov asked, a hectoring note all too evident in his voice. "Who knows?"

"A young woman I met. Greta Engel."

"Oh, that young woman. In any event, mind you read well, extemporize little, and do your extra work properly."

3. A Piece of Extra Work

Yuri Maximovich had not really thought very much, until Chupkov's mention of it, about "the extra work." It was folded in an envelope among his documents. The envelope was plain and without distinguishing insignia or watermarks. Ordinary paper, the kind one could buy at the shop where notepaper could be purchased near Pushkin Square. The envelope was sealed, however, a fact which might have made an inquisitor suspicious, but it contained only a poem, a short poem. Chupkov's emphatic mention of "the extra work" recalled to consciousness what had lain there, unexamined but annoying, ever since he left Moscow. He had had little time to consider his extra employment during the two days that remained to him after his charge by Colonel Bobov. He hadn't mentioned it to Yasha Tyutychev, although he realized that somehow his reunion with that remarkable old man was intimately connected to the "poem." Tyutychev was related to Bobov, as undoubtedly heaven was connected to hell, if not by an elaborate chute and trap door, then by way of antipodal contrast, more a conceit of the mind than a literal passageway to the underworld. The point is that in refusing to reflect upon his extra work, Yuri Maximovich was, by that very fact, thinking about it constantly. The refusal had already been evident a half-dozen times—each time, in fact, that he had been obliged to present his documents or examine his itinerary or produce money—for he opened the little pouch which contained those valuables and saw there among other papers the sealed envelope. At first, in the hours after his meeting with Bobov, he had determined to read the poem straightaway, and having accepted its existence, to contend with it merely as another manuscript (an oddity if indeed it was odd, an eccentric expression if indeed it proved eccentric), merely inserting it, reading speedily through the text, and then passing on without comment to a poem of his own authorship. In that way, he felt, having opened the envelope in secret (in the automobile which would take him to his reading or in the lavatory beforehand) and shuffled the poem in among the pages of his own selection, he would come upon it unawares, read it, and be done with the matter. Yuri Maximovich would have liked to have tricked himself into the reading of the poem as innocently as he felt threatened into accepting the charge in the first place.

The resolve to be casual and informal about the little bit of spy work he had been ordered to perform had been thoroughly rationalized. He knew perfectly well that part of the due any privileged Soviet citizen was expected to render to his country was to be on hand to do assorted bits of work whenever his skills or the occasion warranted. The most honored artists of his country were often called upon by the KGB to entertain or recreate foreign visitors being softened to entrapment. It was even known that once in a while the enormously famous—Plesetskaya, for instance—would dance at some embassy party merely to ensure that a certain Soviet agent should be more favorably regarded by a foreign emissary. It could not be that Plesetskaya's toes would warp from guilt or a leap fail in midair for that fact. Artists were innocents and the State protected innocents, but also used them. "Dance a bit for us" might be the appeal, and cheered by the appreciation and of course remunerated with a little something extra for the service, the arms flowed, the legs flexed, the toes went on point. Nothing could be more innocent, almost gracious, if one thinks about it. But then Yuri Maximovich had no such accommodating gift. His was not an intelligent toe or a bow-hand stroking some masterpiece of another century. The real problem lay in the bowels of the art itself.

Yuri Maximovich was a poet. It doesn't matter terribly much that he wasn't a major poet or a productive poet or a poet with a following. He wasn't excused by any of those deficiencies from recognizing that poetry was—he had said it himself that very afternoon—a god speaking from the earth. Whether he was at the top, like Kolokolov, or very near the bottom of the stepladder was irrelevant. It is no wonder that after Chupkov's reprimand and reminder, he lost his appetite that Saturday night. He had risen up the day before to address his colleagues as a musicologist and had sat down crowned as a poet, honored as having made poetry before them. The choices had begun to narrow, and it became apparent that he would have to examine the piece of extra work much more carefully than he had planned.

It was already quite dark. The winter sun had set long ago, while the meetings at the Hilton were still in progress. There was time enough for his visitor to have traveled the considerable distance which he had come after the conclusion of the Sabbath to visit with him. But Yuri Maximovich was otherwise preoccupied when he heard the knock on his door. He opened it to a considerable surprise. An old man bent like a blasted olive tree, his hands clasped over the silver head of a fine Malacca cane, hobbled into the room, assisted by a young boy not over nine or ten, whose face, dominated by hazel eyes, was partially covered by untrimmed earlocks which fell in natural curls down his cheeks. The old man was dressed as Yuri remembered from his Kievan boyhood, in white stockings, silver buckled shoes, a long black silk coat. The old man was led by the boy to the only soft chair in the room, and without speaking, he motioned to Yuri to take the hard-backed desk chair and draw it close to him. Before he seated himself he drew off his fur hat with the velvet crown, handed it to the boy, and sat back in the chair to examine Yuri.

"So, my old friend," the white-bearded patriarch began in Russian.

"You know me?" Yuri asked with amazement.

"And you know me, for a certainty. We are like brothers meeting after many years, like Joseph reunited with his brothers, although neither you nor I have done harm to each other. Although I should say it was because of what I did for him, your dead father, that I disappeared."

Yuri Maximovich was overwhelmed. He jumped up from the seat and came over to the old man, bent down and kissed his crippled hand. Of course it was the same man, the rabbi who had buried his father, the same Mendel Iskovitz.

"You do remember me. I knew you would. I told the Rebbe you would remember me. I am grateful for that. It would have been very hard for me—I am so old—to have undertaken to convince you if you had chosen to forget. But you didn't. Jews have long memories."

"But here, what are you doing here? In New York, in the United States? What are you doing?"

"A long story. A short story. I will give you the short story. They took me away and when I returned, I left."

"But how? How did you get out? How?"

"You don't need to know. The point is that I escaped, shall we say? I got out, but not before I had spent eight years out in that wilderness. Eight years."

"Tell me, Reb Mendel. Have you ever heard of Tyutychev, Yasha Isaievich Tyutychev?"

"Of course, he's one of us. That great and marvelous old bluster of a Jew. Tyutychev. He wasn't in my camp, but he was in one a dozen miles away. He came later, when my term was almost up, but I had known of him from Kiev. He was one of Rappoport's disciples. He persevered after Rappoport went away from us. Are you a friend of Tyutychev?"

"Yes. He's living in my apartment while I'm here. We've adopted each other."

"But then you plan to go back?"

"Yes."

"Why?"

"It is my home."

"Jews have no home there. We are being destroyed there."

Yuri Maximovich hadn't expected this. Greta Engel had begun the inquiry, but he had turned aside her insinuations. Reb Mendel, however, was no young girl with a project.

"But what about the others?" Yuri asked. Reb Mendel did not understand his allusion. Actually Yuri Maximovich was continuing the argument he had had with Greta Engel in the cafeteria. "The others like me, with half minds—half Jew, half Russian. We call Russia our home, even if it's an ungrateful house which starves and beats us. It's still a home. One loves a mother and father even if they beat you."

"Beating's one thing, Yuri Maximovich. Killing's another. They do more than beat us. They're out to kill us."

"So you want me to flee the killers."

"I don't want anything from you. I'm asking you to consider alternatives. You are given a breather from the Russian claustrophobia, a day outside the steaming bathhouse, and you have to use it, you have to decide whether you intend to return and continue to sweat out your life's blood or live a full Jew's life outside the furnace."

"But, you see, Reb Mendel, there's one other thing. I'm also a Russian poet. I write in that language. I think in that language. It's my tongue. If I sweat, yes, if I sweat, my tongue pants in Russian."

"I understand. That's why I never forgot my Yiddish and always study and write in Hebrew. Oh, my Russian is fine for innkeepers and tradesmen, but I decided when I was a little boy in the last century that if I wanted to keep my freedom—even though I lived under the Russians—I had better keep another language as a secret vault where no one but I knew the combination. It's worked. It didn't matter to me whether they threw me in jail or sent me to the East or brought me back and helped me get away (yes, I was helped to get away by one of them), all they had was my body to play with, but my language, where all the thought worked itself out, was foreign to them. I kept my language out of their prison. But you, you're trapped by them. The only way Jews like you try to get away without a language is by changing religions. That you see is both sad and a betrayal. What began in ignorance and dereliction ends in deceit." Reb Mendel was closer to his life than he imagined. He had converted and he had become a poet in order to escape, but it proved to be no escape, only a burrowing deeper into the Russian bowel. The conversion was a stupidity, but the old trunk with the skeletons of the poets, that was something else.

"So what do you want of me?"

"I want nothing of you. You are free to find your life. You are free to lose it. That is one freedom that is guaranteed in Russia. No. What I think you should do is merely consider whether it is worth the price to return and quite possibly be destroyed or to remain behind and learn to become a free Jew."

The old rabbi, he was more than eighty, Yuri calculated, lifted himself out of the sofa, the young boy helping him to rise. "My great-grandson, would you believe, Yuri Maximovich? A great-grandson. My granddaughter's husband, I'm afraid, has not been successful in leaving that wretched homeland of yours. He was shot several years ago. But others survive and the work goes on and our pride and tenacity is undiminished." Reb Mendel moved slowly to the door, looked about quietly, and bowed his head to Yuri Maximovich; as the latter came forward to take his hand, the old man reached into the pocket of his frock coat and withdrew a card on which he had printed his name and a telephone number, and handed it to Yuri. "If you should decide to speak with me. Otherwise, I bid you goodbye. Undoubtedly I will be dead by the time you return to this country, if you return, if you ever leave that country again. But however fortune decides, I give you my blessing and wish you peace."

If one had doubts about the ever-narrowing whorls of time, curious ellipses which shave away the irrelevances of a man's life and confine its significance to fewer and fewer events, it could not be doubted after the visit of Reb Mendel Iskovitz.

What an extraordinary confluence of fortune, from the voice of Comrade Bassinova less than a week ago to the nighttime manifestation of Kievan shades in New York City. But it remained unclear, certainly unspoken, why the old rabbi had taken the trouble to visit him. He had really told him nothing or offered him anything or provided him even with an explanation. He had merely appeared on the arm of a young lad and described certain alternatives in the most general and ambiguous terms. It was almost as though Reb Mendel already knew that it was pointless to suggest to Yuri Maximovich that he defect. He hadn't really argued that point. He spoke of being a free Jew, which meant little more than granting Jews the privilege of an elective bondage, for that was the way Yuri remembered it from his father's house. His mother never tired of telling him how difficult it was to be a Jew, and his father, a free thinker who had no capacity for thought, would discourse on occasion, usually at the conclusion of their Passover feast, upon the yoke of the commandments and the bondage of the Kingdom of God and would advise his son (for their daughter never listened at all) that it was best to be without observance and ritual, but that he should never forget he was Jewish because if he did forget, the world would be sure to remind him with a kick in the behind. Yuri had found that piece of advice to be true. Even Father Arkadi Ignatiev had called Yuri a thankless Jew when he threw him out of the monastery after his baptism. But the real turn in the conversation had been Yuri's declaration of fidelity to the Russian language. Even if, as Reb Mendel suggested, it was a perilous betrothal—that romance with a language—there was no possibility of taking a new and younger bride. Of course, he could learn Hebrew and master his forgotten Yiddish, but it would be indecent, like David taking the Shunammite maiden. He would never be able to master it, no more than David could his lissome bedwarmer. A language is always young in a new mouth, but not all mouths have the light tongue and the adventurous palate to enjoy it. The older one grows, the more hopeless the enterprise, and Yuri was fifty-four. He might succeed in saving his soul (if the Jewish religion bothered with that), but he would never be able to write a new poem.

And the more he considered his life the more he was convinced, as all this telling is intended to make clear, that poetry was rather more than the attitudes of poets. Poetry possessed for Yuri Maximovich a kind of durable essence, a *prima materia* which the ancients were always hunting to find and which finally, elusive and indefinite, was identical with the requirement of truth. Clearly not abstract or theoretical truth, not truth about general things and empyrean realms, but truth which is immediately to hand. That's why his favorite poets—the ones who shaped his imagination in the Russian language—always began their best poems examining something very definite and there, right in front of their noses, like a horseshoe, a willow tree, a twisted nail, or a glassful of gritty wine. Not simply the quotidian, for that carries with it the task of bearing boredom and supporting its reality, but the diurnal, which suggests a rhythm not at all boring, one which pulses through everything. Hard as it was in his country to concentrate on such little rhythms when the nation was constantly engaged in large and world-shaking enterprise, he took the little rhythm to be the poet's truth. It was, moreover, the little rhythm which for so many years had eluded him and made his poetry trivial and impersonal.

It pleased Yuri Maximovich that no one had come to his room. He hadn't seen Ilia Alexandrovich since the evening before, and Vovka Bedkin had gone, he concluded, to his room after the congress ended its second day's deliberations; even Greta Engel, whom he had half hoped would renew her invitation for dinner that evening, had apparently made other plans. He was left to himself on a Saturday night in New York City. The following days would be busy enough, busy enough. Sunday at the congress and in the evening at the testimonial dinner for the grand poet, and Monday and Tuesday the work of the congress, which he had begun to enjoy, and Wednesday his reading. Thursday morning he would leave. For the moment he had no doubt of that. None at all. Of course, he had to decide what poems he would read to Professor Simonson's seminar. He would give Saturday evening to that, and then of course there was "the extra work."

From the journal of Yuri Maximovich Isakovsky
January 22, 1972

Outside of our country there is a vast body of writings that absolutely thrill Westerners in which the anonymity of the prisoner, the vagueness of the charges, the impersonality of the system are presented with such deadpan exactness that a shiver of terror becomes the appropriate expression of literary triumph. Those writers over there seem to think that unless everyone is given a name and a condition and charges are specific and well documented (the rules of evidence, they say) the world collapses into frothy hysteria. I know this is not so. Whatever the grand metaphysical, theological, or aesthetic constructions which others elevate to interpret a world in which people are known by letters of the alphabet and crime consists in breathing, I am aware that in my country people are letters of the alphabet and often the greatest crime is breathing.

How shall I deal with this poem—so-called—of Colonel Bobov? Our country is not interested in acts. No one commits acts against the state. There hasn't been an act against our state in a very long time. Not at all. Any act that is done against our state couldn't be harmful. How could a single person do a harmful act, and why would anyone do such a thing? Counterrevolution (as the phrase has it) or anti-Soviet behavior or the expression of sentiments or feelings which are against the State really has a different spirit behind it. Only Westerners think about acts and work out complicated systems for evaluating good and bad actions, right and wrong actions, calibrating them on a scale from 1 to 10, from moderately pleasant to positively saintly around the top, and then down again to the demonic. My Russia, my Soviet Russia legislates against interior conditions that are by definition vague. It worries about states of being, habits of mind, conditions of emotion, timbres of feelings, resonations of language. It goes to the heart of man. My Russia arrests actions before they become actions. And that's where I'm caught, dead to rights. I assume my guilt, or rather (which is the way I understand this acute perception of mine), I recognize that my guilt will be revealed ever so slowly, emerging out of the system of my nature until it is the manifest reality of what was present, unrecognized, all along. In other words, if I were to be arrested for what I do, I am guilty. Ipso facto. The guilt was in my bones long before I was aware of it. That's why poets are all dangerous. Every poet is guilty before he says a word. If he weren't guilty of breathing against the order of things, why would he love nature (nature can't do anyone any good—it's only there, nature is, and utterly useless to us unless you trap her, strip her of her valuables, and make them work for us humans) or ancient and dead gods (ugh! how revolting to think that I would invoke Gaea on her knees when everyone knows Gaea and Demeter and all the rest of the earth gods and spirits don't exist except in the poet's worthless imagination) or spend his time celebrating love or intimacy or independence (when it is indubitable that such things are perfectly all right in the bedroom or by the fireside, if one has earned one's rest by hard work, but certainly have no place on good imported paper or even on commonplace wood pulp)?

The opening of the sealed envelope was undertaken with ritual care. The end of the envelope was cut with a little pair of scissors, and a half-inch of paper deposited in the wastebasket, the envelope expanded with a blast of air, the folded paper withdrawn with pincered thumb and index, and at last unfolded. The poem was typed. Fourteen lines, three stanzas, an opening fortissimo and a concluding whisper. Yuri Maximovich stared at the words, reading them first as the poem of another, a casual poet who drops a page or two in your mailbox and asks for an opinion, or like the young poets up from the provinces who used to accost Mandelstam in the park and ask for a reading. The words before him were not his own. They were words delivered in a sequence and order, a typographic arrangement which means "poem" to nonpoets. (Take any ordinary piece of paper, center the pen or adjust the margin release, and begin to compose straight down—like the poem of Apollinaire in wich the letters of the words descend like streaks of rain upon the page, appropriately entitled "*Il pleut*"

—except that here, nonpoet, not letters but whole words are arranged in little sequences which signify poem, poetic, poetical.)

The cipher machine, genius of memory, storage bank of the system, is still a child when it comes to poetry—not even a child (Rimbaud was a child), but a preliterate, an idiot with habituated intentions. The cipher, given the units of information and the code of the alphabet, can devise a sequence of imagery which, loosely considered, constitutes a poem. Mandelstam would send away the accosting poet in the park with instructions to continue his engineering studies and leave poetry alone. For poets like Mandelstam, poetry was a beleaguered castle, not requiring additional manpower from the countryside, but better training and greater devotion from those already raised up at the manor table. It was preferable that the castle fall, overwhelmed by the odds of the world, than be subverted by innocents and rude soldiers with blunted broadswords.

"The dry earth / Strangled with dust."

The opening words told the story. Quite passable, really. Passable, just passable. Yuri could read them, but he would choke up; indeed, he would strangle on the silt of language which filmed the page before him. Before he knew it, inconsiderate of the sensibilities of the preliterate cipher machine and its walleyed programmer slotting cards into its mouth, Yuri Maximovich had begun to work. The poem was a mangle, but by the time its lines had passed through his brain—a brain, a conjunction of tubes and micro-miniaturized synapses and cortical equipment—the poem about the strangulation of the earth before the "October morning" of the revolution had been transformed. "If there's a message there, they'll get it, but now it's a poem, not a machine." That's precisely what Yuri said to himself about ten-thirty that Saturday night as he put the new manuscript back into the envelope of Colonel Bobov.

Strangely exhilarated, again light-headed (from hunger perhaps), he went immediately to the door when he heard the knock. It was Vovka Bedkin, weeping copiously, his jacket torn, his face dirty, a thin trickle of blood running from one nostril. "I have been attacked. Hooligans. Dirty, rotten fascist hooligans attacked me and took my money and my wrist watch."

Yuri Maximovich was sympathetic. He couldn't imagine why, but he was undeniably sympathetic. The man was in pain, and wretched person though he was, all things considered, Yuri considered pain as pain, not as retribution. Yuri helped Bedkin into the room and led him to the bed. He knew every reason for laughing at Bedkin's condition, hobbling now from his wounds, dragging his leg like a badly sewn appendage, but he was unable to feel either divine justice or perverse pleasure at Bedkin's misery.

"I hurt. I ache. My nose is a bloody sausage. Damn city," Bedkin moaned.

Yuri had gone to the bathroom and returned with a rag soaked with warm water. Bedkin fell down upon the bed, his legs no longer touching the rug, a middle-aged baby blubbering from his wounds. Yuri dabbed his nose until the blood stopped. Only a swollen nostril remained behind. He wasn't badly hurt, not badly hurt at all, but he needed some comforting, so Yuri took him down into the street and across from the hotel to a bar for a cognac and a sandwich. The bar was dark and cavernous; a flickering purple neon light advocating a beer and a life-size cutout of a Rheingold maiden were virtually its only decorations. A jukebox illuminated like a pleasure ship hung outside the limits of the booths and tables where a dozen—no, fourteen serious drinkers were at work organizing their Sunday hangovers.

The two seated themselves in a secluded booth in the rear and ordered liverwurst sandwiches and cognac. When they arrived, Bedkin steadied his glass with both hands, lifted the tumbler to his mouth, and swallowed. After a second drink he felt better, and Yuri asked, "How did it happen? What became of you? If you had stuck with me as you said you would, it might not have happened. No?"

Vovka Bedkin squinted at him. Another thought had obviously presented itself, and he was coping with it. Vovka Bedkin was the kind of person who could sustain only one thought at a time: the former occupant of his brain had to be shunted to a siding before the express movement of a new idea could be signaled through. Yuri had asked a question with subparts and contingent unities, and Vovka Bedkin was obliged to clear his head of any other distraction.

"Which first?" Vovka replied, smiling uncertainly.

"What which?"

"Your questions. Which first? The how or the why?"

"Vovka, old man, it doesn't matter a bit to me. I'm not being inquisitive. You can tell me what you want or nothing at all. I'm quite content to sit and say nothing."

"Yes?" Bedkin looked up at Yuri Maximovich, his eyes squinting again, as though by narrowing the field of his eyes, he could guarantee concentration. "Well, I believe you."

"What's that?" Yuri was watching a woman at the bar, whose flowered hat had fallen to one side of her face, composing a ridiculous counterpoint to her drained and empty face. "What? You believe what?"

"That you're not being inquisitive."

"Listen, Bedkin, let me be clear about one thing. I'm not a spy." He finished the sentence and shivered. "No. I'm not a spy," he repeated. "I have no interest in what you do. I am upset that you are hurt. I am sorry that you were attacked and robbed. But that's the end of my curiosity."

"I'm not going back, Comrade. No!" Vovka spoke without looking at Yuri Maximovich, then drank off the remains of his cognac, motioned to the bartender for another, and bit into his sandwich.

"Where?"

"Over there," Vovka motioned vaguely to the street.

"To the hotel?"

"No. You know what I mean. You're an intellectual."

"What's that to do with anything? Intelligentsia, anyway. Not an intellectual."

"What I mean is, you understand serious things."

"Yes?"

"That is to say, I don't have to be more specific."

"About what?" Yuri was hardly paying attention. He had begun to think about the extra piece of work again, no longer extra, but enlarged and amended.

"About not returning."

It became clear. Like a minesweeper that he remembered seeing in the harbor of Odessa going through its maneuvers in a choppy sea, zigzagging at perilous angles, he realized that Bedkin had been communicating, saying the most precarious and compromising of things in a language that skirted clarity and directness without overturning into ambiguity. Bedkin was telling him that he wasn't returning to Russia.

"I can't listen to this, Bedkin." Yuri was afraid. The man opposite him was a flunky of Internal Security. He could be telling the truth, but why to him? A nobody in the machinery of the State. Or he could have been put up to it. "Sound out Isakovsky, see if he's planning to jump ship," he might have been told. "So am I, old Bedkin," he might be expected to reply, trusting the gimpy fool of a spy, and then he would have to watch out—the speeding car, the abduction, the drugged return to Moscow. It was so improbable. It was improbable. Why the confession to him? "I can't listen to this, Bedkin. I have to tell Chupkov. I'm obliged to tell Chupkov." Yuri rose from his seat as if to slide out and go promptly to the telephone as Chupkov had instructed. Perhaps that was the right maneuver. If he began to laugh, Yuri would know he had been put up to it, and having planted the subversion and waited for it to take root, had changed his mind. Bedkin was, after all, an incompetent, and so was he, Yuri concluded. Quite right, he thought, for them to set Bedkin at his heels. But precisely the opposite occurred. No sooner had Yuri stood up and begun to slide out of the booth, Bedkin whispered with terror.

"Don't. Please, God, don't. Don't turn me in. Don't. They'll kill me for sure."

"You're serious, aren't you?"

"I have to be. It's my only chance of having a life."

"You mean it. Bedkin means to defect."

"It's all about my leg. I've been promised an operation on my leg. They can fix it, don't you understand."

"Don't tell me any more. I don't want to hear it. No. Don't say another word."

"I have to tell you this. You're the only person I can tell it to. You told me about poetry. Don't you remember? You're the only person who ever told me something about poetry."

Oh, God, Yuri thought. How ridiculous. The idiot had taken his ironies and sarcasms for instruction. He had become his friend. How miserable. How mean and stupid.

"You understand me. You see that I'm more than a rotten little cripple, that I'm something more than that."

Yuri sat down again. It was hopeless. He had to listen, somehow, listen and not listen, answer without replying.

"The two men who beat me up and robbed me, kicked me in the side, right where the bone is off. That didn't hurt much, not more than usual. I'm always in pain. That's why I drink a lot sometimes—to ease the pain. They don't give me good jobs any more because I drink too much to ease the pain. Try to walk the way I do. Try to run, God forbid. Try to run. I tried to run away from those hooligans. I was like a car moving with a flat tire, clumpy-clump, ridiculous. I just stopped. They caught up with me and knocked me down and kicked me and called me words I didn't understand, but they were harsh and hissing words. Right then and there, lying on the pavement near the hotel, I made up my mind to accept the offer. I want to have my hip fixed. I want my legs to be legs, real legs, don't you see. Back there, they told me I could have an operation one day. Promised me after the Moysevich turn-in, but you know what happened to that one. Everyone got it in the neck and I got it both places, neck and hip. No hip operation. Everything's a reward or punishment back there. Turn in your quota, and get your packet, get your leg fixed. Fail, lose your buildings, go to jail, stay a cripple. I'm fifty-eight. I have time. I can do something here. Oh, yes, but get my leg fixed. That's first."

"What's to say?"

"Nothing. There's nothing to say. I have to do it. It's not really a defection. Not a betrayal. I'm always Russian, always.

I could never leave that behind, but I can't leave my leg behind. My leg has no socialist feeling. It's only pain."

An incontrovertible assertion, incontrovertible, and Yuri made no reply. Bedkin was drunk by now and the pain had passed. He had had a half-dozen cognacs, the bartender had appeared and disappeared with frequency, bringing a filled tumbler of brandy to replace the empty. If Bedkin was lying, if it was another one of Chupkov's manipulations and temptations, Yuri had not succumbed. Of course, Yuri was guilty by the complicity of hearing, but that couldn't matter.

Yuri Maximovich didn't continue the conversation. He didn't reply. Defecting the Soviet Union was not uncommon. Intellectuals, artists, anti-Communists, now Jewish intellectuals, Jewish artists, Jewish anti-Communists, non-Jewish intellectuals with Jewish friends, and cosmopolitans with one Jewish parent, poets without parents who read the poetry of Jews with parents, any and all mutants of *Homo Sovieticus* were begging for passports to leave, or having been given permission to visit abroad, dropped out of sight and turned up at the foreign office of some other county to renounce their citizenship, or hunger-struck, sat down in protest, wrote endless unanswered letters to members of the Praesidium asking to be let go, to be banished, to be exiled. It was not uncommon. Bedkins, however, were uncommon. Usually Bedkins didn't have the imagination to want other or differently than peasants anywhere. If they had roots they stayed put, down in the earth the roots stayed, even if they were withering from the soil up. But Yuri Maximovich? He had some reasons to leave—some reasons, but not a great many, not even as good reasons as Vovka Bedkin. He couldn't leave without a reason.

4. Relieving Oneself

From the journal of Yuri Maximovich Isakovsky
January 23, 1972
Kolokolov disapproved of my clothing. He disliked the disheveled appearance of my collar tips, their tendency to spread and shine, their capitulation to hard water and scrubbing. But I had no time to buy a new shirt. I had no wish to buy a new shirt. It never occurred to me in Moscow. It certainly never occurred to me during the first three days of my visit to New York. Shirts and collar tips were far from my mind. And scuffed shoes and bagging trousers and jackets whose pockets seemed weighted with stones. I did not have an appearance, since there was no one to whom I had ever wanted to appear. These seemings and appearances were totally irrelevant, but of a sudden they had become very important. I recognized people who cultivated street habits of observation, who lounged like drapery upon the sofas and benches of the Hilton, and others who became indistinguishable from the street lamps, their eyes shifting to the trajectories of moving heads and torsos. They observed appearances and dreamed the implication of clothing, the angles of hats, the friction of dresses, the hug of

trousers. To their appraisals, clothing was revelation, but I could not understand when Ilia Alexandrovich criticized my shirt. He knocked at my door and I opened it to his antelope jacket and his black silk tie, recumbent upon a field of sky-blue crepe de Chine. He was a magnificently elegant poet. Before I could manage my huzzah of congratulation, for I would have been pleased that Ilia would be splendor to American intellectuals, he snapped, "You can't wear that shirt." I looked down at my shirt. The workshirt which I had bought from the French itinerant I had soaked in perspiration during my talk. It was drying out in my bathroom. I had worn it into the shower the day before and washed both of us. I had only one other presentable shirt, a white cotton thing that was streaked and dingy. Yes. Admittedly unattractive. But so what? No one would have commented on it. They would have taken it in stride and it would have been hidden behind my no less unfashionable suit coat, whose pants had long ago been discarded. I was an unmatched poet. Ilia Alexandrovich was all match and contrast. He planned his effects, whereas I, alas, had no choice but to happen upon them. It was already six o'clock Sunday and Ilia was to make his entrance by six-thirty. There was no time to fiddle with my clothing. I explained to Ilia that we would be late, and a glance at his gold wrist watch confirmed my sense of time. I promised that I would keep my jacket buttoned, that no one would see my dubious shirt. He suggested that I try a shirt of his, but I pointed out to him that I was fifteen pounds heavier, that my girth would burst its buttons and that it was preferable to wear a closed shirt of an unpleasant hue than a new shirt flawed by absent buttons. Already I knew that I should have a precautionary pee, but Ilia stood over me, impatient to be off, undoubtedly annoyed that he had promised me a seat at his table. (During the afternoon while I was sitting with Greta Engel in the lobby—we had arranged to meet there and converse in public, for I had no wish to be further compromised by anyone—Ilia Alexandrovich had swept in, trailing his trench coat and what I took to be a young American poet behind him, and both disappeared into the elevator, but not before Ilia had appraised Greta Engel and observed to me that the head table was crowded. I would have let it pass. It didn't matter to me where I sat, since truth to tell and obviously, I could have done without the affair entirely, but Greta Engel had become my emissary and she replied immediately, "But, Mr. Kolokolov, you promised." Ilia had grunted with resignation, picked up his coat, and handed it to the young American poet, who had kept his distance from the encounter.) "I should pee. Do we have time?" "No. No more time. You had time for a clean shirt and you've used that up. Let's be off." I resolved to forget my bladder. Another foolish resolution!

The university was obviously not in the habit of organizing affairs of magnitude. An important academic institution whose reputation derived in part from the solicitude it had shown a generation earlier to refugee intellectuals, to whom it had offered its facilities, it was today, like many American universities, situated in a major metropolis, totally confused by the multiplicity of demands it was expected to satisfy—not merely to educate the young with vigor and discipline, but to provide diversion for restless adults, vocational guidance for youthful malcontents, and stimulation for the aging. It was therefore less a university than an intellectual agora, a species of marketplace where everyone was encouraged to mark the ostraka of approval or condemnation. Plato would have fared as badly at the hands of this constituency as he did at the hands of Athenian free men. The university was, if not sensitive to the confusions of its own identity and charter, enormously sensitive to the pulse of the times, quick to pick up on anything from classes in batiking and macramé to Ilia Alexandrovich Kolokolov.

Kolokolov was good public relations. He was, the administration had been told, a poet of great power and daring, an honest poet (that is, one who spoke his mind, whichever mind that happened to be at the moment), and he was sponsored in the English language, not alone by journeymen translators, but by many of the most admired American poets, those who traveled regularly to European literary conferences, enjoyed the confidence of the State Department and Central Intelligence Agency (and by implication, of the Senators and Congressmen who voted funds for adult education and vocational training), and always charged PEN for their junkets, presenting meticulously kept accounts of every zloty and drachma they had expended in the cause of literature. The university was quite delighted, therefore, with the suggestion of Anderson, Warfield, and Paris that it sponsor the dinner, and since Mr. Paris was on the Board of Trustees of the university, it was speedily arranged, the program announced, the invitations tendered. Indeed, many intellectuals and poets, those of slight or marginal reputation, begged for invitations and were denied. The crop was generous, the pick exceedingly careful. Not a bruised plum of literature was admitted; only ripe and full reputations were asked.

When Ilia Alexandrovich entered the foyer before the reception lounge of the general administration building of the university where the dinner was convoked, there was applause. The press had attended. There were photographs. There was a television interview, in which Ilia Alexandrovich said something unprepared, although he declined to describe the contents of the talk he would deliver later, promising only that his remarks would be extemporaneous and spontaneous, more a response to the proceedings than a prepared statement.

No one spoke with Yuri Maximovich. It was just as well. He saw no one that he recognized. Vovka Bedkin had not been invited. Where would he be this Sunday evening after his Saturday night dismay? Yuri put it out of his mind. Ilia Alexandrovich was surrounded. Several people had brought copies of his books for him to autograph, and he did so, smiling with pleasure. Chupkov arrived with a colleague. Yuri had recognized someone, although the recognition was not precisely filled with satisfaction nor was it reciprocated, for Chupkov elbowed his way past him without acknowledging Yuri's stolid presence. Waiters were passing drinks and canapés. The drinks were already prepared. Choose a whiskey, a gin and tonic, or vodka on ice. He drank whiskey. The walls of the foyer were clogged by little knots of people chatting among themselves; an occasional head turned to Ilia Alexandrovich and examined him. It appeared to Yuri that a considerable number of these people had turned up less from the wish to celebrate a Soviet poet than from the wish not to appear to have been uninvited. One young woman with a program of the proceedings and the guest list arranged by tables was checking off the people she identified and observing to her companion upon their credentials and achievements. One had a Pulitzer Prize, another wrote for *Partisan Review*, while another had written one extremely famous first novel and for twenty years had been working on its successor, and yet another was just out of the tank or about ready for the tank, or released from Payne Whitney or about due to enter it again. The young woman was exceptionally well informed, and although Yuri had no idea to whom her information referred, he was impressed by the variety of her annotation. It seemed to him that indeed he was among extraordinary people.

An hour later, nearly eight o'clock, the guests assembled at their tables. The lounge was attractively arranged. Round tables seating ten, each appointed with a floral arrangement and rented silverware, dotted the room. At its head there stood a long table, traditionally rectangular, with Ilia Alexandrovich in command, two other gentlemen whom Yuri did not know and whose place cards he had not been able to read, their wives (he imagined), Mr. Paris and his wife (most definitely), an unattached woman of middle age, a single gentleman with a rubicund complexion who always kept his hand on a drink, and Yuri Maximovich. Behind the head table was a curtained stage on which presumably the talks and commendations would unfold.

"And who are you?" the lady to his left asked.

Yuri had speared a piece of grapefruit and his mouth was full of juice. He couldn't speak but used his spoon to turn his place card toward the woman.

"Yes, indeed. So you're Mr. Isakovsky."

Yuri swallowed. "You know me?"

"Doesn't everybody?" she replied, smiling. Clearly she was a woman of inexhaustible politeness.

"Harold, this is Mr. Isakovsky. My husband's Mr. Paris. Ilia's publisher, you know." Yuri knew perfectly well. Undoubtedly the woman did know something of him, if not from the report of his Soviet publishers, who had long since forgotten his existence, then from Mr. Paris, Ilia's publisher, who most certainly remembered him.

"Yes, we've met. How have you been enjoying New York?" Yuri admitted he had seen virtually nothing of the city except a cafeteria, an Italian restaurant, a bar, and the Hotel Hilton. "We have to remedy that. May I have a car take you about the city tomorrow? I'd be happy to arrange it." Yuri said he would think about it overnight and call him in the morning if he felt in need of touring. The idea was not unpleasant, but somehow he had no particular interest in experiencing more of New York. Mr. Paris was not offended; Yuri's temporizing was so obviously unstudied and maladroit. Mr. Paris dismissed him as gauche and probably vulgar as well. Yuri sipped some of the white wine which had been poured into his glass and again felt the urge to pee. He was about to ask a waiter the direction to the lavatory when Ilia called down; "Yuri, my old friend Panitz here thinks the suffering of Russian poets is one of our five-year plans."

Yuri put down his glass, looked at Panitz—a small man with an ardent, endlessly moving chin which he stroked as though to keep its agitation in check—and smiled. "We don't plan it at all. It just happens." But Panitz had no intention of being put off either by Ilia's wit or Yuri's dismissal.

"Quite seriously, my friends," he began, and there was silence, grave silence, for Panitz was to be reckoned with by many. "Akhmatova was quite struck by my sense of the Russian suffering. I think she rather agrees that the predicament of Russian poets is unique and their suffering a spiritual yeast to the language." Ilia Alexandrovich had stopped smiling. The mention of the great Anna always stopped him. He couldn't bear female poets. He had been married to one whom some thought much better than he. Yuri Maximovich knew perfectly well that Ilia would be unnerved by any reminiscence of that splendid woman and would have joined Akhmatova in acquiescence (more, Yuri suspected, to avoid a confrontation with the fervid Panitz than because he agreed with such pious flapdoodle), but there was something about Panitz, a certain quality of being on his toes, alert like a scavenger bird, which put him off.

"Sir," Yuri countered, deliberating his words, "there is nothing admirable about suffering. Nothing at all. It's not suffering that makes poetry. It's work and gift of the gods."

"Nonsense," Panitz rejoined. "Gift of the gods. Pure sentimentalism. Suffering has tested the Russian character."

"I? Sentimental? I beg to disagree. First of all, not single one bone of sentiment in my body, not one brittle bone of sentiment. Suffering is sentiment. Poetry is something quite different. Ask Ilia Alexandrovich. Have you suffered, Ilia?"

Ilia wanted no part of the conversation. Mrs. Paris was smiling ardently, a dumb smile smudging her teeth with lipstick. She loved high argument. Mr. Paris, the publisher, was mentally publishing. Understanding nothing, he was considering a book idea on Russian suffering and hoping he would find the authors right there—a symposium, a round table on suffering, and he would publish the proceedings. It wouldn't sell much unless the controversy could be fanned. "What do you think of all this, John?" Mr. Paris turned to the brave alcoholic on his right, who faced Yuri across the table. John was all Yuri knew of the man. He was never introduced and he felt certain after John's reply that there was nothing to be gained by addressing him.

Both Ilia and John replied at the same time, and nothing could be heard. For once Ilia was happy to be ignored and John took over: "Tish-tosh" was the way he began, and Yuri neither knew nor cared about the meaning of "tish-tosh." "Balls, that's what it is. Poetry is suffering if you don't sell and a miracle if you do. Ilia is the most famous poet Russia has because he outsells everyone. Now that's a fact. I know. I was there. Everyone knows Ilia. He's like a general or a commissar. Everyone knows him. I copped a plea on a speeding ticket because the policeman recognized Ilia's book on the front seat. Now, that's not suffering." An indomitable silence followed, broken only by nervous coughs, cigarette lighting, drink drinking, and similar motions of evasion.

"That's very insightful," Mrs. Paris chirruped.

"That's pure nonsense, John, and you know it perfectly," Ilia snapped with annoyance.

Panitz grumbled that John was drunk already, but John didn't hear him. Throughout the exchange and the main course of chicken braised with small onions and garnished with peas and potato sticks, Yuri had listened. He couldn't eat. He was too excited to eat. It was marvelous. The quality of universal inanity overwhelmed him. Stupidity was universal, without national boundaries; the perception of that fact was overwhelming and delicious.

"Forgive me for saying one more word on subject, sir." Yuri was addressing Mr. Panitz. "I wish to clarify my feelings. It would help me and hope not bore you. I think suffering luxury, not capitalist luxury, not socialist luxury. Simply human luxury. If one needs audience and misses one, the loss can be made suffering. If one needs love and not find love, absence can be made suffering. In summary, if one has to go outside oneself to fill up oneself, to make self whole and healthy, the lack is called suffering. I think poets can suffer, but so can shopkeepers without customers, and restaurant managers without hungry people. Oh, yes, people can suffer for what they lack, but work of artist is good or bad and suffering has nothing to add to it. I tell you one thing, sir, you are lucky man to be able think about suffering. There are countries where people have worry whether they're going to stay alive at all, whether they can survive famine or change in politics or whim from police chief. Suffering, I think, is just indecision, waiting for sword to fall, or luckily, for sword to be put away in sword holder and hidden in closet. But art—art has no merit from suffering. Bad art is bad art. I think you the sentimental man, Mr. Panitz."

"Well, Mr. Isakovsky," Panitz said dourly, having assimilated nothing of Yuri's remarks, "the great Akhmatova didn't agree with you."

"But the great Akhmatova could also be very human and very wrong." Yuri drank off his glass of wine at that point and nearly spilled it, for the waiter had begun to remove his untouched plate and the lock of arms and dishes, moving with contrary intention, had almost produced an accident.

"If the wine had spilled on my pants, that would be great suffering, I tell you!" Everyone laughed. Yuri Maximovich was rather more charming than he knew and Ilia Alexandrovich uncomfortably realized it. Turning to Mrs. Panitz, a thin woman with black hair in bangs, who listened to everything intelligently, Ilia commented, "My friend's English is very good, isn't it? No?"

"Oh, excellent, Ilia. Excellent."

The dinner was nearly completed; a sherbet, coffee, and petits fours appeared. Yuri felt his strained bladder, massaging it, hoping to redistribute its contents. He had to pee with a ferocity, but all the waiters had disappeared from the dining room, the curtains had suddenly parted, and the stage was illuminated, floodlights from the wings picking up a standing microphone and enveloping it with two overlapping circles of brilliance. Into the center of the beams stepped a gentleman, obviously recognized because he was greeted with applause. Mrs. Paris consulted her program, which she had withdrawn from beneath her dessert plate, and clucked recognition. Yuri found his but knew no one. There were to be four toasts and declamations followed by Ilia's investiture with a doctor of letters and his speech of acceptance.

THE FIRST SPEAKER:
"I delight in knowing Ilia Alexandrovich Kolokolov. He is authentic. As we would say in the big city, 'the real thing.' But I could not have imagined how much of a real thing until I visited him in Moscow. There he is more real than we can imagine. As some of you know, I am a poet, but poetry here is singing in solitude, more like the proverbial nightingale who sings for the sheer wonder of singing, indifferent to being heard, but singing marvelously nonetheless. Unfortunately, poets aren't nightingales, whatever their gifts for song. They are obliged to be heard, and who would know, as the English philosophic Bishop inquired (making a rather different point), if indeed the tree fallen in the forest makes a noise if there is no one in earshot to hear it. Solitary poets are more like sound-

less fallen trees than nightingales. But that is not the situation of our friend, whom we are gathered this evening to honor. You see, Ilia Alexandrovich is really heard at home. His books sell in the tens—no, the hundreds of thousands; the young know his poems like our ancestors knew the Book of Psalms, and recite them almost as their personal liturgy. We poets here are not as splendidly regarded. Our publishers consider us marginal. We are the luxury of publishing, and few there are who can still afford us. We are a truffle (a trifle), certainly not a staple. Publishers can do without us, magazines use us to fill space, and we are confined to universities and little reviews where our readership is our students, our few friends, each other, and old ladies who press poems to their breasts like their mothers pressed dried lavender into family albums. We're slightly silly and useless, whereas in Ilia's land poetry is a blazon and a claxon. A drum and fife corps to the people, leading it, inspiring it, giving its inarticulateness a strong and brave voice. Let me read to you one of Ilia's sturdy poems:

The headwind rattles through the ear of
the Neva
Spurring and bridling the ships
Rising up like horses and settling down like
lambs
Bringing us rag pulp from Finland
Milk-white and flawless as a newborn
Pounded and pressed, heated in the viscous sap
of the mould-makers' vat.
Drawn forth like braids of sticky candy
Cut, refined, winnowed of impurity
Until before us (the pen shived like the
pulp) it is ready for the imprint of the eye.
Words, conjured like a magician, spark
Through the point as if a million tons
of water generated that power
And Finnish whiteness receives the mottlings
and markings of Russian words."

THE REACTION:
The speaker concluded, dropping his long head over the microphone, awaiting the sound of the applause which clattered like hooves over the room; his blond hair streaked with gray fell over his eyes, and shambling to the wings, he smiled with delight, being replaced by a youngish man, thin, intelligently ugly, who gripped the neck of the microphone as though to strangle it.

Yuri Maximovich had listened to the speaker, understanding less than he had understood since his arrival in the country. The words, so they sounded, were not so much conjoined as fused, streaming elegantly like shades of the color blue, each shade and hue of language indeterminate, all blue, all pale-blue, all pale. And what the audience applauded, applauding the poem—a poem felt, but not felt as the audience received it, for Yuri remembered the circumstance of its composition. Ilia Alexandrovich had received a little reward once—a reward not many Russian poets had received before or since. He had behaved well, and for a change a limited edition of his fourth book had been printed on fine Finnish paper, paper that wouldn't blanch before the sun or retire into beige before the light or hide in yellow embarrassment in an attic trunk. Finnish paper, decent paper for a book of poems. Ilia Alexandrovich was celebrating a decent edition of a book of poems.

THE SECOND SPEAKER:
"I have set myself to thinking about a curious fortuity. At approximately the same time as I published my first novel, Ilia Alexandrovich published his first book of poems. The same year. The same month. Three days apart, we have discovered. My first novel was about growing up in Maine. His first book of poems was about growing up in Moscow. The differences are already obvious. My first book had somehow to work its way down from Auburn to Bar Harbor to Boston and points south, and his, well, his started out in the capital and went like a sound wave to the barriers of the nation, bouncing back like sound, reverberating, shuddering. I published a book of

poems, lyrics, and gambits a few months after he published his little autobiographic essay. And the same thing happened. Mine trickled. His streamed. Now, what was the difference? Really, what is the difference? It isn't that Russians read and Americans are illiterate. It isn't that the word matters more to them than to us. It certainly isn't any longer—although sometimes I wish it were—that the Russians believe in their messianic Muscovite Jerusalem. They may, but they don't use that language any more and the language they presently use isn't one that yields to such purely religious potencies. It was useful for esoteric—they would say elitist—thinkers like Chadaev, Soloviëv, Berdyaev, but not for the Russian that was born with a Mayakovskan thump and thunder. There are—let us be accurate—many Russian poets who didn't, as the expression goes, make it. They had no constituency. They had admirers, but no voting delegation. Some of them were quite exceptional poets, but they didn't represent, as my friend just finished saying, an unarticulated voice. They found their own voice, but no one else's. That perhaps is the difference between a personal poet and a people's poet. My friend Ilia Alexandrovich is certainly a people's poet. Not simply because people read him. They wouldn't read him if he wasn't somehow their man. But to be their man, he had first to be his own, and, well, it's a real pleasure, being able to celebrate that kind of manhood."

THE REACTION:
The speaker raised his arms above his head, precisely the gesture which Ilia had used only a few days before, and waved them down at him; Ilia flushed with delight, the skin upon his flat cheekbones spreading into a smile, stood up, and bowed quickly. The applause this time was splendid, breaking waves, choric whistling (Yuri remembered the lone whistle in the aula). Ilia Alexandrovich was a great people's poet. Most assuredly, Yuri thought. He belched sourly. His groin was anesthetized. He felt a slight pain and looked around, thinking to slip out, but the third speaker had gained the platform. It was drunken John from his table, and drunken John would have noticed him.

THE THIRD SPEAKER:
"Now, what does one say for a Russian comrade? I don't really know. They gave me a dinner in Moscow before I left, but all the toasts were in Russian and I didn't understand a word. They could have said anything, anything at all, and it wouldn't have mattered a damn to me. I didn't understand a word of Russian, you see, and what's more I'm afraid the potables had gotten to me long before the formal part of the toasting had begun. I kept up with the toasts, but not with the toastmaster. So now then, what to do now? I'm afraid I've enjoyed this dinner a bit too much also. Can't be helped. Well, you see, as I was saying during dinner to a friend of Ilia's, the truth of the matter is that Ilia's a star. The reason we're here tonight is that Ilia's a star. His poetry hasn't improved over the last book or two. As a matter of fact, it doesn't really matter at all. Even if the poems were rotten, most of us would still be here. Invited guests. Good dinner. Drink. Camaraderie. We're all writers up against it. And we'd still be proud that someone like Ilia Alexandrovich can be a star, and a star, mind you, not in Hollywood where stardom is a matter of course or on Broadway in lights or a personality, as television calls its curious brand of faceless nonentities, but a star in a country where presumably being a star is not only uncommon, but sometimes dangerous. I'm proud of Ilia for having brought it off, having gotten away with it. Well, that's enough from me."

THE REACTION:
"You bet it is," someone shouted as the speaker moved dizzily as a moth toward the wings, holding a hand before his face to shield it from the lights. The applause was nervous and perfunctory. It was apparent that the audience was embarrassed by the remarks of drunken John, but Yuri was somehow pleased with them. Not simply that they restored blood to the pallid proceedings, but he sensed in drunken John a kind of misery not incapable of heroism, a plain-speaking verging on the dangerous which was at least compatible with gallantry.

THE FOURTH SPEAKER:
"Friends, this is all a gesture. All of us, most of us, certainly those of us who like myself are poets in their middle age, have passed through five decades of war, revolution, depression, war, cold war, other wars and revolutions and depressions which gave birth in the Russia of the czars to Socialist Russia and in this country have seen us at long last to the beginning of the end of war in Southeast Asia.

"The history of the Russian people and the American people has coalesced and separated many times, bringing us together in uneasy alliance during the Second World War, parting us for more than two decades, and now once again resuming civil communication, defining the possibilities of pacific disengagement. We Americans have had to face up to Russia. Russia has had to face up to us. None would have thought this possible—or even, I might add, necessary—a half-century ago. Very few Americans took the Russian Revolution seriously in 1917, but within ten years there were Americans who had become partisans and revolutionaries, and the repression of dissent had begun here. Well, we can now draw breath again. There's not much of a revolutionary movement left in this country, but there are millions of Americans who remember what it was like in the thirties. The rise and fall of movements have little or nothing to do with the continuity of memory. Memory is much longer than most people imagine.

"Throughout these long fifty years, while the politicians argued and the militarists armed and the spies spied, the intellectuals have continued to think and write and read each other's stuff. I knew about Kolokolov long before he knew about Panitz. Quite right, too, since he's still a boy and it's the business of young men to work at their craft without giving too much time to what others, thousands of miles away, are doing. But people like myself who've been writing for decades get awfully tired looking at a piece of paper day in, day out. We look up out of fatigue, we pay attention to what's out there and try to figure out something about the topography of poetry elsewhere than in our own neighborhood.

"I first read a poem of Ilia Alexandrovich in a French magazine—published, I think, in the late fifties, about a month after his first book of poems was published in Russia. What struck me about it—and it's hard making certain that a poem is virile and tough when it's filtered through the fine mesh of the French language—was that it said what it had to and nothing more. It was direct, forceful, spare. I didn't say then, "Here is a poet." I was quite content to say, "Here is a poem." I asked several people over the ensuing months about this Kolokolov, friends who followed Russian literature, and they told me that he was young and promising. Well, he was more than that, it appears. He was also daring and courageous. He said happy and joyful things to his people, but he also said things that young people alone dare to say, things which made his own establishment nervous and uncomfortable. I thought to myself, Here's a man with blood in his body, someone whom Whitman, for instance, might have admired. And then his first selected poems appeared in this country, poems drawn from his first three books, and I was delighted. He understood that the revolution in his country wasn't just a matter for Marx and Lenin, but that human lives were at stake, and everything human mattered to him down to the least worker who died building a dam across the Dnieper or the gypsies who were killed by the Germans or a stupid censor's mark over a good manuscript.

"Ilia Alexandrovich got the point of being young, of not having had to live through the five decades of getting to this year. He made up for his inexperience by paying attention to the experience he had had and making a powerful body of poems out of it. We don't have poets like him in this country. We don't have poets like him because our poets can't get into trouble even if they try. They get into trouble if they break the law or get caught with a minor in the back seat, but that's not unique poet trouble. Poets here don't get into trouble with poetry. They don't make a dent. In Ilia's country they make a dent, and making dents means making trouble and making friends. I guess Ilia has more friends and more enemies than most of our cities have people, but that's the way it is in his vast homeland.

"I am happy to be an admirer of Ilia Alexandrovich, to be among his translators, to be a sponsor of this dinner and to be a public testifier to his gifts. The only thing I can say to him is 'Keep it up,' 'Keep the pressure on.' It not only ennobles you. It purifies and strengthens us, your fellow poets."

THE REACTION:
Panitz had panitzed as he had been known to panitz for a generation. Snotty critics had invented the verb "to panitz" to describe a kind of full, grandfatherly rhetorical style. Used in another form, as an adverbial modifier, writers had been known "to have panitzed" their prose (this requiring an orthographic enlargement). The preferred form was the past definite: "panitzed" and sometimes "to panitize," as when speaking extemporaneously, using hands to calm the air and fingers to tickle words, a speaker would be coaxing and folksy. Panitz had cultivated the air of being everyone's father, of having been through it all, not with a wince but with a wisdom; and having survived everything the world had to offer in the way of obscurity and notoriety, he had come to the time when he would confer his benefice. His own poetry, difficult and obtuse, had remained a constant threat to understanding and was consequently protected from the higher judgment of its otiosity. Panitz had made certain that he kept his truth sufficiently wrapped in layers of imagery so that no one could be certain if he was really first rate. Persistence in a democracy scores points. If you keep at it, putting friend to friend end to end over the years, eventually they run out of names to honor, and if the prize money lasts, you'll get yours. That's the way Panitz had managed.

All Yuri Maximovich could think of was "super-Chocham," the contemptuous phrase his mother used to describe a garrulous old bookseller in the Podol. Panitz was precisely that, "a super-wiseman," and he was irresistible. The audience applauded generously, warmly, looking not at Panitz but at Ilia Alexandrovich, the child benefacted, the young man heroized, the poet panitized. But Yuri Maximovich was frowning. A half-hour of this had gone by, and he was having enough. The anesthetized groin, stabilized by inactivity, accommodated to its distension, would at any moment collapse. The university president had made the presentation, had handed Ilia his hood, had saluted his gifts to world literature, and had passed from the stage as the audience stood to applaud. Ilia Alexandrovich dropped his head into a bow, pleasure like a liquored syrup seeping over his face until, laughing with delight, he calmed the enthusiasm with his hands and struck a pose before the microphone, feet apart, body loose, jacket open, scarf flowing, hair falling.

ILIA ALEXANDROVICH KOLOKOLOV:
"I am honored. I am pleased. I am—is correct?—touched. (*He looked up, smiling, and applause broke out and withdrew.*) Yes? Yes! So what is best way for me to speak with you than by reading you a poem I wrote this afternoon. It is long poem, not finished by any means. A draft poem, but I wrote it in a heat, a passion to tell you something about the man and the poet you honor and the people from whom he comes as an emissary and a spokesman.

Don't drop upon my head a laurel crown
Like an ancient general come to visit
Conquered territory, saluting the enemy
In shackles, stripped of clothing,
Naked in humiliation.

I don't desire your iron wreaths,
Their leafy bullets bright with the
smiles of napalm.
No. Keep those gifts for your own heroes,
Those you honor for destroying peasant towns,
Making rivers of blood out of hill streams
Where old men and women used to wash
The turned earth from their tired bodies.
Keep those wreaths for your own.

Give me the little I deserve
A smile of recognition as your brother,

Someone you did not know but learned
Had ancestors from the same village as yourself.
I am the child of those ancestors
Now lying under clean soil, down among the
Slugs and worms, conversing about the
Upper world where struggling life
Goes on until the final call to sleep."

Yuri Maximovich had begun to squirm. He squirmed and his eye twitched. He knew those images. Ilia had already used them in a poem never translated but circulated in manuscript, had used them to describe his reaction to an earlier depredation, the entry of Russian troops into Budapest. In fact, Yuri had a copy of that *samizdat*. Later the poem had been denounced and denied, copies called in (not all, most assuredly). Ilia had claimed that only the first stanza was his own, that he had thrown the notebook away and some scavenger, some enemy had retrieved it from the ashcan, added the outspoken stanzas and put them abroad. Since the notebook was empty except for that poem, earlier versions of other poems, and poems copied out from other poets he no longer fancied, the notebook was genuine. It is only that the offending stanzas, now recharged and refurbished for another war and another criminality, had been repudiated as a forgery. And here he was, that honest voice, that "blazon and claxon," owning up to his past, retrieving from the scrap heap of his own history a dreadful poem denouncing a dreadful treachery, and substituting a new culprit, a few words of advanced technology (for not napalm but fire explosives had been used in Budapest), and hero, daring spokesman, emissary of his people, he was letting the Americans have it after a good dinner.

Yuri looked around, trying to figure out what the audience was thinking, but they sat slack-faced, unnerved as the poem unfolded. It wasn't the poem, to be sure, it was Ilia Alexondrovich which got to him. Suddenly, leaning back in his chair, Yuri let a little groan escape. Mrs. Paris turned, flickered at him, and departed. Yuri slipped out of his chair, and with his back to the stage, began to edge his way through the tables. He had two to pass before he could escape through the exit door. He managed it. He believed he made no fuss. What he did not realize was that against the illuminated stage, his own body in the darkness of the room appeared as though a tortoise was ambling across the apron of the stage, a little bump rising and falling as he sneaked by. Someone tittered, and Ilia Alexandrovich paused for an instant, noted Yuri's departure, and flung himself more daringly into the poem, slashing the air with one hand for "slugs" and the other for "worms." Yuri disappeared to take a pee and never learned the outcome of the poem. He knew the poem. It denounced and thundered, but it was no poem. Even the feelings lied, even the feelings lied, he said to himself as he peed. It was a long and good pee.

He could not return. He would not remain behind to greet and be greeted. He didn't want his opinion asked. It was better to disappear into the Sunday cold. His sense of direction had improved. He walked back to his hotel slowly, thinking to himself about the city, about living in the city. He could learn English and teach poetry in a college. He could, but how foolish. To defect out of failure, to give political reasons for human failings was too disgusting. He knew a good poem, but he hadn't written one, and he owed his own language and the spirit that wrestled in the language a last chance to speak.

5. Doing Love

The voice began to scream at Yuri Maximovich a little after eight o'clock on Monday morning. "You're a disgrace. A disgrace, Comrade. I can't even bear to call you Comrade, I'm so enraged with you. Bedkin's gone. You know that. Gone! You had drinks with him two nights ago in a bar opposite your hotel. Oh, yes, we know. We know everything. We couldn't hear what you were saying. We tried, you may be sure, but we couldn't pick it up. But he told you. We are certain of that! Our operative said that at one point Bedkin wept. The weeper. The damned fool. I don't understand why they sent him at all! They thought it would do you both good—him keeping track of you, since Bedkin said you confided in him. Well, so much for Bedkin. A child of kulaks, he shouldn't have escaped at all. Two busted legs would have been forbearing. Shot. He should have been shot, that's what. And you, you idiot. How dare you walk out on a Soviet poet, a great poet, *our* great poet? How dare you? To pee, you say? To pee? We'll piss on you. You'll learn once and for all, you damned

Jew poet. You'll learn. If we didn't need you, you'd read your poems to jackals in the zoo. Damn you, you stay right there. You stay where you are. You're not to go out of your room until I can get there . . . I don't care if you have meetings to attend. You'll go late. Now, listen to me, don't call me Comrade Chupkov. Get it through your head that I am Lieutenant Colonel Chupkov and I've dealt with your kind a thousand times."

Yuri Maximovich put down the receiver and shook his head vigorously. The sound of Chupkov's voice rang in his ears. It wasn't until he stepped into the shower, turning on the cold water and dancing from the icy pricks, that he drove Chupkov away. But not for long. A half-hour later he was seated before a pot of coffee in Yuri's room and more calmly, deliberately, abusing him. "You're quite unreliable. It's clear that you're quite unreliable."

"I don't think so, Colonel. I don't think so. I'm unsteady, a bit shaky, but not unreliable," Yuri replied, buttoning his shirt.

"You don't seem to understand that you've humiliated us. You were entrusted with Vovka Bedkin and you let him slip."

"What are you saying? I? I, entrusted with Bedkin? My friend, you have it backwards."

"I have nothing backwards ever. It is not my business to have things backwards."

"But—" Yuri began to laugh.

"You laugh. How dare you?"

"But it's ridiculous. You are making me crazy. I loathed Bedkin. I can't stand the Bedkins of the world. They're grub worms. They're toadies and flunkies. All they want is a piece of cake, the crust of a piece of cake. Bread they don't want. Beer they don't want. The least bit of cake is what they want. And for cake, they'll betray everything, every last bit of human decency. I pitied and loathed Bedkin, but responsible for him? Not me."

"Listen! You confided in him. You made him your ally."

"Who says that?"

"Bedkin said it. We have a recording of you telling him about poetry."

"Oh, you do. Listen to that recording, will you? Listen to it. I confided? *You're* mad, Colonel."

Colonel Chupkov stood up abruptly and slapped Yuri Maximovich. Yuri Maximovich apologized. The reflexes of two generations of life in his homeland returned to him. He had never before sat in a foreign hotel drinking coffee with an officer of State Security. He had lost his head. He apologized. He rephrased his comment. The slap hadn't hurt, but he knew that a slap in New York would most certainly become something else upon his return.

"I too, I shouldn't have lost my temper. I apologize to you as well, Comrade. Not that you didn't deserve it, but it wasn't dignified."

"Yes, well, sometimes we lose control." The two men were strangely embarrassed by the passion with which they invested their disagreement. Undoubtedly Lieutenant Colonel Chupkov had received a critical signal from Moscow about Bedkin and a complaining harangue from Kolokolov. Whom else to assault but Yuri Maximovich?

"The point remains as before. A simple delegation to a congress, a simple visit of a Soviet poet has become a botch. Someone has to be blamed."

The omniousness of the logic was palpable. Yuri shivered. "Why a someone? Why not chance, reality, the way things are?"

"There's always a someone."

"I don't think so. Normal fatality has no need of new victims. History isn't a god to whom we sacrifice."

"It is. It's the way we humanize history. We transform it from an energy into a little god with a voracious appetite. The god is grasping and hungry. It requires sacrifice and propitiation."

"Am I the offering?"

"Maybe yes, maybe no. It's not determined until the sequence is completed. You've two more days of meetings. You have your reading and your piece of work. Do them well and perhaps the decree can be averted and another name inserted in the blank space. That's your only hope."

"A curious system."

"You think so? Not really. The system requires a quota. A quota of merits and demerits: a fixed number are rewarded, a fixed number condemned. The names don't matter. The good works don't matter, nor do the crimes. The documents could even be printed in advance—the confessions, the condemnations. It could all be anticipated. The only thing life supplies are names. You, my friend, are only a name. History is a universal, with its own law and logic."

"I am, then, at best a random name to be inserted if needed? Yes?"

"Correct!"

"At last I understand the system."

"Does it frighten you?"

"Of course. Doesn't it frighten you?"

"No less. One day I run the system. The next, I could be a name for a blank space. Oh, yes. It frightens me. But for the moment it should frighten you more, much more."

Lieutenant Colonel Chupkov stood up, saluted Yuri Maximovich with his cup, and drank off the coffee. "Try to be good, Yuri Maximovich." Chupkov said this last with an almost paternal affection. It was unintelligible. The only explanation for the curious reversal was Yuri's sense that indeed the conversation had confirmed as much to Chupkov about the nature of their common world as it had revealed to him.

Yuri completed dressing and left the hotel, taking the street uptown, again walking. He passed an automobile accident (a taxi driver shouting with a truckman), a knot of people listening to a salesman extol a remarkable vegetable peeler in front of a food market. He had walked two blocks, not more, when Greta Engel caught up with him.

"What's become of you?" She took his arm and linked it to her own.

"I? Well, I suppose the answer is that I've been occupied." Yuri Maximovich was irritable. He was impatient. He wanted to be alone, but Greta Engel was unavoidable. He hadn't seen her for a whole day and indeed had not remarked her absence until she reappeared, but at that instant, feeling her weight upon his arm, the rub of her body against his side, he felt attended, accompanied—more accurately, shared. Yuri Maximovich sighed, allowing himself a bit of pity and sadness.

"Occupied?" Greta asked. "You disappeared. Naturally I wasn't invited to the dinner. I waited outside, but you never came out. What became of you?"

"I left early."

"Were you ill?"

"Yes. I think I was ill."

They crossed the street. They had a mile and a quarter to go. Greta Engel explained that approximately twenty city blocks made a mile. "You're being evasive, Yuri. Very evasive."

"Not evasive. Is evasive avoid? Yes. Well. I am avoid. There is much I wish to avoid. I should, you understand, speak with no person. None. Everything I said since arrival has been ridiculous mistake. Don't you see, dear Greta Engel, I am in big, serious trouble."

Greta Engel gripped the fabric of his coat more tightly as though Yuri might suddenly disappear, leaving behind an empty coat sleeve. "Can you tell me?"

"Why you? I tell no one. There is no one to tell. Everyone dead. My mother gone. My father. My sister. I don't even know where she is or what name she has become. Only Nastya and Yasha Isaievich. Maybe a rabbi? I don't know. Nothing to talk about. It is beyond conversation."

"Let me hypothesize for you."

"You do what? I don't know what you say."

"Hypothesize? Let me guess. Guess. Make up possibilities for you. It will make it easier for you to confide in me."

Yuri grunted. They stopped before a window and Yuri Maximovich noticed a reflection in the glass. A man with an ill-fitting overcoat and a tight-fitting homburg had come to a stop twenty feet away and lit a cigarette. Yuri knew who it was. Not by name. He had no name that mattered. He was being followed. The agent, whoever he was, made no effort to conceal his presence. He followed closely, stopping a minute later when Yuri checked again to confirm his suspicion. The agent was obviously instructed to be visible and explicit. Another form of warning. In Moscow there would be six agents, on different corners, waiting for him to descend from his apartment, picking him up and leaving him, waiting until he made a move somewhere, anywhere. The task of such agents was to harass and unnerve, not to produce information. Greta Engel was aware of the sudden strain. Yuri's body had tensed, and he reached a hand into his overcoat and tapped his heart, which had begun to race wildly. He had never before been aware of being followed. At one time or another he had perhaps been followed, but nothing had come of it. Every Soviet citizen above a certain rank or responsibility is followed. That's also part of the invariant law. "Let's follow Isakovsky today. See what he does. Write up a report. Fill in the blanks. File it." Nothing comes of it. Yuri Maximovich walks from Pushkin Square to his office. (Nothing peculiar.) Doesn't stop to buy a newspaper. (Curious. Nothing remarkable, however.) Goes out for soup. Returns to his office. Returns home by eight. Doesn't malinger. Doesn't stop for a drink. File it. Tomorrow try Pavel Meledin. Who's Pavel Meledin? Does it matter? Not really, but follow him. In New York, however, there aren't many Soviet citizens walking about. American agents didn't appear to be following Yuri Maximovich. Not that they wouldn't, given half a shove. It's simply that they don't even know who he is or why he would matter. Maybe tomorrow they'll begin to follow him, after Vovka Bedkin tells them he's in trouble. But then Bedkin doesn't know much trouble. Bedkin defected before the fabulous pee. But Bedkin knows about the extra piece of work? Bobov said so, but was it true? Not likely. An operative, an agent, but not a man likely to receive the confidences of Bobov and Chupkov.

"What's wrong?"

"Nothing. I'm being followed."

"By whom?"

"Agents."

"Whose?"

"Ours."

"Does that include me? Yours and mine?"

"No."

"Soviet?"

"Yes."

"But you're in New York. What does it matter? They see a woman on your arm. That's not unusual, is it?"

"It's not you. They know about you. Chupkov's mentioned you. It's not you. It's me. They mean to fear to me. You see. They want Yuri Maximovich full of fear."

"Are they successful?"

"Very."

"Poor Yuri." Greta Engel smiled at him. She fell silent and hugged at his coat sleeve. "Yuri, may I ask you something?"

"Yes, please. Ask. But do not think rude if I say nothing."

"Well, yes. Don't go to your meetings today. Come to my apartment?"

"Why?"

Greta Engel looked out into the street. She didn't dare to say it directly. A curious modesty. "Well. The fact is I want to make love to you. Do you understand?"

Yuri Maximovich heard the word "love," but the specific formula was unfamiliar.

"What is that? Precisely. How is 'make love.' English idiom?"

"Yes. A polite English idiom. To make love. Well"—Greta's voice had dropped to a whisper and her head rested for an instant on Yuri's shoulder—"to make love is to kiss, to hold, to enter, to leave, to fall asleep, to wake up and go through the whole thing all over again. That's what it means to make love."

"I see." The predicament was that Yuri Maximovich saw but did not understand. He saw the phrase before his eyes, misspelled. A colligation of words dropped like a caress into the midst of his fear. The agent had no doubt stopped behind them when Greta Engel had summoned her description of this curious English gentility. Slowly it became clear to Yuri that this girl had conceived some passion for him, unfamiliar at best, appealing, slightly frightening (but in a different way, although love and death were the coupled frights of man), astonishingly inappropriate.

"But the meetings?"

"Yes. I know. The meetings. Listen, Yuri, Mr. 'Also a Poet.' I have thought about you a great deal since I met you Thursday. I don't know what it is. You're old enough to be my father. Familiar phrase—even in Russian, I suppose. But then my father's a boozer and you're a sober man. But not quite sober. I think you're as dizzy and vague as he is, but the dizziness—"

"What's dizzy?"

"Stop it." Greta Engel put a hand to Yuri's mouth and covered it.

Yuri smiled. He caught on for the first time. This woman had somehow managed to fall in love with him. With him?

"Is this love part of project?" Yuri asked through the mesh of her fingers, laughing. She pinched his lip and removed her hand, hugging his arm once more.

"You're wretched, wretched. The article is out of my head completely. I swear. You're no longer a project."

Yuri Maximovich was whirling with excitement. He admitted to himself again that he found the woman lovely and slightly mad, a combination fatal to him. There was about Greta Engel the same unpredictability, the same daring and self-indulgence that had originally delighted him with Irina Alexandrovna. Irina had really behaved no differently than Greta Engel. Irina had invited him back to his own apartment after his reading and didn't leave for two years until she was good and ready. Yuri knew perfectly well that Irina had planned it that way. Yuri wasn't the calculated beginning, and the major the anticipated end. It had just turned out that way. Yuri was simply an opportunity to be seized, a matchless opportunity to gain stability, a residence permit, an apartment. In her own way, Irina had really enjoyed Yuri. She wasn't monogamous, but she was faithful to their two rooms, to the old-fashioned stove, to the bookshelves. She cleaned them from time to time, she cooked when she felt in the mood, she read once or twice. And Yuri, part of the movable furniture, was shifted about as it suited her, but not a single one of her lovers failed to treat Yuri with respect. Yuri was a significant lover, *primus inter pares*—first among equals and in that respect preeminent. The defect of Yuri's nature was his inability to consider himself with the same dedication and fidelity with which Irina considered her own pleasures and satisfactions. If he had been able to manage a mistress or two while she was pursuing her lovers, it might have turned out differently. Unfortunately, he couldn't manage it all. Writing poems he thought indulgence enough, a sufficient obsession. If you want, he thought of the muse as his mistress. He was finally, unavoidably, a man belabored by duties and obligations, a bit tedious and lugubrious, too grave and serious perhaps, but on the right track.

"All right. Yes. But now now. Later." Yuri Maximovich saw the hotel a block away and knew that the agent was behind him. He couldn't just flag a taxicab and go to the apartment of a young woman. He had to make an appearance, sit through the meetings for a bit, and then, hopefully, slip away, confuse the agent, and disappear. Greta Engel's face became pained. The disappointment was obvious. "Look, Greta, look, dear Greta Engel. It is not simple. Making love is simple in your country? (Not simple for any person, I guess.) Perhaps more simple here. I don't know. I have no experience. You make up mind and say come, make love in my apartment. Just like that. Same at home. Very easy. But I am here on visit. I am expected to be Soviet editor and intellectual. God save me. I have Colonel give me hell this morning. I have agent at feet constantly. How does look, you think, if I am—correct?—seduced from my Soviet tasks. Not very good. So I go to meetings and I come to you at intermission. And not go back in afternoon. I spend afternoon with you. I spend evening with you, night perhaps. And we do love." Yuri Maximovich spoke gently, looking down at the young woman, whose pain had changed to frowns and lovely pouts of disappointment. Greta thought over his words and then shrugged her shoulders in assent and kissed him. The agent turned away.

"All right. I understand. Here's the address." Greta took out of her coat pocket a slip of paper on which she had already written the address and handed it to Yuri Maximovich. She had been prepared. He glanced at it. A number on a Second Avenue. "A few hours from now, yes? Two o'clock. Yes? Plenty of time to get rid of that silly fool behind you. He has a face like a cuckoo clock. I expect that when the hour strikes he sticks his tongue out. How disgusting he is, Yuri." Yuri stroked her cheek gently, feeling the smooth curve of her jaw couple with his palm, fitting perfectly.

The meetings were already in progress when Yuri Maxmiovich, bundled in his overcoat and scarf, settled himself into a seat in the fifth row of the conference room. He was plotting, carefully and precisely, the most effeftive and intelligent means of losing the agent, who had taken a seat in the rear of the room. He fully realized that it was one thing to escape an agent and quite another to leave the agent with the confused feeling that his charge had not betrayed him and escaped but had simply vanished from view. The essential thing was to persuade the agent that Yuri Maximovich had not contrived to escape, that Yuri was not the culprit, but he, the agent, had failed. Obviously if Yuri succeeded, the agent would not report his disappearance, recognizing that he himself, not Yuri, had been derelict. The common assumption which both pursuer and pursued shared was that both knew of the existence of the other. The agent had made his presence manifest. In such cases, the pursued, knowing that he is followed, must play according to different rules than one who is covertly surveilled. He has an obligation to assist the pursuer. He must not speak with the agent, but he must give the agent full warning and information in advance of his next move. In that way the pursuer manifests his correct sense that as a Soviet citizen it is proper, legitimate, right that he be followed, that the agent is doing his job and that the pursued is cooperating as well as possible. In other words, Yuri had to construct a situation in which the decision to disappear—to be absent for an afternoon, an evening, a night—becomes something out of his control, beyond his ability to prevent, and therefore impossible to communicate to his guardian watchdog.

Yuri Maximovich hardly followed the proceedings. A succession of speakers in different accents, the thud of boredom, the bright lights and the half-filled auditorium, the comings and goings of visitors were so many distractions of the conference, but all the while Yuri was considering his options and alternatives. He realized that the task of evading the agent and keeping his rendezvous was not due simply or even sufficiently to the anticipation of Greta's ministrations. It wasn't just passion that drove him. He was quite fully aware that this small affair would be the last of his life. Thursday morning, when he stepped aboard the Soviet aircraft to return to Moscow (assuming, of course, that he did not elect Bedkin's way, choosing instead surgery upon his native tongue), such human joys would definitively end. Whether he was arrested or not, whether he was interrogated and tortured or not, didn't matter. Yuri Maximovich knew quite well, whatever the course of events, that the Moscow days which would follow to the end of his life would be constructed differently, that the evasion he had managed for decades was over. He had no idea in what the new Isakovsky would consist, but new he would most certainly be.

The meetings drew to a close and adjourned until the afternoon. Yuri Maximovich joined the line of conferees streaming down the center aisle to the exit. It was at that moment that the idea came to him. Yuri was not a tall man—just modest height, one would say. At the instant that he joined the people leaving the auditorium he was surrounded momentarily by three rather tall men, one of whom, in tribal robes which flowed about his body, carried a swathe of cloth over his arm. Yuri ducked low and noticed as they passed that the agent was suddenly confused by Yuri's apparent disappearance. He couldn't find Yuri in the line. It wouldn't do to seize that opportunity. It wouldn't have worked. By the time the group reached the elevators, the crush of the giants had been relieved and Yuri was revealed once more. The agent found him, and Yuri noted in the mirror panels about the elevator that he seemed relieved, although his habitual implacability had immediately returned. Clearly the only way to lose the agent without seeming to have lost him intentionally would be to enter a crowd, to disappear in it, and then to exit from it unobserved. It would take time, but crowds are inevitable in a city, and without a covey of agents passing the pursued along from one to the other it would not be difficult, only time-consuming. The main thing was to begin to walk, to follow congestion and hope for a crowd. Yuri turned down from the Hilton in the direction of what he learned later was Times Square, a crossroads of a number of streets where people congregated for their luncheons and additional recreation in the endless succession of bars, stand-up restaurants, and peep shows.

It was after one o'clock when Yuri arrived in what was called a square. He stood beneath the tower for a moment and read the news circling the girth of the building. People swirled about him—thousands of people, no doubt—but they did not stop. They formed no crowd into which he might duck and disappear from view, innocently vanishing. They moved, always moving, very rapidly, shouting raucously, slapping each other's palms in a strange salute, wearing astonishing clothing which made Yuri's drab seem uncommon and singular. The agent had stopped across the street and was drinking a beverage at an outdoor counter, one foot resting upon a chrome rail—rather casually, Yuri thought. The news continued its uninterrupted trail around the building. About him the people moved, some crossing the intersection and parting to disappear down different avenues, others threading down into the subway station only a few feet away.

As it happens, if one is patient, happy chance intervened. Yuri had been standing more than a half-hour. It was twenty minutes to the hour by then. A young man taking steps by twos emerged from the subway entrance, and looking about, began to run up the avenue. An elderly man, his eyeglasses broken and falling over his face, his lip streaming blood, followed him, shouting for him to stop, calling out, "Thief, thief!" The swirl of people slowed. Toward the young man came a crowd of adolescents just disgorged from the entrails of a movie theater. There must have been a dozen of them. As the young thief ran toward them they, in cruel high spirits, converged upon him and encircled him. Two of the group seized his arms and broke his flight, lifting him into the air, releasing him, catching him, and throwing him up again. Within minutes the shouts of the old man were taken up by the crowd, which began to surround the group. Some thought the boys were circus performers, their movements seemed so assured. The young thief, his face strained with fright, screamed for them to let him go; the victim, his face bloody, continued to shout. Police cars, sirens shattering, came up the street from different directions and blocked the scene. Yuri had no difficulty in escaping. He went down through the crowd of people before the subway entrance and disappeared.

A half-hour later Yuri Maximovich stood before the white door of Greta Engel's apartment and knocked. The door opened and Yuri announced, "Here is Isakovsky." Greta laughed with delight and Yuri entered. He was excited. He had not only evaded the agent, but to his pleasure had managed the subway easily. When he purchased his token of admission he asked the attendant where she thought the address on Second Avenue might be. The attendant was uncertain, but instructed him that he had to go east from the square to another line of the subway moving uptown. Yuri Maximovich managed the details, followed the arrows, asked questions of only one more person, an elderly woman who was bemused by his accent but helpful, and managed it without too much confusion.

"Yes, Isakovsky is here but is not certain why."

"Come in," Greta said, ignoring his confusion. "Take off your overcoat and put it on the sofa. I'll be right back." She disappeared and Yuri heard a whoosh and sizzle from the kitchen, followed by a quiet "damn." "The coffee overflowed. Nothing serious," she called out, explaining. It didn't matter. Yuri was absorbed by the room. Large, he concluded, although it was not that large, a rectangle containing perhaps six hundred feet, but the two windows looking out over the avenue were agreeable and the profusion of plants wandering about the room gave it a generous and unplanned quality which relieved the sobriety of the wall of books which flanked the entranceway. Greta had disappeared into the kitchen to the right and another passageway to the left augured the bedroom. So three rooms for a single woman who did some kind of odd work for a newspaper. Luxurious, he concluded.

"And you have your own bathroom, or do you share one?" Yuri Maximovich called out.

Greta Engel reappeared, matting her forehead with a dish towel. "Share one? Really. Of course not. If you need to use the bathroom, it's down the hall off the bedroom."

"No. Curiosity is all. How do you manage it? You must be very rich?"

"Rich? You're teasing me, Yuri. You have no idea how the rich live, my dear. It's understandable, but this isn't rich. I do it very modestly. I have some money in a trust fund from my grandmother, but that's almost gone. I do some writing for the newspaper. I had a rich lover once upon a time who furnished the apartment. That's how it's done. Bits of inheritance and passion."

"It's beautiful, though. It's completely who you are, intimate and vague. My apartment is Yuri Maximovich, *disjecta membra*—same in your language, yes—that don't add up to a whole body. But I love it there and I love it here. Good place to live, dear Greta."

"Very good place to live," she agreed. "Will you have a drink before lunch?"

"What? A wine? Yes. White wine. It's festivity today, no?"

"I should think so."

A moment later they were both seated on the sofa clinking their wine glasses, and passing from amenities and nerves to the pleasure of looking about, Yuri admired the books, the shelf of records, the complicated tuner and turntable that produced music from speakers at opposite ends of the room, an African mask with white eyes and a beak nose, and a deck of eighteenth-century French playing cards with which Greta explained she played solitaire, delighting more in the random revelation of the baroque costumes than in the outcome of the game.

"When were you last with a woman, Yuri?" Greta asked pouring herself another glass of wine.

"Long ago." Yuri was shocked by the question, but found it easy to answer. After all, the girl wasn't Russian. "Not that I have no desire for woman. Much desire. Little occasion. I stay with myself, I guess. Unhappy life. Not remarkable."

"But if you need a woman, why not have one?"

"It's not easy for me. I didn't pay attention. I had great fright of being overwhelmed by woman. When I was young boy, I always went to parties with book in my pocket. Stupid, I think now. But found more comfort reading. People fright me. People still fright me."

"Do I?"

"Yes. Of course. Do you think it easy come here? And fright double, three times ordinary. Not only woman—my elementary fright. But what? American woman and journalist. Two fright. I come here when I am to be at conference. I disappear into subway and trick Soviet agent. Three fright. And Comrade Chupkov gives me a big trouble this morning for leaving dinner during Kolokolov's speech, and also, you know, Bedkin . . ." Yuri was about to tell her about Bedkin's defection but decided against it. She didn't notice. His description of his fear must have delighted her. She kissed him lightly on the forehead. She had undoubtedly known men before who found her somewhat fearsome. Greta was after all a Greta, and like her name, her personality was assertive, foreign, gritty. She took a cigarette from a box on the side table behind her, and Yuri Maximovich, remembering, reached for the lighting mechanism, shaped curiously like an ancient Roman oil lamp, and produced a flame.

"I am not afraid."

"And what you should be—afraid, is it?—what should *you* be afraid?"

"Nothing. There is nothing frightening in the world as long as one knows the most one can lose is one's life." She laughed.

"The most? One's life. And that's trifle, you think. Losing life."

"Yes. Isn't it? I remember reading in college a section from a book by Spinoza. You know Spinoza? Nothing of it was clear to me. Much too demanding for my mind. But one thing stuck. Spinoza was always saying that this or that must be regarded '*sub specie aeternitas*' which I guess means 'in the light of eternity.' After that, whenever I felt a pain or a despair, anything that would bother me, I would sit myself down and think about it 'in the light of eternity.' It didn't take long to disappear. Eternity clears the mind. It's a long, long, time. Eternity is a long, long no-time. Not much point measuring my thirty-four years against eternity, or your fifty odd years."

Yuri Maximovich grunted to himself, thinking about Greta's eternity, approving it, but finding that the wince inside him kept up a steady pressure against eternity. Only his dying father had picked up Greta's message, and again Reb Mendel, who had visited him two days before. But they were unequal testimony. Millions upon millions seemed to say, quite the contrary, deny death, accommodate to it at most regretfully.

"Yes. I understand what is said. But easy for you to be so philosophic, so tranquil, here where you seem to be free?"

"That's just the point. It's all a tissue of seeming. You seem to be unfree. I *seem* to be free. It's a bit more muddled than that. What drives us in this country is a compulsion no less militant and destructive than your own. We don't lose our body life to it, but the mental institutions are full and bursting. In your place it's the reverse. They can't even pretend to cure you of your unhappiness. They say it's anti-Soviet and throw you in prison. What the hell's the difference? Losing your mind or losing your body. The quality of freedom is doubtful in any case."

Greta stood up abruptly and returned to the kitchen. Yuri Maximovich followed her. He wanted to watch her in the kitchen. She began to ladle a soup into mugs and dropped coconut chips into its murk. Salads of shrimp like crooked baby fingers lying on beds of lettuce were ready on a sideboard. They ate the luncheon in the living room, reclining like ancients on the sofa, the food displayed on colored mats before them, the bottle of wine perspiring. The conversation flagged during eating—just small comments about the taste of the curried soup, the texture of shrimp, the difficulty of getting seafood in Moscow—but, the eating finished, Greta returned her plate to the table mat.

From the journal of Yuri Maximovich Isakovsky
January 25, 1972

I have gotten to my fifty-fourth year without a scratch. Now that I think about it, it is quite remarkable, since objectively speaking, there are any number of reasons which should have made me at the very least questionable since my birth. I was, first of all, a Jew. We all know, that is, the system and the self (we share this recognition), that despite reluctance to be officially anti-Semitic (our Soviet Constitution forbids such an official doctrine), a great many Russians are mediocre enough to imagine that if things don't go right, it has to be someone's fault, and why not the Jews. Why not indeed? When the price of cabbage used to soar in the Podol and potatoes were scarce, I remember how the peasants used to grumble that the Jews were hoarding them to drive the prices up and skin the poor folk. Stomachs were very anti-Semitic in those days. My mother, whose blood was socialist and who would never buy a single thing more than she needed to feed Papa and us (my sister and me) the same day. She said it was unjust to stock up just because we had extra kopecks with which to put away a bit for the next day. No. No. She knew perfectly well what the gossip of the Podol was like and she wanted none of the muck thrown at her. I guess she was right, but she started me off very early with the notion that it wouldn't do for Jews who had working papas with a steady job looking like they were rich people who could afford to keep an extra piece of salted fish or a piece of fruit that could easily go bad. So I have no guilt on that score. I know that there are millions of Russians who think that everything that goes wrong is the Jew's work, but that doesn't bother me. Russia is not a bit different there than anyplace else. At least when Russia is anti-Semitic, it's old-fashioned. Its anti-Semitism is still straight out of czarist times and before. It's not an up-to-date anti-Semitism like the Germans, for instance. It doesn't roll on well-greased rail tracks straight to the ovens. (Too many witches in German fairy tales feeding children to the oven. No wonder!) The genius of Russia isn't anti-Semitism. So finally, even though I was prepared from childhood for this bit of nastiness, I can't lay it at the door of anti-Semitism.

I have to take it much more seriously than I have thus far, that the complaints Chupkov and before him Bedkin brought against me make sense only because the powers at the top are so insecure about holding onto the system they've built up for us. They have no way of knowing what we really think of them. We don't have elections. We don't have a free press. There are no radio programs like I heard at Greta's (we'll come to her in a moment), where people call in and speak what's on their minds to an all-knowing voice who hears them out and then gives it to them. The letters columns of our newspapers are all organized and coordinated to elevate or denounce some preselected target. My God, I pity our poor rulers. They're up there all alone. If they gave us the chance of telling them what we think, they might be very pleased. Most of us would say that it is just fine, that things are going well—although it would be nice to have better clothes in the stores and fewer line-ups for food and perhaps private bathrooms where even if you couldn't lock the door at least you could be certain a stranger wouldn't wander in on you when you're thinking the deep thoughts that accompany lavatory pilgrimage—that they're much better than they were in the twenties, that we haven't been at war in thirty years and our young people aren't dying far away in countries whose names we can hardly pronounce. We'd vote the rulers in again and again. But they just don't believe it, so they won't risk it. The result of all their loneliness up there is that they start living their lives looking over their shoulders. How can the bosses get any work done? They sit down at their desks to go through the papers and all they can think of is someone spying at their back. At the beginning, all of them had to patrol their own rears with swiveling eyes and gun to hand, but when they were done with the Whites and the Mensheviks, and the SD's, they began to employ others to keep eyes open for them, and before they knew it they had millions of people at work keeping watch on their rears. When the capitalist countries have an economic setback they put the employed back to work on big public jobs—building roads and clearing forests and such like—but we manage it by recruiting more people into security work.

Everyone with half a brain makes up the difference between his needs and his income by spying. More and more spies spying on fewer and fewer people.

Will they end up with me? With me! I can't think of anything more ridiculous and wasteful. Granted "ridiculous" is a subjective point of view, and all subjectivity, however light bends, is only my own angle of vision (and hence perhaps against Soviet "objectivity"), it is nonetheless true that waste can be objectively documented and bundles and bundles of spies working on a Yuri Maximovich Isakovsky doesn't quite add up. I can't think of how many people are being employed on me—staging a going-away party for me, organizing Irina Alexandrovna, Liudmila Brilova, Kolokolov, a ranking colonel, an overseas lieutenant colonel, banal Bedkin, a tail, and finally the receiver who is to take my poem—all to do what? To prove that I will or I won't, that I can but I can't, that I might but I didn't do what I was supposed to do. And if it works? Comrades, if it works? What will be proved? I'm not going to be made the director of the Soviet "disinformation" service for poetry, am I? So to what advantage to waste all those people trying to find out whether someone like me is a useful tool? I'm not. I'm no good at it. If they'd asked me straight away, looking me face-to-face, "Yuri Maximovich, are you able to use poetry as a cover?" I would have had to answer, "Oh, no, friends, try to get someone else for the job." Didn't I just about say that very thing to Colonel Bobov? Didn't I? And what did he do. He threatened me. How ridiculous!

One last thing on this point. About bureaucracy (and that's what I'm talking about—bureaucracy). The system has decided to drop its whole bureaucracy on me, like an elephant walking on a forest rodent. *What the system doesn't know about elephants*: If an elephant stamps on a mouse, the mouse survives. That's what it doesn't understand. Only larger creatures get crushed by the elephant's foot. Field mice, however, survive. They aren't brittle like larger creatures. They get flattened into the earth and the earth opens a teeny bit for them and they hide there until the elephant has passed over. I am the lowliest Soviet rodent. I survive. I continue to think. I continue to imagine and dream even though the whole system has fallen on me.

. . .

Yuri Maximovich was not gifted at making love. He had nothing of the knowledge of the flesh which, whatever its inexperience, knows instinctively the magic connections of the body, aware that a touch on the ear registers in the lumbar vertabrae, that the body has no visible logic, but that whatever occurs to a toe, to the flesh behind the knee, to the crossroads of the creasing flesh beneath the vagina shakes the brain and washes the heart with a rush of blood. He had no such knowledge. He thought the bodies of others were like his own, diagramed like the charts of acupuncture by a magisterial anatomist who throws shafts of light down upon men's heads, piercing them at the juncture of eyes and nose—in a word, that the vulnerable, soft mush of brain controls everything. He thought. He thought. Irina Alexandrovna, that first night long ago, had contested his assumption, but it was not long before he regained its serenity, locked more securely in the iron shackles of his slow, pondering intelligence.

Greta lay back upon the sofa, her head falling into the pit between his legs, her hair flooding down his legs. He looked down at her, smiling, amazed, and his hands began unsurely to stroke her forehead, feeling like a blind man about her eyes and lips, describing like a portrait painter the outline of her face. When the fingers had learned what they could understand, he bent down to her and kissed, exploring with his tongue the cavity into which he had once made frequent pilgrimages, wandering among the descending and rising formations of porcelain as a geologist coming upon a secret cave marvels at the strange configuration of stalactites and stalagmites that circle its interior. All touch and tenderness; the eyes have no part in wandering through openings of the body. Greta clasped her hands about his waist, and satiated with his kisses, pinched the bumps of flesh which haunched about his thighs. Yuri Maximovich sighed, threw back his head, and began to laugh, explaining that her fingers tickled him, but Greta understood his nervousness and with sureness stood up and without a word took his hand and led him stumbling toward the bedroom. It was there amidst the afternoon sunlight, their bodies slatted with bars of sun and darkness printed upon them by the angled blinds, they made love.

Yuri undressed neatly, folding his trousers but forgetting to remove his socks, while Greta—held together, by a single snap (or was it a clasp?)—was naked with a single pull, virtually all her clothes except the sheerest of panties dropping off. Upon their bed, the one explored scandalously, devising the game of pursuit and discovery as though it were the first time she had ever pushed a tongue up the knoll of flesh toward its nippled center ("Ah," she sighed, capturing the promontory; Italian operatic style would have been "*Vittòria! Vittòria!*") or allowed finger to promenade the gluteus, occasionally dropping precipitously into the delicious buttock cavern. She did not play capriciously nor did she mock. The movement was slow and languorous, and Yuri Maximovich, at first unnerved, settled down, buried his face in her pillow; he smelled the drift of her sleeping hair, the slightly musky odors of solitude; and he thought again of Irina Alexandrovna (hoping she would envy his pleasure) and Nastya eating his warm soup; even Lydia Yegorovna pinning him to his desk at *The People's Voice* suddenly took on the slow and deliberate movement of an embrace. Yuri Maximovich gave himself up to this obviously talented lover, surrendered quite completely, accepting it as somehow mysterious and beyond him.

There came a moment, sometime after it began, when Greta fell back from her ministrations, tired of kneading this inert matter (and panting from exhaustion, her forehead moist, her hands sticky from spittle), she whispered to Yuri, "You. You now! You, Yuri." Yuri might have asked why or what she meant and an interlocution could have ensued, part semantic, part simple confusion, but fortunately Yuri understood that he had been lying in this bed for some time now, wakefully asleep, allowing a stranger to him, someone who didn't even speak Russian or read its poetry, to make love to him. Not a vain exercise, since he, like many men, was sufficiently compliant, testifying and rewarding the endearments he received by the beacon torch of his erect member, fluttering with excitement, waving spasmodically as if to say, "Behold." It is, after all, not quite enough.

Greta repeated her plea and Yuri, roused from himself, turned to her and smiled gratefully and replied that he understood. But understanding, such as it was, seemed to mean little more than that the time had come when it was expected that he should work his way into her body and discharge himself. Greta groaned as he turned himself upon her. Yuri took the groan for pleasure and pressed on, but Greta had another idea; she pried his hand from his penis, where it was busy trying to guide it in its blindness, and conducted it upon a different tour, placing it first upon her breasts, where it rolled over her stiff nipples, and then drawing it down the curve of her side, where it crossed the slight ravine into the knoll of her pudenda, once more to the inside of her legs, stroking all the while, and finally lifting his index finger and conducting its nail edge in a delicious arabesque up and down the flesh that joins the buttocks to the vagina, all the while like any adept cicerone congratulating the sightseer upon his excellence and perspicacity. "Ah. Wonderful. Again. Once again. More. Oh, Yuri dearest. Again. There. Right there, Yuri. Yes. Yuri. Now. Oh now Yuri. Yesssss. Yes, beloved." At last, some time beyond the familiar time at which Yuri Maximovich would have been done with his pleasure, they completed the festivities: the final display, the rockets, the rockets exploded, and dizzy from a thousand lights they fell apart and stared up at the ceiling, numb with exhaustion.

The telephone must have jangled several times, but they slept through it. The third time it began to ring, Greta removed her arm from Yuri's chest and began to stroke her forehead, passing it lightly over the rim of her eyes, until with these strokes like the feints of a magician she had transformed herself from sleep into consciousness, brushing herself awake. It was then, on the fourth ring, that she heard the phone, and cursing its insistence, reached to the nightstand and picked up the receiver. "Hello . . . Oh, good God, it's you, Mother . . . What? What? What are you talking about? . . . He wants to commit suicide? Oh, good God, Mother. What are you doing calling me in the middle of the night? . . . It's not. What time is it then? . . . Seven-thirty. I must have lost track. . . . No. That's impossible . . . I don't know what I'd do if he killed himself . . . He can't make up his mind whether to jump out of the window or cut his wrists? Well, give him some black coffee first, call the doctor, and sit tight . . . He won't drink black coffee? Well, then, tell him to walk it off . . . He's too drunk. He can't walk? Well, I imagined that he was . . . He's drinking all the time now . . . I'm sorry, Mother. I really am sorry, but, Mother, I can't come up . . . That's not true, Mother. I'm not the only person he listens to. He listens to nobody. If he did, he might hear something, but he doesn't . . . It won't be on my conscience, Mother, it damn well won't be. Stop that. You're blackmailing me . . . Oh, shit, Mother, I *know* he's my father. But let me repeat slowly what I've told you both a thousand times: he had to be your husband first before he became my father. Now don't forget it. You chose him. He chose you. *I* was the accident. *I* was the accident. I didn't have any choice. So it's on both your consciences, not on mine . . . Yes, I know, Mother. I know I'll feel guilty. I'm sure of it. But I'll be much more miserable if I leave this apartment now to come up and talk Papa out of killing himself . . . Why? Well, Mother, let me tell you why. I'm lying in bed at the moment and a marvelous man is lying next to me and we've just made love. Do you understand? Can you understand? Goodbye, Mother."

Greta fell back upon the bed and began to cry. Yuri had heard most of the conversation. He had awakened just before the phone rang and the words had filtered through to him, and as he understood them, he understood much more. "I am sorry, Greta. You certain you not go to see them?" She stopped crying and reached over to him, hugging his chest and burying her face in his stomach, resting there for a moment.

"Yes. I'm certain. It happens very often. Mother can't handle him. He can't handle himself. One day I guess he will kill himself. He's so humiliated, so humiliated."

"But tell me, tell me, Greta, why is it upon you?"

"It's always that way. You know, to the third and fourth generation."

"I don't think so. Old people at home are different. We love our old people as much as our young people. Is it true, as we are told, that here—in West, that is—old people are considered failed young people. To become old and tired and weary is quite natural. No? Sometimes I think that young people the unnatural ones. But you do it the other way. Old people hang onto their life by dragging on coats of their children. Pull down everything, everyone. Yes?"

"Yes. Yes. It's true."

"That is very terrible. Very terrible." Yuri Maximovich shook his head. "Very bad way to end up life. I would not want to be old man in this place."

"Will it be better in Russia?"

Yuri Maximovich had no answer. It might have been different. It might have been different if he had married another woman, if he had had children, if he had made his peace with the Russian vastness, but he had done none of these things.

"Why don't you stay with me?" she said at last. It was a question he knew would come, and even though meaningless—for he persuaded himself the affair would have blown away if it had been obliged to dry out in a normal sun—it was nonetheless inevitable and he was grateful for it.

"Greta, dear, I could say yes. I could say"—Yuri leaned on his elbow and watched her as she lit a cigarette—"that it would be wonderful, that Yuri Maximovich loves the idea to stay with Greta, but I think it would be to tell great and unforgivable lie. What you have done for me marvelous. You give me treasure I never forget. This afternoon. But truth is that this man, Yuri Maximovich, is tied to another world, another fate. I think out loud. What would I do in this country? I would arrive and mistress would take me in? I look for work. Where? No one needs someone who speak bad English and perfect Russian. So I teach Russian poems and work hard to learn English. In the time between, inside me, more and more of what is Yuri Maximovich would turn to stone. I read newspapers about my lost country, my lost friends, and I begin to write letters to people for help. I pretend I am loyal to them, but all the time I live from plate of my mistress, teach Russian poems, and try, my God, try, write poems in what—English? I not even manage poem in Russian. My stomach knot is Russian. You think English untie me. No. Not possible. I end up like Greta's father, drink myself to humiliation. Terrible. Beautiful gift your love give me, Greta, but Yuri would die in the hands of your loving."

Yuri had gotten up to pace about the room while he spoke. His chest heaved and his stomach, only a little inflated by inattention and the ballast of his thousand soups and fruit compotes, jumped, but his legs—enormous thighs set upon white and almost hairless spindles—distracted Greta, and when he finished she was smiling with delight. She lifted herself onto her knees, and as he passed, saying his last words referring to her loving hands, she extended them again and they began once more to make love.

When Yuri Maximovich left Greta's apartment it was just after dawn. The buildings were still in shadows, warming themselves in the dark, but the sky had moved from purple to dirty white and the air was heavy with rain. He had come out into the street, leaving Greta behind sleeping on beautifully, her face calm, her hair like spume protecting her face from the cold of the apartment. Yuri had written her a note and left it by the coffeepot on the dining room table. It said only: "A thousand of thanks. Yuri." Yuri remembered how the subway might work, but decided it would be more sensible to take a taxi to the hotel. He wanted to rest for a few hours, to write in his journal, to be ready for the morning meetings. He had to attend those meetings, although he already anticipated his rendezvous with Greta at noon. He stood in the street before the apartment breathing in the air, surveying the streets, weary but deliciously happy. Across the street was a diner, already open. A lone customer sat at the counter, leaning over his coffee. Yuri stepped out into the street and lifted his arm to flag a taxi, but it was off-duty and passed him. The lone customer paid for his coffee and came out into the street. Yuri noticed him just as another taxi braked to a stop. It was his agent. He was about to greet him and invite him into the taxi, but prudence prevailed over his high spirits. It wasn't difficult to figure out how the agent had found him, not difficult at all. It annoyed him to think that he had listened at the door to make certain he was inside, but undoubtedly he had retired to the street to await his reappearance. That was *their* problem. If they insisted on spying, they had to suffer the inconvenience. The consequence, of course, was no less severe. It didn't matter that his disappearance was innocent, that it was only a lovely American girl who admired a Russian poet, that it had no significance beyond what appeared. Such simplicities of feeling meant little or nothing to his superiors. What was clear was that he was not conducting himself as a Russian who had a "little piece of work" to do for Colonel Bobov.

6. A Crime

Tuesday evening Yuri Maximovich was obliged to descend from the heights to which he and Greta had climbed. The thirty-six hours which had passed since their magnificent Monday afternoon were a hum of pleasure, only briefly interrupted by the meetings of the Congress, but even those became light-headed, even enjoyable. Yuri passed his time diligently furrowing his forehead in concentration upon the papers and discussion, once even volunteering to ask a pointed question of an Islamic scholar that reconfirmed his familiarity with the literature, but principally opening his mind to the warming recollection of sensations and pleasures, the times when he was with her, touching, embracing, making love.

At the luncheon recess on Tuesday, when the other delegates made their way solidly and calmly to the restaurants of the hotel, Yuri Maximovich managed a semblance of bonhomie, bid goodbye to the few delegates whom he had met, descended into the street, and having made certain that his agent was behind him in readiness, dashed for a taxicab, threw himself into the back, calling out the number of Greta's apartment, and sped there to make love—instantly, and with that done, eat a cake, drink coffee, and return.

Yuri Maximovich had brought the manuscripts of his poems to Greta's apartment, and after supper, in anticipation of the reading the next day, he laid them out and began to go through them, grunting with displeasure or nodding grimly as he worked through the texts. He imagined that he should read about three hundred lines in all, perhaps less, since his translator would be standing by his side and offering a sight rendering of the poems and undoubtedly some of the apportioned hour would be lost as the translator mumbled his way through the poems.

It was shortly after ten o'clock when Greta's phone rang. She answered it and without a word handed the receiver to him.

"Professor Simonson. Pleasure . . . Yes. How you did find—never mind. It doesn't matter . . . Yes. Tell me about arrangements . . ." There was a long silence while Simonson explained. When it was done, Yuri acknowledged that the arrangements were excellent, thanked the professor, and hung up.

Yuri Maximovich should have been elated, but he was suddenly overcome by the stupidity of the situation. It was quite worthless. It wasn't for his sake; it wasn't for his Russian poems that the special gathering in Professor Simonson's seminar had been arranged. It was simply a stage setting for transacting the piece of work, for hearing the right words, offering the right manuscript, passing the text of a poem from one hand to another, from one coding instrument to another. Of course, it wasn't at all clear to him why the procedure was even necessary, why the elaborate device, if indeed it was one, had to be invented, since Moscow could cable in a thousand codes, could transmit to its own cipher band without resorting to such an intricate mechanism. Why, indeed? He speculated for a moment, but found no ready answer. It remained a confusion to him. Spying was meaningless, an enterprise which consumed vast energies in his country, in this country, requiring imponderable resources, inhuman discipline and obedience, submissive intelligence, deathly self-denial—everything, in fact, which made his enterprise as a poet seem in principle more significant, but at this moment left him with a feeling of helplessness. And besides all that, what possible point was there in standing up and reading, in his strong and clear voice, poems which couldn't be understood unless one had been at the Russian language for more years than the assembly of literature enthusiasts whom Professor Simonson would convoke could possibly have aggregated? So, then, what would he do? He'd go through with it, naturally, but he could just as easily recite names from the Moscow telephone book, with deep sonority and feeling, and then hand his translator a prose summary of the mood and image and tell him to read it off. It wouldn't do. He'd have to endure it like all the others who preceded him in the decades of visiting Russian poets, Esenin, Yevtushenko, Vosnesensky, Kolokolov, flashing their smiles, their teeth, striking poses, feet apart, making Russian sound like the tumbling Volga instead of making sense, and hope for the best. It didn't do his spirits any good to know that Mr. Bateson, the professor from the press conference who had known his poems, would stand at his side making up prose replicas of his poems.

The poems through which Yuri Maximovich had read that evening acquired a species of fatal logic, as though their composition from the earliest, written just after the war, to the most recent, the little lyric at the Krimsky Bridge, were linked not alone by his imagination, but by a webbing of events which compelled them to be reviewed and selected for this specific occasion. He could not read all of them. Some had to be left behind. They had traveled through the skies and come to rest upon a coffee table. There were sixty bits of paper, some whole sheets, the final version written in a neat and unadorned hand, others with small corrections or the addition of stress marks in a different ink.

Yuri Maximovich had become habituated to preparing his final manuscripts in two colors of ink, writing out the body text in blue-black, and then after several extended sessions of elocutionary practice reading out the poems to the head of Pushkin, completing the text by indicating in red ink the modulations and elisions which stressed the poem, leaving to no chance, not even to his own, the accenting of the poem. It was not that he thought his poems sacred text which, like the Holy Scripture of his ancestors, was sealed into stone by the system of those called Masoretes, who had devised the vowel marks to stress the divine word for all the generations of men who had lived and will ever live. No. Not that he thought his poems were such writ. Nor even like the conventions of primitive tribes who train the tribal singers of tales to know by heart the whole saga of its creation myths, the names of all the monsters to be slain and the women who become mountains, the sea nets of fishermen which dried out into stars and who recite the cycle, singing for four, five, eight hours at the annual spring palaver and failing by a single word, losing one syllable, are put to death, their young acolytes rising in turn to the position until they, too, inevitably fail. The assumption of the tribe, the primitive tribe, the great tribe of Israel, the tribal genius of the entire human race is that all men know the words, but not all have the gift of speaking them. Otherwise put, Yuri Maximovich, like the Masoretes, like the primitive tribes, believed that men knew the truth, the whole truth even, but did not know (or had forgotten) how to speak it. They had forgotten the stress marks, the accent, the right rhythm of the speaking. And the right rhythm? That came from inside, from the honest gut, from the deepest tummy gorge of the race where men had no choice but to admit that the whole business was about living and dying well.

It was for these reasons that Tuesday evening, expecting some word about his Wednesday reading, Yuri Maximovich had gathered his manuscript together and brought it to Greta's apartment, and when supper was over had begun to go through the poems, speaking them aloud, stressing them with the true stress, until he knew which poems had endured, which had failed, which still enforced the truth and which—staled by time, dried up—deserved to be left behind, although Yuri also believed that at another time they might be brought back to life, read again, stressed to the right beat of the world, and renewed.

Throughout that evening and into the early hours of the morning, Greta Engel had sat beside him, hardly speaking, playing solitaire. Only once had they spoken with each other before she disappeared into the bedroom to sleep. Yuri had separated the poems that he would read from those to be left behind. The others, arranged now in the order and sequence of their movement and sense, he had returned to his briefcase. "I want you keep these poems, Greta. I do not read them. They are poems left behind by me. Yours. You keep them. I remember them. I will never forget them. But they are your poems." Greta had begun to cry as she accepted the little sheaf of papers. "Ridiculous to cry. Don't cry over poems. Don't cry over Yuri. Point of gift is to tie you up, tie you tight to me whatever happens now. I could not stay to give you child, but long enough to give you old part of me, old poems of me."

It was shortly after this that Greta went to sleep. Several hours later, cold now in the unheated apartment, he undressed and slipped in beside her and fell asleep.

Professor Simonson was distinctly unpolitical. He had no interest in politics, no talent for its intricacies, but unfortunately he had unhappy enthusiasms which lent themselves to Soviet employment. Poor man, he had been caught one evening many years before, when he was still a graduate student in Russian literature, dressed from head to toe in black leather, seated in his room on floor 9B of Moscow University reading pornographic literature. He had never even had the courage to wear his little uniform, all elaborated with metal studs and lengths of clanky chain, into the streets, even in the dead of night when absolutely no one would be about to squint their eyes at him in disbelief, so he gave up all fantasy of encounter and reconciled himself during those long months in Moscow to periodic dress-ups before the mirror and readings of his furtive literature. To his ultimate dismay and misfortune, the old maid who cleaned his room came upon his costume folded under the mattress of his bed, and reported it to the authorities, undoubtedly imagining that Professor Simonson was some kind of foreign agent rather than a harmless and pathetically unoriginal masochist. The outcome is predictable. He was arrested on the occasion of his next masquerade and blackmailed, and although it facilitated his career, since he was allowed to return frequently to Moscow and even given the opportunity of inspecting rare manuscripts and documenting unfamiliar literary codices, he was also employed, his classes used for occasional transmissions to Soviet agents, his examination papers sometimes pricked with pins above certain letters or supplied with microdots and distributed to one or another student who had above-average competence in the Russian language. In that way Professor Simonson was allowed his unhappy enthusiasm undenounced and the KGB their little class in Russian literature.

It was arranged that Yuri Maximovich would arrive at the university campus at three-thirty in the afternoon and would proceed to Professor Simonson's office to be briefed and to meet with Roger Bateson, the translator, and together they would enter the classroom for the reading. He awakened late in the morning, breakfasted with Greta, and left her about noon to return to the hotel. There were no messages for him at the desk, but when he arrived in his room, he found a letter from Kolokolov under his door:

Yuri Maximovich. I'm off for a few days. I won't be able to wish you bon voyage in person. If it had been a few days earlier, I might have hit you instead of simply wishing you a good journey. But that's passed. I can't say I understand your behavior at my dinner. I can't say I understand anything about you. You seem determined to end badly. That kind of determination commends charity, not indignation. Forgive me for giving you a small piece of advice, but I'd suggest you watch your step. Your old friend,

Ilia Alexandrovich Kolokolov

From the journal of Yuri Maximovich Isakovsky

January 26, 1972

What do you make of such advice? How does one "watch one's step"? Clichés are useful only if you know instantly what they mean. Otherwise, what is one to do? If I were to decide to watch my step, how would I go about it? I would not, for example, behave like poor old Pythagoras, who never watched his step and fell into a pothole. Pythagoras was interested in stars, not potholes. The outcome was foregone and inevitable, but I have never been interested in star-gazing, nor for that matter in charting potholes.

I have tried only to keep my head above water. Now that's another cliché, but much more applicable to me than watching steps. If Ilia Alexandrovich had advised me to keep my head above water, I would have known what he was talking about. Water clichés work with me. Keep out of hot water! Keep your head above water! For someone prone to head colds, that kind of advice is practical. Keep your boots dry, stay away from water (hot or cold), keep afloat, etc. Now all that makes a great deal of sense to me. But watching steps, how very boring, how uninteresting! My footwork doesn't fascinate me (that's what finally ended my brief flirtation with soccer—poor footwork).

What I'm saying is that Ilia Alexandrovich uses dishonest clichés, clichés that don't fit. If he had said to me straight out, "You're in trouble, old friend," I would have gotten the point. Not that I can do anything about it.

Not that I can do anything about it! This is very important. I can't do it any differently than I am. It isn't enough to chide me by saying that I could do it differently if I remind myself of my socialist obligations, my clear-cut responsibilities to the system, the society, the nation. It doesn't work that way for me. It never has. I didn't stay out of trouble all these years because I never did anything significant or important enough to be considered troublesome. I didn't have interesting or provocative friends until now. I read my unpopular books privately, neither borrowing them nor lending them. Nobody ever knew I had them until Colonel Bobov discovered their existence. In a word, I was a private man, totally private. I could have remained that way quite happily, working away at my poems, but that secrecy, too, is at an end.

I didn't have to watch my step until others started putting stones in my way. And now, if I fail to please, it's others, not I, who have chosen to be displeased. Yuri Maximovich is the same as always.

The same Yuri Maximovich Isakovsky ran from the taxicab through the ponderous iron gates at the university. The taxi man had apologized for being late, but it was not his fault. The traffic jammed; a fire engine followed by an ambulance had beaten back the movement of the automobiles. Fifteen minutes Yuri and Greta sat perspiring in Herald Square. He couldn't believe the hopelessness of the traffic. Greta had agreed to meet him at the hotel to take him to the university, but she'd had trouble finding a taxi and had ended traveling on the subway downtown and then catching a taxi westward to the hotel. When she arrived, a half-hour late, Yuri was pacing nervously in the lobby. She rapped on the revolving doors and he rushed out, following her into the waiting vehicle, which turned illegally and moved up the avenue. But in Herald Square they were becalmed and when they finally arrived at the gates of the university it was sixteen minutes until four. Yuri imagined that everyone had gone home; the professor had given him up for lost, the reading been canceled. He dropped his money into the driver's lap, more bills than were necessary, thanked him for nothing too many times, clutched his briefcase to his chest with one hand and held onto Greta's coat with the other and ran with her into the quadrangle. They saw a university policeman ambling across the quadrangle and Greta called out to him the building Professor Simonson had named. He pointed to a building on the other side of the campus. When they arrived in the foyer of the building, a thin man approached Yuri, and ignoring Greta, greeted him in Russian and began to chat amiably about the difficulties of using taxis in such a congested city.

"Then I am not too late?" Yuri asked diffidently.

"Of course not, Mr. Isakovsky. We wait for you. You're the guest." Professor Simonson replied, eyeing him pleasantly, enveloping him with a knowing arch of his right eyebrow.

Yuri Maximovich was relieved and withdrew a folded handkerchief with which he wiped his damp forehead. He looked around for Greta Engel. He wanted to introduce her, but she had undoubtedly seen the announcement of Yuri's reading on the bulletin board and had gone ahead to the classroom. In all events she had disappeared, but Yuri's relief effaced his discomfort at her absence.

"Follow me, if you please. You can talk for a few minutes with Rog Bateson before we go to the seminar room." Roger Bateson, in slacks and sweater, was waiting for them when they stepped off the elevator on the third floor.

"So good to see you again, Isakovsky," Bateson said, waving to Yuri. "I hope you've enjoyed this place," he asked, motioning presumably to the whole of Manhattan. Yuri mumbled something inaudible, anxious to be finished with the amenities and get on with the poems. "How do you want me to do it? You don't have a second copy of the manuscript, do you?" Yuri answered that he didn't. "How many pages have you got there?" Yuri opened his briefcase and withdrew the manuscript of the poems he had selected and began to count.

"Twenty."

"Easy enough. Let's run them through the machine and get a copy." Professor Simonson called his secretary, who appeared and for some dubious reason removed her eyeglasses in order to greet Yuri Maximovich, replacing them only after their hands had shook. She took the manuscript and was about to disappear into another room off the office when Yuri Maximovich remembered the extra poem.

"Wait for minute, please," he called. "One more. A new one that I read." The envelope with the text of "Ripe Times" appeared, typed unlike the other poems, neatly typed with Yuri's corrections written above the struck words, and lines moving like emaciated arms from the body of the text to grasp and encircle bunches of words which he had written in the margins. "Please, this one." The secretary nodded and disappeared, returning a few minutes later with two neat scripts, separated and squared off. Harold Bateson took his and began to read through it, nodding, clucking, noting with a pen this or that in the margin (instructions to himself), and once consulting a large Russian dictionary which lay open on a swivel stand in the office.

The classroom was filled with the students of Professor Simonson when they entered a few minutes after four o'clock. There were perhaps forty people in the room, their faces turned vaguely in the direction of the little platform on which two small desks had been placed side by side like friends. Professor Simonson led Yuri Maximovich and his translator to chairs in the front row and invited them to be seated. Yuri was so nervous he did not look around. He stared straight ahead at the blackboard. He couldn't possibly have seen Greta Engel, in the very last row near the window, hidden in a corner where mistresses invariably secret themselves at the performances of their lovers. After the shifting of chairs and the rustling of papers had subsided and the students—varying in age from youngsters to the white-haired or bald—had come to attention, Professor Simonson began to speak, dryly clearing his throat after every orderly paragraph of thought or rapping with the back of his pen against the desk to strengthen one or another point, describing the unfolding of the postwar generation of Soviet poets, their indebtedness to the classic tradition, the impact of the poets of the twenties, the precariousness of poetry under Stalin, the resurgence under Khrushchev, the predicament of literature in general and poetry in particular during the present period.

"One poet who has been noticeably silent during the past decade is our visitor today, Mr. Yuri Maximovich Isakovsky. Isakovsky was born in Kiev in 1918. He was a child during the Revolution, and quite literally as Russia has matured in the revolution so has our guest. He was educated in Kiev, and for many years, not unlike other poets and writers of his generation, he wrote for newspapers as a literary critic and musicologist. Shortly after he became the editor of *The People's Voice*, the most influential periodical of ethnic music in the Soviet Union (and the occasion for his visit to the United States as delegate to the recently concluded Congress of Music and Ethnology), he published his first, and to date only, book of poems, *The School of Song*. The poems which Mr. Isakovsky will read to us today are poems written after *The School of Song*—that is, during the past sixteen years. Mr. Isakovsky will read in Russian, and our friend, Mr. Roger Bateson— who as you know is the translator of many books of modern Russian poetry—will offer sight translations of the poems. If we have time at the conclusion of the reading, Mr. Isakovsky has kindly consented to answer questions." Professor Simonson smiled at Yuri Maximovich as he said this last, for he had never asked Yuri to respond to questions. It didn't annoy Yuri. He had been pleased with the introduction and with Professor Simonson's familiarity with him and his career, and more than these (for it was evident to Yuri how he might have come by his knowledge), he had delivered the introduction with the kind of fluency and respect that betokened a more-than-casual interest in his work. Simonson and Bateson exchanged places and Yuri Maximovich seated himself at the empty desk.

Yuri Maximovich looked out at the room and for an instant became dizzy, but he gripped the desk and held on, turning after several moments to the manuscript before him, arranged now in the paged sequence he had determined, the extra poem seeded out of numerical order as chance and the secretarial sorting had devised.

Yuri spoke the name of the first poem, a mongrel sestina which he had written some years earlier, employing two quatrains and a concluding rhyming couplet, in which the stress words of the concluding couplet recalled the last words of each line of the quatrains. Originally he had thought to eliminate this poem as being hopeless for sight translation (or blind translation, if that signifies the use of book and dictionary in contrast to lightning intuition and hope), but finally decided to include it, placing it at the very beginning of the group of poems he would read, since it was for him an emblematic poem, dealing with the effort of a poet to sing sanity into the head of a mad emperor and failing. He knew the poem had its origins in his reading the saga of David and Saul in his father's Russian Bible, and he had set out to replicate the accent words of the Russian translation in his own vision of the poet as healer.

Roger Bateson threw up his hands at the translation of the poem, giving way to such meaningless evasions as, "The poet is trying to say here that" . . . and a stream of "as if to say" or "wants to say," when in fact what he meant was that the poet has said, but that he, Roger Bateson, cannot, in his language, with his experience, with his well-shielded version of the real world, bring himself to understand that the world stops short of being healed. Yuri Maximovich realized the difficulty, apologized to the audience for the problems he had created for his translator, and asked their indulgence.

And then he announced the next poem, cleared his throat, and remembering the purple light at dusk in the city park at Tashkent, he read:

TASHKENT MEDITATION

A bare room in Tashkent:
flies graze upon my face,
even the coffee is brackish.
Alone with half my life, sudden
blackout is what I fear.

Death's a factory, bees know.
All their lives they never
do anything alone. But die.
One sting, one singular moment, and then
back to the mass grave again . . .

The more I fear, the more
I'm busy: dusting the picture frames,
tinkering poems, scouring the teapot.
My hands push at the clock, the time
slipping through my fingers like fog.

Nothing that lives wishes to die alone.
Hermits have kept lions without teeth.
Giacometti slept with his night lamp lit.
In the last resort even the skinny breast
of madness would be warm enough for me.

But this!? These scribblings?
Comfort enough.

Does beauty beat down death?
Beauty beats down nothing.
Beauty is the rainbow, the sidereal light,
the sign of what has passed.
To speak by signs is beautiful,
it is the human thing to do.

No one sees.
Make, make anyway.

No one hears.
Say it anyway.

God hears, God sees.
For Him I make these.

Roger Bateson improved. The images were sharp and he produced them without cutting himself and bleeding. Yuri watched him translate and smiled to himself. The Russian was mashed and stomped into English.

LOVING PUSHKIN

Every last one of us
loves Pushkin.
Not with the usual love
that picks and chooses:
a beech copse, say, set off
in a field of wheat;
a stream that keeps and keeps
a childhood picnic
fresh and clear as it was;
or a summer pergola
to ward off bluebottle flies
rising at dusk;
or steaming mounds and lumps
of groats and butter;
or a waltz, scratched
and rattly as tin

so that in memory
it's loved more than ever . . .
These simple things, we love.

The love we love Pushkin
with, is different.
Pushkin . . . is loving a whole
heaven of constellations.
It's all there. And if a single star burns out,
a single line is lost
or the least feeling unfelt,
it's a hole in our lives.

We poets love Pushkin
the only way we can:
by giving him back
what gift we have.
A half-decent line or two
if that's all we can do.
What's possible, is enough.
Every poet loves him,
because Pushkin
makes poetry possible.
He shows it can be done.
Thank God, thank God.
With the help of God, Pushkin
allows us all we do.

"These people like this poem," Yuri recognized when Bateson had finished. "There is something wrong with it, but I am too far along in life to fix it."

POEM

This, our generation
flies, obsessed.
A packed suitcase
is all the home we have.

At the beginning, and in the end: a chaos
of worn-out overshoes,
and shirts
threadbare at the collar, the wrist.
Poems we saved like postage stamps
are canceled. Yet
they're all the memory we have
of far-off places that we visited
and left.

We had a childhood, before
the twentieth century began
in 1922.

Then
we packed.
But stripped down.
Postage stamps? we gave away
to new children. But this time
without the involved baroque accounts
of pyramids and the Acropolis.
The space saved
we used for passports, visas.
We'd no use for letters.
We were sending ourselves instead.

I knew a poet and his wife
who flew from the birch trees
into nights dripping with jasmine.
In Kiev the ravens called to them
caw more caw caw more
while they lived on and on
as excess.
They lived nowhere.

Roger Bateson stumbled in the translation, but recovered. He managed it once, reworked it, and tried again. He happened upon the caw of the ravens and it worked, although Russian ears heard ravens differently in the fields about Kiev and Bateson had no idea of what it meant to be an excess in the Soviet Union.

The poems were making Yuri Maximovich immensely sad. The hopelessness of it all, the hopelessness of writing poems in this age struck him brutally, and he recoiled. Before him lay another poem, the one about his empty picture frames. He had collected more than thirty in every style and from every period of the decorative arts, and these had ranged the shelves of his bookcase during the years of his marriage. He had thrown them in a box when Irina Alexandrovna had departed. They lay empty in a box, awaiting images.

EMPTY FRAMES

Mother told me. Her father and mother
and theirs, and theirs, and theirs
were stricken by fear—
at the upside-down, black-for-white
photographer's art.
A fear, I thought, rooted in the first
awful fear of graven images.
But that's not it.

My desk like a graveyard is lined
with picture frames.
Wood, with strips of tin.
Silk rims like lips
around an oval void,
and cut stone
like the tablets we must lie under.
And silver, silver tapped into fish and fruit
in the French style.
Eight frames in all.
One, still wrapped in tissue,
waits for the uncle who lives in Murmansk.

I work my verse,
the way craftsmen

cutting and molding and carving
made these empty frames:
that they might wait for death
to stare out from them.

This grandmother died in Kiev
thirty years ago. In bed,
a rare occurrence even then.
Her gnarled hands are folded, rooted
in what seem to be festive lights.
Her death was a slow guttering flame.
The cedar frame from Palestine
holding her now, recalls her piety.

Another froze to death: tripped
and fell into a snowdrift.
Feet up no less. And found
now, colder still, in this ivory frame
tamed by lion's feet, of all things!

I go on engraving images
our fathers have forbidden.

My own father, that counterrevolutionary saint,
never thought an issue to its end.
He died with prayers on his lips
he never understood.
No matter. It was enough
he savored them,
grateful for his poor dish of groats.

And mother, my mother of mothers,
whose breasts billowed
like the tents of Jacob—
she brooded over me
and three aunts, all unmarried.
I keep them, keep them all
festooned in the desolate space

of two damasked traveling frames,
fit for ikons.

And Fanny, and Rose:
rosy Fanny
round and firm as a plum,
and fanny Rose, big-bummed
but delicate, like a circus horse . . .
They kept a tea shop near our mother's house
and died of cholera, before the men
could scrape away their lice.
God, my God, I keep them too.
One pewter frame with curlicues.
One tin, incised with roses.
And my wife, poor shiksa,
who left me during the purge,
but first declared my verse was safe,
uncontaminated by anything
including the muse.
Having saved me, she found
a booted Major from the Kremlin
to save herself from the gloom
of uninspired poems.
Until a tiny splinter from a German mortar
pierced her tiny heart.
Her I commemorate
with the cut stone tablet.

My frames, my empty frames, my ungraven
images I recall—

when other images, those
an angry stomach and a broken heart
refuse to give up,
to arrange,
to frame,

when those images
glare and reflect

He read the poem with unmistakable passion, his body lying behind each word like a hammer, his large head falling upon the opening life of each stanza, almost grazing the manuscript, which he had lifted up to hide his face. Roger Bateson recognized, following as Yuri read, that it was an intricate poem, and breaking through the cast of knowing languages and vocabularies, he achieved, even if imperfectly, the ideal of translation, which is the permutation of spirit.

AND WHO WILL KEEP MY POEMS?

And who will keep my poems, who
commit them to a memory
or to a music?

Every night, I hide another phrase or two
in the goosedown pillow
no one will ever burn,
I scribble
stanzas in the family cookbook
no one will throw away—

that they be kept, or passed
on, as from a mother
to a daughter,
from broken household
to pushcart,
and from there
into another kitchen, another
bed or chair—

that they might pass from hand to hand
though I myself disappear

THE WORD

The word buried in my brain
might be a slug
burrowed in the earth.

Under so many memories like monuments
the dead weights
of other ages
it scavenges what it can.
Dumb thing: with no cavernous throat
to crawl through, singing
up into the light

What good is such a word!

And yet, the word can wait.
If not this mouth
then another
or another or another
will give it up: will let it, shining, out

But someday. Not now.

Not now, but when
graverobbers should break open this tomb
and find a tiny slug
scudding
glistening in the porcelain mouth,
because the slug endures.
And then will be the miracle.
What will be heard
will be incredible:

for when the slug speaks
it sings,
and when the slug emerges in the blinding light,
we all sing, stunned and trembling

we sing at last our word

Roger Bateson, improving, received the last two poems and made them sensible, catching the words better, caught the words like butterflies that flew directly into his mouth and died there, coming forth once again as words.

Shortly before the last poems, Yuri Maximovich realized that he had not yet come to the "extra piece of work." He had finished reading "The Word," and as Bateson finished rendering it, Yuri lifted the manuscript page which he had been following attentively as Bateson translated, and placed it at the bottom. "Ripe Times" came up, the next-to-last poem.

Yuri Maximovich looked around the room, scrutinizing the faces, trying to discover which face was waiting for the poem. They seemed implacable—some attentive, some bored, some strained with uplift and elevation. Greta Engel caught his eye and looked away, embarrassed, Yuri thought.

RIPE TIMES

Walking through that dying land
(a battlefield of corn stalks,
wounded like soldiers)
I stepped upon a clod of turned earth.
It shattered into dust and did not cry.

The sounds of the carnage that reached
the Moscow offices far away
Were recorded as unidentified bodies,
dried-out skin and bones.

On an October morning,
someone understood that even earth
remembers and can settle old accounts.
Water flowed and planters turn the furrows,
Threshers waited for the right time.

The old gods and the new men, tense,
prayed. Gaea was on her knees
for the coming of ripe times.

Yuri Maximovich was grateful that the poem was not the last. He had ordered the sequence of the poems, and where it fell by chance it also appeared by necessity. It came between "The Word" and a small poem he had written in his icehouse after hearing a description of the suicide of Marina Tsvetaeva.

The last poem which he read was called "Suicide."

Seven five-year dreams ago
a poet buried his poems.
His voice went out, blind,
like a song with its throat cut.
There are many suicides among poets
but only one reason makes sense:
why should a poet wait
for death to bury him?

Roger Bateson translated this last poem like his last piece of work, his voice unquavered, and when he finished, he gathered up the manuscript, handed it to Yuri Maximovich, and began to applaud. Yuri Maximovich had finished his reading. The applause was intense and strained and then stopped quite suddenly. He would have been relieved if someone had asked him a question. He hoped someone would say something, but no one spoke.

Professor Simonson stood up and turned to face the class. He saluted Yuri Maximovich and called his poems deeply moving; he said that they were sad, reflective, speculative poems; he annotated the despair of the poems, citing a line here and there through the poems which signaled an uncommon lament, a mood which recalled earlier poets, and then, addressing Yuri Maximovich, asked, "Tell me if you will, Mr. Isakovsky, does this selection of your poems represent your sense of things, your vision, if you will allow me that labored word?"

Yuri Maximovich was uncretain of the word. "Vision?" he asked.

"Yes. Vision is the right word. What I mean is this. You have written many more poems than these, and yet you have chosen only these to read to us. In some sense, then, these poems reflect your basic way of seeing things, isn't that so? And it seems a tragic vision."

"Tragic? No. Not at all. I read much criticism about poems. Naturally. It seems, in my mind, that critics very happy with tragedy, more happy than poets. If poets tell the truth, all they do is cut back the world to bone, take away nice pink flesh, wash off all cosmetic, all paint, all dress-up of the world. Telling truth very simple. Telling truth comes down to this: difficult to live well, difficult to die well. Poets are ancient educators. They say to people: now, try to think life like this (and poets use image) or life like that (use different image), or death like this (then poets use image 'big storm,' 'wind,' 'hurricane') or death like that (and use image 'whisper' or 'breeze' or 'tinklebell'). Poets simply take naked universe and try—with all might, power, clearness—to force us see it. That is all we do. That is my opinion. Eh? Do I make clear? Yes?"

Professor Simonson nodded as though he understood, again thanked Yuri Maximovich for the reading and stood to applaud him. The students rose, applauded politely, gathered up their books and papers, and began to leave. A few edged forward to the desk where Simonson and Bateson stood talking with Yuri Maximovich. Yuri had completely forgotten the piece of work. An elderly gentleman with a hat much too small for his head edged forward to thank Yuri in broken Russian; several men and women waited to one side trying to make up their minds to come up and address him; some younger students began to smoke in the rear of the classroom. Greta Engel waited until the conversation had subsided and then interjected, "Yuri, it was marvelous. Your voice is incredible. The poems take you over. I loved the poem with the ancient earth god."

"Which poem?" Yuri demanded, his voice suddenly choked with anger.

"What's wrong?"

"I said, which poem? Which poem is it?"

"The poem before last. The one that ends with Gaea on her knees."

"You like that poem?"

"I do. Yes, I do. I'd like to have that poem with the others you gave me."

"You, then. You?"

"No, indeed," Roger Bateson interrupted, speaking over Yuri's dismay. "That's my favorite, too, Isakovsky. Let's compete for that poem, young lady." He smiled at her, his regular but wearying good looks inviting her to a combat to which she was unequal. Greta fell silent, confused by the situation. "Oh, well, the times are ripe, don't you think, for a little gift to the hard-working translator. This young lady can have other rewards for her admiration." Bateson winked at Yuri Maximovich, who mistook his irony, thinking it but another confirmation of Bobov's code line.

"I'm sorry, dear Greta," he said, looking at her wearily. "I think the gentleman is right. He's earned this present. He's welcome to it." Yuri took the poem from the bottom of the manuscript and handed it to Bateson, who received it, glanced at the title to confirm the transfer, and folding it, put it into his pocket.

"A fine poem. Thank you for it," Bateson remarked as he shook Yuri's hands.

"I'm afraid it isn't. It's the one poem I doubt."

Roger Bateson looked Yuri in the face: "Poets very often fail to know their best work."

Yuri Maximovich and Greta hardly spoke during their last dinner in the city or on their way back to her apartment. She was hurt and offended. No. Not that, precisely. She was offended and amazed. Something had transpired in the conversation which eluded her. Yuri Maximovich for his part breathed in short little gasps, groping for air, as though passing through a minor heart seizure. When they reached her apartment he asked for a drink of whiskey, opened his shirt, and slumped forward on her sofa, trying to compose a presence all but shattered by the experience. The whole of it was a parody, a monstrous parody.

He had spoken his poems intending the world, and this man, this translator Bateson, went through the gestures of translation, waiting only to collect his piece of work and be off. A job to do. A job finished. Yuri Maximovich was finished with the United States of America. A job done. He was finished.

"What happened there?" Greta handed him the whiskey and sat down besides him, resting her hand on his shoulder. She asked quietly, without importuning his answer.

"You really do not understand? Really not?"

"No. I do not, but you must tell me."

Yuri drank off the whiskey and put the glass on the table. He turned away from her and looked over his shoulder out of the window toward the lights of the city. "That poem was not me, Greta. That poem not belong to me. That poem was theirs, invented by them. Written by them on their damned machine. The poem tells a story. Oh, yes. A story poem. Poem with a meaning. Profound and deep poem. But not my poem and not my meaning. Do you see what Yuri tries to explain you?"

"No, my dearest, I do not."

"That poem was spy poem. They gave that poem and said, Yuri Maximovich, you give that poem to person who asks for it. That poem had message inside it. I said to them 'No.' But you saw it. That man ask for the poem and I give it. You understand now?"

Greta ran her hand over Yuri's eyes, bringing them to rest upon his lips. She thought she heard her father on the ledge calling for her. "But, Yuri, how can you go back to them?"

"That's what you do. Go back to them. Go back to them and say whatever a person can say. It's not right do this thing to a man. You must not do this thing. How you said it, Greta? Under eternity, it not really matters very much what they do to me, not really matters."

"But to me? You found me. That's something."

"Yes. Something for another time, a different world. Heartily sorry. Heartily sorry."

"Heartily sorry." She couldn't explain that contrition. She was going to ask why he was sorry, but the buzzer to her apartment sounded. She didn't answer it, but minutes later she heard footsteps outside her door and a knuckle rap against the frame. She went to the door and looked through the peephole. She recognized the caller. It was the agent who had been following them for three days. She opened the door and blocked the entranceway. "Who are you?" she demanded bravely.

"Have you here, Yuri Maximovich Isakovsky?"

"Who wishes to know?" she asked, her voice ridiculously strong.

"Miss Engel, please tell Mr. Isakovsky that he has a visitor."

Yuri appeared from the living room. "Enough, Greta. Let me speak with him."

"Mr. Isakovsky," the agent said in Russian, "Lieutenant Colonel Chupkov requests that you join him in the car below. You have five minutes."

"I will be there. Five minutes? In five minutes. Thank you."

The door closed and Yuri Maximovich smiled. "It comes on schedule. Everything on schedule. They found out."

"What?"

"I changed the poem. I made decent poem out of lie. Already they know. Well, love, time Yuri Maximovich go home."

It doesn't matter particularly how they managed to say good-bye, what instructions he left behind, whether he adjured her to remember him, whether he received pictures, exchanged promises, swore to write. None of that matters particularly.

It was early in the morning, after a sleepless night at the Soviet Mission, that the plane departed for Moscow. Yuri Maximovich closed his eyes as the aircraft sped down the runway. If he was arrested and tried upon his return, he was reconciled. He had done the only thing he could. Yuri Maximovich preferred to be classic. He wanted the poem more than he wanted to please. In all events, he knew the system had no canon of pleasure, but a poet, a poet sticks with the canon of poetry or ceases to be a poet. There would be nothing to confess except perhaps to a millennial crime. Being a poet, even a minor poet, has to be a crime. Of that Yuri Maximovich was certain. He contemplated the future, prepared, perhaps for the first time, to invest its trial with the kind of tenacity often mistaken as heroism. He looked forward to Yasha Isaievich Tyutychev. He might not see him alive again, but he was going home to the land that brought forth Tyutychev.

"Help me now," he said soundlessly, tapping against his knee with a pencil. "Help me now, Yasha Isaievich." The stewardess passed him speaking to himself, his eyes closed, concentrating on Tyutychev's ugliness. She noticed his lips moving and frowned.

Works by Arthur A. Cohen

Fiction:
The Carpenter Years (1967)
In the Days of Simon Stern (1972)
Acts of Theft (1980)
An Admirable Woman (1983)
Artists and Enemies (1987)

Nonfiction
Martin Buber (1959)
The Natural and the Supernatural Jew (1962)
Osip Emilevich Mandelstam: An Essay in Antiphon (1974)
A People Apart: Hasidic Life in America (with Philip Garvin) (1974)
If Not Now, When? (with Mordecai M. Kaplan) (1975)
Sonia Delaunay (1976)

Editor of
The Anatomy of Faith: Theological Essays of Milton Steinberg (1960)
Humanistic Education and Western Civilization (1966)
Arguments and Doctrines: A Reader of Jewish Thinking in the Aftermath of the Holocaust (1970)
The New Art of Color: The Writing of Robert and Sonia Delaunay (1978)
The Jew: Essays from Martin Buber's Journal, *Der Jude* 1916-1928 (1980)

Other Phoenix Fiction titles from Chicago

The Bridge on the Drina by Ivo Andrić
Concrete by Thomas Bernhard
Gargoyles by Thomas Bernhard
The Lime Works by Thomas Bernhard
The Department by Gerald Warner Brace
Lord Dismiss Us by Michael Campbell
Acts of Theft by Arthur A. Cohen
In the Days of Simon Stern by Arthur A. Cohen
Solomon's Folly by Leslie Croxford
Fish by Monroe Engel
In the Time of Greenbloom by Gabriel Fielding
The Birthday King by Gabriel Fielding
Through Fields Broad and Narrow by Gabriel Fielding
Concluding by Henry Green
Pictures from an Institution by Randall Jarrell
The Survival of the Fittest by Pamela Hansford Johnson
The Bachelor of Arts by R. K. Narayan
The English Teacher by R. K. Narayan
Swami and Friends by R. K. Narayan
Bright Day by J. B. Priestley
The Good Companions by J. B. Priestley
Angel Pavement by J. B. Priestley
A Use of Riches by J. I. M. Stewart